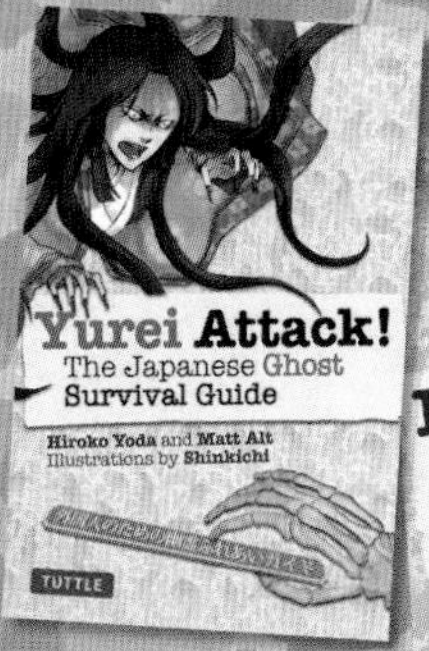
Yurei Attack!
The Japanese Ghost
Survival Guide
Hiroko Yoda and Matt Alt
Illustrations by Shinkichi
TUTTLE

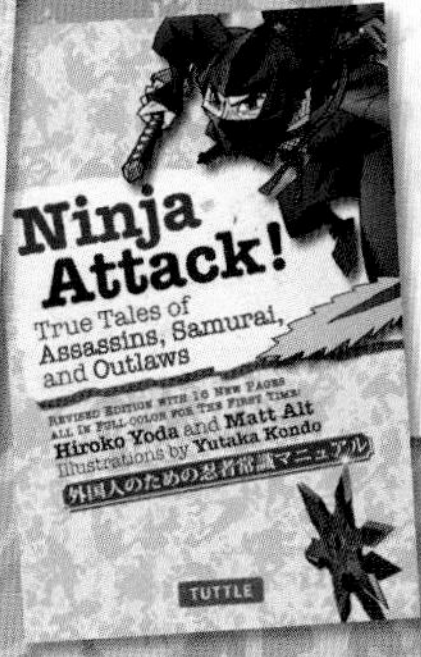
Ninja
Attack!
True Tales of
Assassins, Samurai,
and Outlaws
REVISED EDITION WITH 16 NEW PAGES
ALL IN FULL COLOR FOR THE FIRST TIME!
Hiroko Yoda and Matt Alt
Illustrations by Yutaka Kondo
外国人のための忍者常識マニュアル
TUTTLE

MAKE SURE YOU ALSO CHECK OUT THESE OTHER BOOKS BY HIROKO YODA AND MATT ALT

Yurei Attack! The Japanese Ghost Survival Guide and *Ninja Attack! True Tales of Assassins, Samurai, and Outlaws*

Hiroko Yoda and Matt Alt are a husband and wife team who run a Tokyo-based translation company that specializes in producing the English versions of Japanese video games, comic books, and literature. They are the co-authors of *Yokai Attack!*, *Ninja Attack!*, and *Yurei Attack!*.

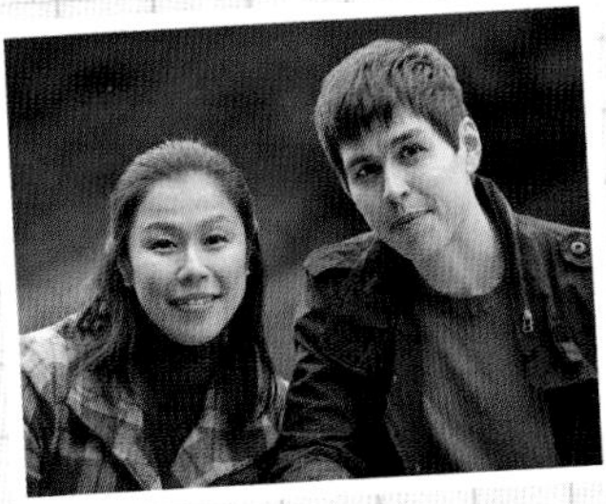

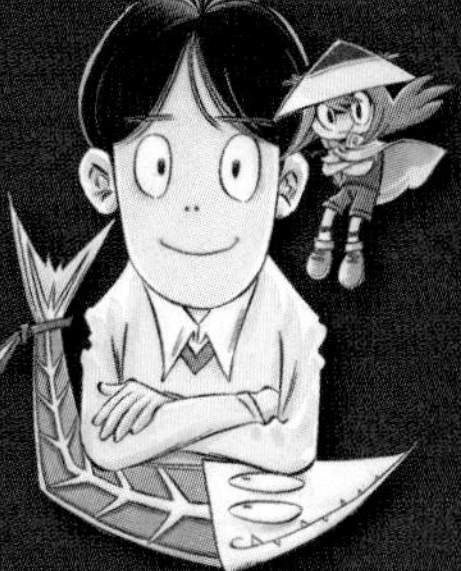

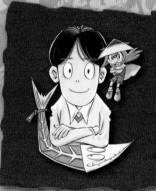

Tatsuya Morino served as an assistant to manga artist Shigeru Mizuki for over ten years before striking out on his own in 1994. His works include "*Kibakichi*" (2004), "*LEGENTAIL Sennenta*" (2009), and creating the characters for the web-anime "*Trip Trek*."

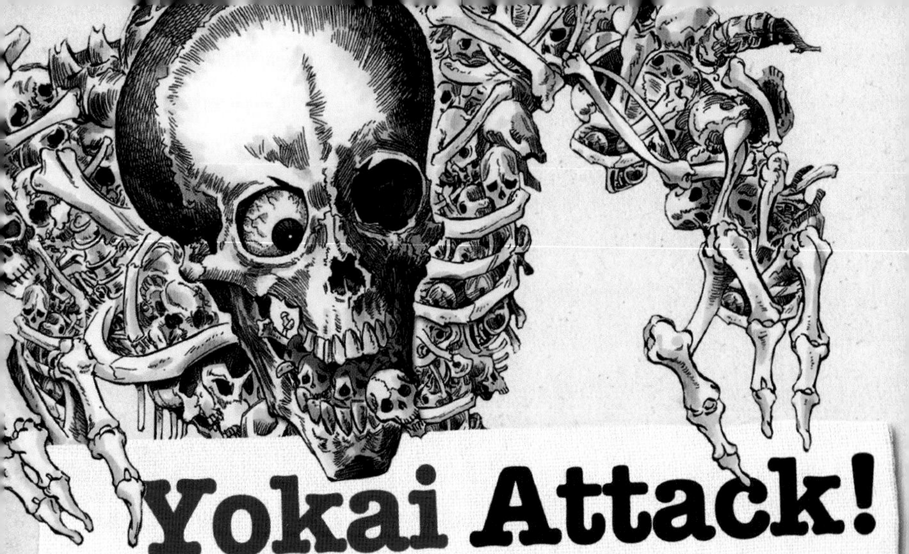

Yokai Attack!

The Japanese Monster Survival Guide

Hiroko Yoda and **Matt Alt**
Illustrations by **Tatsuya Morino**

外国人のための妖怪サバイバルガイド

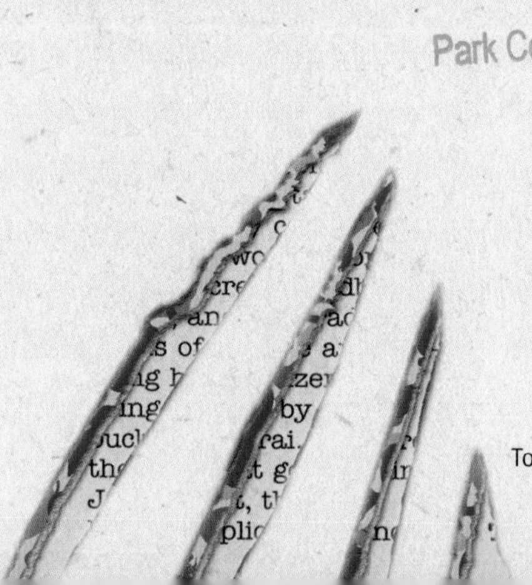

TUTTLE Publishing
Tokyo | Rutland, Vermont | Singapore

Published by Tuttle Publishing, an imprint of Periplus Editions (HK) Ltd.

www.tuttlepublishing.com

Copyright © 2008, 2012 Hiroko Yoda and Matt Alt
Illustrations © Tatsuya Morino

Library of Congress Cataloging-in-Publication Data

Yoda, Hiroko.
  Yokai attack : the japanese monster survival guide / Hiroko Yoda and Matt Alt ; illustrations by Tatsuya Morino. -- Rev. ed.
     p. cm.
  Includes bibliographical references and index.
  ISBN 978-4-8053-1219-3 (pbk.)
  1. Yokai (Japanese folklore) I. Alt, Matt. II. Title.
  GR340.Y63 2012
  398.20952--dc23

                        2012009752

ISBN 978-4-8053-1219-3

Distributed by

North America, Latin America & Europe
Tuttle Publishing
364 Innovation Drive,
North Clarendon,
VT 05759-9436 U.S.A.
Tel: 1 (802) 773-8930
Fax: 1 (802) 773-6993
info@tuttlepublishing.com
www.tuttlepublishing.com

Asia Pacific
Berkeley Books Pte. Ltd.
61 Tai Seng Avenue #02-12
Singapore 534167
Tel: (65) 6280-1330
Fax: (65) 6280-6290
inquiries@periplus.com.sg
www.periplus.com

Japan
Tuttle Publishing
Yaekari Building, 3rd Floor
5-4-12 Osaki, Shinagawa-ku
Tokyo 141 0032
Tel: (81) 3 5437-0171
Fax: (81) 3 5437-0755
sales@tuttle.co.jp
www.tuttle.co.jp

15 14 13 12   6 5 4 3 2 1
1205CP

Printed in Singapore

TUTTLE PUBLISHING® is a registered trademark of Tuttle Publishing, a division of Periplus Editions (HK) Ltd.

Contents

For Setsuko and
Yakumo Koizumi,
a.k.a Mrs. and
Mr. Lafcadio Hearn

Preface

The *yokai* are the spookiest Japanese monsters you've never heard of, and it's high time they got their due.

 Written with the Japanese characters for "otherworldly" and "weird," the word "yokai" has typically been translated in a great many ways, from "demon" to "ghost" to "goblin" to "spectre"—all of which are about as imprecise and un-evocative as translating "samurai" as "Japanese warrior," or "sushi" as "raw fish on rice." Yokai are yokai.

The yokai in this survival guide are mythical, supernatural creatures that have populated generations of Japanese fairy tales and folk stories. They can be seen in museums worldwide on scrolls, screens, woodblock prints, and other traditional forms of Japanese art, menacing hapless citizens or being skewered by swashbuckling samurai. They are the things that go bump in Japan's night, the faces behind inexplicable phenomena, the personalities behind the strange hands that fate often deals us. They represent the attempts of the fertile human imagination to impose meaning and rationality on a chaotic, unpredictable, often difficult-to-explain world. This is essentially what the yokai are: superstitions with personalities.

For centuries they have stalked the mountains, forests, fields, rivers, and coastlines of Japan. Some are animal-like, some are human-like. Others are inanimate objects that have taken uncanny sentient form. Some are personifications of natural phenomena. And still others are obviously tongue-in-cheek flights of fancy—physical incarnations of jokes, puns, or idioms. Some are considered helpful. Many are mischievous. And more than a few are thought to be very, very dangerous. They are Japan's bogeymen, and once the lights go out, they are always there.

The term yokai wasn't always as widely used to describe these creatures as it is today. Until the end of

the seventeenth century, they were more commonly referred to as *mononoke* (ghosts) or *bakemono* (monsters). Many were originally of foreign provenance, having come to Japan via Chinese religious and academic texts. Others were purely native creations.

The single most famous collection of yokai illustrations can be found in artist Sekien Toriyama's 1776 satire *Gazu Hyakki Yako*, or the "Illustrated Demons' Night Parade." It featured descriptions of more than fifty yokai, some rooted in tradition, but many crafted by Sekien himself to poke fun at various social conventions. Its success led to a series of sequels and heralded a growing public interest in the mysterious creatures.

The real heyday of yokai was in the early to mid-1800s, from the end of what is known as the Edo period through the Meiji era, just before Japan re-opened to the West and began modernizing. Raised in the fertile soil of Japan's polytheistic, animistic culture, polished by generations of rural storytellers and eventually given form by urban artists and illustrators, the folktale creatures enchanted people of the day. They quickly emerged as popular subjects for the burgeoning mass media, which at the time included books, woodblock prints, scrolls, and public storytelling. Adults perused tabloid publications brimming with lurid descriptions of purported real-life yokai encounters, while children collected yokai *karuta* (game cards) in a trend that is startlingly evocative of the Pokemon fad that swept the world in the late twentieth century.

Yet for all the fascination and even terror they induced in generations of Japanese, the strange creatures proved no match at first for the inexorable march of progress. In the late nineteenth century, Japanese philosopher and university professor Dr. Enryo Inoue saw the widespread belief in yokai as such a threat to modernization that he established *yokaigaku*—"yokai-ology"—a systematic, science-based approach to cataloging and debunking purported yokai sightings. Slowly but surely, yokai began to disappear from the public consciousness around the same time that Japan began to

industrialize and institute a formal educational system. (Ironically, Inoue's painstakingly collected data is a treasure trove for those interested in yokai today.)

For a while it seemed as if this complex bunch of bogeymen, some of them strong and voracious enough to rip a man's entrails out by hand, were fragile enough to be driven away by the advent of electricity, flush toilets, and the trappings of an industrial society.

But yokai never die—they just fade away until the moment suits their return. While the lights may never truly go out in modern Japanese cities, the yokai never stopped prowling the pages of Japanese literature.

It was a foreigner who rekindled the Japanese love affair with yokai: Lafcadio Hearn, the eccentric journalist who published in English under his given name and in Japanese under the name Yakumo Koizumi. His compilations of Japanese legends, produced with the assistance of his wife and interpreter, Setsuko, include *In Ghostly Japan* (1899) and *Kwaidan* (1903). When translated back into Japanese, they influenced a new generation of local folklore scholars.

Kunio Yanagita's *Tono Monogatari* ("Tales of Tono"), a collection of folktales and yokai stories from the northern reaches of Japan, proved tremendously popular on its publication in 1912, and remains in print even today. Comic books featuring yokai characters sparked another fad for things yokai in the 1960s, most notably artist Shigeru Mizuki's hit series *Ge Ge Ge no Kitaro*. Many of Mizuki's characters are based on the same folktales and classic art that were consulted for this book.

Children raised on this fearsome fare grew into adults that remained fascinated with the creatures. Yokai-like characters appear in several of the novels written by bestselling Japanese author Haruki Murakami, including the mysterious Sheep Man from *A Wild Sheep Chase* and the *yamikuro* (translated as "Infra-Nocturnal Kappa" in the English edition) that infest the Tokyo sewer system in *Hard-Boiled Wonderland and the End of the World*. The internationally acclaimed films of director Hayao Miyazaki feature abundant yokai-related imagery—

including *Spirited Away*, *The Princess Mononoke*, *Pom Poko*, and even *My Neighbor Totoro*, the eponymous main character of which could be considered a yokai of sorts. And hundreds—perhaps thousands—of yokai took the stage in director Takashi Miike's 2005 film *Yokai Daisenso* (*The Great Yokai War*). Yokai may not have the hold over the public consciousness that they once enjoyed, but they continue to subtly inform the aesthetic rhythms that pulse beneath the surface of Japanese pop culture.

Learn about yokai and you will understand a critical piece of the puzzle that Japanese culture often presents to outsiders.

That's where this book comes into play. *Yokai Attack!* is your one-stop guide to understanding Japan's traditional creepy-crawlies. Yokai are ethereal sorts of beings, nearly always encountered at night, so everyone has their own take on how they might look in real life and what sorts of characteristics they might have. This book represents an attempt to reconcile descriptions from a variety of sources, including but not limited to individual accounts of encounters, Japanese vintage woodblock prints, and microfilms of vintage illustrations stored in the National Diet Library in Tokyo.

All-new illustrations, created by the talented Tatsuya Morino, detail the potential appearance of each yokai. In many cases, they're portrayed in a traditional manner; in others, we decided to have some fun exploring how they might look in more modern settings. Alongside each illustration is a series of "data points," allowing you to take in key characteristics at a glance. And most importantly, we've provided information about how to survive meetings with these strange creatures—handy for any potential close encounters.

A quick word about what this book is *not*. It is not intended as an authoritative last word on the origins or purported behavior of these creatures. It is a collection of conventional wisdom (perhaps "uncanny wisdom" would be a better term?) concerning the yokai—the sorts of things the average Japanese individual might know about them. Think of it as a springboard for further exploration

on your own, and a leg up to understanding the many references and allusions to yokai that appear in modern Japanese films, literature, and even everyday speech.

In traditional Japanese "yokai-ology," the creatures are classified by where they generally appear. Typical habitats include in and around houses (both functional and abandoned), mountains, forests, Buddhist temples, the banks of lakes or rivers, coastal waters, and such. But to make things easier for the first-time reader who isn't as intimately familiar with these traditional settings, here we group a small selection of the most famous and visually appealing yokai by personality. **Ferocious Fiends** are the sorts of creatures you wouldn't want to encounter in a dark alley (or a bright one, for that matter). **Gruesome Gourmets** are yokai with peculiar eating habits. **Annoying Neighbors** are the sorts of things you pray never move in next door. **The Sexy and Slimy** enchant their prey with slithery svelteness or carnal charms. And **The Wimps** are just what their name implies: monsters who are probably more afraid of you than you are of them.

So forget Godzilla. Forget the giant beasties karate-chopped into oblivion by endless incarnations of Ultraman, Kamen Rider, and the Power Rangers. Forget the Pocket Monsters. Forget Sadako from *The Ring* and that creepy all-white kid from *The Grudge*. Forget everything you know about Japanese tales of terror.

If you want to survive an encounter with a member of Japan's most fearsome and fascinating bunch of monsters, you've got some reading to do.

—*Hiroko Yoda & Matt Alt*
Tokyo
2012

Yokai Terminology

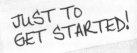

Bakemono: This extremely broad term can be used to refer to any monstrous or supernatural creature. Often used as a synonym for "yokai," it was once exclusively used to refer to the types of creatures depicted in this book.

Biwa: A traditional, short-necked Japanese lute that was introduced to Japan via China around the eighth century. It is based on similar Middle Eastern instruments.

Edo: Also spelled "Yedo." The name of Tokyo until it became Japan's capital city in 1868.

Edo Era: Lasted from 1603 to 1867. Yokai-related art, including paintings, woodblock prints, and *karuta* cards, became quite popular during this period of Japanese history.

Hearn, Lafcadio: (1850-1904) A journalist, author, and educator, Hearn is best known for introducing Japanese ghost stories to the English-speaking world. Born in Greece and educated in Ireland, he spent much of his career in the United States and the West Indies before coming to Japan. He took the name Yakumo Koizumi after marrying his wife Setsuko and taking Japanese citizenship.

Heian Era: The period of Japanese history that began with the movement of Japan's capital to Kyoto in 794 and lasted until 1185.

Heiankyo: The former name of the city now known as Kyoto, which was the capital of Japan for more than a thousand years. In 1868, the capital moved to Tokyo.

Inoue, Enryo: (1858-1919) Japan's foremost investigator of supernatural phenomena. His life work, a philosophy and book series called *Yokaigaku* (Yokai-ology) earned him the nickname "Dr. Yokai." Although his research and educational efforts were dedicated to stamping out belief in the occult and supernatural, his collections of local superstitions are a treasure trove for folk researchers.

Kaidan: Occasionally written "Kwaidan" (a regional dialectic variation), this term refers to spooky stories and tales of terror.

Kami: Literally, "god," but the concept differs from the Western monotheistic usage. Kami can be used to refer to an almighty creator, but is also used to denote nearly any spirit, deity, or otherworldly presence. In times of old, it was often used to describe the divine forces of nature.

See photos from Shinto shrines in the sections on Kitsune (p. 154) and Hanadaka-tengu (p. 22)

Karuta: Derived from the Portuguese word for "card," these decorated paper (later cardboard) cards are used in a traditional Japanese game. Karuta featuring monster motifs became popular during the Edo era.

Koto: A variety of floor-harp, roughly six feet long. Some versions are native Japanese creations; others are derived from similar Chinese instruments.

Mononoke: A supernatural being. See also Bakemono and Yurei.

Obake: Literally, "honorable monster." A softer, cuter, colloquial version of Bakemono.

Oni: Often translated as "demon" or "ogre," Oni carries connotations of extreme power and does not always necessarily indicate an evil or harmful creature. Common throughout Japanese folklore, they are often described as clawed, fanged humanoids with red or green skin, tiger-striped loincloths, and a pair of short horns growing from their heads.

Shamisen: A traditional three-stringed musical instrument that is played with a weighted plectrum.

Shinto: The native religion of Japan is a polytheistic, animistic belief system with a strong emphasis on nature worship. While the majority of Japanese would not identify themselves as active practitioners, Shinto shrines are extremely common throughout the country, and the core beliefs remain deeply entwined with the culture.

Shoji: A sliding screen consisting of a wooden lattice overlaid with paper. A traditional sort of home furnishing in Japan.

Toire: Pronounced "toy-ray," this is the Japanese version of the English word "toilet."

Toriyama, Sekien: (1712-1788) A talented woodblock print artist with a knack for portraying subjects from folklore. His pioneering illustrations of yokai and other supernatural creatures remain popular even today. Several reproductions of his work can be found in the pages of this book.

Yanagita, Kunio: (1875-1962) Author of the influential 1912 book *Tono Monogatari* (Tales of Tono), which re-introduced rapidly modernizing Japanese to a variety of folktales, legends, and superstitions from the far north of their country.

Yokai: See Preface.

Yurei: A spirit that has, for whatever reason, not entered the afterlife. Essentially, a ghost.

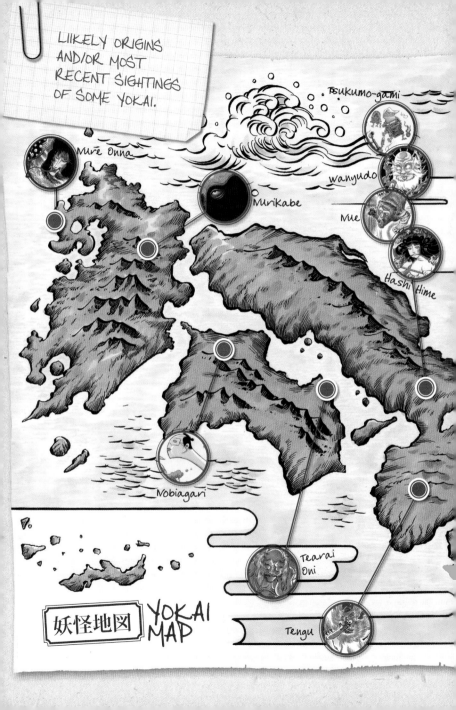

LIIKELY ORIGINS AND/OR MOST RECENT SIGHTINGS OF SOME YOKAI.

Tsukumo-gami

Mure Onna

Nurikabe

wanyudo

Mue

Hashi Hime

Nobiagari

Tearai Oni

妖怪地図 YOKAI MAP

Tengu

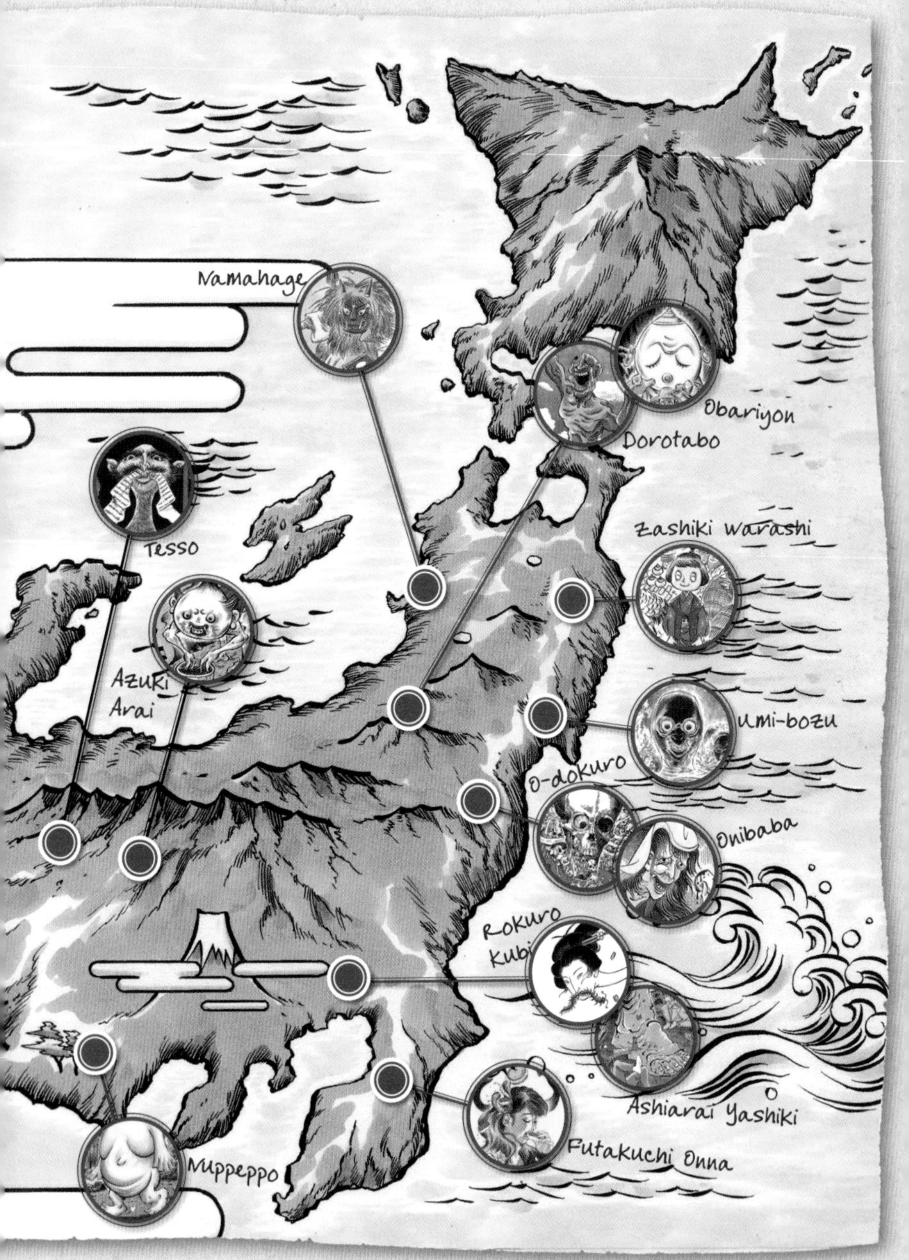

Namahage
Obariyon
Dorotabo
Tesso
Zashiki Warashi
Azuki
Arai
Umi-bozu
O-dokuro
Onibaba
Rokuro
Kubi
Ashiarai Yashiki
Futakuchi Onna
Nuppeppo

輪入道

車の轂に大なる入道の首つきたるがかた輪をかけてめぐりありくありこれを見る者魂を失ふ此所勝母の里と紙にかきて家の出入り

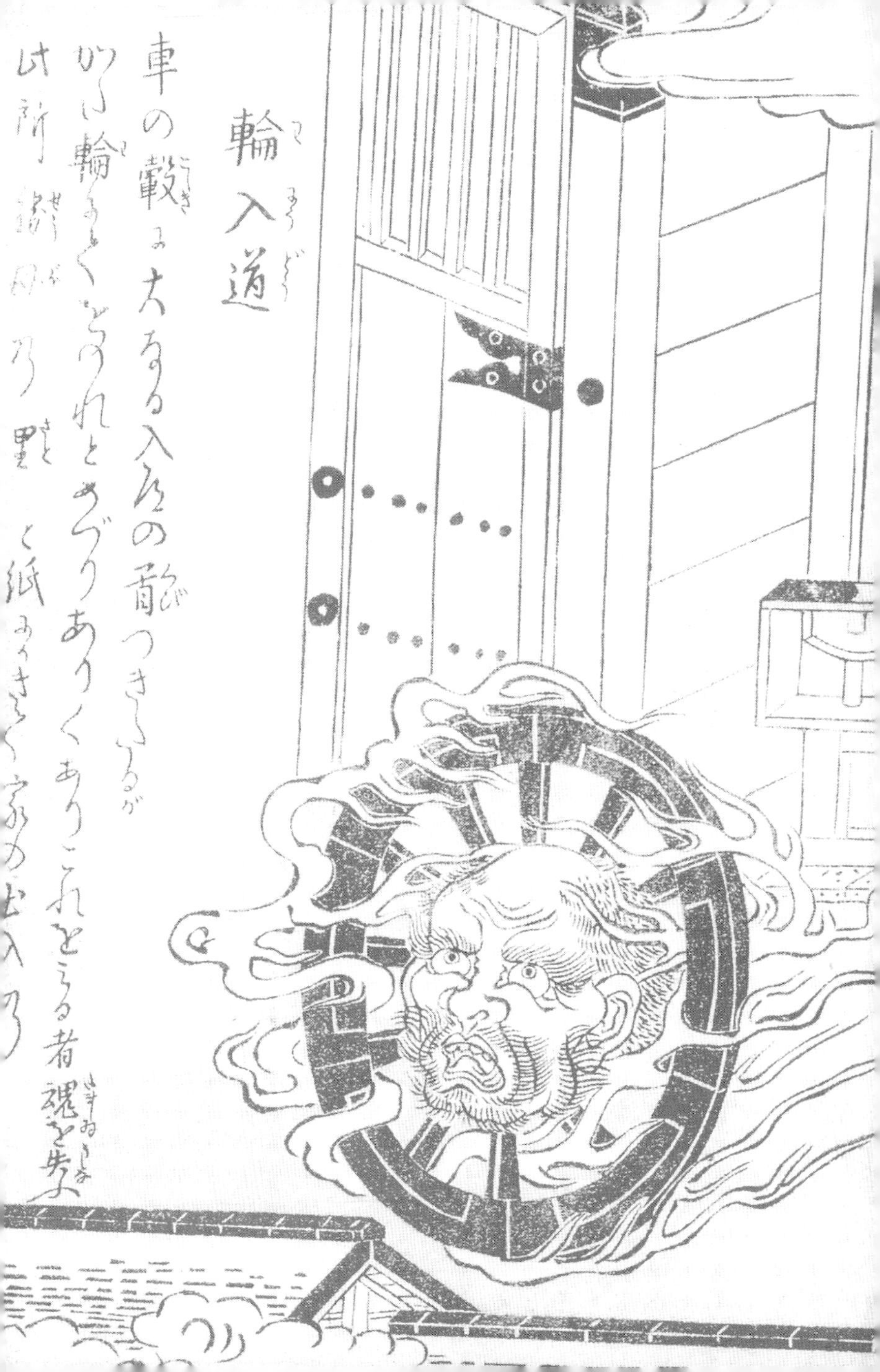

Ferocious Fiends

Make no bones about it: a run-in with one of this fearsome crew will send you to the hospital if you're lucky . . . and the grave if you're not.

YOKAI NO: 0 0 1

Karasu-tengu

鳥天狗

Pronunciation:
(KAH-rah-soo TEN-goo)

English Name:
Raven-tengu

Gender:
Male/Female

Height:
5 to 6 ft. (150 to 180cm)

Weight:
Unknown

Locomotion:
Bipedal, flight, teleportation

Distinctive Features:
Generally humanoid
Bird-like or dog-like face with beak. When clothed, attire is similar to that of a Buddhist monk

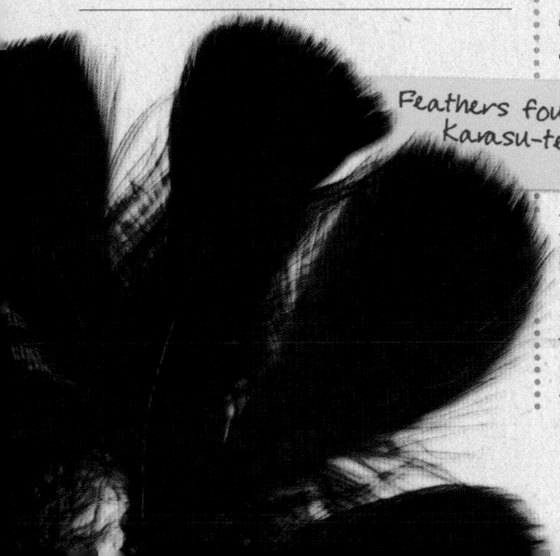

Feathers found near a Karasu-tengu sighting

Offensive Weapons:
Tremendous strength
Ability to cloud human minds
Possession of human hosts (according to some tales)
Claws and shape shifting!

Abundance:
Prevalent

Habitat:
Mountainous regions

Claim to Fame:
The wings on their backs may be reminiscent of angels, but the similarities end there. Crafty, adroit, and extraordinarily dangerous, these unpredictable tricksters are a constant presence in Japanese myth and folklore. Their portrayal has varied greatly over the centuries since their first recorded appearance in eighth-century Japanese literature, but let us boil those thousand years of history down for you: Tengu equal trouble.

According to the *Tale of the Heike*, a twelfth-century chronicle of Japanese military and political intrigue, the

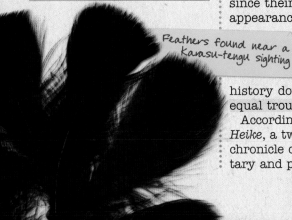

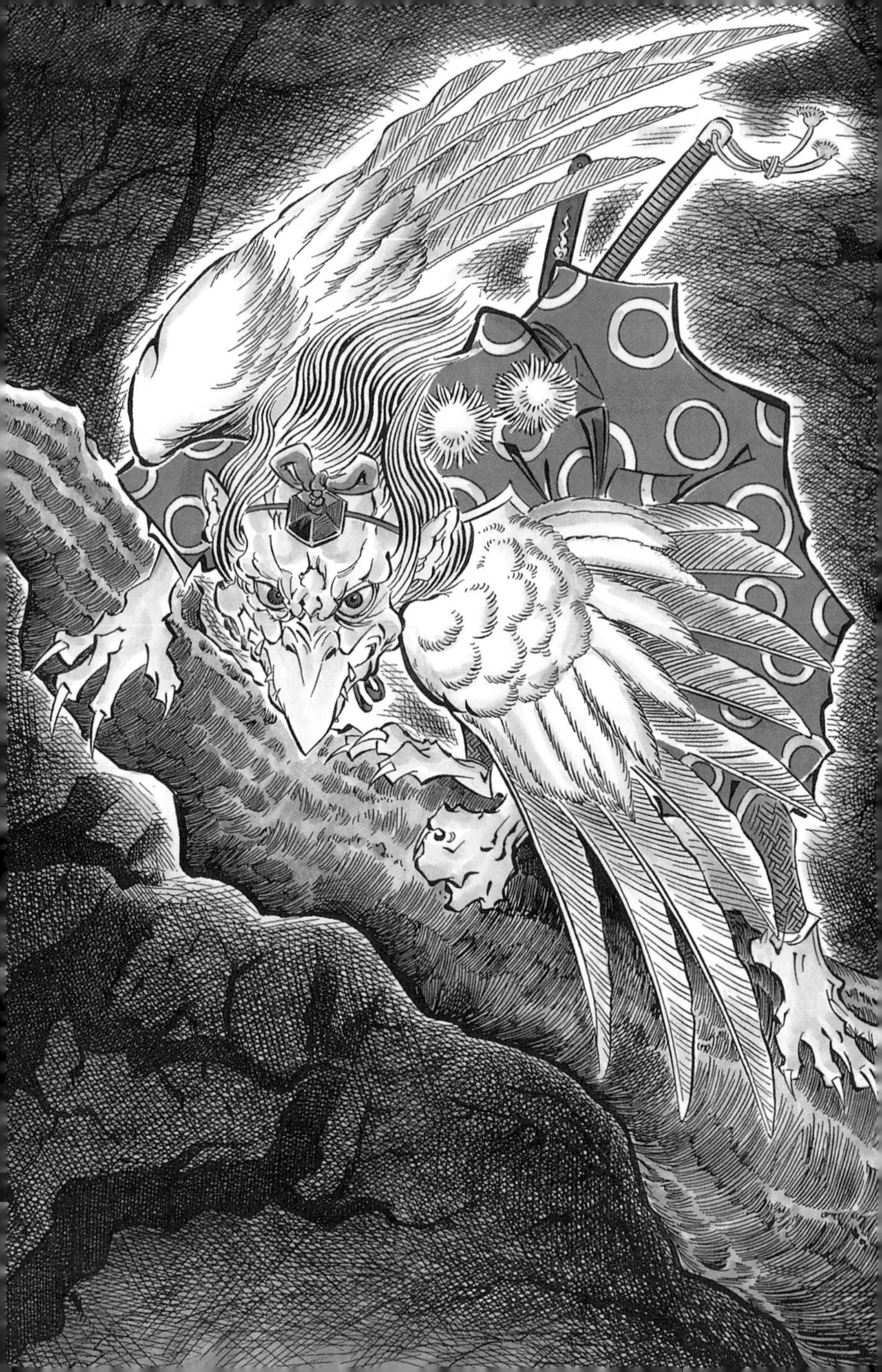

Karasu-tengu are "men, but not men; bird, but not bird; dog, but not dog; they possess the hands of a human, the head of a canine, a pair of wings, and are capable of both flight and walking."

The Karasu-tengu are, essentially, a metaphor for the travails of becoming a Buddhist monk. In their earliest incarnation, they were death and destruction. They are also famed for their skill with a variety of weapons and are credited with having taught some of Japan's most renowned swordsmen their skills.

It is not exactly clear how Karasu-tengu reproduce, but the population includes females as well as males. They are said to hatch from enormous eggs, occasionally found deep in the mountains by wayward travelers.

Tengu Trivia: Popular legend has it that the famed general Minamoto no Yoshitsune (1159?–1189) learned swordsmanship and military tactics from a variety of Tengu in the mountains near Kyoto.

portrayed as taking great pleasure in playing tricks, spiriting disciples away to far-flung locations, and taking various forms to tempt holy men and believers from the path of virtue. They were also said to have the ability to possess human hosts, causing madness or inciting political intrigue. Over the years they have been blamed for causing all manner of catastrophe and mayhem, including the spreading of plagues and other natural disasters. That being said, Karasu-tengu are not always viewed as harbingers of

The Attack!

Karasu-tengu are the foot-soldiers and enforcers of the Tengu world. Unlike the related Hanadaka-tengu (p. 22), who generally eschew random violence, the Karasu-tengu instigate disaster on scales both widespread and personal. They are fiercely protective of their territory and will relentlessly attack those who insult them or their masters.

If you find yourself face to face with an angry Karasu-tengu, you are in serious, serious trouble. Its proficiency with a wide array of

man-made weapons is dangerous enough. But its ability to shape-shift and take flight makes it far more deadly than any human opponent, and its raptor-like claws and beak are as capable of disemboweling you as any sword.

Surviving an Encounter:
If you happen to live in an area where a Karasu-tengu has decided to spread a plague or other form of mass calamity, with any luck you can pack your bags and get out. If one is targeting you personally, you're going to have to take your medicine. No human power can halt a Karasu-tengu on the warpath.

As a preventive measure, you can avoid incurring the wrath of a Karasu-tengu by treating the mountainous areas in which they dwell with care and respect. And who knows—if you're lucky, you might even earn yourself some lessons from one of these undisputed masters of martial arts. In 1806, villagers in Gifu prefecture reported that Tengu kidnapped a fifteen-year-old boy named Jugoro. He returned three years later, completely unharmed, but had become an expert marksman with the *tanegashima*, a flintlock rifle that represented the cutting edge of Japanese weaponry at the time.

Some Scholars Say:
The roots of the Tengu can be found in the Hindu deity Garuda, a similar avian-humanoid hybrid, tales of whom arrived in Japan along with the importation of Buddhism in roughly the same era.

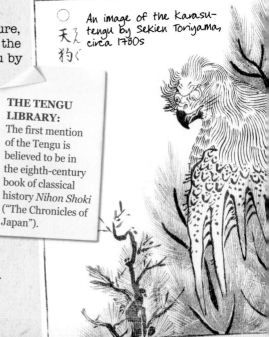

THE TENGU LIBRARY:
The first mention of the Tengu is believed to be in the eighth-century book of classical history *Nihon Shoki* ("The Chronicles of Japan").

天狗
An image of the Karasu-tengu by Sekien Toriyama, circa 1780s

YOKAI NO: 0 0 2

Hanadaka-tengu

鼻高天狗

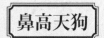

Pronunciation:
(HAH-nah-dah-kah TEN-goo)

English Name:
Longnose Tengu

Gender:
Male

Height:
6 ft. (180cm) and up

Weight:
Unknown

Locomotion:
Bipedal, flight, teleportation

Distinctive Features:
Enormous nose
Large feathered wings
Bright red skin
Barefoot or wearing single-toothed "geta" clogs

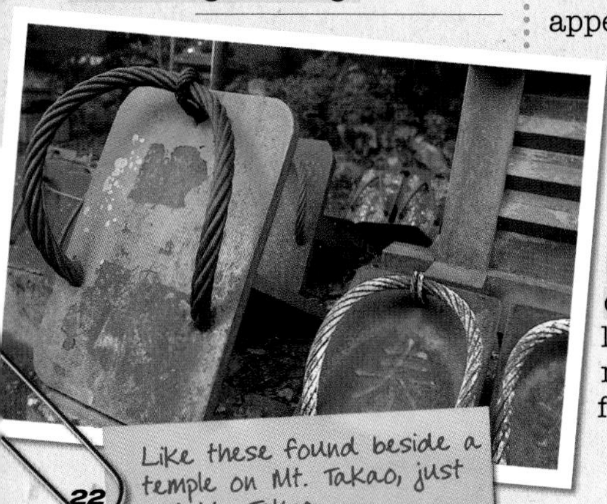

Like these found beside a temple on Mt. Takao, just outside Tokyo

Supernatural Abilities:
Telepathy
Teleportation

Offensive Weapons:
Weapon-based martial arts, particularly swordsmanship
Ability to generate strong winds using leaf-like fans
Shape-shifting and mimicry

Abundance:
Prevalent

Habitat:
Mountainous regions

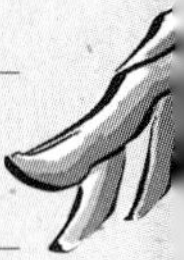

Claim to Fame:
The more recent of the two distinct "species" of Tengu that are known to inhabit the Japanese islands (see Karasu-tengu, p. 18). The Hanadaka-tengu's physical appearance is based on that of the *yamabushi*, practitioners of Shugendo, a religion dedicated to asceticism and training in isolated alpine monasteries. Tengu are enormous, muscular creatures, with spectacularly long noses, bright red skin, and massive feathered wings. The most

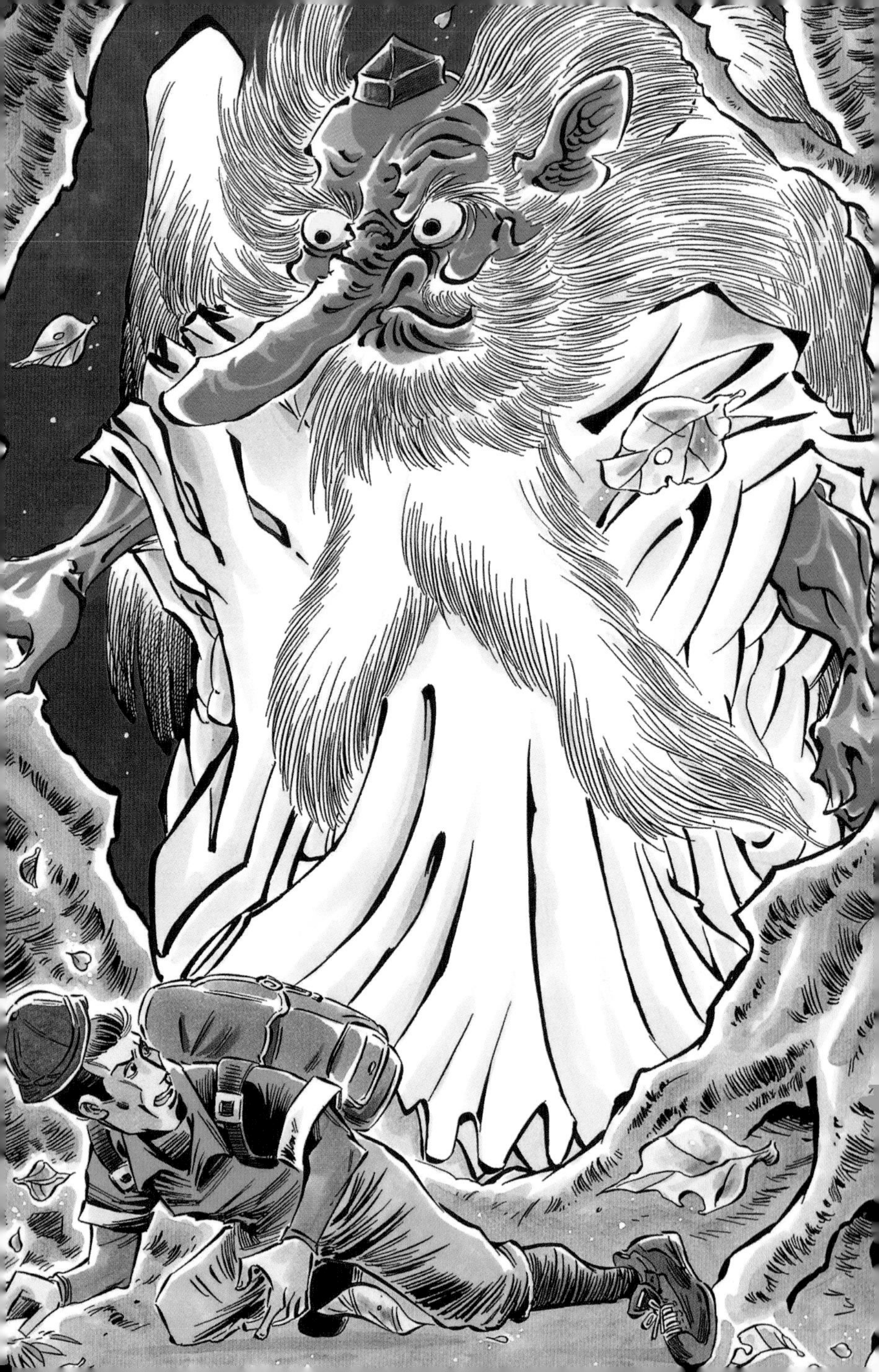

FIENDS

sive feathered wings. The most powerful are called O-tengu (Great Tengu), and are said to be the leaders of Tengu clans. The Hanadaka-tengu are said to be superior to the Karasu-tengu in the pecking order of the Tengu hierarchy.

Famed for vanity, they are known to love showing off their vast knowledge and, like the Karasu-tengu, have been credited with teaching some of Japan's top martial artists their skills. Boasting an elaborate culture and deep ties to Japanese mythology, religion, and the martial arts, the Tengu are often described as minor gods. Even today,

traditional masks featuring their visages are common sights in Japan.

These yokai have a wide variety of startling abilities—including the power to communicate without moving their mouths, and a flight speed reportedly on par with a jet aircraft.

The Attack!

Famed for an obsession with discipline and spiritual training, a Hanadaka-tengu would rarely engage in acts of wanton violence. Instead it prefers to play tricks on its prey, often in an attempt to teach a wayward soul a lesson. Quite often the victims of this mischief are spirited away to some far-flung location. In one notable incident in 1812, a stark-naked man fell from the skies over the streets of Tokyo's Asakusa district. Disoriented but uninjured, he claimed his last memory had been of hiking on a Kyoto mountainside long known as a home to the Tengu.

A tengu mask

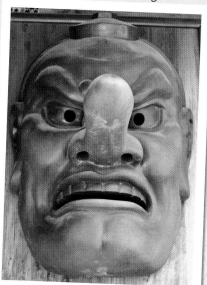

TENGU PROVERBS:
"Tengu ni naru"—in keeping with the Tengu's love of teaching and displaying their skills, this idiom means "to show off" or "to act overconfidently."

Surviving an Encounter:
The humble and pure of heart have nothing to fear from a Tengu, but woe betide those who are pompous and self-important. If you've angered one, chances are you're beyond any help we can offer here. May we suggest a change in attitude and lifestyle?

Being dropped nude onto the streets of Tokyo is merely embarrassing; you could well find yourself without clothes atop a remote mountaintop. And these sorts of pranks assume you haven't upset a Hanadaka-tengu enough to make him truly angry, in which case you might well find yourself facing the point of an extraordinarily sharp *katana* blade—or being sent flying by a wave of his fan, which when swung forcefully can create a blast of wind more powerful than a hurricane.

Bottom line: your best bet for survival is to appeal to the Tengu's sense of mercy. Beg for your life.

TENGU TRIPS:
Mt. Takao is the site of a temple dedicated to the Tengu. It was (and is) home not only to practitioners of Shugendo but a large population of Japanese giant flying squirrels. Some scientists theorize that the combination may be responsible for the large number of nocturnal Tengu sightings that once occurred here.

Tengu Tips:
Know your Tengu hierarchy. The Edo-era book *Tengu-Kyo* (The Book of Tengu) describes forty-eight Japanese mountains as being associated with specific Tengu clans. For example, Kyoto's Mt. Atago is the home of a clan led by Tarobo; nearby Mt. Kurama, Sojobo. Even Mt. Fuji is home to the Daranibo clan. The total clan member population is estimated by the book's author to be some 125,500 Tengu, giving a sense of the sheer prevalence of these creatures.

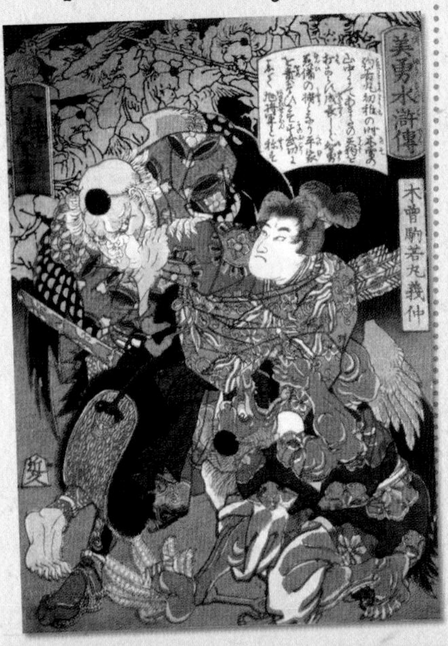
美勇水滸傳
木曽駒若丸義仲

An 1867 print by Yoshitoshi. Talk about taking the Tengu by the nose! (Not recommended for amateurs.)

Kappa

河童

Pronunciation:
(KAH-pah)

English Names:
Literally, "River Child";
Water Sprite, Water Imp,
Water Goblin

Alternate Japanese Names:
Gawappa, Kawataro, Sui-
tengu, Suiko

Gender:
Male

Height:
3 to 5 ft. (100 to 150cm)

Weight:
65 to 100 lbs. (30 to 45kg)

Locomotion:
Bipedal or quadrupedal (on
land), webbed fingers/toes
(in water)

Distinctive Features:
Beak-like mouth; Tortoise-
like shell on back; Frog-like,
removable skin; Water-filled
depression on top of head;
Three anuses *and strong*
"fishy" odor

Offensive Weapons:
Claws, extensible arms,
extreme flatulence

Weaknesses:
Dehydration, particularly of
the "head dish," which when
spilled drains the kappa's
strength. Strong aversion to
iron, deer antlers, and mon-
keys

Abundance:
Prevalent *But may be in decline*
due to global warming?

Habitat:
Rivers, lakes, swamps, wet-
lands, and coastal areas

Claim to Fame:

If you've heard of any one
yokai, it's probably the
kappa. Easily the single most
famous yokai in Japan, this
amphibious creature has
long been feared as a vicious
scourge of Japan's rivers,
swamps, coastlines, and other
bodies of water. They are also
known to take refuge in man-
made structures such as cis-
terns and garden ponds. They
are occasionally encountered
on land in mountainous areas
during the winter, when their
watery homes freeze over.
They can be tracked by their
pungent body odor, said to be
reminiscent of rotting com-

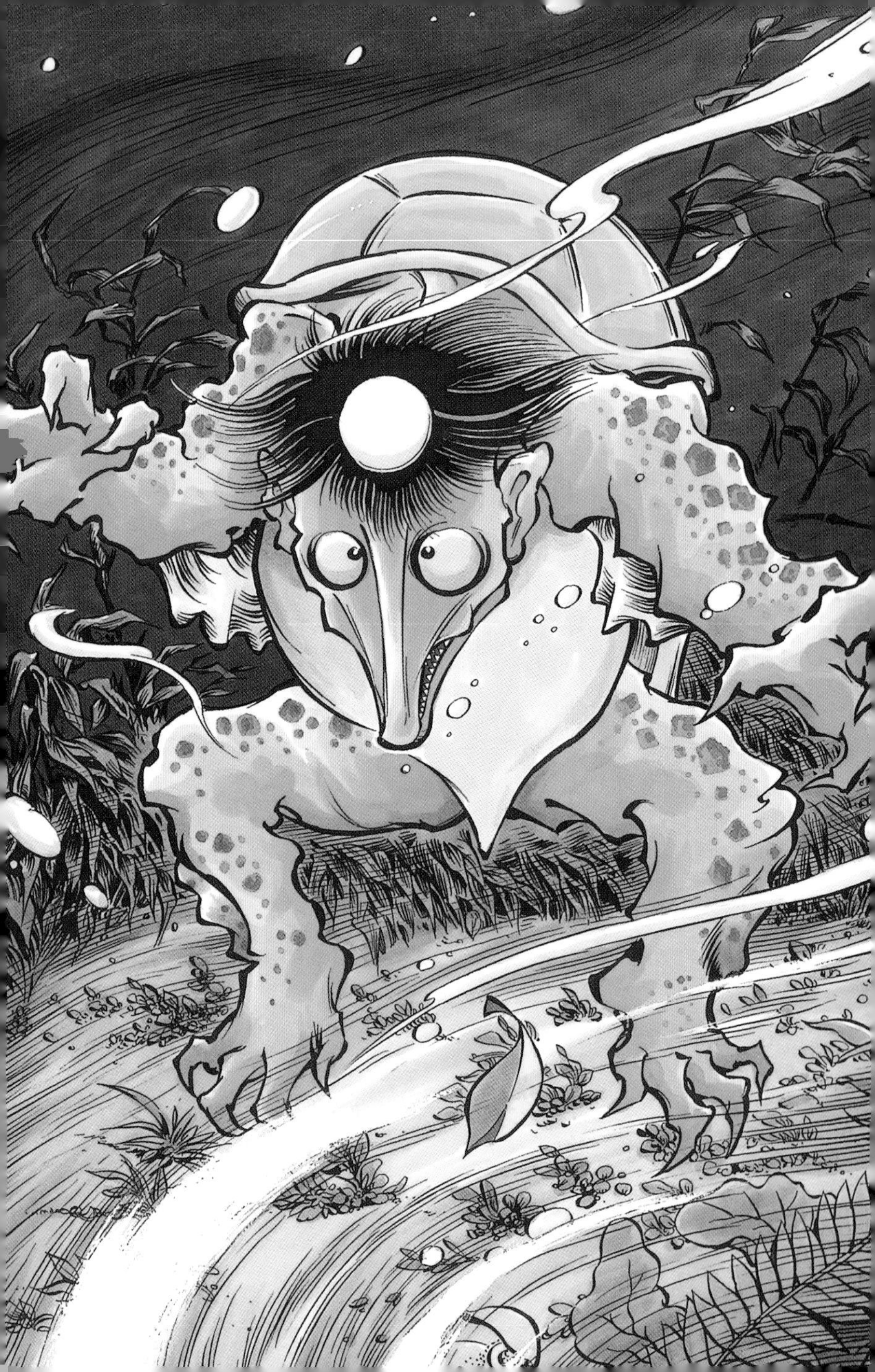

post. Kappa are the traditional "bogeymen" invoked by Japanese parents to frighten young children away from playing near lakes and rivers unattended.

According to one story, some nine thousand of the creatures swam en masse from China to Japan around the fifth century. Whatever their true origin, they have become the signature yokai of the Japanese folk pantheon.

KAPPA PROVERBS:

KAPPA NO KAWANAGARE: —"Even a kappa can drown"—is an idiom that means even experts make mistakes.

RIKU NI AGATTA KAPPA:—"Like a kappa on land"—is a saying that refers to situations where someone is out of their element.

HE NO KAPPA:—"Like a kappa fart"—is the Japanese equivalent of the American idiom "a piece of cake!"

KAPPA-HAGE—Term for a man with a round bald spot on the top of his head.

The Attack!

Although generally considered unaggressive, a kappa can be absolutely vicious when angered. While particularly famous for challenging unwary passersby to *mano a mano* wrestling matches, they are also notorious for ambushing and drowning those foolish enough to swim in isolated or fast moving waters. One strategy is simply to drag a victim below the surface. Another is to remove a swimmer's intestines from below, by punching a slimy hand through . . . well, use your imagination. The kappa isn't after the entrails themselves, but rather the *shirikodama*, a mysterious organ said to be located in the colon.

Surviving an Encounter:

If challenged to a wrestling match:

1) Grit your teeth and graciously accept.

2) Bow deeply (you're in Japan after all). This will make it spill the contents of its head-dish, draining its power like water from a bathtub.

3) Insist on wrestling under bright sunlight to speed up evaporation. (Warning: this only works on sunny days.)

4) In a real pinch, fling a fresh cucumber—one of the kappa's favorite foods—into the ring. This should distract it long enough for you to beat a hasty retreat.

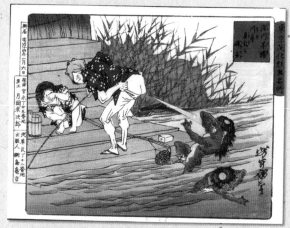

Can Kappa be repelled by farts? This 1881 woodblock print by Yoshitoshi seems to suggest as much.

If you're confronted by a kappa in the water:

1) Don't panic.

2) Work your way calmly back to shore.

3) The creatures have occasionally helped drowning children to the shore, so try acting childish. Who knows? It just might let you—and your colon—off the hook.

Kappa Couture:
Kappa must leave the water and remove their waterproof skin—called *amagawa*—in order to sleep. A kappa without its amagawa is totally defenseless: it can't enter the water without it! Because of this, raincoats are also known as *amagappa* in Japan.

Kappa Sightseeing:
The Kappabashi (Kappa Bridge) area of Tokyo has, as its name suggests, a deep connection to these strange aquatic creatures. Legend has it that the very first Kappa Bridge was built by a raincoat merchant who enlisted kappa as laborers. The former site of the bridge is now occupied by the local Buddhist temple, Sogenji, also known by its nickname, Kappa-dera (Kappa Temple).

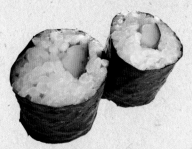

Kappa Maki Rolls

Kappa Cuisine:
The popular sushi dish *kappa maki* (cucumber roll) takes its name from this yokai.

Zashiki Warashi

座敷童子

Pronunciation:
(ZAH-she-key WAH-rah-she)

English Name:
Literally, "Child in the Room"

Gender:
Male/Female

Height:
Same as a human five-year-old

Weight:
Same as a human five-year-old

Locomotion:
Bipedal

Disctinctive Features:
Resembles a normal human child in traditional Japanese dress

Offensive Weapons:
Bankruptcy, social ostracism *and family strife!!*

Weaknesses:
Neglect

Abundance/Distribution:
Uncommon/Northern Japan

Habitat:
Happy households

Claim to Fame:
A cute and cuddly countenance cloaks this yokai's startling ability to destroy people's lives. But don't get the wrong idea: it isn't angry or out for vengeance. In fact, most of the time it's downright playful.

Taking its name from the Japanese term for a traditional tatami-floored room and an archaic term for "child," when happy, the Zashiki Warashi is a pleasant sort of poltergeist. It is especially fond of pranks and tricks, including climbing atop sleeping people in the dead of night, flipping over pillows and unmaking beds, causing music to issue from otherwise uninhabited rooms, and hiding in the midst of large groups of children during mealtimes.

In essence, this is one yokai you want to have haunting your home, for the Zashiki Warashi's presence is a sign of good fortune. The problems come when it leaves.

SEE MAP ON PAGE 32

FEROCIOUS FIENDS

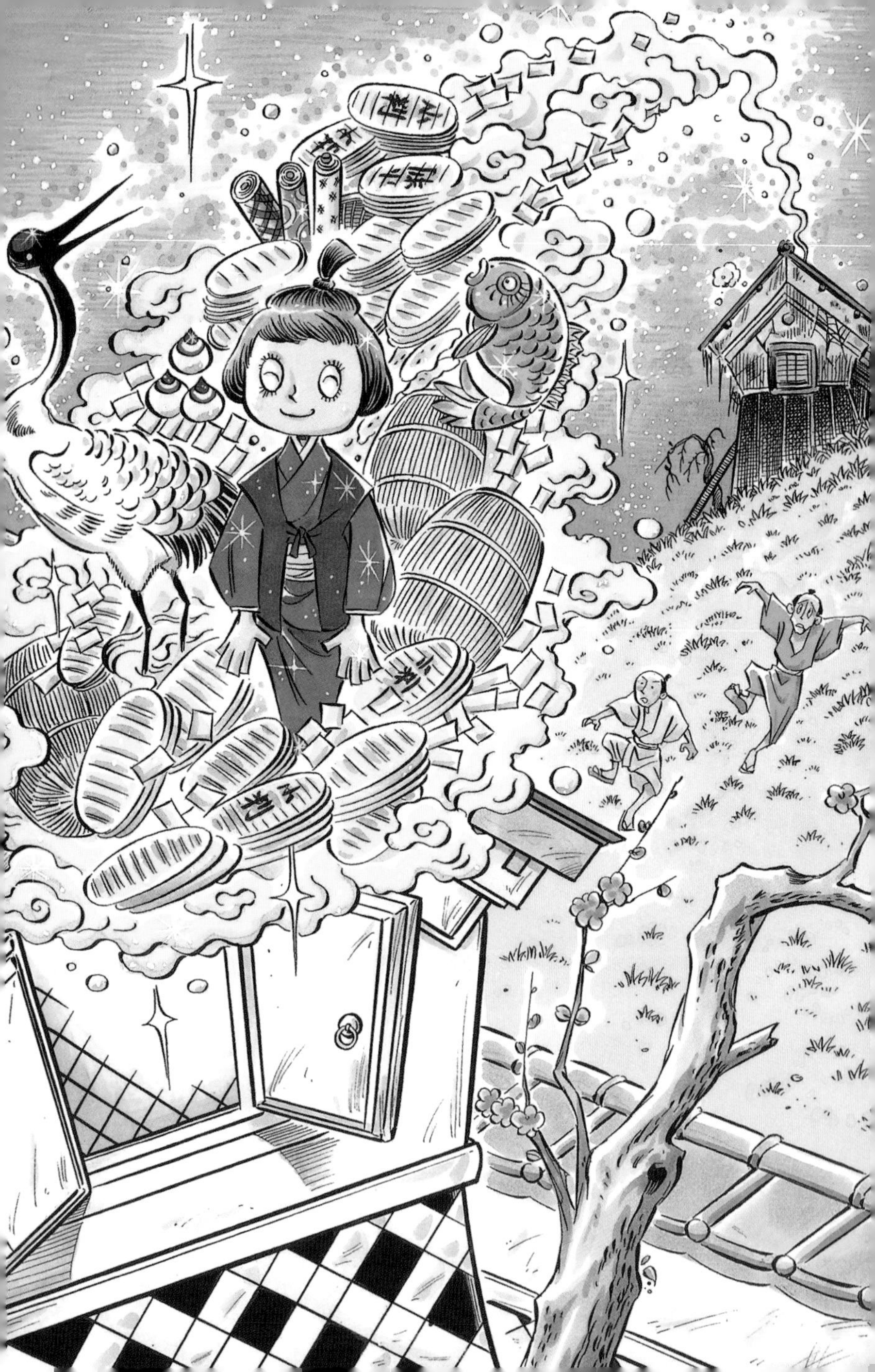

YOKAI NO: 004 ZASHIKI WARASHI

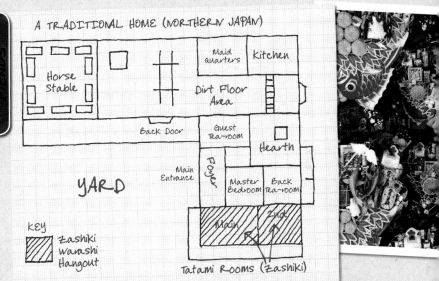

A TRADITIONAL HOME (NORTHERN JAPAN)
Horse Stable
Maid quarters
Kitchen
Dirt Floor Area
Back Door
Guest Tea-room
Hearth
Main Entrance
Foyer
YARD
Master Bedroom
Back Tea-room
Main
2nd
KEY
Zashiki Warashi Hangout
Tatami Rooms (Zashiki)

The Attack!
The Zashiki Warashi isn't aggressive. It looks like a harmless little kid. So what's to be afraid of? That's the trick. Zashiki Warashi's glowing good fortune only lasts as long as it's in your home. Its very presence is a silent demand for respect and care. If it—or more specifically, the home it inhabits—is neglected, it will leave. And when a Zashiki Warashi leaves, you and your family are most definitely in trouble, for bankruptcy, disaster, and domestic strife are certain to follow. A home deserted by a Zashiki Warashi is on the road to ruin.

Surviving an Encounter:
Think of the Zashiki Warashi as an adopted child. Take care of your home and everyone in it, and the Zashiki Warashi will take care of you. This yokai is essentially a reflection of the level of happiness of a household. If it leaves, it's already too late for you and your family.

Tracking the Zashiki Warashi:
In spite of its penchant for fun and games, the Zashiki Warashi is actually a timid sort, tending to hide from all but the residents of the homes it inhabits, and more

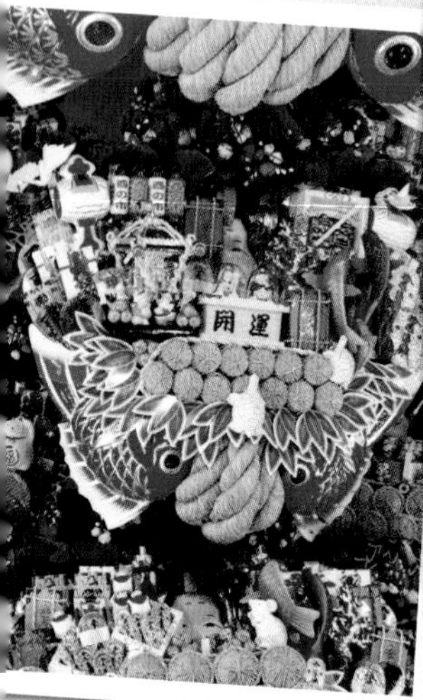
開運

"Rake of Prosperity" offerings are sold at temples to beckon the kind of fortune that the Zashiki Warashi can bring.

Zashiki Warashi in "Tales of Tono"

TOHOKU, JAPAN—In 1910, Japanese folkorist Kunio Yanagita published a compilation of stories told to him by inhabitants of Tono, a remote village located deep in Japan's northern "snow country." One of these concerned the Zashiki Warashi.

According to an old villager, the Yamaguchi family was so prosperous that many believed their household was home to not one but two Zashiki Warashi. One day as a young man, he happened to encounter two strange little girls crossing the bridge into Tono. They walked in unison and appeared deeply absorbed in thought. Since visitors were quite uncommon, he asked the girls where they were from. They replied that they had just departed the Yamaguchi household. Intrigued, he inquired further as to their destination. They answered that they were bound for a new home, the name of which the man recognized as belonging to an affluent family in a neighboring village.

Several days later, twenty members of the Yamaguchi family perished in a freak accident, mistakenly consuming poison mushrooms for dinner. Only the Yamaguchis' seven-year-old daughter survived. At the time the man told Yanagita the story, many years later, the daughter had passed away childless and in ill health, while the family in the neighboring village continued to thrive in prosperity.

frequently only making itself visible to very small children. Scattering ash on the floor in the evening may capture its tiny footprints come morning.

Those who want to come face to face with this yokai should visit a certain room in a hotel by the name of Ryokufuso in the Kindai-Ichi Onsen area of Iwate Prefecture. It is fabled as the home of a Zashiki Warashi. There is apparently no shortage of individuals who want to make the acquaintance of this gentle yokai, for the hotel is often booked solid for two years in advance.

Wanyudo

輪入道

Pronunciation:
(Wah-NEW-doh)

English Names:
Firewheel, Soultaker

Gender:
Male

Size:
Roughly 3 ft. (1m) in diameter

Locomotion:
Airborne

Distinctive Features:
A flaming wagon-wheel with a human face for a hub

Offensive Weapons:
Gaze of death

Weaknesses:
Ofuda (paper talismans)

Abundance
One of a kind

Habitat:
Urban areas

looks like someone got too close!!

Claim to Fame:

One of the oldest yokai; the origins of the Wanyudo extend back more than a thousand years to Japan's Heian era. When a tyrannous nobleman with a penchant for viciously mistreating townspeople was assassinated during an ox-drawn wagon tour of the city, his vengeful spirit returned in the form of the Wanyudo. Some say it continues to haunt the streets of Kyoto and other cities even today. Taking the form of a spinning, flaming wagon-wheel with a furious human face in place of the hub, the Wanyudo is generally encountered in large cities, particularly residential areas.

The Attack!

Those unfortunate enough to find themselves in the path of the Wanyudo as it traces its furious trajectory through the night are mercilessly run down and ripped limb from limb, their remains left smoldering in the streets. In fact, it is said that those foolish enough to gaze upon

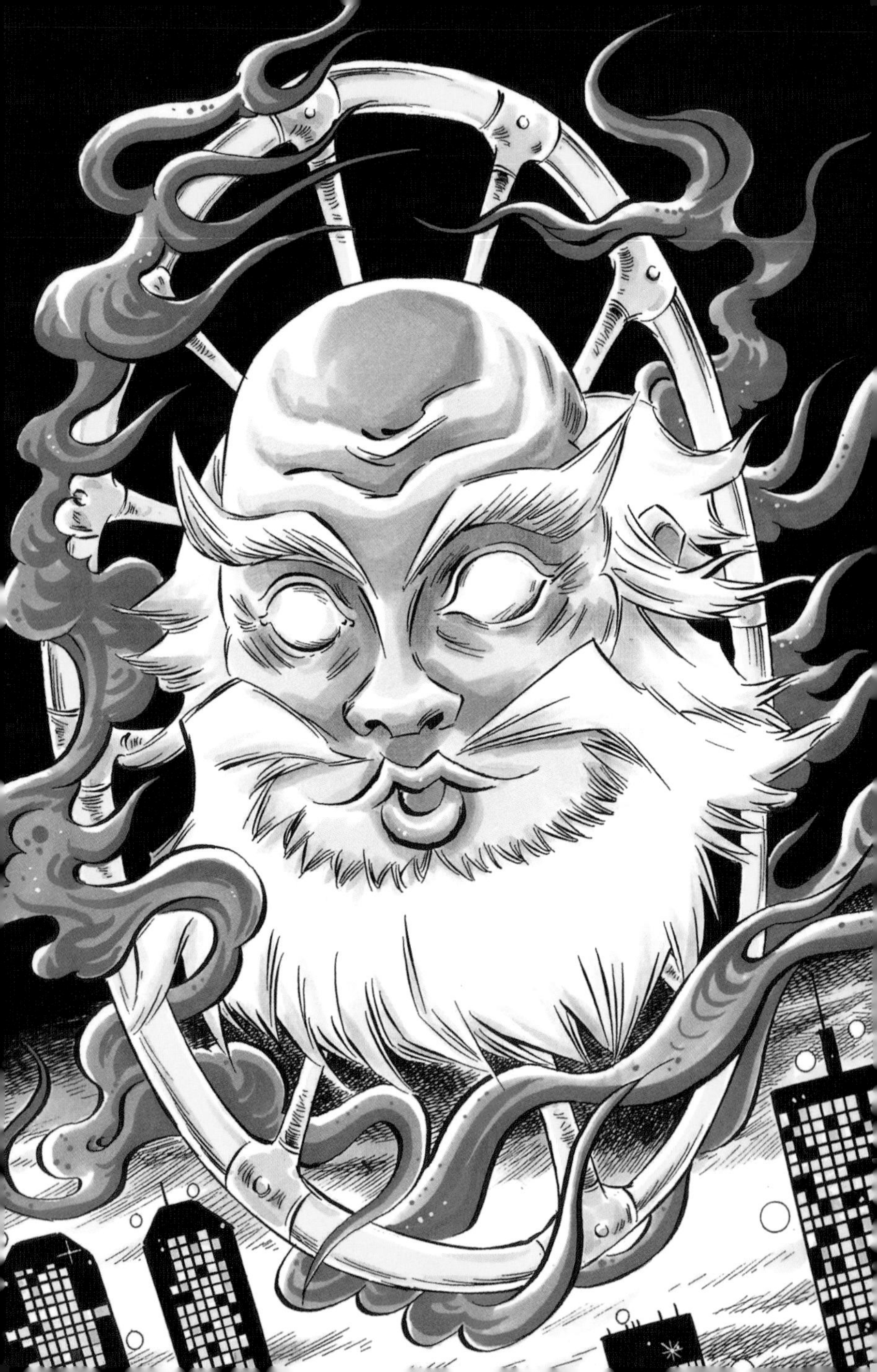

the Wanyudo as it rolls and flames its way through city skies and streets will forfeit their lives—and their souls—to the angry creature. Such is the power of this ferocious yokai's countenance that even the shortest, quickest glimpse is enough to induce a raging and life-threatening fever in the observer.

In one famous urban legend involving the Wanyudo, a woman who peeked out of her home to get a glimpse of the creature was spared death, but startled to see tiny human limbs dangling from its spokes. "If you have the time to gaze upon me, tend to your own child!" it is reported to have roared at her. When she did so, she discovered to her horror that her infant's legs had been reduced to bloody stumps.

Surviving an Encounter: Averting one's eyes is the traditional expedient. And if you do happen to catch a glimpse, take heart: some people merely faint from the sight of the creature rather than dying. Hey, life's a crapshoot.

Another traditional method of surviving Wanyudo encounters is hiding. The Wanyudo is a creature of the night; when day breaks, it heads for the mountains, where it apparently slumbers in anticipation of another night's terror. In the meantime, whatever you do, no matter what you may hear or how tempted you might be by the fury raging outside your door, *do not look at the Wanyudo*.

The safest place to hide from the Wanyudo is indoors. When you have located a suitable

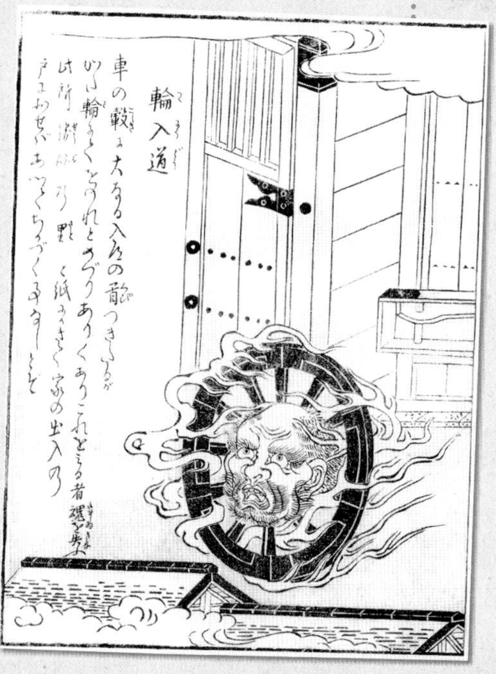
輪入道

sekien's wanyudo

HEY, KIDS! CUT OUT AND POST THIS OFUDA TO KEEP THE WANYUDO AT BAY!

structure, paste *ofuda*, slips of consecrated paper inscribed with the term "kono-tokoro-shobo-no-sato," on the doorways to keep the beast at bay. Even if the commotion outside seems to have died down, the safest course of action is to remain hidden until sunrise. The Wanyudo is too dangerous to tempt fate by leaving earlier.

Warding off the Wanyudo: Both the legend of the inattentive mother who allowed harm to come to her child and the writing on the ofuda paper have a distinct Confucian bent. The Chinese philosopher Confucius advocated (among many other things) respect for one's elders, and his teachings spread widely throughout Asia. The text, "kono-tokoro-shobo-no-sato," literally, "this is the town of Shobo," refers to a parable involving one of Confucius' disciples avoiding the Chinese town of the same name because the characters "Shobo" can be read as "triumph over one's mother."

For those interested in creating their own ofuda to ward off the Wanyudo, the specific kanji characters are:

此所勝母乃里

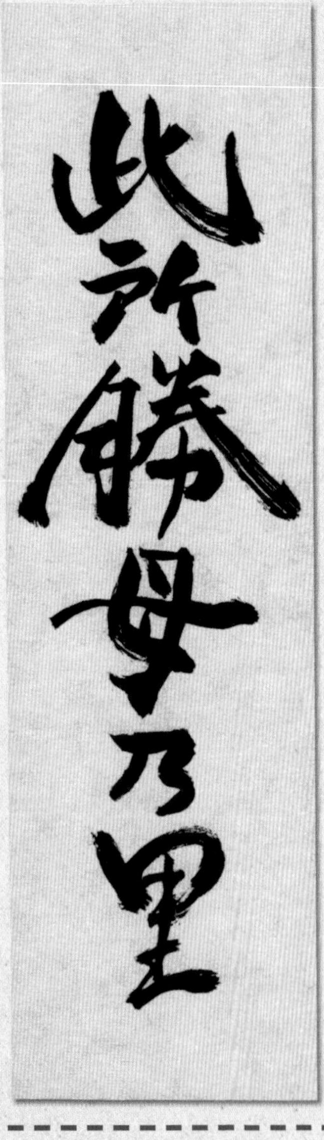
此所勝母乃里

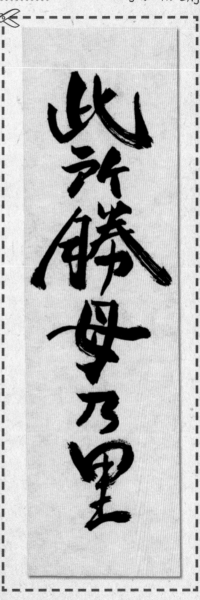

Neko-mata

猫又

Pronunciation:
(NEH-koh MAH-tah)

English Name:
Literally, "Forked Cat"; Two-Tails

Gender:
Male or Female

Length:
Housecat-sized to two or three times housecat-sized

Weight:
Unknown

Locomotion:
Quadrupedal or bipedal

Distinctive Features:
Two tails or a forked tail

Offensive Weapons:
Shape-shifting, claws, teeth

Abundance
Prevalent

Habitat:
Anywhere cats live

Claim to Fame:
In a twist on the Western concept of cats stealing babies' breath, Japanese superstition holds that cats need to be kept away from the recently deceased, lest they breathe new life into the corpses.

Set against this macabre background, it is said that once a cat reaches a certain age—according to some sources, more than forty years; in others, as little as eleven—its tail naturally splits into two and it acquires supernatural powers. Other legends hold that cats that are mistreated or killed by humans will return as vengeful spirits. These paranormal felines are collectively known as Bakeneko (literally, "monster cats") and Neko-mata.

A Neko-mata interacts with the human world in all sorts of ways. Often spotted dancing or conversing in human speech, they have also been cited as the source

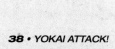

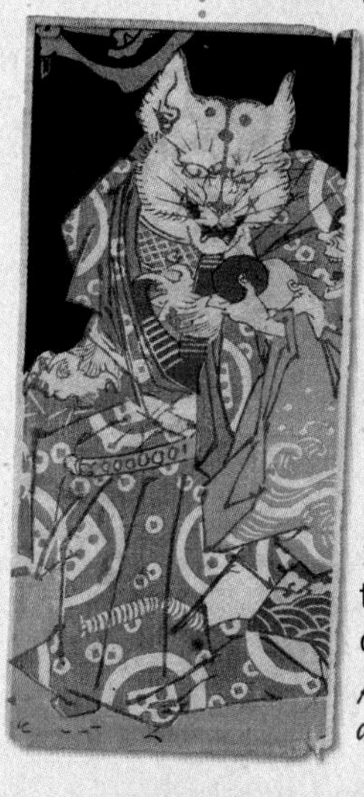

A well-dressed Bakeneko in a vintage woodblock print.

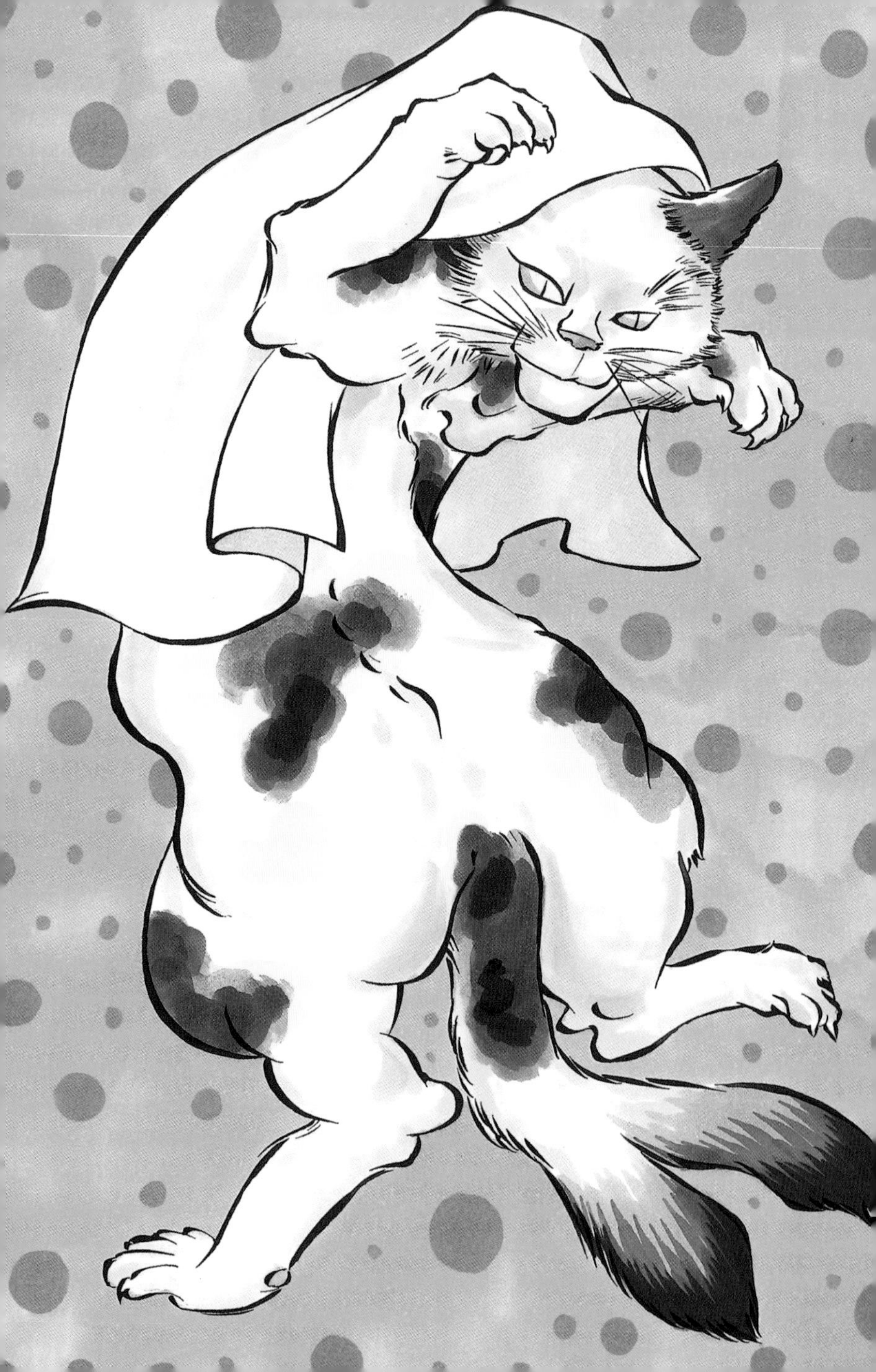

of ghostly fireballs and other forms of supernatural environmental phenomena. Similar to Kitsune (p. 154) and Tanuki (p. 126), the Neko-mata is believed capable of mimicking the forms of other creatures. Although it prowls the streets as a normal-looking cat, it can make itself significantly larger than the average feline.

The Attack!

A Neko-mata is particularly feared for its voodoo-like ability to raise and control the dead. They achieve this feat by leaping over the heads of fresh corpses, using the reanimated bodies to take revenge on individuals or families that they believe have wronged them.

A Neko-mata has been known to attack and even devour living human victims. *Meigetsuki* ("The Record of the Clear Moon"), a thirteenth-century diary written by a Kyoto aristocrat, recounts a terrifying attack in which a furious Neko-mata consumed seven or eight individuals over the course of a single night. Meanwhile, the 1708 document *Yamato Kaiiki* ("A Record of Strange Phenomena in Japan") describes an incident in which a hefty specimen measuring some five feet (1.5 meters) from head to tail pounced on a samurai relaxing in his own home.

Surviving an Encounter:

The traditional expedient for avoiding the wrath of a Neko-mata is simple. Don't abuse cats. Or any other animals, for that matter. At its

Tail Trivia:
A great many cats in Japan are of the bobtail or tailless variety. Some speculate that the relative rarity of long-tailed cats gave rise to the legend of the Neko-mata.

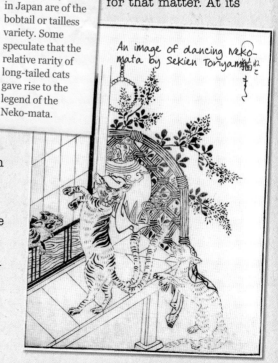

An image of dancing Neko-mata by Sekien Toriyama

heart, this yokai is a metaphor for the consequences of mistreating those smaller and weaker than yourself.

For concerned pet owners, there is an easy expedient for preventing one's beloved housecat from turning into a Neko-mata. Before taking any cat in, you must clearly state to it: "I will only care for you for three years." This establishes a contract of sorts, after which the cat is free to stay or go as it pleases. And don't forget to stock up on catnip while you're at it.

Lamp-Lickers:

Neko-mata are famed for their peculiar dining habits, which include not only the occasional human but also a thirst for lamp oil. Before the age of electricity, metal lamps that burned vegetable-based oils were a major source of light, and it was said that phantom kitties would drink the fuel from lamps left unattended. But why lamp oil? Back then, meat was not a fixture of the Japanese diet, which consisted largely of rice, and this extended to pets as well. A cat hungry for a little extra fat and protein but too lazy to head outside for a mouse was apt to sneak a quick slurp of oil from the

fuel-dish of a nearby lamp instead. As lamps were usually placed on tabletops, a cat needed to stand on its hind legs to reach the treat. When glimpsed in silhouette through a paper shoji screen, the looming shadow of an average housecat could easily pass for a yokai feline that walks on two legs instead of four.

TOP SIGNS YOUR PET MAY BE A NEKO-MATA

1) Appearance of second tail

2) Thirst for lamp oil

3) Preference for walking on two legs

4) Sudden rise in conversational ability

5) Newly discovered repertoire of songs

6) Overly fond of hitting the dance floor

7) Insatiable hunger for human flesh

YOKAI NO: 007

Nue

鵺

Pronunciation:
(NU-ay)

English Name:
Japanese Chimera

Gender:
Unknown

Locomotion:
Quadripedal, flight

Distinctive Features:
Variable. See below.

Supernatural Abilities:
Riding inside storm clouds
Breathing fire

Weapons:
Unsettling screech

Abundance:
Rare

Habitat:
Storm clouds

Claim to Fame:
A harbinger of bad luck and illness, the fearsome Nue was first described in the twelfth-century epic *Tale of the Heike* as comprising a monkey head attached to a *tanuki* (Japanese raccoon-dog) body, with a tiger's limbs and a snake for a tail. Over the generations other hybrids have been described as well, including one with a monkey's head, a tiger's body, a tanuki's legs, and a fox's tail. Occasionally it even appears as a bird-like creature with a human face.

The Nue is a vague and volatile sort of being, elusive and difficult to pin down with any specificity. Because of the extreme danger in closely approaching this yokai, it remains unknown whether the differing appearances represent one or multiple "species" of

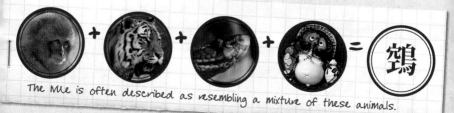

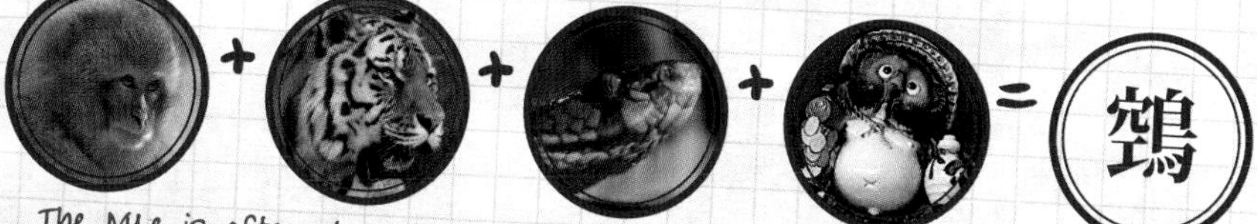
鵺
The Nue is often described as resembling a mixture of these animals.

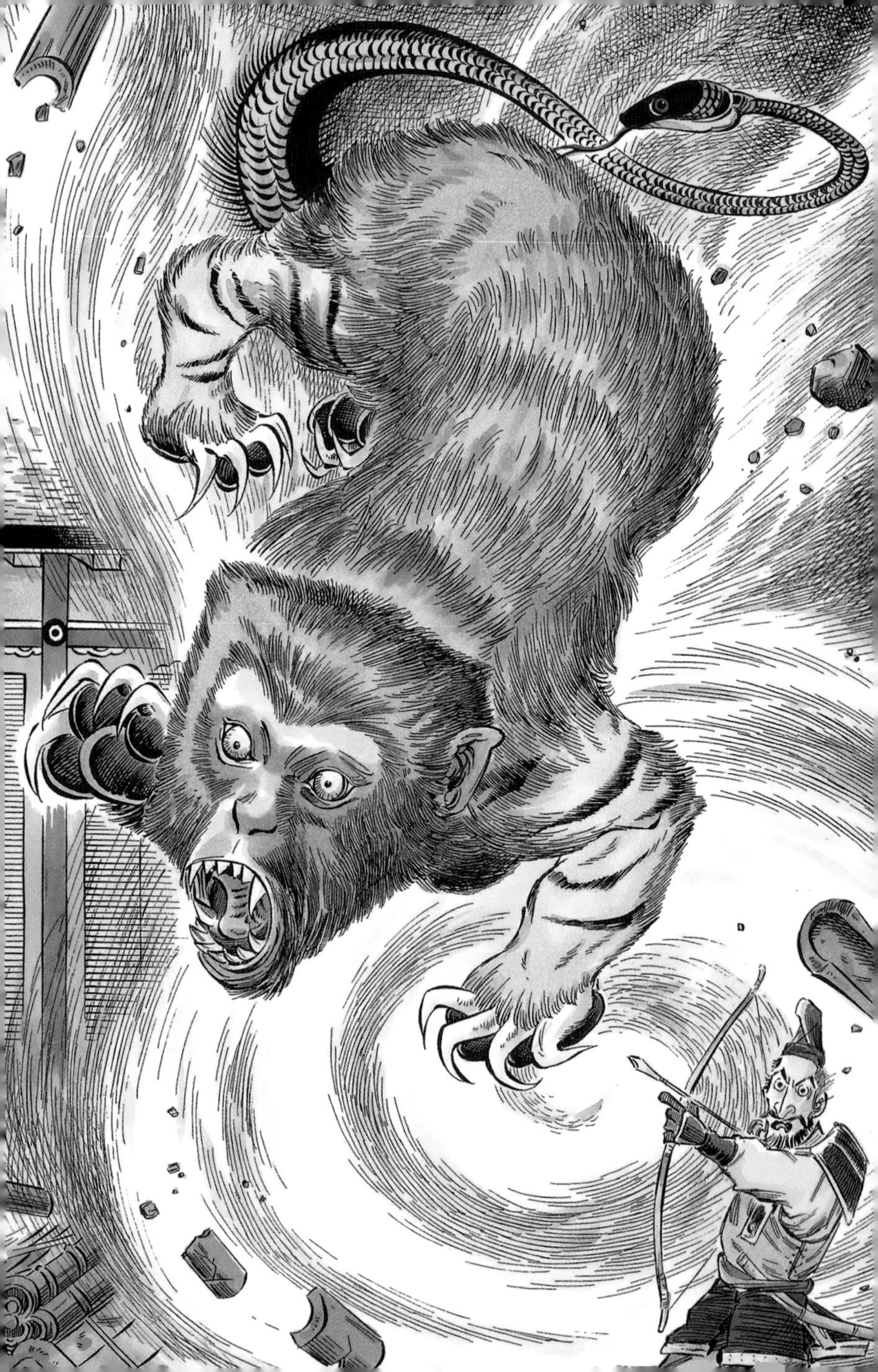

creature. Some theories hold that the bizarre appearance of the otherworldly Nue is actually a type of optical illusion. The human mind is unable to assimilate the true form and nature of the beast, resulting in a visual patchwork of different animals as the brain attempts to come to terms with what, exactly, it is seeing. If this is the case, its true form must be even stranger than we can imagine.

A great many sightings of the beast have been reported over the years. Morihiko Fujisawa's *A Collection of Japanese Folklore* lists no fewer than eleven appearances between 905 and 1774. The most notorious occurred in the spring of 1153, when a strange black cloud appeared over the Imperial Palace night after night, disturbing then-Emperor Konoe's sleep with constant and terrible nightmares, slowly but surely sapping his health. Eventually, an exasperated royal retainer fired an arrow into the heart of the cloud, causing a mortally wounded Nue to drop from the sky.

The Attack!

Close encounters are extremely dangerous. Although it is theoretically capable of causing serious injury via tooth, poison fang, or claw, the real threat isn't physical violence but rather the Nue's ability to induce illness in those who come into close or repeated contact with it. It is unknown whether the creature actively intends humans harm or if sickness is a mere side effect of the human mind attempting to reconcile the Nue's strange quintessence and physiognomy. Whatever the case, there is no question that any sort of contact with the crea-

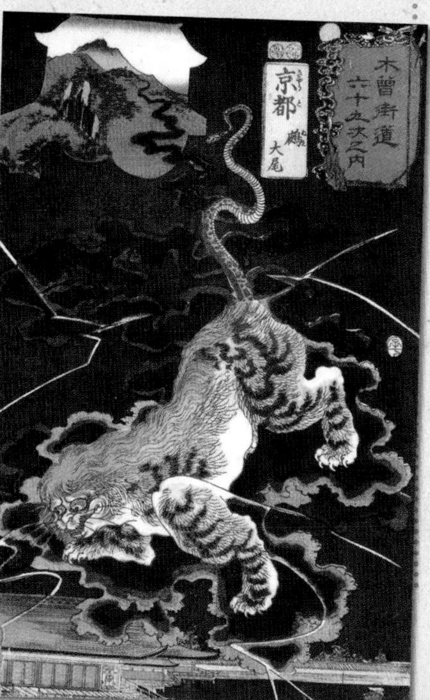
木曽街道
六十九次之内
京都
大尾

Utagawa Kuniyoshi's 1852 depiction of the Nue.

NUE NAMING:
The Asian Thrush (*zoothera dauma*), currently known as toratsugumi in Japanese, was long ago known as the Nue. It's call was said to resemble that of a mysterious and as-yet unnamed yokai then plaguing the countryside. Over the generations, the yokai came to be known as "Nue" rather than the bird.

ture is hazardous to your health.

Fortunately, the vast majority of Nue encounters occur at a distance, "attacks" taking the form of an unsettling, bird-like cry that scares the daylights out of people. Like most yokai, it generally appears at night, making it even more difficult to make sense of the Nue's already confusing forms. Even at some remove, repeated contact can drive victims over the brink into illness, as was the case with Emperor Konoe.

Surviving an Encounter:

1) Follow weather reports to track storm clouds.

2) Brush up on your skills with the bow and arrow.

3) Invest in a pair of ear-plugs.

4) Look an the bright side and consider yourself fortunate: sightings of this strange and dangerous creature are extraordinarily uncommon in the modern age.

Yokai Party:

Japan is a nation of festivals, and more than a few of them are related to the Nue. For example, every January 28th a festival intended to keep the creature at bay is held in Shizuoka Prefecture, roughly one hour south of Tokyo by bullet train. It is called the *Nue-barai Matsuri*, or "Nue Exorcism Festival."

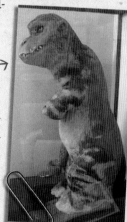

A stuffed Nue on display in Nagoaka, Shizuoka Prefecture

Funa-yurei

Pronunciation:
(FOO-nah YOO-ray)

English Name:
Literally, "Ship-Ghouls";
Sea Phantoms,
Marine Spirits

Alternate Japanese Names:
Hiki-funandama, Obako,
Yobashiri, etc.

Gender:
Male

Height:
Average adult male height

Weight:
Unknown

Locomotion:
Floating, swimming

Distinctive Features:
Skeletal humanoids

Offensive Weapons:
A fisherman's ladle

Abundance:
Prevalent

Habitat:
Coastal waters, lakes, rivers

Claim to Fame:
The Funa-yurei are the lonely, restless souls of those who have drowned at sea. They rise from the depths as the sun sets, banding together in small groups to seek out and sink the boats of living fishermen and travelers. They are common in coastal waters throughout Japan; in land-locked areas, they are known to prowl lakes and rivers.

According to one tale, the Funa-yurei simply want others to share their sad fate. In other tales it is said that the individual souls cannot leave their phantom boat until they find a living victim to replace them.

They can appear in a range of forms, from fairly healthy-looking individuals to skeletal humanoids clad in tattered and waterlogged clothing, their flesh picked clean by aquatic creatures. From this it could be theorized that the length of time since death affects their outward appearances. In nearly all cases their heads are crowned with white triangular headdresses of the sort used in Buddhist

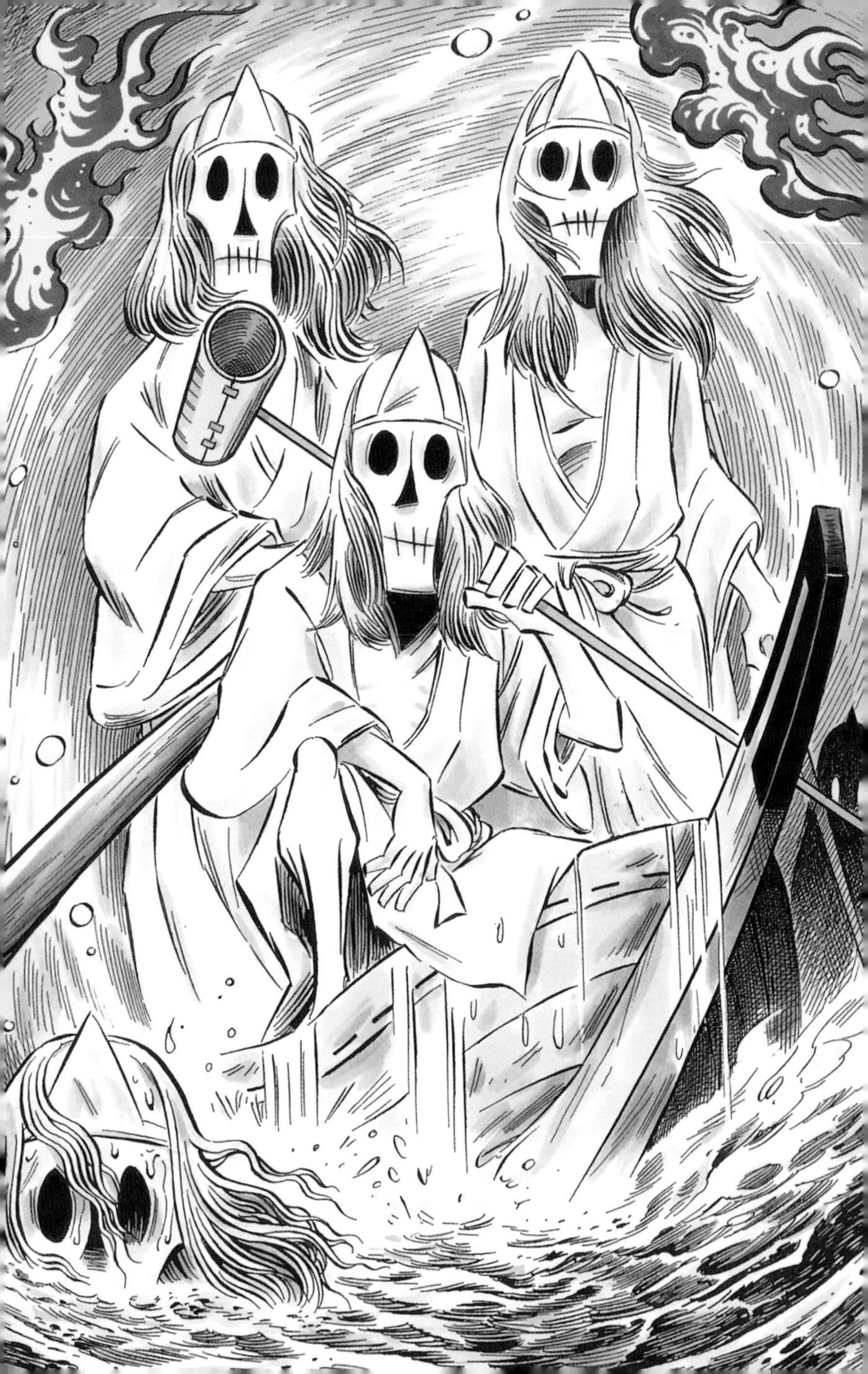

FIENDS

funeral rituals to prepare corpses for their journey to the underworld.

The Attack!

Funa-yurei always appear at twilight or in the predawn hours, often in reduced-visibility conditions such as stormy or foggy weather. Encounters follow a predictable pattern. You are bobbing along in your fishing boat when you notice a faint light approaching you. These lights are often (but not exclusively) accompanied by a steady, rhythmic drumming, creating a processional atmosphere. As the light moves closer, you realize that it's attached to a small fishing skiff with several individuals aboard. It pulls alongside and something seems amiss. In a ghostly voice, one of the "men" intones, "Ladle. Give me your ladle."

WEATHER WATCH:
Funa-yurei appearances often accompany strange weather patterns, such as a sunny day suddenly turning cloudy or waves and whitecaps developing in a dead calm. Nights of the full moon and the time period corresponding to the Japanese holiday of O-Bon, the festival of the dead, also raise your likelihood of encountering these yokai.

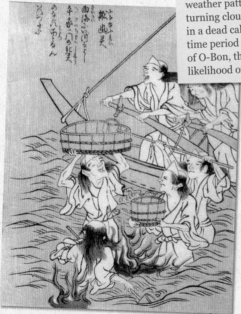

A 19th-century print showing the Funa-yurei in action. Note the ladle.

Do not be fooled by outward appearances. While some Funa-yurei look like reanimated corpses, the recently deceased may look surprisingly like normal humans. The key is to watch the headgear. If the inquisitor is wearing a triangular funeral headdress, you are up the proverbial creek without a paddle: damned if you do, damned if you don't. Hand over the requested ladle and the Funa-yurei will

use it to scoop a tremendous quantity of water into your boat, scuttling it. Refuse—or simply happen to not have a ladle on hand—and they will capsize your vessel in fury. In either case you're going on a one-way trip to the Japanese equivalent of Davy Jones' Locker.

Funa-yurei are known to exploit the use of lighthouses (or signal fires in the old days) by generating false lights to confuse and lure fishing vessels farther out to sea. Seasoned navigators know to keep careful watch: the position of human-generated lights remains fixed, but the phantom glow of a Funa-yurei tends to flicker, bob, and weave.

Surviving an Encounter:
To this very day, many a Japanese fisherman refuses to leave port without a bottomless ladle aboard. You would be advised to do the same. Scoop as they may, Funa-yurei won't be able to lift any water into your boat.

Yokai Trivia:
So why a ladle? It's a play on words. *Inata*, a variation on the Japanese word *inada* (ladle), is slang for "fisherman" in some regional dialects.

Funa-yurei do not necessarily appear in boats. Cases of them surfacing from the sea, either individually or en masse, have been reported as well.

Nearly every fishing village in Japan has its own legends of Funa-yurei claiming family, friends, or neighbors. Even today, there are occasional reports of what appear to be brightly glowing boats effortlessly skimming through waters known to be too shallow for any normal vessel to move.

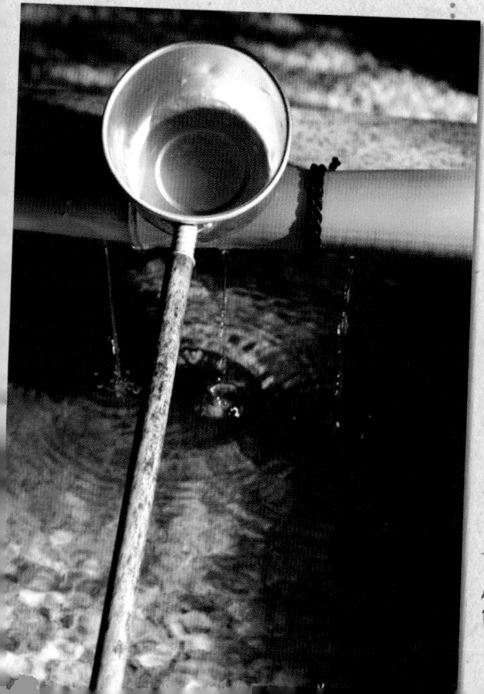

A traditional ladle. Don't forget to poke holes in the bottom!

Umi-bozu

海坊主

Pronunciation:
(OO-mee BOH-zoo)

English Name:
Literally, "Sea Monks"; Pelagic Phantoms

Gender:
Unknown

Height:
From 4 in. (10cm) to over 100 ft. (30m)

Weight:
Equivalent to equal mass of seawater

Locomotion:
Wave motion

Distinctive Features:
Domed, jelly-fish-like body
Smooth, pitch-black skin
Glowing eyes

Offensive Weapons:
Water

Weaknesses:
None known

Abundance:
Prevalent

Habitat:
Open seas

Claim to Fame:
In spite of the cute-sounding name, the Umi-bozu have long struck terror into the hearts of Japanese mariners. Some say they are the vengeful spirits of drowned sailors; others say they are strange mutations of deep-sea life taking monstrous supernatural form. Whatever the case, the Umi-bozu look nothing like any creature from this world, taking the form of jet-black, dome- or drop-like beings with glowing eyes. It has been suggested that they may actually be composed entirely of water, which would explain the near-total absence of any other distinguishing features. Although many seem to lack mouths, they are often described as issuing an unsettling

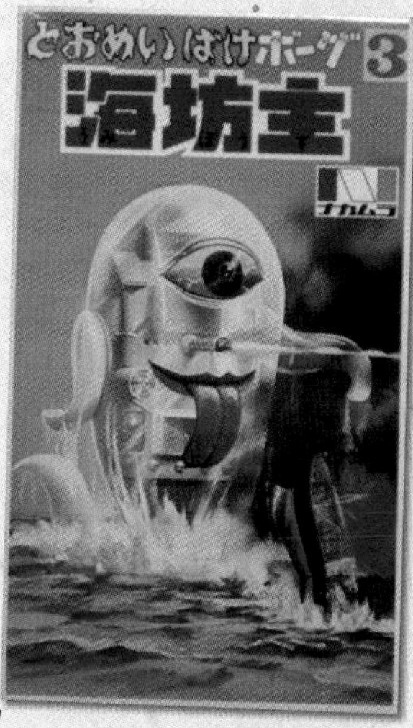
3
海坊主

This 1970s Robo-Umi-Bozu model kit is an interesting variation.

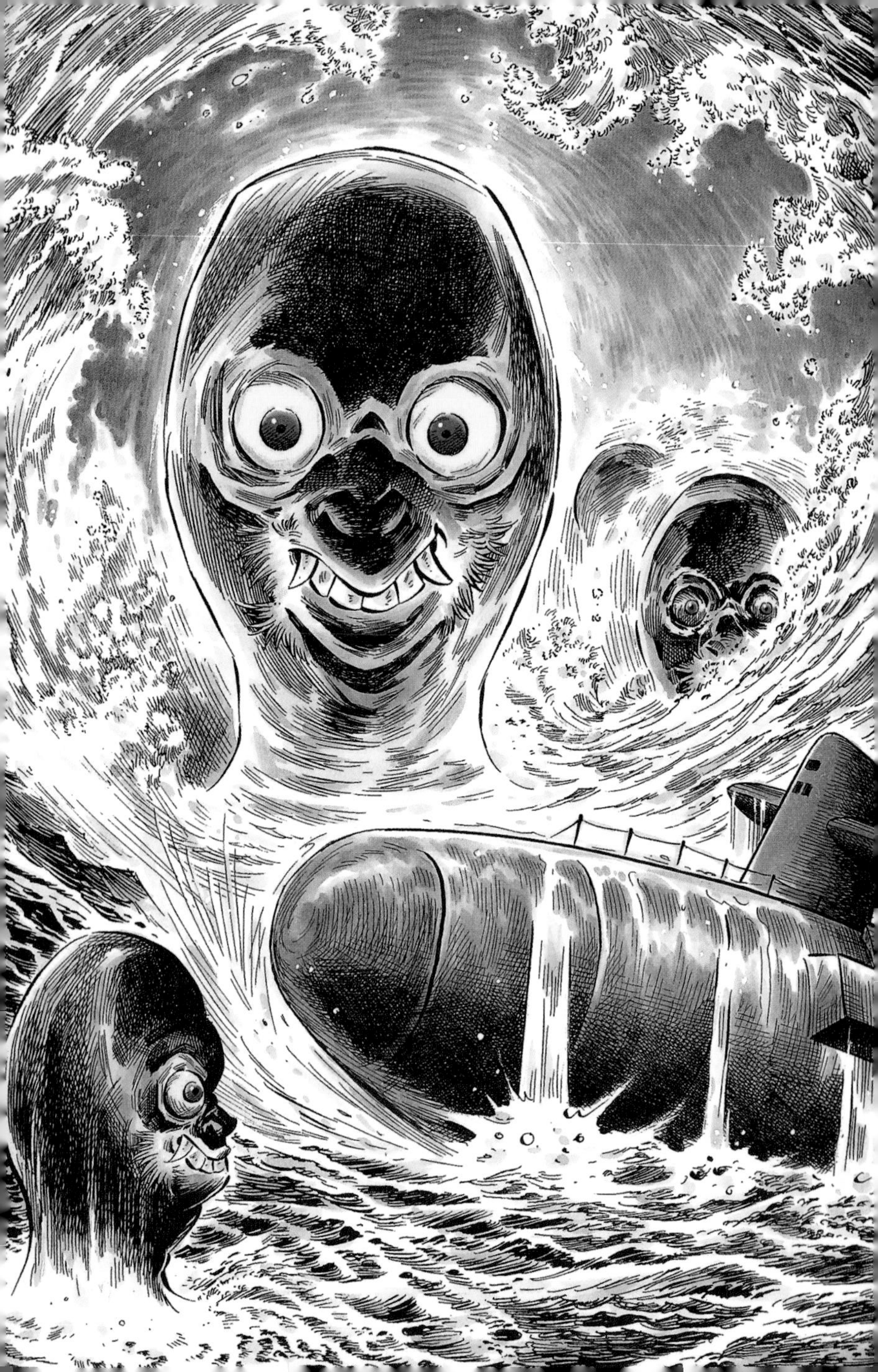

YOKAI NO: 0 0 9 UMI-BOZU

sighing or moaning sound.

Umi-bozu come in a variety of sizes; the smallest, roughly four inches, are occasionally caught in fishing nets. Perhaps these are the juveniles of the species. Medium-sized Umi-bozu are large enough to menace fishing boats; at their largest and most fearsome, they tower over the surface of the water.

The Attack!
Unlike the Funa-yurei, (p. 46), which only appear at night and in coastal waters, the Umi-bozu appears far out to sea and shows itself at any time of the day. It sometimes accompanies (or is accompanied by) strange atmospheric or oceanic phenomena such as storms. Umi-bozu rise from the surface of the ocean; fed by its limitless waters, it is capable of growing in size until it looms over even the largest of ships. It prefers brute-force attacks, attempting to engulf individuals, ships, or even entire fleets, depending on their size.

Surviving an Encounter:
This probably goes without saying, but avoid putting out to sea when strange weather is on the horizon. Smaller Umi-bozu respond with cries of pain when hit with poles or oars, meaning it is theoretically possible to injure them. It may be possible to fend off small or medium Umi-bozu with whatever tools are at hand, but a full-sized specimen is another story. If you see one on the horizon, finding a safe harbor is your only hope for survival.

Don't let your guard down once you've reached shallower waters, however, particularly if darkness is

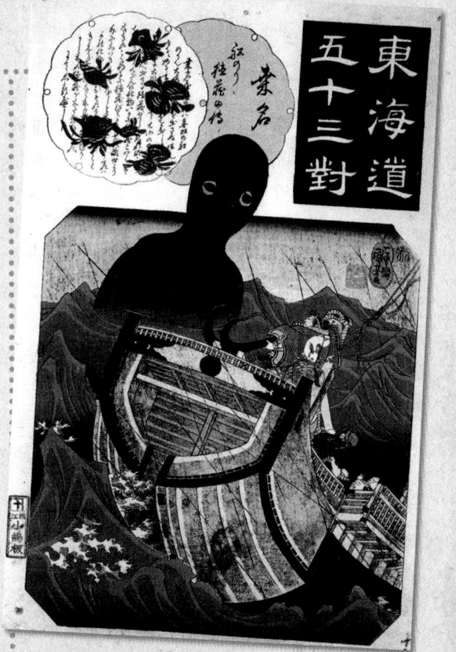
東海道
五十三對
桑名

A woodblock print by Utagawa Kuniyoshi depicting an Umi-bozu

falling. If conditions are right for the Umi-bozu far at sea, chances are you may well encounter Funa-yurei on the way back.

Marine Monster Mating?

According to *Kanso Jigo* ("Speculations on Natural Tales"), an eighteenth-century text composed by historian Norimitsu Yanagihara, smaller and medium-sized Umi-bozu very occasionally appear close to shore. Residents of the town of Izumi in Osaka reported that one remained in some nearby shallows for three days before returning to sea. During these times the townspeople took pains to avoid the coastline, but those who caught glimpses said that the Umi-bozu took on an almost humanoid appearance. Yanagihara did not propose any sort of explanation for this behavior, but we speculate that it may be a form of mating ritual for the creatures.

Country Cousins:

Although most commonly referred to as Umi-bozu, this yokai is given a variety of names throughout Japan. Fishermen on the island of Sado, located off the west coast of Japan, speak of the Tate-Eboshi, a sixty-five-foot (twenty-meter) tall creature that attempts to swamp any boat it encounters. Meanwhile, fishermen in Shiriyazaki, at the northeastern tip of Japan's main island of Honshu, have a tradition of mixing miso paste with water and pouring it into the sea to drive away the Mojabune, another towering yokai of the high seas.

BEARDED BOZU

Some accounts describe the skin of the umi-bozu as being covered in ultrafine hair. The veracity of these claims remains unknown. If true, an umi-bozu's "pelt" is probably similar to that of other marine mammals such as the sea otter, the dense fur of which contains some one million hairs per square inch of skin! (By comparison, an average human has only one hundred thousand hairs on their entire head.)

O-dokuro

大髑髏

Pronunciation:
(Oh DOH-koo-row)

English Names:
Giant Skeleton,
Skeleton Spectre

Alternate Japanese Names:
Dokuro-no-kai, Mekurabe

Height:
Up to 150 ft. (45m)

Weight:
Variable depending on size

Locomotion:
Bipedal, quadripedal

Distinctive Features:
A giant skeleton, or a body
composed of many bones

Offensive Weapons:
Fearsome appearance; a
vengeful appetite

Abundance:
Rare

Habitat:
Unspecified

Claim to Fame:
These titanic skeleton-mon-
sters appear over battlefields

and other places where large
numbers of human bodies
have been left to rot without
proper burials. The collective
infuriation, sadness, and
sense of neglect can, in rare
cases, result in spontaneous
reanimation in the form of
an O-dokuro. They sprint
along on two legs or on all
fours for greater speed, hunting remorselessly for fresh
human bones to add to their
bodies.

The roots of the O-dokuro
are a synthesis of a wide
variety of folktales and legends, some of them extending back more than a
millenium. At their most
basic, O-dokuro are simply
oversized human skeletons.
In other tales, they are
titanic, re-animated conglom-
erations of the bones from
innumerable human bodies.

The Attack!
Whatever its origin, this
vengeful yokai is said to
seek out and feast upon the
flesh of living humans. When
it manages to catch one, it
devours the skin, entrails,
and other soft portions, then
incorporates the flayed-clean

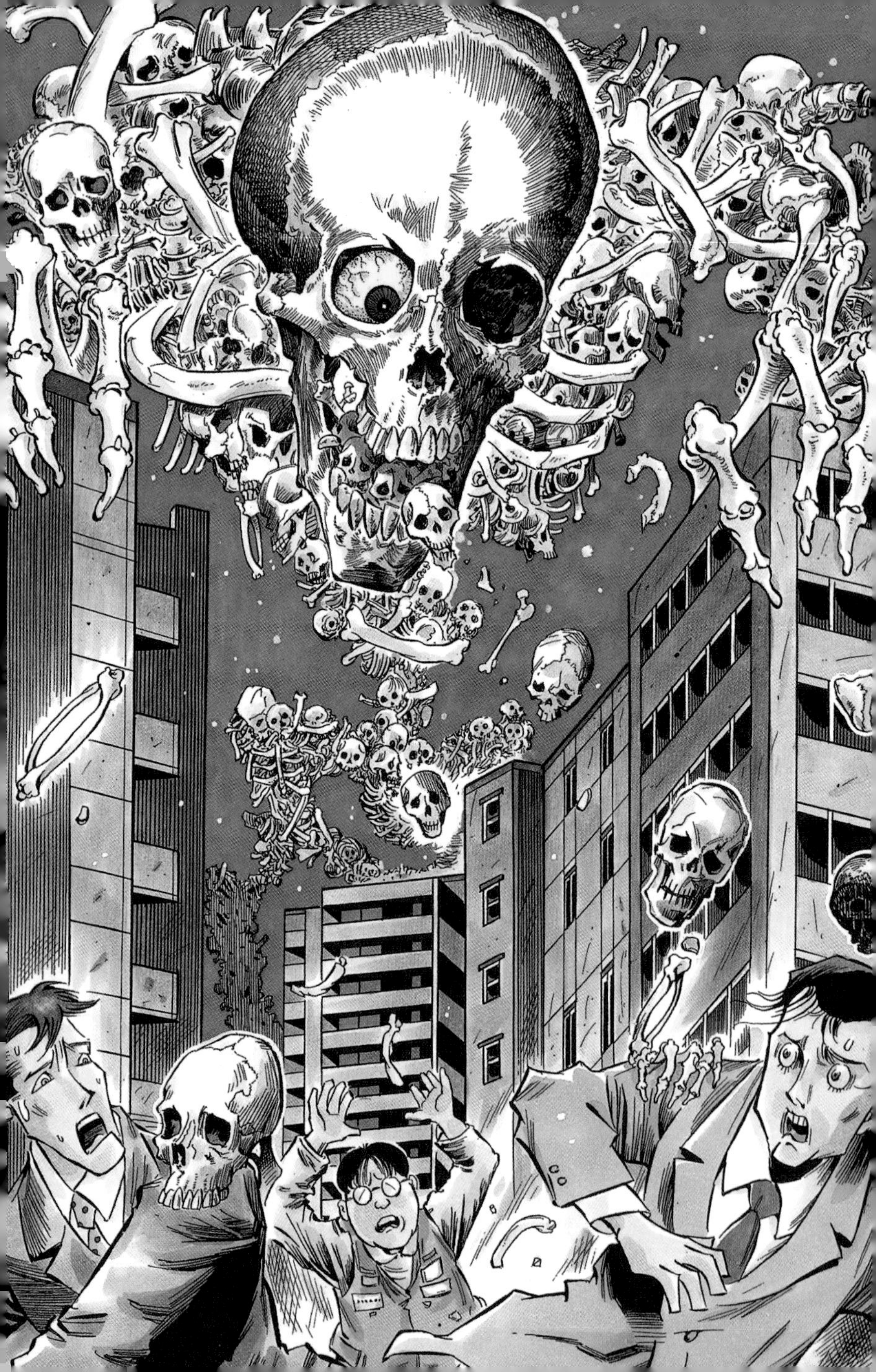

bones into its own skeletal body.

Surviving an Encounter: Unless you feel confident in taking on a giant skeleton many times your size in hand-to-hand combat, find a suitable location to hide until sunrise. The O-dokuro will disappear when day breaks. In the meantime, pick your hiding place well. The O-dokuro is capable of partially disassembling itself to reach into places too small for its oversized body to fit.

O-DOKURO SIGHTINGS IN POPULAR CULTURE

In the Studio Ghibli animated film "Pom Poko," a clan of shape-shifting Tanuki (p. 126) terrorize their human neighbors by mimicking the form of an o-dokuro. The motif is also popular in tattoos and as a decoration on silk jackets.

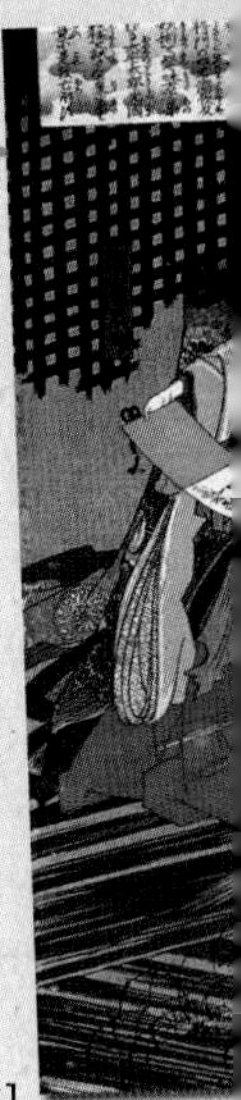

The O-dokuro's Revenge: Famed woodblock print-maker Kuniyoshi Utagawa's nineteenth-century rendition of a giant skeleton menacing a pair of samurai, "Mitsukuni Defying the Skeleton-Spectre," is a signature image of traditional Japanese art that forms the foundation for most modern portrayals of this creature.

The illustration is based on a true story from the tenth century. A provincial warlord by the name of Taira-no-Masakado led a coup d'etat against the imperial court until he was captured, beheaded, dismembered, and displayed as a warning for several months after his death. Legend holds that Taira-no-Masakado's severed head continued seeing, grimacing, and even occasionally laughing the entire time, eventually flying off in search of its body.

Infuriated at his death and the treatment of his corpse, his daughter prayed at Kyoto's Kifune Shrine for revenge. (Incidentally, this shrine, which still exists today, is the same one that is said to have created the fearsome Hashi Hime [p. 162]. Her fury and that of her

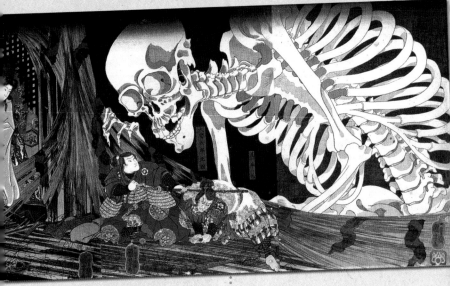

The most famous picture of the O-dokuro is Utagawa Kuniyoshi's "Mitsukuni Defying the Skeleton-Spectre."

defeated father combined to grant her supernatural powers, which she used to summon an O-dokuro and attack the imperial court. Utagawa's woodblock print describes the scene.

A shrine to the place where Taira-no-Masakado's head is said to have eventually landed still exists today. It is called Masakado Kubizuka ("The Hill of Masakado's Head"), and can be found in the Otemachi section of Tokyo.

Garden Ghoul:
According to the fourteenth-century classic *Tale of the Heike*, an O-dokuro appeared in the city of Fukuhara (now Kobe) in the mid-1100s. Taira-no-Kiyomori, a brutal shogun, awakened one morn-

ing to find the garden of his residence filled with human skulls. When he called for his retainers, the skulls quickly began assembling into a massive skeleton, said to tower some 150 feet (45 meters) off the ground.

It is reported that even though the glow in its innumerable hollow eye-sockets tracked Kiyomori's every move, the general stood his ground, returning the gaze and eventually causing the O-dokuro to dissipate without a trace. This method of staring down an O-dokuro is absolutely not recommended for novices.

Tsuchi-gumo

Pronunciation:
TSOO-chee GOO-moh

English Name:
Earth spider, Ground spider, Dirt spider

Alternate Japanese Name:
Yatsukahagi ("The Long-Legged Ones")

Gender:
N/A

Height:
Upwards of 10 feet

Weight:
Upwards of 10 tons

Locomotion:
Six or eight legs

Distinctive Features:
Varies, but generally take the form of enormous spiders or crickets

Abundance:
Prevalent (in times of old)
Rare (now)

Season:
N/A

Preferred Habitat:
Mountainous terrain, caves

Distribution:
Broadly distributed in scattered remote areas ranging from Southwestern Kyushu to Northern Tohoku

Claim to Fame:
An enormous, insect- or spider-like yokai. Emphasis on enormous: most historical depictions portray them as significantly larger than an African elephant, which is the real-life animal we're using to guess at the height and weight. (Few are brave enough to approach a fully-grown Tsuchi-gumo with a tape measure.) Some resemble insects such as crickets; others appear more menacing, with body-plans similar to those of tarantulas. Distorted human or animal facial features are common. Presumably these different appearances represent sub-species of the same yokai.

They dwell in natural caves or in holes that they have dug themselves, preferring to remain hidden in the presence of human activity. They are nocturnal creatures, said to possess territorial and hunting behaviors similar to wolves.

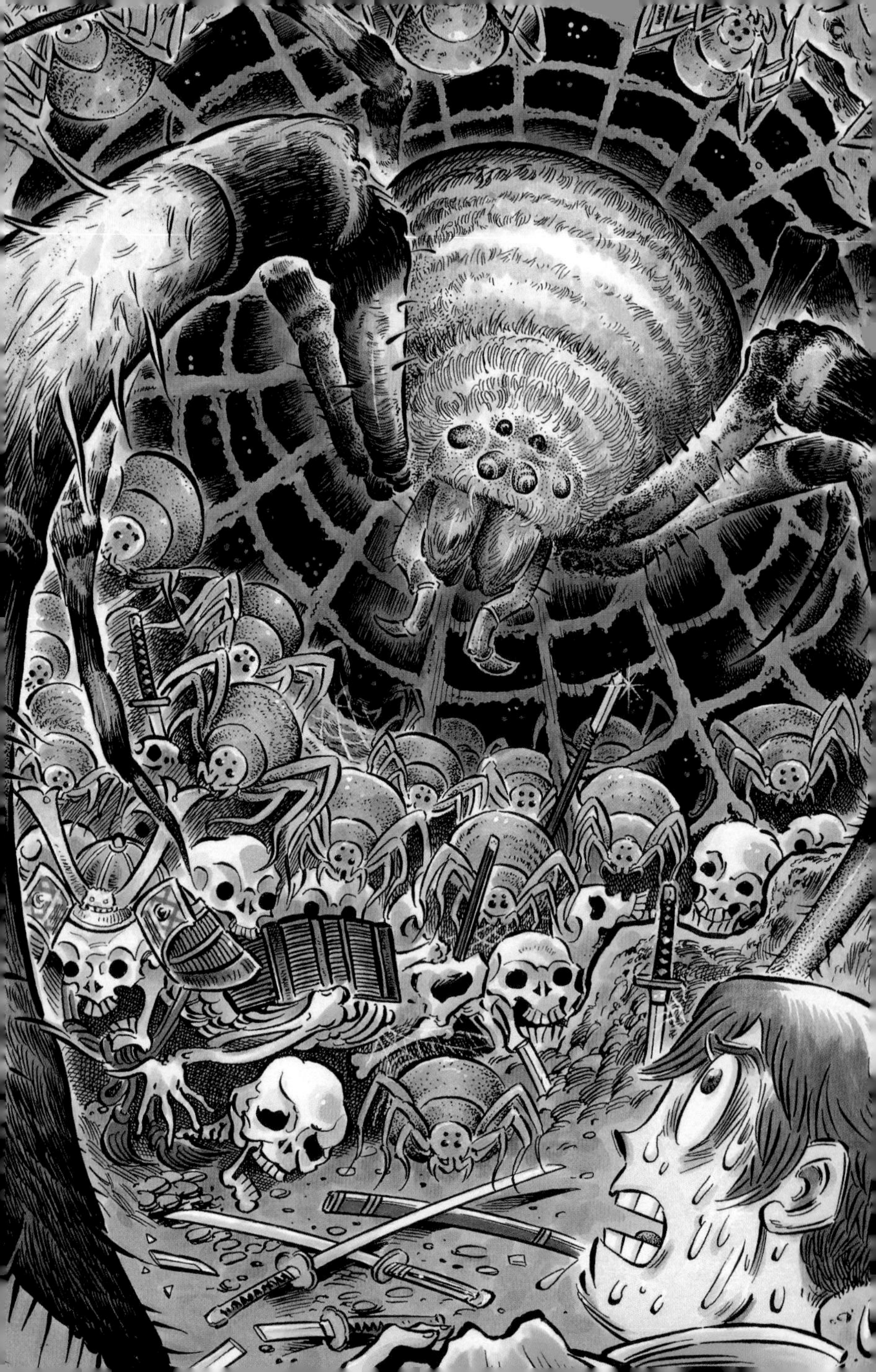

Once far more prevalent than they are today (for reasons we'll explore below), Tsuchi-gumo are usually shown locked in mortal combat with armored samurai. References to the creatures pop up again and again in the Japanese historical record.

Where Tsuchi-gumo Come From:

Long, long ago, Japan was a hodge-podge of various tribes and villages. Sometime around the 5th or 6th century AD, a single group emerged as the dominant force in the country: the Yamato people, whose increasingly powerful emperor began to conquer his rivals and unify the country. His armies waged war against those who refused to pledge allegiance, killing or chasing them from areas that the Yamato Empire controlled.

There were many such refugees, who scattered throughout the Japanese islands seeking the isolation they needed to preserve their own cultures. The Yamato people coined the derogatory term Tsuchi-gumo ("ground spiders") to portray these "rebel" tribes as savage cave dwellers too primitive to submit to civilized authority. The word is a catch-all, covering everything from different ethnic groups to those who simply resisted Yamato cultural imperialism. But they were probably less like barbarians and more like political refugees who simply wanted to live their lives in peace.

Alas, it wasn't to be. These pockets represented a thorn in the side of any emperor or warlord who wanted to claim that they ruled everything under the Rising Sun. And so for a time, ventures to wipe out one or another Tsuchi-gumo enclave became the standard feather in any would-be Yamato hero's cap.

Over the years, the combination of the gruesome-sounding "ground spider" nickname and the ferocity with which some tribes attempted to defend themselves from Imperial crusaders gave rise to many legends about the Tsuchigumo. Chief among them was that they had mutated into giant insects and spiders over the centuries, laying traps for any who dared invade their territories. These creatures are often referred to as "yokai Tsuchi-gumo" to distinguish them from the actual tribes.

Although Tsuchi-gumo settlements persisted for centuries in the deep coun-

tryside, Yamato emperors and warlords eventually succeeded in subjugating and assimilating them into mainstream Japanese culture. Today, hazy tales of yokai Tsuchigumo are essentially all that remain of these outlaw tribes. These visual caricatures are essentially political cartoons created by the "winners" of history.

The Attack!

Much like their human counterparts, yokai Tsuchi-gumo are not aggressive unless provoked. However, caution is required as they are voracious predators that become extremely violent when agitated; their lairs are inevitably filled with the skeletons of animals and humans who have accidentally wandered too close. Their webs are usually woven within caves, but sometimes found stretched out in the open, in rare cases large enough to transect entire valleys. They seem to cause injury in the same way their smaller insect/spider cousins do: with mandibles or poison fangs.

Surviving an Encounter:

Nobody has run into a yokai Tsuchigumo for generations. But Japan is nation of mountains and cave sys-

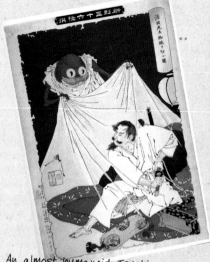

An almost humanoid Tsuchi-gumo, as portrayed by Tsukioka Yoshitoshi in 1892.

tems, some of them still fully unexplored. Should you plan to go poking around in any of them, take a page from the samurai and brush up on your bushido ("the way of the warrior"). If old stories and art are any indication, the yokai Tsuchi-gumo can be felled with swords, spears, and other weapons.

But ask yourself: why would you want to? Remember that the Tsuchi-gumo are essentially tragic figures, the original outsiders (and some would say anti-heroes) of official Japanese history. If you happen to encounter one, keep your distance and marvel at a rare glimpse of cross-cultural drama given physical form.

Konaki Jiji

児啼爺

Pronunciation:
(KOH-nah-kee JEE-jee)

English Name:
Literally, "Old Man Who Cries Like a Baby"

Gender:
Male

Height:
1½ ft. to 5½ ft. (0.5 to 2m))

Weight:
6 lbs. (2.5kg) to unfathomable

Locomotion:
Bipedal

Distinctive Features:
The wrinkled, aged body of a tiny elderly man, or the body of a helpless infant

Offensive Weapons:
Variable mass

Weaknesses:
Being ignored

Abundance:
One of a kind

Habitat:
Mountain fields and forests

Claim to Fame:
Don't be fooled by this pint-sized phantom's infantile appearance and wimpy-sounding name: the Konaki Jiji is a baby that doesn't simply tug on your heart-strings—it will make your heart explode. Normally, it appears in the form of an ordinary, if unusually small, old man. In such cases it is entirely harmless and virtually impossible to tell from a human. However, it is also capable of transforming itself into the shape of a wailing, abandoned infant, using the power of pity to lure human victims, much as an angler-fish uses its glowing lure to capture prey.

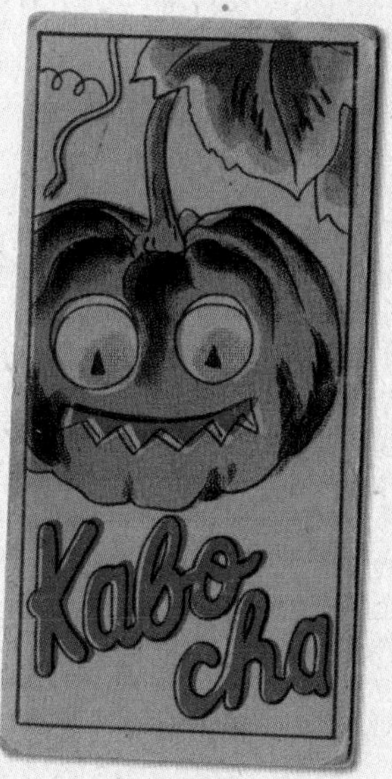
Kabo
cha

A pumpkin patch is an ideal (but by no means the only) spot for this yokai to hide.

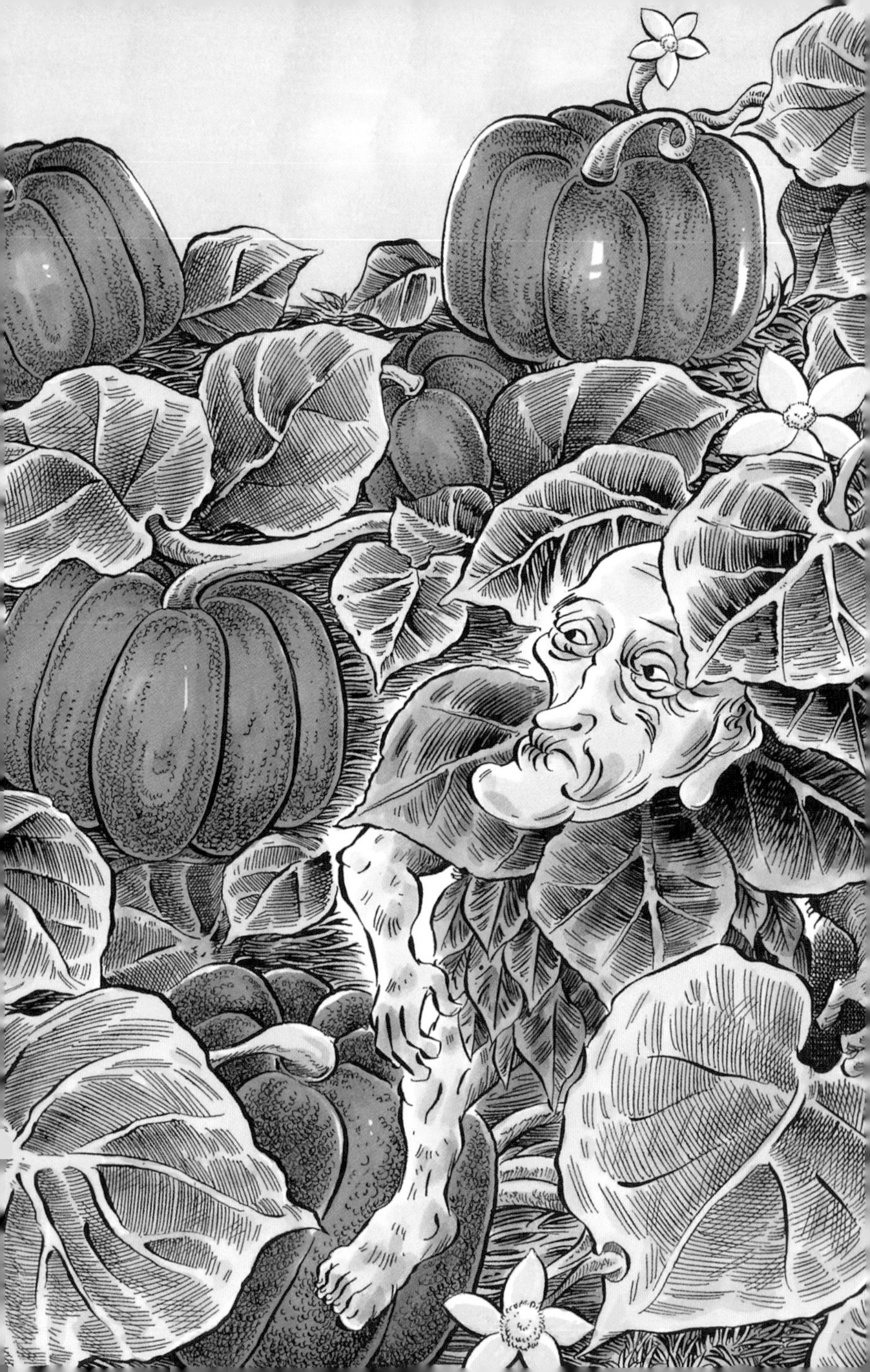

The Attack!
Once picked up by a kindly stranger, the "baby" Konaki Jiji cannot be set down. It begins increasing in weight, slowly at first and then unbearably quickly, crushing the life out of the hapless individual who attempts to save it. In the world of this yokai, it seems, no good deed goes unpunished.

Surviving an Encounter:
It goes against human nature to suggest that one should ignore abandoned babies, but if you happen to encounter a bawling infant in an unlikely location—say, high atop a mountain, in a field, or deep within an uninhabited forest—you might consider approaching it with extreme caution.

Konaki Composting:
Konaki Jiji is inevitably encountered in remote mountain regions or deep within forests. Individuals who happen to stumble into areas that contain large amounts of dead and decaying vegetation could conceivably be overwhelmed by the carbon dioxide and methane released by the composting process, leading to a feeling of light-headedness and eventually an overwhelming sense of heaviness. This has led some to dismiss the Konaki Jiji as a naturally induced form of hallucination by those panicked at being lost in the woods, while others believe that the Konaki Jiji merely harnesses the effect to enhance its own strange abilities.

TEARS OF ALARM:
Some say the cry of the Konaki Jiji is said to either precede or directly cause earthquakes.

Yokai Trivia: Although this yokai is commonly attributed to the folktales of Tokushima prefecture, natives insist that it is not of local origin. In fact it is believed that the tales of the Konaki Jiji are the synthesis of a wide variety of rural myths and legends from across Japan.

Gruesome
Gourmets

A smorgasbord of fiends with a taste
for the strange . . . and often human.
If you accept an invitation to dinner,
don't say we didn't warn you.

Tesso

鉄鼠

Pronunciation:
TEH-soh

English Names:
Literally, "Iron Rat"; the Rat-Monk

Height:
Roughly that of an adult man

Weight:
Roughly that of an adult man

Locomotion:
Bipedal or quadripedal

Distinctive Features:
Rat body
Tattered monks' robes

Favorite Food:
Sacred holy texts and this one!

Offensive Weapons:
Metal fangs
Army of rats

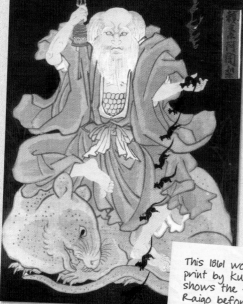

This 1861 woodblock print by Kunisada shows the furious Raigo before his transformation into the Tesso.

Weaknesses:
Unknown

Abundance:
One of a kind

Habitat:
Temple libraries

Claim to Fame:
The Tesso is the Pied Piper of the yokai world. Its saga dates back to the Heian era of Japanese history, and more specifically to the reign of Emperor Shirakawa, who ruled from 1073 to 1087. Tesso, whose name

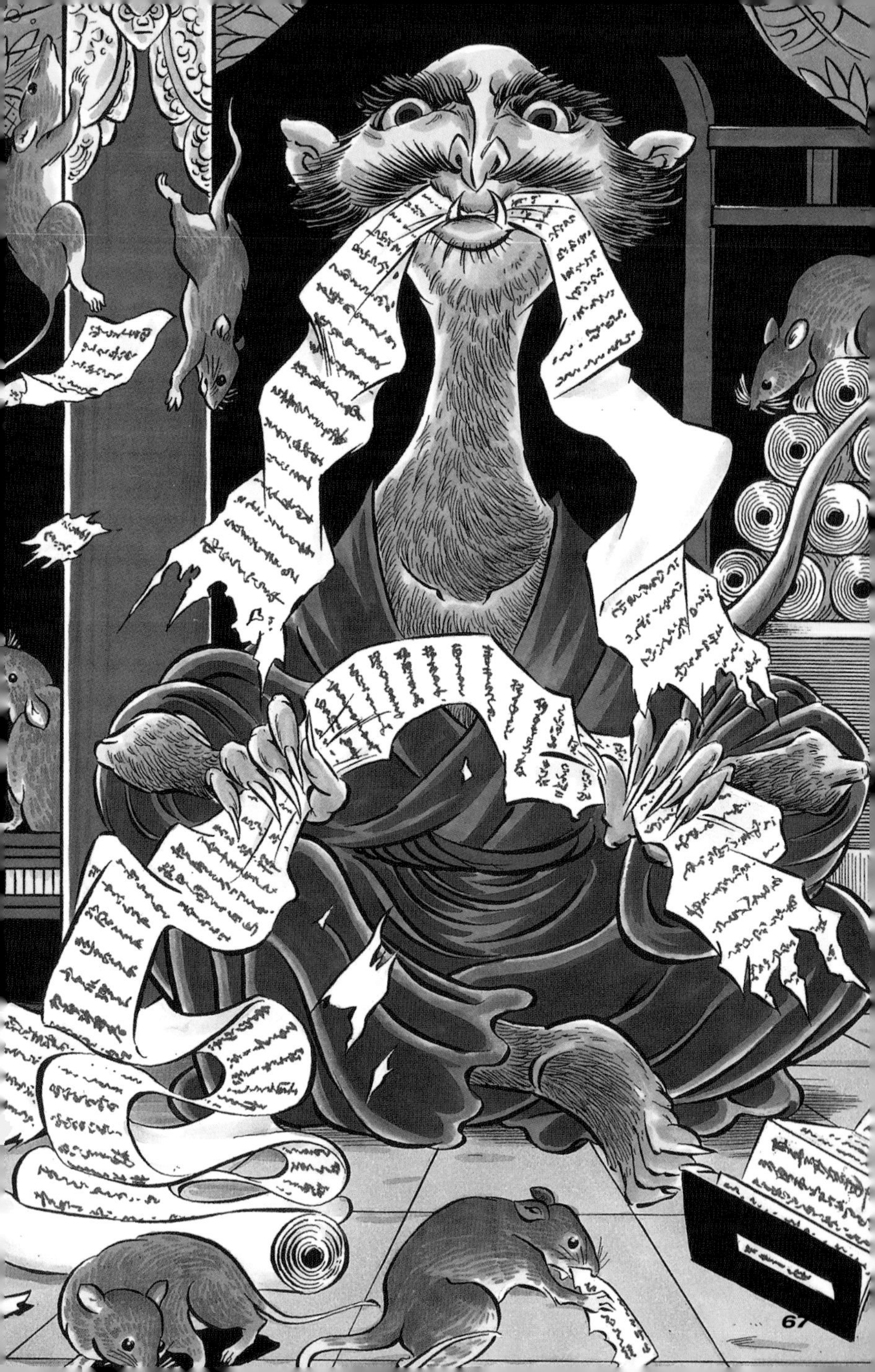

literally means "Iron Rat," was once a Buddhist monk by the name of Raigo. He was ordered to pray for the birth of a royal son with a promise to expand his temple if the prayers were answered, but in spite of a successful birth, the expected reward was denied. Infuriated at the political rivalries that upset his plans, Raigo went on a hunger strike that ended in his death.

He was reborn as the Tesso, a strange hybrid of human and rodent with a mouth full of indestructible iron teeth. But perhaps even more frightening was its ability to summon and control rats at will.

The Tesso led a plague of rats—according to one account, upwards of eighty thousand of them—on a rampage through the temple libraries of Raigo's rivals, most notably that of Enryaku Temple in Kyoto. With its rat underlings, it consumed uncounted numbers of Buddhist effigies, holy sutras, and other important religious texts.

Some accounts claim that the Tesso and its army of rats were eventually lured into a pit and buried alive. Others say the scourge finally abated on its own, meaning the Tesso remains at large even today.

TOOTHY TRIVIA

Humans have thirty-two teeth, while rats have only sixteen. It remains unknown whether the number of teeth in Tesso's iron jaws correspond to human or rodent, but his enlarged incisors would seem to indicate the latter.

The Attack!

Being a giant rat, the Tesso is more than capable of inflicting injury by iron tooth and claw. But its interest is piqued not by human flesh but rather human knowledge; it consumes scrolls, books, and art—literally and with gusto.

Surviving an Encounter:

Fortunately, the Tesso seems to have spent its fury back in the eleventh century. In the unlikely event of a reappearance, temple librarians have more to fear than most people. The best chance for avoiding property damage from the Tesso's rat horde is to move your institution's valuables to a distant location. But if time doesn't permit this expedient, the fol-

lowing steps may help. First, check the building and plug any small openings that might accommodate the passage of rats. Barricade the doors and place mousetraps liberally around the walls, windows, and any other place rats might work their way into the structure. And for an absolutely impenetrable defense, use construction equipment to dig a deep trench around the building, toss some texts you're willing to sacrifice in as bait, and bury it when it gets stuck at the bottom. Hey, it worked in the eleventh century.

More Tesso Tales:
Raigo's temple, called Mii-dera, can be found in the city of Otsu, in Shiga Prefecture. The dirt mound that is the supposed final resting place of the Tesso is said to be located in the city of Oyama in Tochigi prefecture, though the exact location has been lost to the mists of time.

On a side note, the Tesso is not Emperor Shirakawa's only connection to the yokai world: One of Shirakawa's heirs, Sutoku, was deposed from the throne and, after a lengthy insurrection known as the Hogen Rebellion, was exiled to a distant island where he died in misery. Japanese legend has it that upon his death Sutoku became an O-tengu (p. 24) hell-bent on haunting the new emperor in an attempt to avenge his maltreatment.

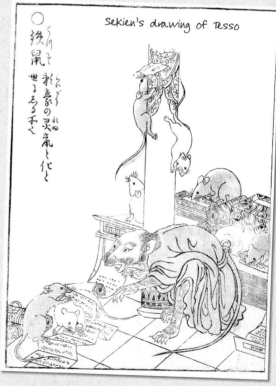

Sekien's drawing of Tesso

Tearai Oni

手洗鬼

Pronunciation:
TEH-ah-rye OH-nee

English Name:
Literally, "Hand-Washing Demon"

Alternate Japanese Names:
Dendenbome

Height:
Mountain-sized

Leg-span:
7.5 miles (12km) estimated

Locomotion:
Bipedal

Distinctive Features:
Enormous size
Hirsute
Fur loincloth

*Often caught in awkward arched-back pose

Favorite Food:
Unknown

NOTE: See map on page 72

Offensive Weapons:
Sheer size

Weaknesses:
Polluted or dirty water

Abundance:
One of a kind

GOURMETS

Habitat:
Mountainous regions

Claim to Fame:
A literally mountain-sized yokai with a predilection for washing its hands in rivers—often (but not always) bent backwards in a precarious-looking upside-down posture (p. 73). In spite of its huge size it remains one of the most mysterious of the yokai. It appears to be closely related to the creatures known variously as Daidarabo and Daidarabochi, legendary giants referenced in folk legends throughout Japan. Aside from its peculiar habit of washing its hands in deep river canyons between mountains, the Tearai Oni is virtually identical in description.

It is difficult to estimate the exact size of the Tearai Oni. One account describes it as straddling two mountains separated by a distance of some seven and a half miles; another, almost twelve.

Although there is no hard data as to this yokai's specific diet, if any, its excellent manners of thoroughly washing

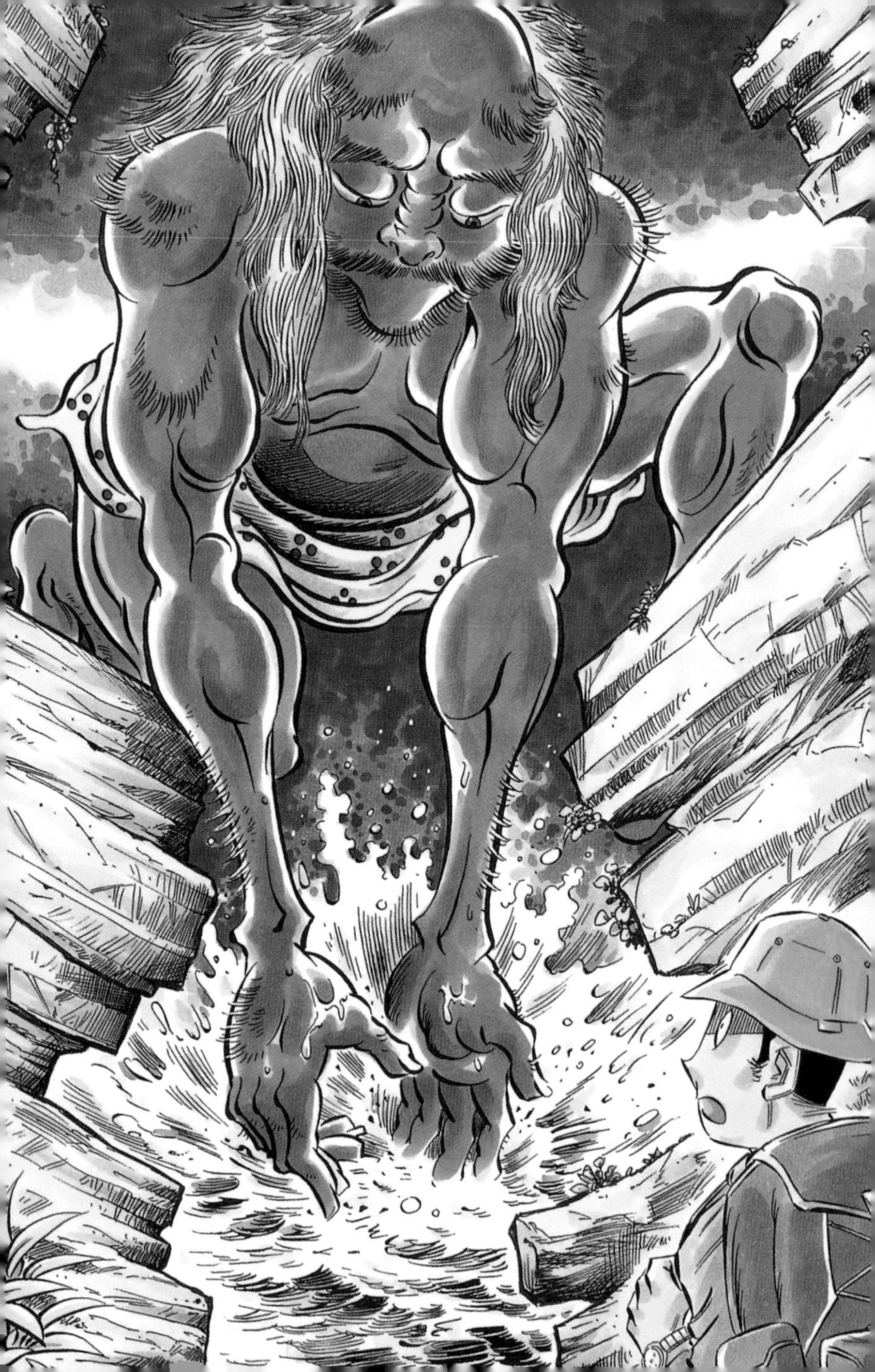

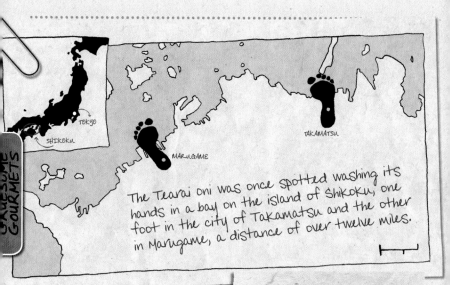

YOKAI NO: 014 TEARAI ONI

TOKYO
SHIKOKU
TAKAMATSU
MARUGAME
The Tearai Oni was once spotted washing its hands in a bay on the island of Shikoku, one foot in the city of Takamatsu and the other in Marugame, a distance of over twelve miles.

its hands would make it a perfect guest at any dinner table . . . provided it was the size of a skyscraper. The area of Shikoku where it was last sighted is famed Japan-wide for a noodle dish called sanuki udon. Perhaps the Tearai Oni has a taste for it? One can only imagine the portions that would be needed to satisfy such a titan.

The Attack!

A secretive and rarely encountered yokai despite its titanic size, there are no reports of individuals being injured by the Tearai Oni. Caution is still required due to its extreme size, however. Although it does not seem

SCHOLARS SAY:

Yokai aren't created by random chance; they inevitably have some connection to the way humans see the world. Many yokai are anthropomorphic representations of natural phenomena (such as the Azuki Arai, p. 90) or of abstract concepts (such as the Mokumoku Ren, p. 98). Similar to the Dorotabo (p. 114), which is a personification of a once-popular slang phrase, scholars of Japanese folklore believe that the Tearai Oni may in fact have its roots in a turn of phrase or metaphor. However, the specific details have been lost to the mists of time, making this yokai an intriguing linguistic artifact—and an example of how quickly human language changes over the centuries. Whatever the case, the Tearai Oni could be called a living testament to the concept of "cleanliness is next to Godliness"!

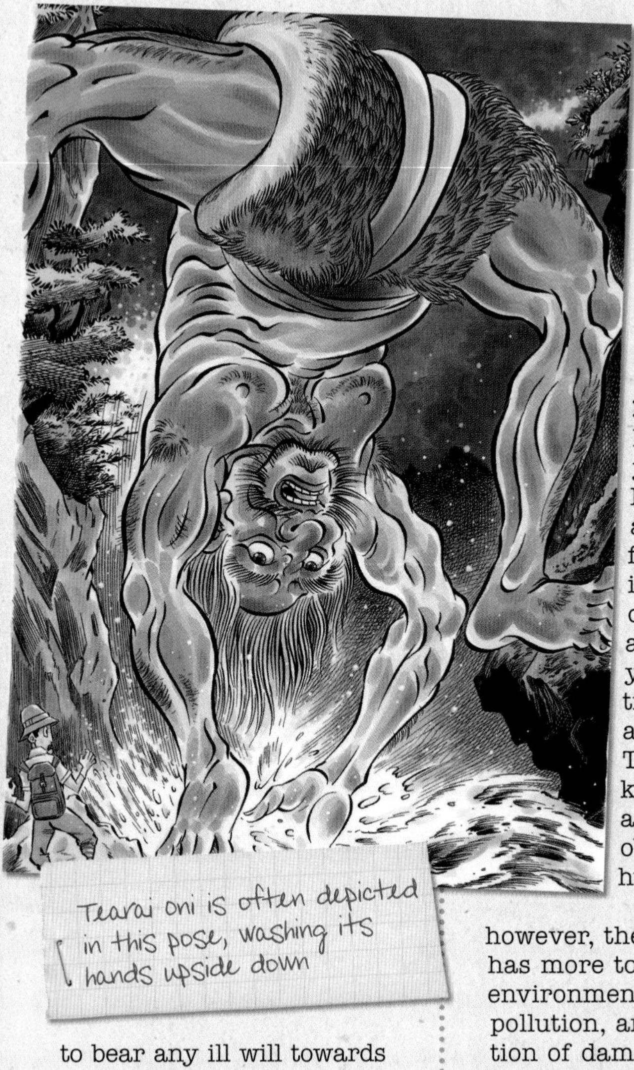

Tearai oni is often depicted in this pose, washing its hands upside down

tively, if you happened to approach by raft or canoe, your vessel could easily be capsized by its enormous hands roiling the waters.

Surviving an Encounter: Maintain your distance. Remain quiet and refrain from attempting to disturb or otherwise attract the yokai's attention. By all accounts the Tearai Oni keeps to itself, apparently oblivious to the human world.

Ironically, however, the Tearai Oni has more to fear from us: environmental damage, pollution, and construction of dams have greatly reduced the potential habitat for this yokai. Sightings are extraordinarily rare; if you happen to spot this gentle giant, consider yourself extremely fortunate.

to bear any ill will towards humans, the Tearai Oni appears deeply absorbed in the act of washing its hands. You could easily find yourself absentmindedly crushed by one of its giant feet. Alterna-

YOKAI NO: 015

Futakuchi Onna

二口女

Pronunciation:
(FOO-tah KOO-chee OHN-nah)

English Name:
Literally, "Woman With Two Mouths"

Gender:
Female

Height:
Average for a Japanese adult female

Weight:
Average for a Japanese adult female

Locomotion:
Bipedal

Distinctive Features:
Second mouth located on back of head
Tentacle-like, prehensile hair
Voracious appetite

Number of Teeth:
64

Number of Tongues:
2

Favorite Food:
Just about anything
but sweet things in particular

Offensive Weapons:
None

Abundance:
Prevalent

Habitat:
Anywhere humans live

Claim to Fame:
It is a supernatural star, one of the most well-known and instantly recognizable yokai in Japanese folkore. The Futakuchi Onna—the Woman With Two Mouths—is a yokai of many contradictions. It at first appears to be a normal-looking woman, yet it has a second, perfectly formed mouth hidden between the locks of flowing black hair on the back of its head. In fact, the mouth has a mind of its own, insolently mumbling comments and curses. Sometimes it is said to feed incessantly to satiate the second mouth; in other tales, it is described as eschewing food.

According to one rather dark legend, they are cursed beings, once human. They are the result of extreme cases of mothers favoring their own offspring over

GRUESOME GOURMETS

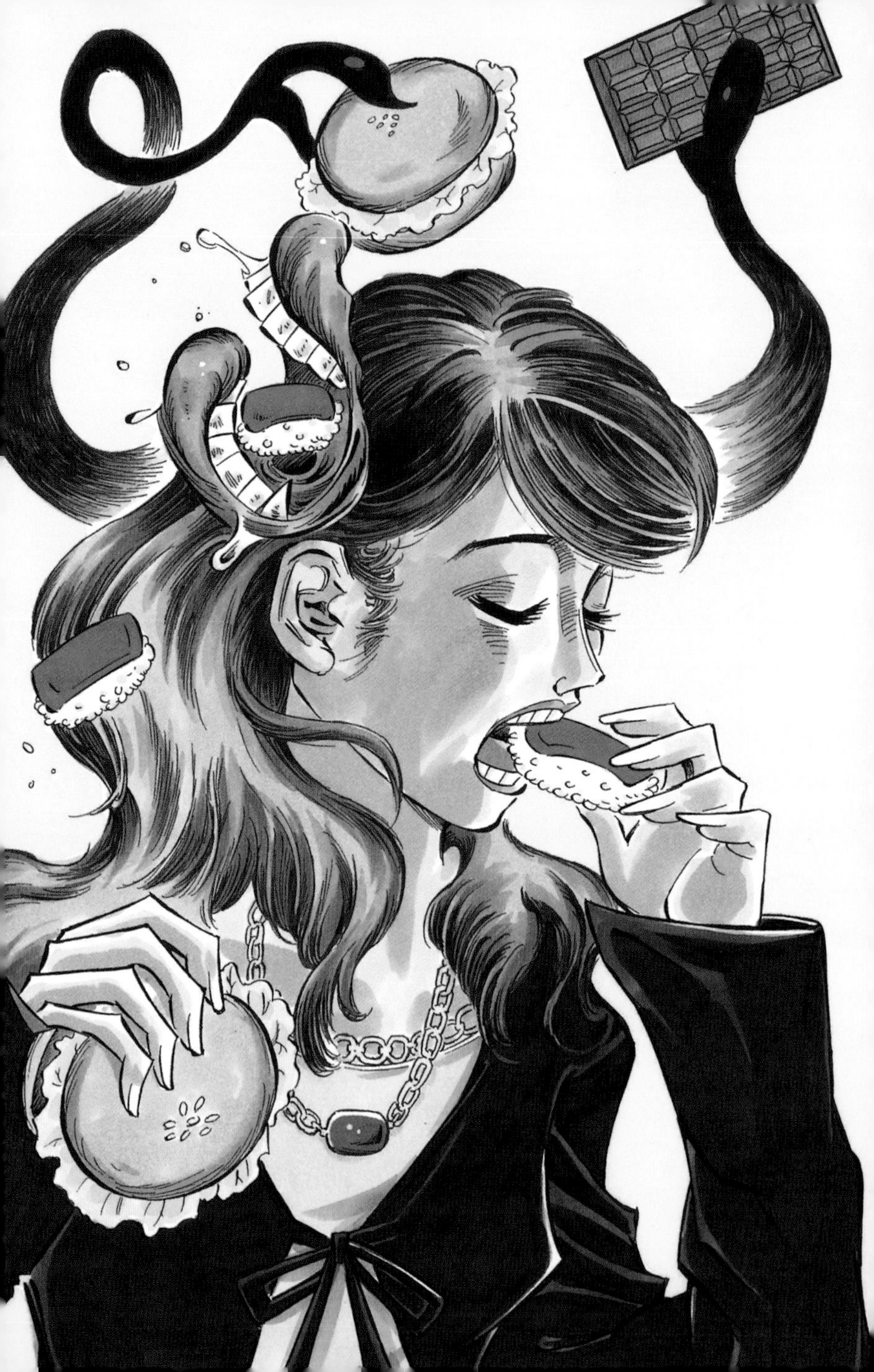

their stepchildren; more specifically, in situations when the stepchildren are neglected to the point of starvation. In a "karmic boomerang" of sorts, forty-nine days later the soul of the departed child comes to inhabit the body of his or her tormentor, transforming her into an insatiably hungry Futakuchi Onna. (Forty-nine days is the traditional length of mourning in Japan.)

One famous tale describes the case of a woman who allowed her stepchild to perish of starvation. Forty-nine days later, she was struck in the back of the head by an errant swing of her woodcutter husband's axe. The wound, while not particularly deep, refused to heal; before long, it formed lips, teeth, and a tongue that began intoning the phrase "you must apologize" over and over again. In another version of the tale, the mouth begins an incessant refrain of "I killed the child. I was wrong."

Other theories hold that Futakuchi Onna are born from intensely frustrated individuals who repress their true feelings and swallow the words they wish to speak. Over many years this dissatisfaction may eventu-

ally culminate in a spontaneous transformation into a Futakuchi Onna. Unlike the mouths of human beings, the second mouth of a Futakuchi Onna is said to be unable to lie, speaking the truth regardless of situation or etiquette.

The Attack!

Encounters with a Futakuchi Onna are often startling, but to date no fatalities have been reported. The most immediate danger is to your cupboard, as the Futakuchi Onna's serpentine hair seeks out anything and everything edible in your home to feed its voracious second mouth. But these yokai tend to

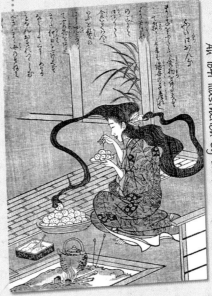

An 1841 illustration by Shunsen Takehara

keep to themselves and only reveal their true natures to a select few, either by design or accident.

Because a Futakuchi Onna is skilled at blending into normal society and its frontal side takes little to no sustenance, there are rumors of them being sought after by oblivious cheapskates on the lookout for a light-eating fiancée who won't put a strain on their food budgets. The joke is on the groom, however, for once he steps out of the house his new bride's second mouth consumes double the amount a normal woman would.

Surviving an Encounter:
Like many yokai, a Futakuchi Onna thrives on shocking victims rather than causing injury. It is likely to avoid revealing its true face (faces?) until it is sure to surprise the person watching her. Generally speaking, these encounters take place one-on-one rather than in crowded environments.

Even after a Futakuchi Onna has revealed itself, you are in no immediate danger. By all accounts it will probably be more interested in eating than in your presence anyway, allowing you to beat a hasty retreat.

If you are female and wish to avoid becoming a Futakuchi Onna yourself, make sure to feed your children well, especially if they're stepchildren. And don't hesitate to speak your mind from time to time.

DANGER SIGNS
Is your bride a Futakuchi Onna? Here are some potential warning signs:

☐ Food disappearing more quickly than it should

☐ Hair in strange places (backs of cabinets, deep inside refrigerator, etc.)

☐ Crumbs and bits of food caught in the hair on the back of her head

☐ her hair curled noose-like around your neck in the morning

☐ More chatty when she's facing away from you

YOKAI NO: 016

Onibaba

鬼婆

GRUESOME GOURMETS

Pronunciation:
(OH-nee BAH-bah)

Alternate Japanese Name:
Kurozuka

English Names:
Literally, "Demon-Hag"; Old Hag, Mountain Woman, The Goblin of Adachigahara

Gender:
Female

Height:
Average for an elderly Japanese woman

Weight:
Average for an elderly Japanese woman

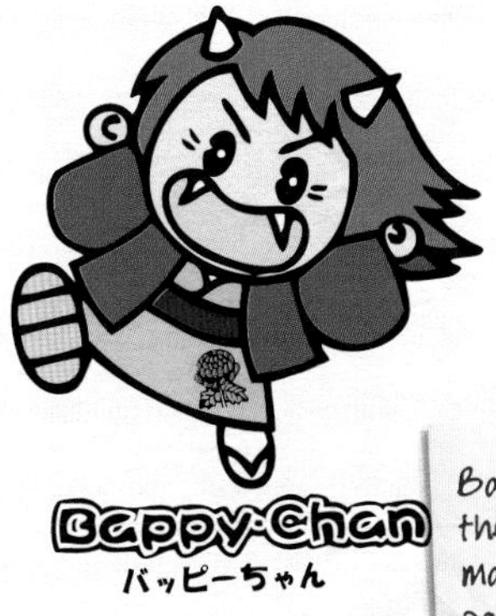

Bappy-Chan
バッピーちゃん

Bappy-chan is the super-cute mascot of a theme park built near the Onibaba's old stomping grounds.

Locomotion:
Bipedal

Distinctive Features:
Disheveled, maniacal appearance
Wild-looking hair
Oversized mouth
Often carries kitchen knife

Favorite Food:
Human entrails

Offensive Weapon:
Knife, teeth

Abundance:
One of a kind

Habitat:
Caves, mountain passes

Claim to Fame:
It goes by many names, but its modus operandi is always the same: a shriveled old woman on a gruesome mission to collect the livers of unborn children. Like the Hashi Hime (p. 162), Onibaba is a once-normal woman turned yokai through ill fortune and madness. For generations, it haunted

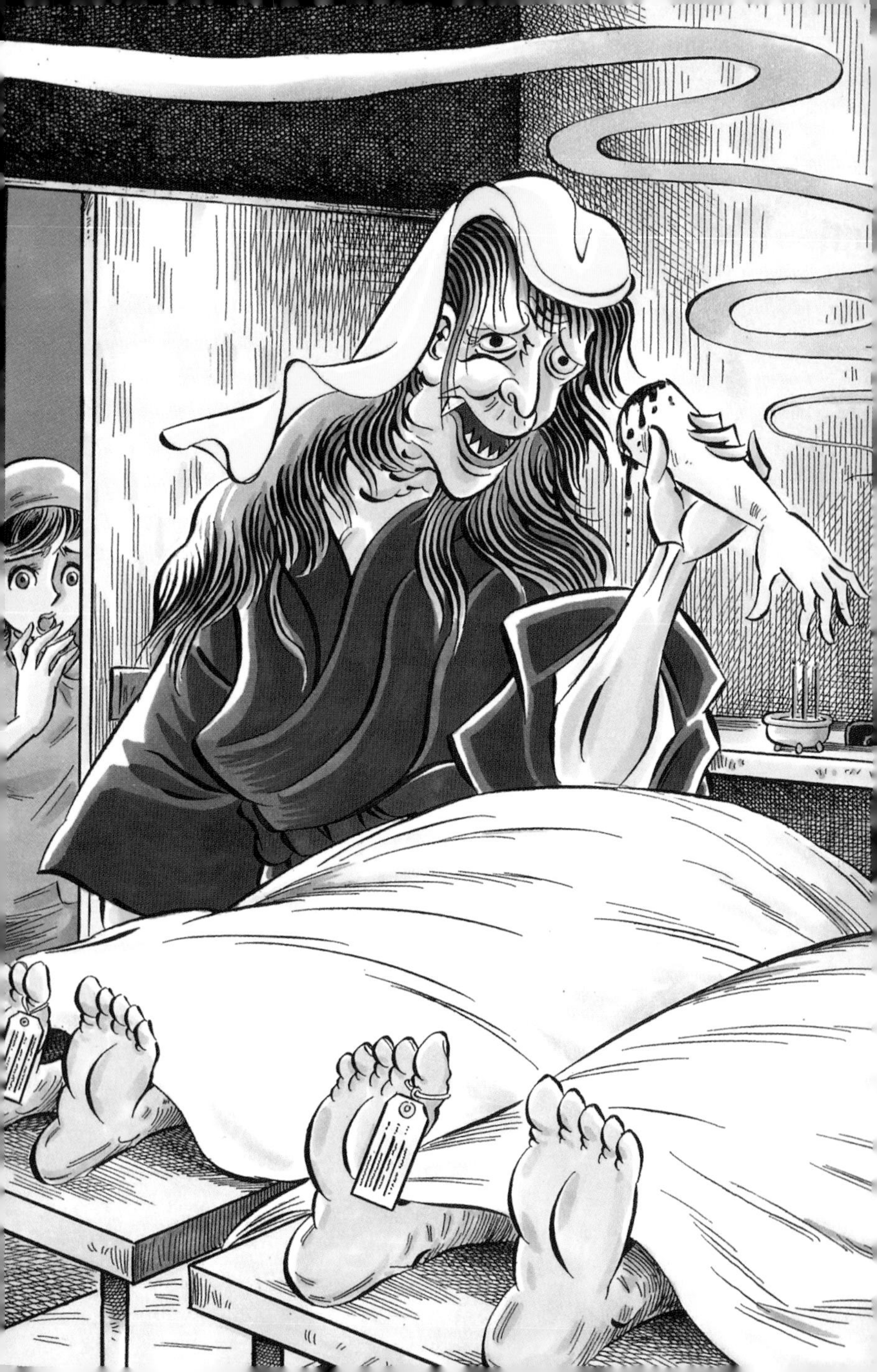

the mountains of Fukushima Prefecture, claiming the lives of uncounted travelers. Its story is as unfortunate as the fates of those who cross its path.

THE TEMPLE OF KANZEJI, also located in Adachigahara, is the site of a small museum devoted to the Onibaba. Not only does it house what is purported to be the grave of the Onibaba but also the knife and the cooking pot she used to prepare the meat from her victims.

The Tale of the Onibaba:
Long ago, a baby girl was born to a wealthy family in Kyoto. She never wanted for anything, but even by the age of five, the otherwise perfectly healthy and happy child had never uttered a single cry or sound. Desperate for some sort of cure, her parents consulted doctor after doctor without success. Finally they encountered a renowned fortune-teller, who consulted his horoscopes and pronounced a terrible cure: feeding the girl the fresh liver from a living fetus.

The girl's nanny, mother of a similarly-aged little girl herself, was given the unpleasant task of locating the liver. Knowing the journey ahead would be long and dark, she left her daughter with an *o-mamori*, an amulet of luck, and headed into the countryside alone.

For long weeks and months she traveled in search of a woman willing to give up her unborn child. Eventually, she reached the distant, hilly terrain of Adachigahara. She resolved to wait, taking a tiny cave as her temporary home. But as luck would have it, many years passed before fate brought a lone, pregnant traveler to her door.

Desperate to fulfill her obligation, the now-elderly nanny pounced without hesitation or remorse, setting upon the young woman with a smile and a hidden knife. It wasn't until after she had retrieved her gruesome prize from the woman's belly that she noticed: her victim was wearing none other than the o-mamori she had given her own daughter so many years previous.

The Attack!
Driven mad by the realization that she had slain her only child and grandchild, the nanny preys not just upon pregnant women but any traveler unlucky enough to cross its path, slaughtering them with its knife and

carving the flesh from their bones for food.

Surviving an Encounter:
In modern Japan, few people set out to cross mountain passes on foot, at night or otherwise. By some accounts it disappeared many years ago, but others believe that the Onibaba has simply left its previous stalking ground of Adachigahara for areas with a higher population density. Who can say what halls it may roam today in search of human sweetbreads and other organ meats?

If you do happen to encounter the Onibaba, you might try convincing it that you're too fatty, stringy, or otherwise unappetizing to be worth the effort. The old Hansel and Gretel trick of presenting a chicken bone as a finger might work. Good luck—you'll need it.

Hanging With The Hag:
Somewhat incredibly, the former stomping grounds of this bloodthirsty cannibal of a yokai have been turned into a theme park. The Adachigahara Furusatomura Village—a replica of a traditional Japanese village created for tourists—is located ten minutes by bus from Nihonmatsu Station on the JR Tohoku Line. Its official mascot character, "Bappy" (which translates into something like "Haggy") is a super-cute portrayal of the Onibaba, and the park's gift shop sells coffee mugs, ballpoint pens, and ear-cleaners featuring its visage. You can even download a "virtual Onibaba" to your computer from their website: *http://bappychan.com/mascot/mascot.html*

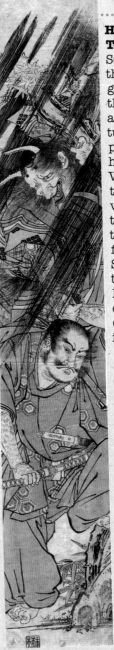

A vintage print: Onibaba on the prowl.

Tofu Kozo

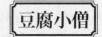

豆腐小僧

Pronunciation:
(TOH-foo KOH-zoh)

English Name:
Literally, "Tofu Boy"

Height:
Approximately 3 ft. (1m)

Weight:
Unknown

Locomotion:
Bipedal

Distinctive Features:
Conical straw rain hat
Kimono
Straw *zori* sandals, wooden
geta clogs, or barefoot
Always carrying a plate

Favorite Food:
One might theorize, tofu

Offensive Weapon:
Somewhat incredibly, a block
of tofu

Abundance:
One of a kind

Habitat:
Urban areas

Claim to Fame:
An unassuming little yokai,
the Tofu Kozo is of relatively
recent origin, having been
first described in the mid-
eighteenth century. It takes
the form of a small boy
dressed in traditional clothes,
armed with but a single
weapon: a jiggly block of tofu
on a plate. Encounters invari-
ably take the same form.

Someone is taking a walk
on a pleasant, uneventful
night. Ahead in the distance,
they can just make out what
appears to be a tiny figure
wearing a traditional straw
hat. As they approach, they
see that it is only a boy bearing a plate. Upon this plate
quivers what appears to be
an expertly prepared and
delicious-looking block of
fresh tofu, adorned with a
momiji (Japanese maple) leaf.

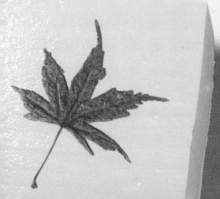

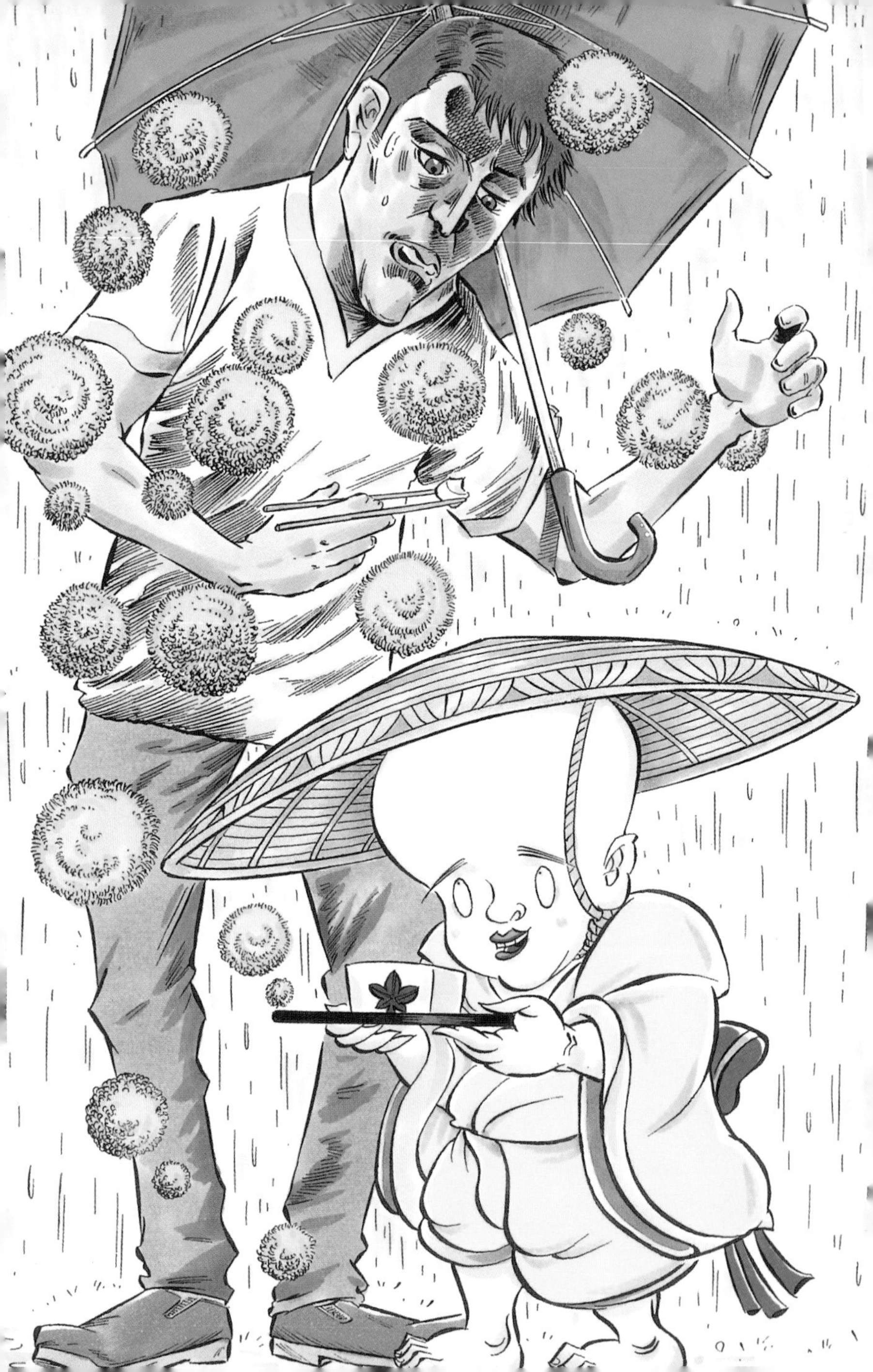

In spite of the late hour, in spite of themselves, they reach out for a bite of the all-natural treat . . .

The Attack!

If anyone tastes the tofu, they've fallen into the otherwise unassuming Tofu Kozo's trap. Results vary. In some cases, those who eat the tofu walk away with absolutely no ill effects. In others, however, once even a morsel of the tofu is consumed, a virulent fungus begin to grow within the victim's body, its fetid spores eventually draining it of all life.

Surviving an Encounter:

Beware of children bearing tofu; not a hard thing to do unless you're in desperate straits. According to some theories, tofu blocks without momiji leaves are totally benign. Try to confirm the presence or absence of the decorative leaves before taking a bite.

Tofu Trends:

Intriguingly, the Tofu Kozo became hugely popular in the early nineteenth century, and illustrations of the otherwise unassuming little fellow began appearing in all sorts of popular periodicals and on collectible cards called *karuta*. Alas, even the most popular of fads are destined to fade: by the dawn of the Meiji era in 1868, the tiny lad had all but disappeared from the public eye.

Kozo Crossover:

Traditionally there has been quite a bit of crossover between the Tofu Kozo and the Hitotsume Kozo ("One-Eyed Boy," p. 170), as both yokai take the form of children with a

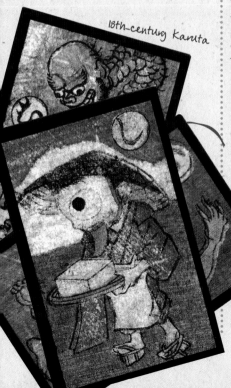

18th-century *Karuta*

GRUESOME GOURMETS

SOME SCHOLARS SAY:
That the presence of the maple leaf may be a play on the word *koyo*, which refers to leaves changing color in the fall. The combination of Tofu Kozo's cute appearance and moniker makes it a direct ancestor of the characters that appear on modern-day collectible card games, many of which feature similarly punny designs and names.

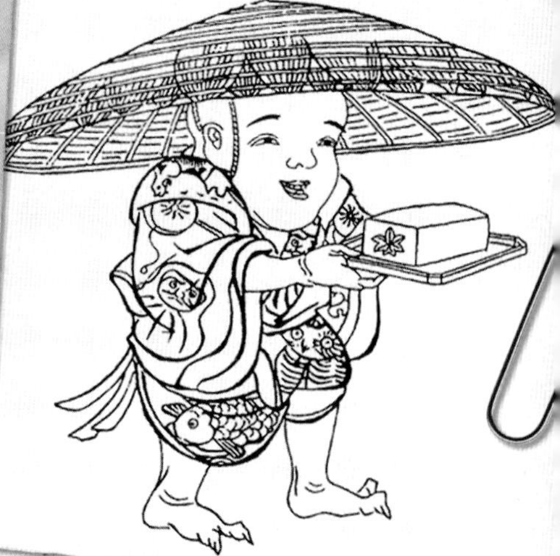

Another version of the Tofu Kozo by Masayoshi

penchant for mischief. As such it is quite common to encounter portrayals of Tofu Kozo with the cyclopean eye and lolling tongue of the Hitotsume Kozo.

Tofu Talk:
Although viewed as a "health food" or occasionally even dismissed as a second-rate meat substitute abroad, fresh tofu is an integral (not to mention delicious) part of the Japanese diet. Most commonly obtained in supermarkets today, it was traditionally handmade and sold through mom-and-pop specialty shops or by vendors plying their trade with pushcarts. Tofu is known as a delicate and highly perishable food, making any association with the forces of the supernatural all the sillier.

TOFU PROVERBS
Although not directly related to the Tofu Kozo, the now-archaic curse "Tofu no Kado ni atama wo butsukete shinjimae!" ("Go hit your head on the corner of a block of tofu and die!") is another example of the amusing concept of tofu causing hazard to life and limb. The absurd image of death-by-tofu, something akin to being killed in a pillow fight, appears to be at the root of the Tofu Kozo as well.

YOKAI NO: 0 1 8

Akaname

垢嘗

GRUESOME GOURMETS

Pronunciation:
(AH-kah-NAH-may)

English Name:
Bathtub Licker, Filth-Licker

Gender:
Unknown

Height:
5 feet (150cm)

Weight:
Average for a small adult

Tongue Length:
Up to one foot (30cm)

Locomotion:
Bipedal

Dinstinctive Features:
Long, tangled hair
Unnaturally tinted skin, often reddish in color
Often quite feral-looking
Long, pointed tongue

Why is the Akaname nearly always portrayed as being red? Because "aka" (scum) is a homonym for "aka" (the color red).

Favorite Foods:
Dead skin, mildew

Offensive Weapons:
None

Abundance:
Prevalent

Habitat:
Filthy bathrooms

Claim to Fame:
This creature comes with the flushed complexion of one who's just stepped out of a hot bath—and an insatiable desire to dine on the scummy residues that build up in and around tubs. Neglect your cleaning duties and you'll increase your chances of running into this disgusting character.

If you want to understand the Akaname, you need to understand the setup of the traditional Japanese bathroom. Generally, bathrooms in Japan are just that: rooms for bathing and nothing else, with toilets relegated to a separate room of their own. Although many modern apartments and hotels use "unit baths" that contain

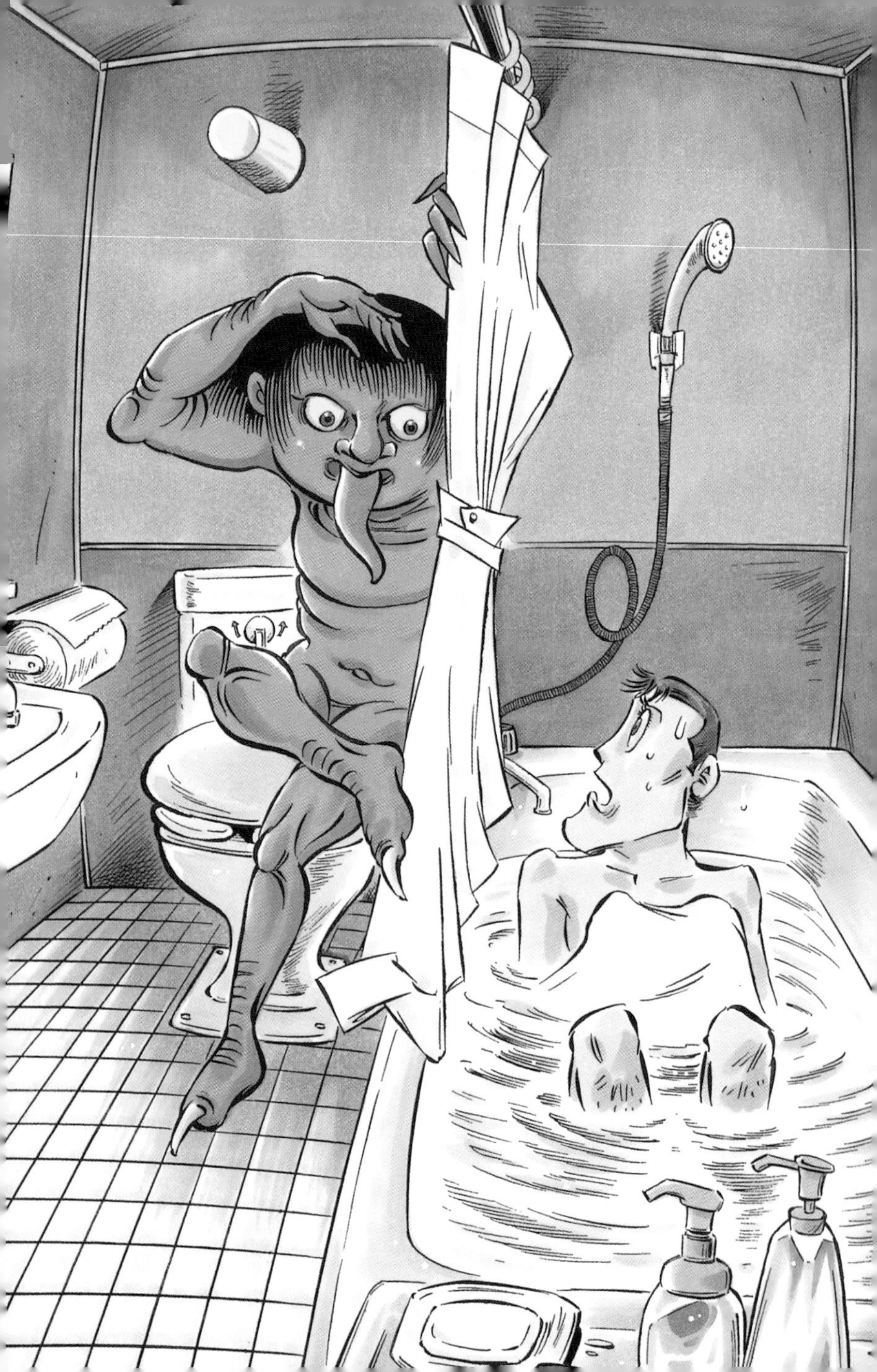

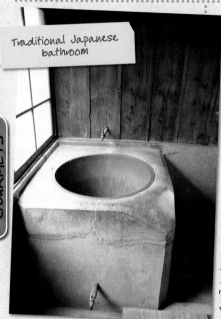

Traditional Japanese bathroom

both bathtubs and toilets, the separated layout remains common in Japanese homes.

In times of old, these bathtubs were built of wood and often housed in their own structures, separate from the main house. Poor air circulation and the resulting dampness and humidity made the enclosed spaces ideal habitats for all sorts of creepy-crawlies during the warmer months. Those who used the facilities in the summer often had to brave encounters with snails, slugs, worms, bugs, spiders, and toads.

The Akaname appears in these kinds of bathrooms late at night, living up to its quite literal name by licking (*name*) the slime (*aka*) out of dirty bathtubs. They are connoisseurs of soap-scum, mildew, and tub-rings. Talk about a cast-iron stomach.

The Attack!
The disgusting thought of having the inside of one's bathtub slathered by a slimy yokai tongue aside, it's hard to describe the Akaname's behavior as aggressive or dangerous. Then again, an Akaname will only appear in long-neglected bathrooms in need of a good cleaning anyway, so by licking out the filth it is actually performing a sort of service, gross as it may sound.

Surviving an Encounter:
For the love of all that's holy, clean your bathtub! Once an Akaname has its sights on a bath it likes, it will continue to return regularly in search of sustenance. Your life isn't in any danger, but if the people next door get wind of the fact that an Akaname has taken an interest in your home, your reputation

certainly is. This probably goes without saying, but once the Akaname has had its fill of filth for the night, it's time to break out the scrub brushes and cleaning supplies.

Although generations of Japanese children (and more than a few adults) once feared a run-in with the Akaname, this yokai is not aggressive or malevolent. Encounters are nearly always limited to the summer months, when the bathrooms are even steamier, moldier, and stinkier than usual. For college students and/or the extraordinarily lazy, simply avoiding the bath until the seasons change is another expedient for preventing Akaname encounters.

Filthy Facts:
At its heart, the Akaname is a personification of the fear of using a dark bathroom late at night. Before the advent of modern baths and flush toilets, the rooms housing these facilities were often considered dark and scary places, particularly by children. The Akaname is but one of many sorts of strange creatures believed to dwell in the bathroom; see also Toire no Hanako (p. 174), who haunts toilets in schools.

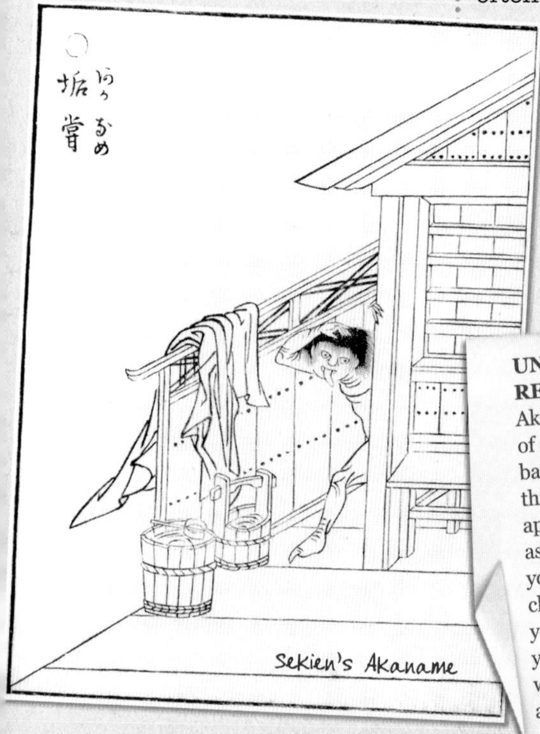

垢嘗

Sekien's Akaname

UNCONFIRMED REPORTS state that the Akaname is deathly afraid of *mujina*, the Japanese badger. Unfortunately this tantalizing weakness appears of limited utility as a countermeasure. Ask yourself: is it really worth chaining a live badger in your bathroom to keep yokai at bay when an hour with a scrub brush can accomplish the same trick?

Azuki Arai

小豆洗い

Pronunciation:
AH-zoo-key AH-rye

English Name:
Literally, "Red Bean Washer"

Alternate Japanese Names:
Azuki-toge (Iwate),
Azuki-togi (Nagano,
Hiroshima, Yamaguchi),
Azuki-koshi (Tottori)

Gender:
Male

Height:
5 ft. (150cm)

Weight:
Unknown

Locomotion:
Bipedal

Distinctive Features:
Strange proportions
Pattern baldness
Facial stubble
Carries a basket filled with
azuki beans

Favorite Food:
Beans and humans, presumably

Defensive Weapon:
Camouflage-like ability
to avoid being seen

Offensive Weapon:
Disorienting song

Abundance:
One of a kind

Habitat:
Isolated banks of
streams and rivers

Claim to Fame:
A furtive little
fellow, often heard
but only very
rarely spotted

GRUESOME GOURMETS

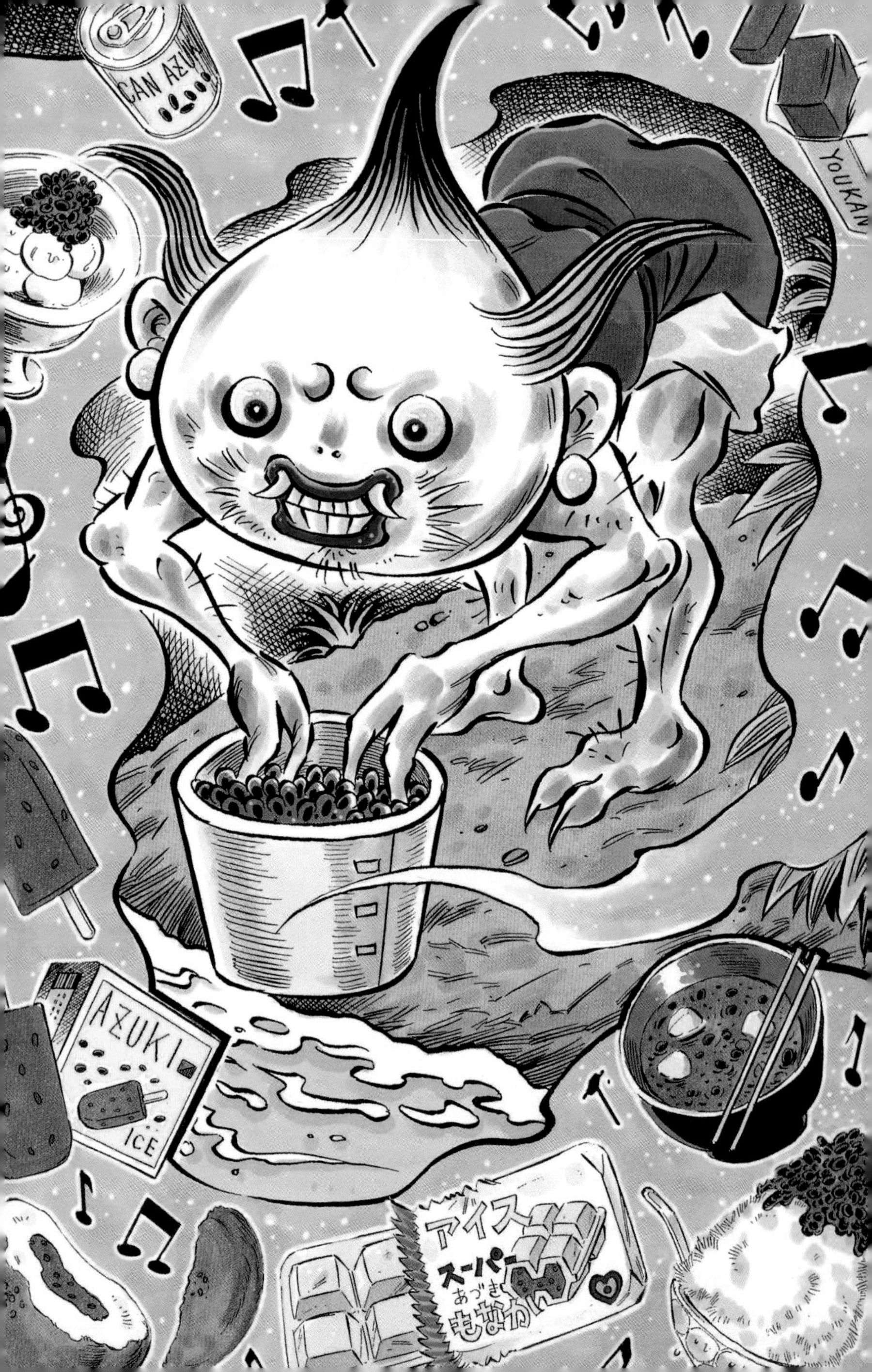
CAN AZU
YOUKAN
AZUKI
ICE
アイス
スーパー
あづき
もなか

alongside isolated streams and riverbanks, the Azuki Arai (literally, "Red Bean Washer") is an unassuming sort of creature that is believed to resemble an odd-looking little human. It is preternaturally engaged in the act of washing azuki beans in the basket it carries for that very purpose, quietly mumbling a weird little tune all the while. When hikers or travelers curious as to the source of the sound make a closer approach, they can make out the words to the Azuki Arai song: "Wash me beans, or catch me a human to eat . . . *Shoki-shoki! Shoki-shoki!*" (The last bit being onomatopoeia for the sound of azuki beans tumbling over one another as they are washed.) It is far more often heard than seen.

The Azuki Arai as depicted by Takehara Shunsen

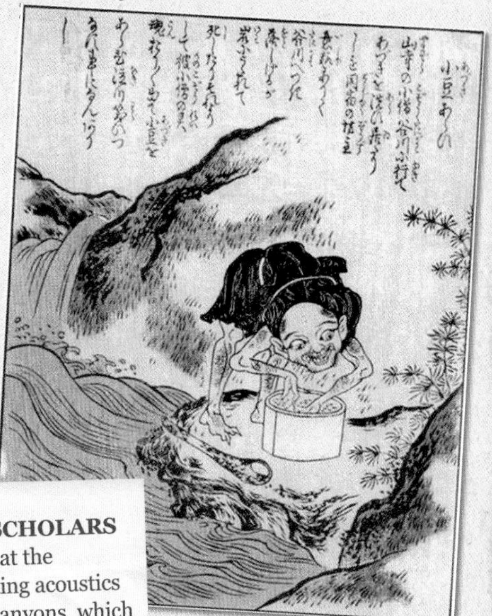

SOME SCHOLARS SAY: That the disorienting acoustics of river canyons, which tend to amplify ambient sounds, are the true origin of this yokai. It is a perfect example of the personification of a natural phenomenon.

Why Azuki?

Azuki beans have been a staple of the Japanese diet for more than a thousand years, and their reddish hue makes them both a favorite ingredient for cooking and a symbol of good fortune. They are often boiled with sugar and mashed into a sweet paste that is used as a pastry filling; they can also be boiled together with rice, another staple of the Japanese diet, to make a celebratory dish called *seki-han* ("red rice"). But first they must be washed, and it is from this step in the culinary process that the Azuki Arai, the Red Bean Washer, takes its name. The whisking of azuki beans and water in a traditional bamboo colander resembles the babbling of the brooks that are this yokai's preferred habitat.

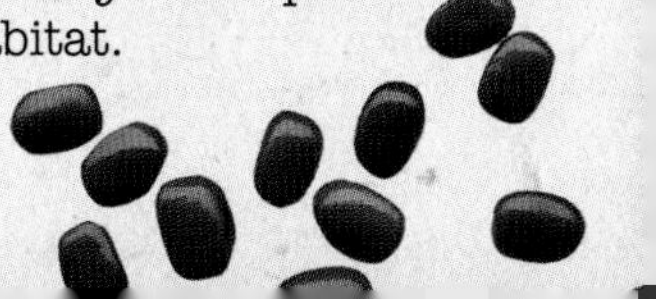

The Attack!

Those who stumble upon the Azuki Arai rarely if ever catch a glimpse of the elusive yokai. Instead they find themselves absorbed in trying to pinpoint the location of the sound and song, eventually becoming disoriented, losing their footing, and inevitably finding themselves sitting in whatever body of water they happened to be near. Whether this is deliberate on the part of the Azuki Arai or a simple side effect of the disorientation caused by spinning around to locate the yokai remains up for debate, but it seems to enjoy watching these pratfalls.

Surviving an Encounter:

In spite of the sinister-sounding lyrics to the Azuki Arai's ditty, the yokai has never been directly implicated in any sort of direct physical confrontation. Rather than violence, this creature takes great pleasure in seeing the look of shock on its victims' faces when they hear the words to its song or wind up in the river.

The Azuki Arai is generally harmless, but those without the ability to swim would do well to avoid this yokai. Although it is extraordinarily difficult to see, avoiding it is an entirely simple task, as the sound of its bean-washing activities is said to carry for almost a mile. If you hear a creek when you are far from water, or a strange song issuing from the woods, move on rather than leaving the trail to try and pinpoint it.

That being said, if you do manage to catch a glimpse of this reclusive loner of a yokai, consider yourself extremely lucky. In fact, it is believed to reside in Japan's forests even today. Rumor has it that hikers who say, upon hearing the sound of a creek or a brook in the forest, "The Azuki Arai used to live around here" are occasionally answered with a disembodied "I'm still here!"

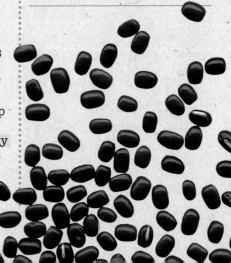

Seto Taisho

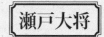

瀬戸大将

Pronunciation:
SEH-toh TIE-show

English Names:
Literally, "General Seto,"
Teapot Samurai

Gender:
Male

Size:
Approximately 1½ ft.
(50cm)

Locomotion:
Bipedal

Distinctive Features:
Sake-bottle head, tea-pot
body, etc.

Preferred Diet:
Rather than eating, it's made
of things to eat from

Offensive Weapon:
Wooden spear tipped with
ceramic

Weaknesses:
Being dropped from a height

Abundance:
One of a kind

Habitat:
Restaurants and home kitch-
ens

Claim to Fame:
This annoying little cuss is
composed entirely of dis-
carded dinnerware. Its head
is a gourd-shaped *tokkuri* bot-
tle for holding sake; its body,
a large teapot; its skirt an
inverted soup bowl; and its
arms and legs a mixture of
whatever plates and spoons
happen to be lying around
at the time. Its origins are
obscure. It remains unknown
as to what exact situation,
idiom, or phenomenon pre-
cipitated this creation.

A diminutive yet feisty
warrior who's always up
for a little skirmish, Seto
Taisho is a tempest in a tea-
pot in every sense of the
word. Being a haunted conglomeration of discarded old
spoons, plates, teapots, and

TAISHO TRIVIA:
In spite of its name, Seto Taisho does not appear directly related
to the city of Seto in Aichi Prefecture which is famed for ceramics.
Much like the term "China," which has come to encompass all sorts
of ceramics from the country of the same name, in Japan "Seto"
was once a catch-all term for nearly any sort of ceramic ware.

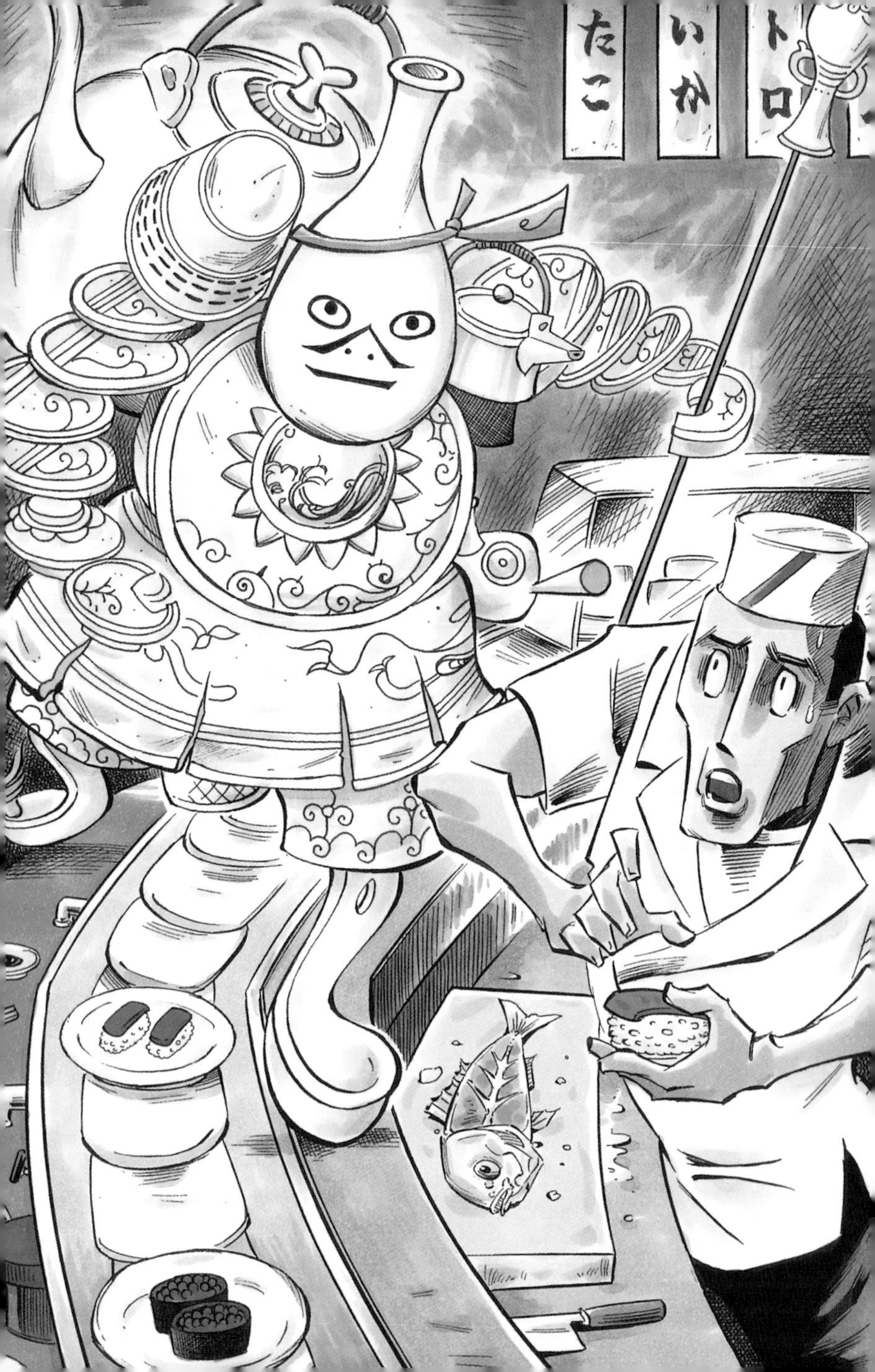
トロ
いか
たこ

other ceramic ware that has taken sentient form, it is essentially a sub-species of artifact-spirit (See Tsukumogami, p. 102). The name is believed to derive from the Seto ceramics that make up the major portion of its body (see note, previous page).

The Attack!

Undaunted by its relatively small size, Seto Taisho is known to fiercely charge his perceived opponents—basically anyone who happens to be within the range of a shouted challenge—with a tiny wooden spear. Unfortunately, it is tipped with a rounded ceramic jug rather than a point, making it fragile and rather useless as a weapon. It can't even make use of the advantage of surprise, as its smooth and hard feet make a loud clacking sound whenever it takes a step. It's a wonder Seto Taisho can even get any traction on the tabletops it uses for its banzai charges.

Surviving an Encounter:

Seto Taisho may be an aggressive little fellow, but it gives the concept of a "glass jaw" new meaning. When it charges, simply lift your arm at the last minute and let it run off the end of the countertop.

Be forewarned: unlike Humpy Dumpty, Seto Taisho is believed to be able to reassemble itself after a great fall. Keep repeating the tactic until it becomes bored and decides to target a new victim.

Sekien's Seto Taisho

IN THE LIBRARY:

Many yokai are based in folktales, local legends, or natural phenomena. Not so Seto Taisho. It was first described in Sekien Toriyama's aptly-named 1784 book *Gazu Hyakki Tsurezure Bukuro*, "An Illustrated Collection of Many Random Creatures." Although created almost as an afterthought, its continued cult popularity among yokai enthusiasts is a testament to the charm of Toriyama's original illustration.

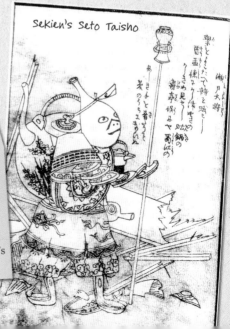

Annoying
Neighbors

Forget "location, location, and location."
The most important thing when purchasing
real estate is to ensure one of these
isn't living next door.

YOKAI NO: 0 2 1

Mokumoku Ren

目目連

ANNOYING NEIGHBORS

Pronunciation:
(MOH-koo-MOH-koo Ren)

English Names:
Literally, "Many Eyes"; Haunted Shoji Screen

Height / Width:
Each panel: 6 ft. 3 in. x 3 ft. (189cm x 94cm)

Eye Color:
Variable

Locomotion:
Lateral sliding

Distinctive Features:
Wooden frame
Torn paper
Eerie Mona Lisa-like eyes

Offensive Weapon:
Blinking

Weaknesses:
Physical impact
Water

Abundance:
Prevalent

Habitat:
Decrepit or abandoned houses

Claim to Fame:
To paraphrase Nietzsche, when you look into the shoji screen, occasionally it also looks into you.

One of the most distinctive members of the yokai pantheon, the Mokumoku Ren appears to be a sliding paper screen of the sort seen in homes and establishments throughout Japan—albeit old, worn out, and full of holes. Upon closer inspection, however, it becomes obvious that the spaces between its lattices are filled with pairs of eyeballs, their pupils eerily tracking the motion of humans that appear nearby.

The Mokumoku Ren is a traditional sort of spook, one of the first things that you might encounter inside a Japanese haunted house. In times of old, when hotels and even villages were few and far between, travelers often found themselves needing to take refuge for the night in abandoned homes, barns, or other creepy man-made structures. It is in precisely these sorts of already unsettling locales that the Mokumoku Ren manifests itself.

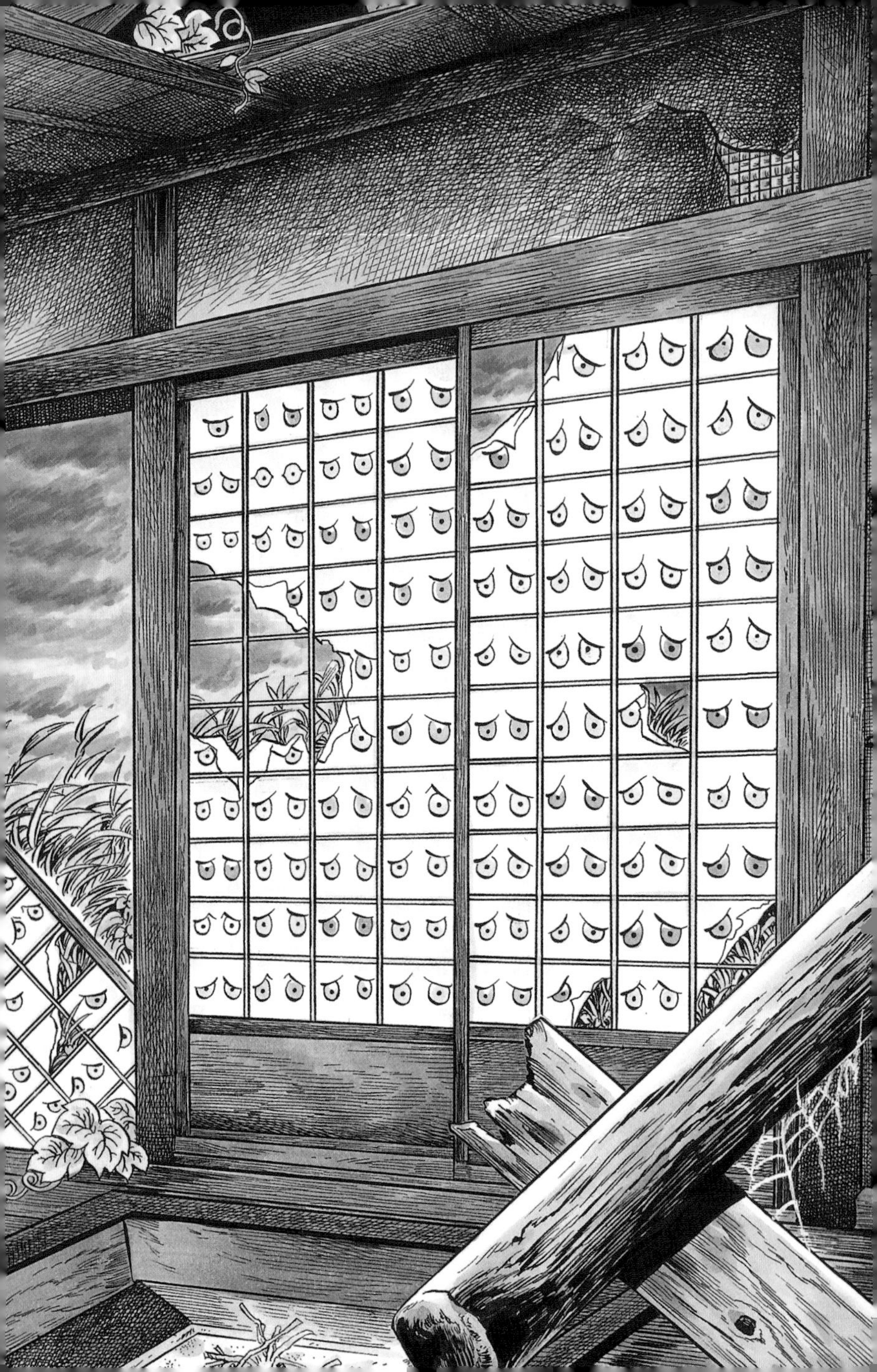

YOKAI NO: 021 MOKUMOKU REN

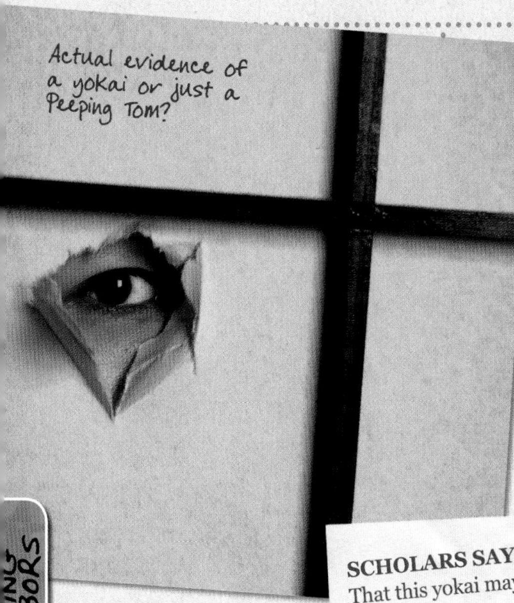
Actual evidence of a yokai or just a Peeping Tom?

Its name literally means "many eyes" or "continuous eyes." It is essentially a conglomeration of disembodied eyeballs that can inhabit a variety of surfaces inside homes, usually shoji screens but also, occasionally, tatami mats and walls. Whether it is a single creature that grows and spreads, or a cluster-like aggregation of many individual beings remains unknown. In any event, its presence is typical of locations with serious supernatural troubles.

The Attack!
Content merely with striking fear into the hearts of its victims (it is said to appear almost exclusively at night), the Mokumoku Ren is not considered dangerous in and of itself. Although it is theoretically possible for the screens it inhabits to slide upon their rails, the Mokumoku Ren generally remains in place, unmoving save for the occasional blinking of its many eyes.

SCHOLARS SAY:
That this yokai may be intended as a humorous illustration of a concept similar to the Western world's idiom "the walls have ears." Others believe it is a visual pun based on the game of Go, in which players focus their eyes on a playing board divided into squares resembling those of a shoji screen.

Surviving an Encounter:
Perhaps save for those with weak hearts, Mokumoku Ren encounters are almost never fatal. Some theories hold that it is possible to dispel the Mokumoku Ren by repairing the shoji screen that it inhabits, but even if true, this expedient presents its own set of problems. For one thing, the average traveler doesn't carry the glue and paper needed to repair

damaged screens, and for another, the Mokumoku Ren itself is the least of your problems. They inevitably appear in locations suffering from one supernatural issue or another, and more often than not indicate places where other yokai are likely to gather—if they haven't already. As such, if you catch sight of a Mokumoku Ren, you should attempt to exit the building and get to safety as quickly as possible.

There are a variety of folk tales involving encounters with the Mokumoku Ren. When a stingy traveling merchant decided to save money by sleeping in an abandoned house rather than an inn late one evening, he was confronted by the sight of countless eyes peering back at him from the building's decrepit screens. Rather than being scared, he plucked out the eyeballs and sold the gruesome collection to a local eye doctor for a tidy sum. Perhaps the Mokumoku Ren have more to fear from us than we do from them.

Or perhaps not. In another and more disturbing story, a traveler

so hell-bent on remaining in an abandoned house for the night attempted to ignore the Mokumoku Ren by wrapping a blanket tightly around his head as he slept. When he awakened, he was horrified to discover that his eye sockets were completely empty, his eyeballs nowhere to be found. Although impossible to verify, the tale should be kept in mind if you are considering spending any length of time in the sorts of buildings that this yokai tends to inhabit.

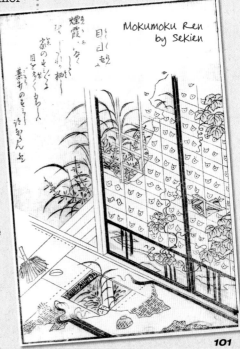

Mokumoku Ren by Sekien

Tsukumo-gami

付喪神

NEIGHBORS

Pronunciation:
TSU-koo-moh GAH-mee

English Names:
"Artifact-Spirits"; "Haunted Relics"; "Thing-Wraiths"

Height:
Variable

Weight:
Variable

Locomotion:
Variable

Distinctive Features:
Too many to record here

Offensive Weapons:
Fear from their sheer presence

Weaknesses:
Unknown

Abundance:
Prevalent

Habitat:
Wherever people live

Claim to Fame:
Taxonomically speaking, this is more of a catch-all term than the name of any one specific yokai. The kanji characters are a homonym for the phrase "ninety-nine gods," a reference to the fact that it was once believed any item that approached ninety-nine years in age would reanimate as a Tsukumo-gami. (Rather than referring to a specific age, here "ninety-nine" is intended to mean simply "a long period of time.") The roots of the Tsukumo-gami are to be found in the animistic tradition of Japan's native religion of Shinto, which holds that not only human beings but all things, living or inanimate, can be repositories for souls.

Conceptually, the Tsukumo-gami can be thought of as anthropomorphic versions of the remorse felt when throwing away an item one has owned for a long period of time. It could be a cooking pot; it could be a well-worn article of clothing or pair of shoes; it could be a hammer, knife, or other tool that has faithfully served its owner for years. It could even be a specimen of a technology that was once popular but

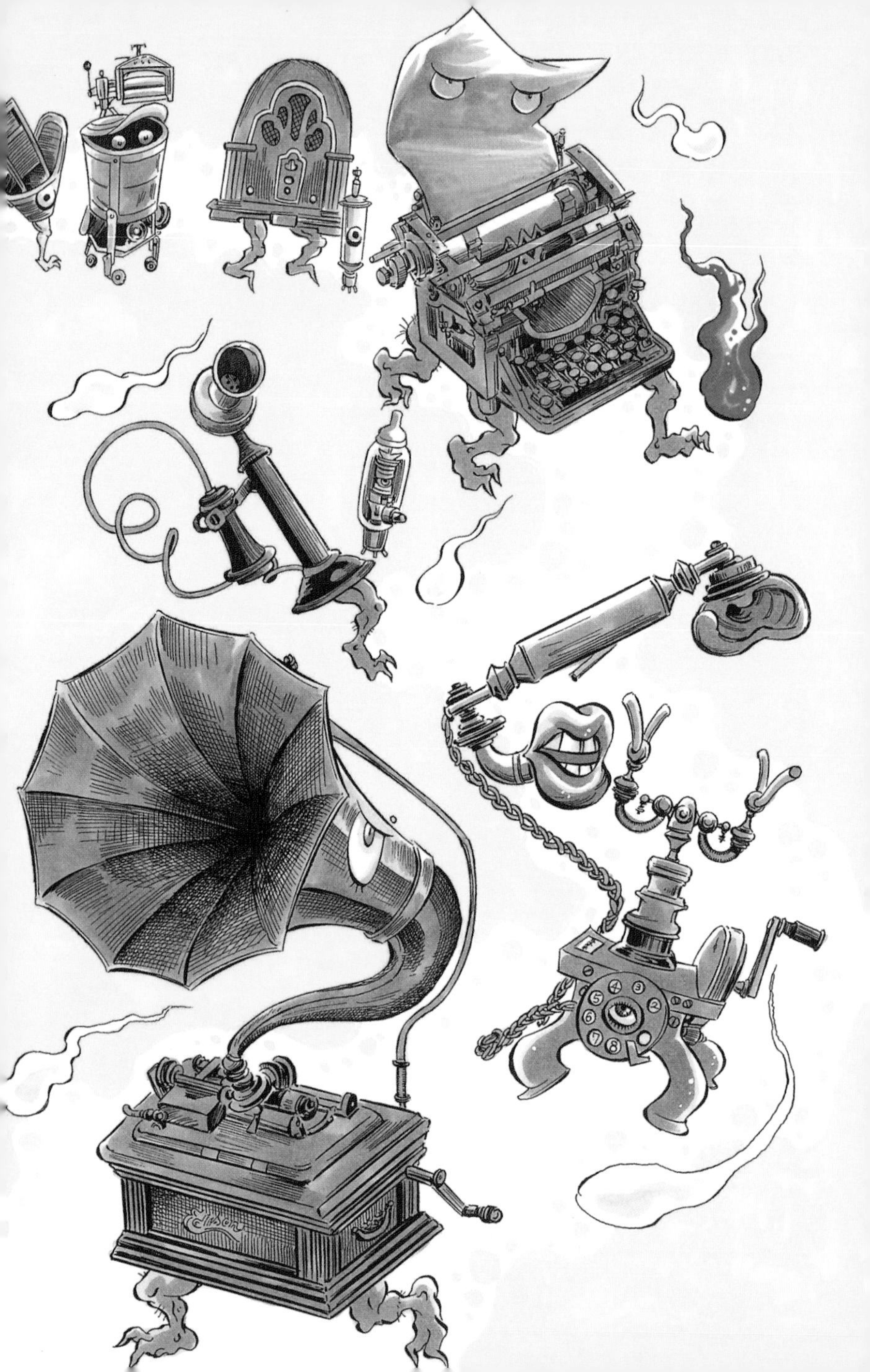
Edison

has since been passed over for newer and better things. Nearly any item that's been in the possession of an individual for an extended length of time can become a haunted, humanoid version of its original self.

The Tsukumo-gami are furious about being discarded after serving their human owners so faithfully. Perhaps their most famous endeavor was the Heian-era Hyakki Yagyo, (literally, "the Demons' Night-Parade"), in which large numbers of haunted items marched along the border of Heiankyo (now Kyoto), striking terror into the heart of what was then Japan's capital city. Legend has it that they were eventually corralled and driven deep into the mountains, safely away from the human population. This may sound cute, but at the time the sight of pots, umbrellas, and other items parading through the streets alongside demons and other monsters was considered extraordinarily inauspicious and a threat to the city's continued survival.

The Attack!

The Tsukumo-gami raison d'être is generally one of reproach rather than out-right aggression. Singly or in small groups, they are content to merely shock by their presence, dancing around, screaming, and doing whatever else they can think of to frighten their victims. They are completely aware that their mere appearance is more than enough to ter-rify human onlookers.

However, in large groups such as the one that took to the streets of Kyoto, Tsukumo-gami are considered

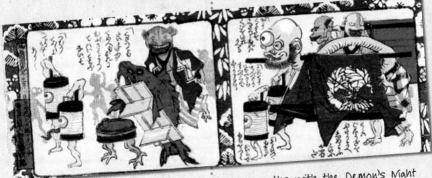

Pray you don't cross paths with the Demon's Night Parade. Detail from a 19th-century print.

to be as potentially dangerous as any mob.

Surviving an Encounter:

The best way to prevent any
of the items in one's possession from transforming into
Tsukumo-gami is to take care
of them. Carelessly handled,
discarded, or neglected items
are more likely to take
offense and reanimate than
those treated with respect.
Once popular but now for-
gotten tools, products, tech-
nologies, and items are the
most likely sorts of things to
appear as Tsukumo-gami.

Tsukumo Tracks:

The path supposedly taken by
the Tsukumo-gami through
Heiankyo still exists in Kyoto.
Ichijo-dori (First Street) long
ago served not only as a
major thoroughfare but also
as a psychological dividing
line between what urbanites
perceived as enlightened
culture and the uncivilized
wilds of rural Japan.

In addition, shrines to
needles, eyeglasses, and
other tools that make the
lives of humans easier can
be found throughout the
country, a clear example of
animistic beliefs and the
desire to show respect to
useful items.

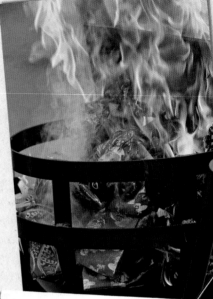

RELATED RITES:

The tradition of SUSU-HARAI
or New Year's cleaning, is
indirectly related to the
Tsukumo-gami in that it is a
time for ensuring the items in
one's possession are properly
cleaned and serviced.

NINGYO-KUYO, the last rites
for dolls, is still commonly
practiced in Japan today.
This involves bringing dolls or
other figural toys that have
spent a long period of time in
the company of humans to a
temple or shrine, where they
are consecrated and burned
in a special ceremony rather
than being simply discarded
with the trash.

Biwa-bokuboku

Koto-furunushi

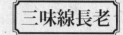

Shamisen-choro

琵琶牧々

琴古主

三味線長老

NEIGHBORS

Pronunciation:
(BEE-wah BOH-koo BOH-koo)
(KOH-toh FOO-ROO-new-shee)
(SHAH-me-sen CHO-roh)

English Names:
Biwa-Monk; Lute-Monk (Lute)
The Ancient Koto (Floor Harp)
Old Man Shamisen (Shamisen)

Height:
Biwa-bokuboku: Roughly
adult human size
Koto-furunushi: 6 ft. (182cm)
Shamisen-choro: 3 ft. (100cm)

Weight:
Biwa-bokuboku: Roughly that
of an adult man
Koto-furunushi: 14 lbs. (6kg)
Shamisen-choro: Weightless

Locomotion:
Biwa-bokuboku: Bipedal
Koto-furunushi: Quadripedal
Shamisen-choro: Hovering

Distinctive Features:
Traditional Japanese musical
instruments
Animal and human form

Offensive Weapons:
Incessant cacophony

Abundance:
One of a kind

Habitat:
Anywhere humans live

Claim to Fame:
A "sub-species" of Tsukumo-
gami (artifact-spirits, p.
102), the Biwa-bokuboku,
Koto-furunushi, and
Shamisen-choro are animistic
"instrument-spectres," old
musical instruments that
have taken humanoid (or in
the case of the floor-harp,
animal) form. They are classic examples of carefully

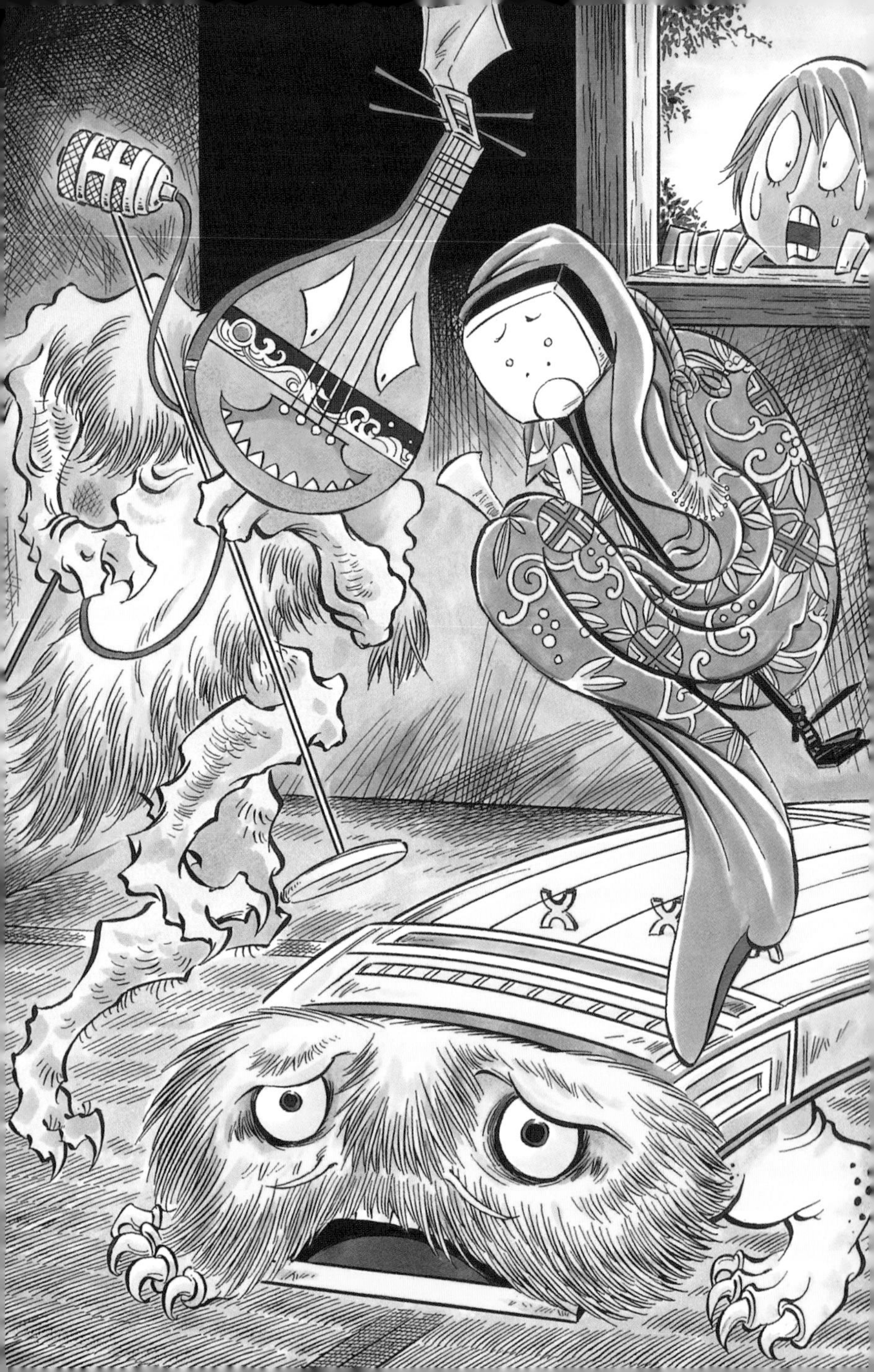

crafted tools attaining sentience after long years of use. Each is traditionally portrayed separately, but they are grouped together here because of their similar nature.

The Biwa-bokuboku:
Takes the form of a kimono-clad humanoid with a traditional Japanese lute in place of its head. As many lute-players in times of old were blind, the Biwa-bokuboku is sometimes portrayed with its eyes pressed tightly shut.

This yokai shares its background with a pair of legendary, long-lost musical instruments named the Genjo and the Bokuba, cultural treasures that were something like the Stradivarii of lutes. The Biwa-bokuboku is an anthropomorphic fusion of the two.

A variety of strange stories surround the Genjo in particular. Only the truly gifted could coax music from this exquisite instrument, as it possessed the mysterious ability to choose who was fit to play it; for those without talent, strumming the Genjo would produce nary a sound.

But perhaps the most famous tale involves the improbable theft of the Genjo from the well-guarded imperial palace. Late one evening some time after its mysterious disappearance, a musician happened to catch the unmistakable strains of the Genjo being played. Following the distinctive sound, he found himself standing under Kyoto's famed Rashomon gate. Unable to find the source of the beautiful music, the musician realized he was dealing not with a common thief but an *oni*, a demon. He shouted for the creature to reveal itself. The music abruptly stopped. Although fearing for his life, the musician stood firm, knowing how much the biwa's loss pained his emperor. Suddenly a rope descended from the highest reaches of the gate. Tied to the end was the precious Genjo, which the musician cut free and returned to its rightful owner. Incidentally, this Rashomon gate is the same as that portrayed in the Akira Kurosawa film.

The Koto-furunushi:
According to at least one source, the Koto-furunushi's provenance dates back to the second century A.D. After the emperor decreed a patch of vegetation be cleared for an outdoor banquet, he was

so pleased with the result that he left a floor-harp, or koto, as an offering of thanks to the site. The koto spontaneously transformed into a large and healthy-looking camphor tree that stood on the spot for many years, and thereafter any who approached it on quiet nights could hear the faint strains of harp strings being plucked. Although the tree's location has long since been forgotten, its spirit occasionally takes up residence in floor-harps, transforming them into Koto-furunushi. Other legends hold that this yokai represents the lonely spirit of a once-popular, now obsolete form of floor-harp that wallows in nostalgia for its "glory days."

FROM THE LIBRARY:
The first widespread illustrations of these yokai appeared in Sekien Toriyama's 1784 book *Gazu Hyakki Tsurezure Bukuro,* "An Illustrated Collection of Many Random Creatures."

The Shamisen-choro:
This yokai has a punny origin. Its name is believed to derive from the Japanese idiom "shami kara choro ni wa narenu," (literally, "a monk in training can't quickly become a master," but more colloquially akin to "Rome wasn't built in a day"). According to some legends, the Shamisen-choro is the spirit of a famed shamisen master who so loved his instrument that he couldn't bear to part with it, even in death.

The Attack!
Although the Biwa-bokuboku in particular is said to occasionally accompany fires or other calamities, such instances are extraordinarily rare. Perhaps "appearance" is a better term than "attack." The theoretical worst-case scenario would be if this traditional Japanese string trio kicks off an impromptu haunted concert when you're attempting to get some shut-eye. On the other hand, if you're a fan of traditional Japanese music, you could well be in for the treat of a lifetime.

Surviving an Encounter:
These particularly needy musical instruments just want to be played. But if you don't happen to be proficient, don't fret—they're more than capable of playing themselves. As with any other artifact-spirit, your life is in no danger. You're just going to have to wait the racket out until sunrise.

Kara-kasa

Bura-bura

Pronunciation:
(KAH-rah KAH-sah)
(BOO-rah BOO-rah)

Alternate Japanese Names:
Kara-kasa: Kasa-bake,
Kara-kasa Kozo
Bura-bura: Bake-chochin

English Names:
Haunted Umbrella
Haunted Lantern

Height:
Kara-kasa: 2½ ft. (75cm)
Bura-bura: 12 to 16 in. (30 to 40cm)

Weight:
Unknown; probably similar to the original items

Locomotion:
Kara-kasa: Monopedal
Bura-bura: Airborne

Distinctive Features:
Kara-kasa: Freakishly large tongue. Single gnarly leg sticking out of umbrella
Bura-bura: Garish lantern

Offensive Weapons:
Bronx cheers, eerie moans, erratic movement

Weakness:
Being ignored

Abundance:
Prevalent

Habitat:
Anywhere humans live

Claim to Fame:
They are a strangely fragile-looking duo: a paper lantern with a leering face and a lacquered-paper umbrella with a creepy eye, bobbing and weaving their way through the air, occasionally leaping out of the shadows to scare the living daylights out of unsuspecting pedestrians. Two of the most commonly encountered Tsukumo-gami (artifact-spirits, p. 102), the Kara-kasa and Bura-bura are often seen together, perhaps because they are found in similar places (both are, or were, everyday sorts of

ANNOYING NEIGHBORS

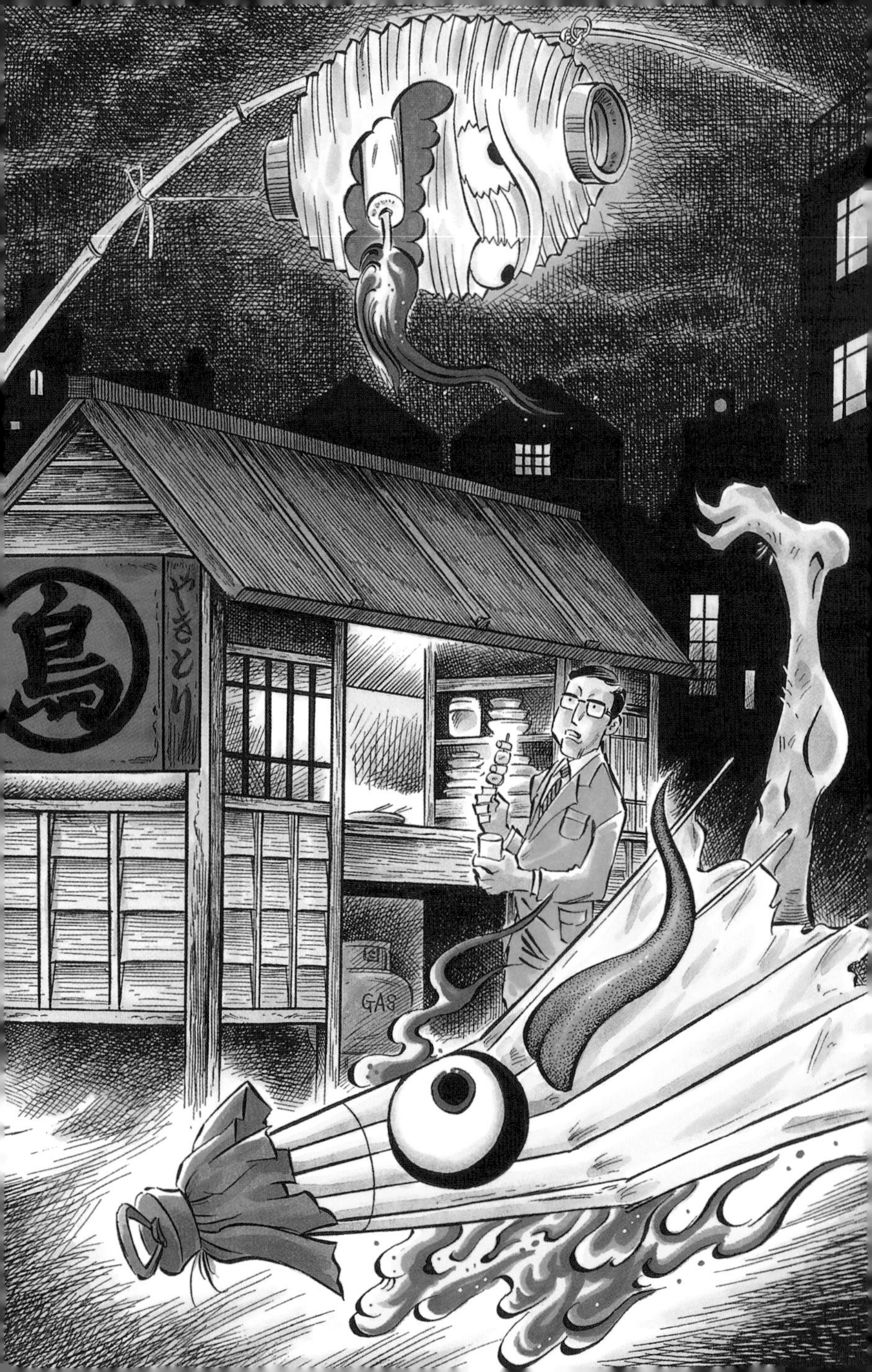
鳥
やきとり
GAS

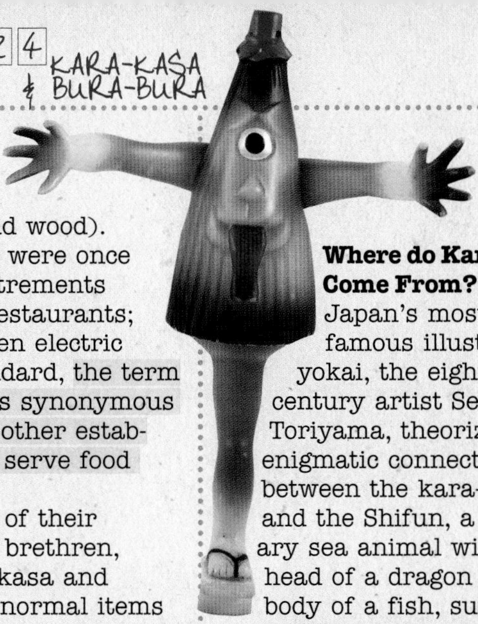

items) and made out of similar materials (paper and wood). Paper lanterns were once common accoutrements for Japanese restaurants; even today when electric lighting is standard, the term "red lantern" is synonymous with pubs and other establishments that serve food and alcohol.

Like the rest of their Tsukumo-gami brethren, both the Kara-kasa and Bura-bura are normal items turned into mischievous spirits, perhaps because of mistreatment or neglect.

Kara-kasa:
The most popular portrayal of the Kara-kasa, whose name simply means "paper umbrella" or "paper parasol," is of a cyclopean umbrella with a lolling tongue and a gross-looking hairy male leg in place of a handle, but other versions—perhaps subspecies?—have been reported as well. The most famous of these, as seen in vintage woodblock prints, features two eyes spaced closely on the ferrule tip and a bent and broken handle instead of the single leg.

Where do Kara-kasa Come From?
Japan's most famous illustrator of yokai, the eighteenth-century artist Sekien Toriyama, theorized an enigmatic connection between the kara-kasa and the Shifun, a legendary sea animal with the head of a dragon and the body of a fish, supposedly able to create clouds and rain at will. Unfortunately, Sekien did not elaborate.

But perhaps there is a more prosaic explanation. It is not uncommon to see obviously forgotten umbrellas left to rot away in the umbrella racks placed outside homes, stores, and other establishments. Is it too difficult to imagine an umbrella becoming disgruntled at being abandoned in some remote and lonely spot, far from home, in spite of having faithfully sheltered its owner from wind and rain?

Bura-bura:
Bura-bura appear in a wide variety of forms as well,

some more reminiscent of a human face than others. Their features are often illuminated from within by a candle, similar to a jack o' lantern.

Paper lanterns were the flashlights of the pre-electricity era, lit up with candles that were, of course, far dimmer than modern lightbulbs. The light they produced was barely sufficient to illuminate the immediate area around a traveler, and certainly not enough to throw light on whoever—or whatever—might go bump in the night, making them ideal props for all sorts of scary tales. The Bura-bura is one such example. Another can be found in "The Guiding Lantern," one of the "Seven Wonders of Honjo," a nineteenth-century collection of urban legends. In it, lanterns carried by what appeared to be human guides but were actually Tanuki (p. 126) or Kitsune (p. 154) in disguise led travelers astray—or to their deaths.

The Attack!
Most commonly, these yokai pose as innocuous umbrellas and paper lanterns, waiting until the last possible second to show their true forms and scare the wits out of victims. Common "attacks" include razzing of tongues, generating eerie keening sounds, and hopping or flying around to create more confusion and fear. These yokai are not known to physically accost individuals, and there are absolutely no accounts of them ever causing direct injury or harm, though it is theoretically possible for victims to injure themselves if they trip or fall during an encounter.

Surviving an Encounter:
Whatever you do, hold your ground. The only thing to fear from these mischievous creatures is fear itself. However, don't let a false sense of confidence lead you into going on the offensive. They are nowhere near as fragile as their humble origins might suggest, and if you do attempt to knock them to the ground, you will most likely find yourself swinging at thin air, unable to actually connect. The Kara-kasa and Bura-bura are only interested in scaring their victims; the less you react, the more quickly they will get tired of you and disappear. Don't worry: they are believed to possess extraordinarily short attention spans.

Dorotabo

泥田坊

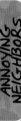
ANNOYING NEIGHBORS

Pronunciation:
(DOH-roh TAH-boh)

English Names:
Literally, "Rice-Paddy Man";
Mud Man

Height:
5½ to 6 ft. (160 to 180cm)

Weight:
Variable

Locomotion:
Bipedal

Distinctive Features:
Composed entirely of mud
Rank, swampy body odor
Dark brown to black color-
ation. A generally lumpy sort
of appearance

Three-fingered hands

Offensive Weapons:
Endless whining, screaming,
moaning

Weaknesses:
Droughts; lazy heirs

Abundance:
Believed to be one of a kind

Habitat:
Rice paddies

Claim to Fame:
Usually depicted as a
humanoid torso emerging,
amoeba-like, from a sodden
rice paddy, the Dorotabo is
believed capable of bipedal
locomotion on land given a
moist enough climate. Rice
fields are essentially shallow
swamps filled with all sorts
of snakes, frogs, insects,
and other creepy-
crawlies, and this
yokai is said to
possess a dark
color and a musky,
peaty body odor
reminiscent of the
fields from which it
arises.

A hairless, golem-
like mud man with
a single eye in the

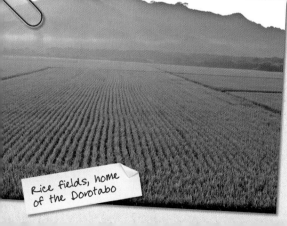

Rice fields, home of the Dorotabo

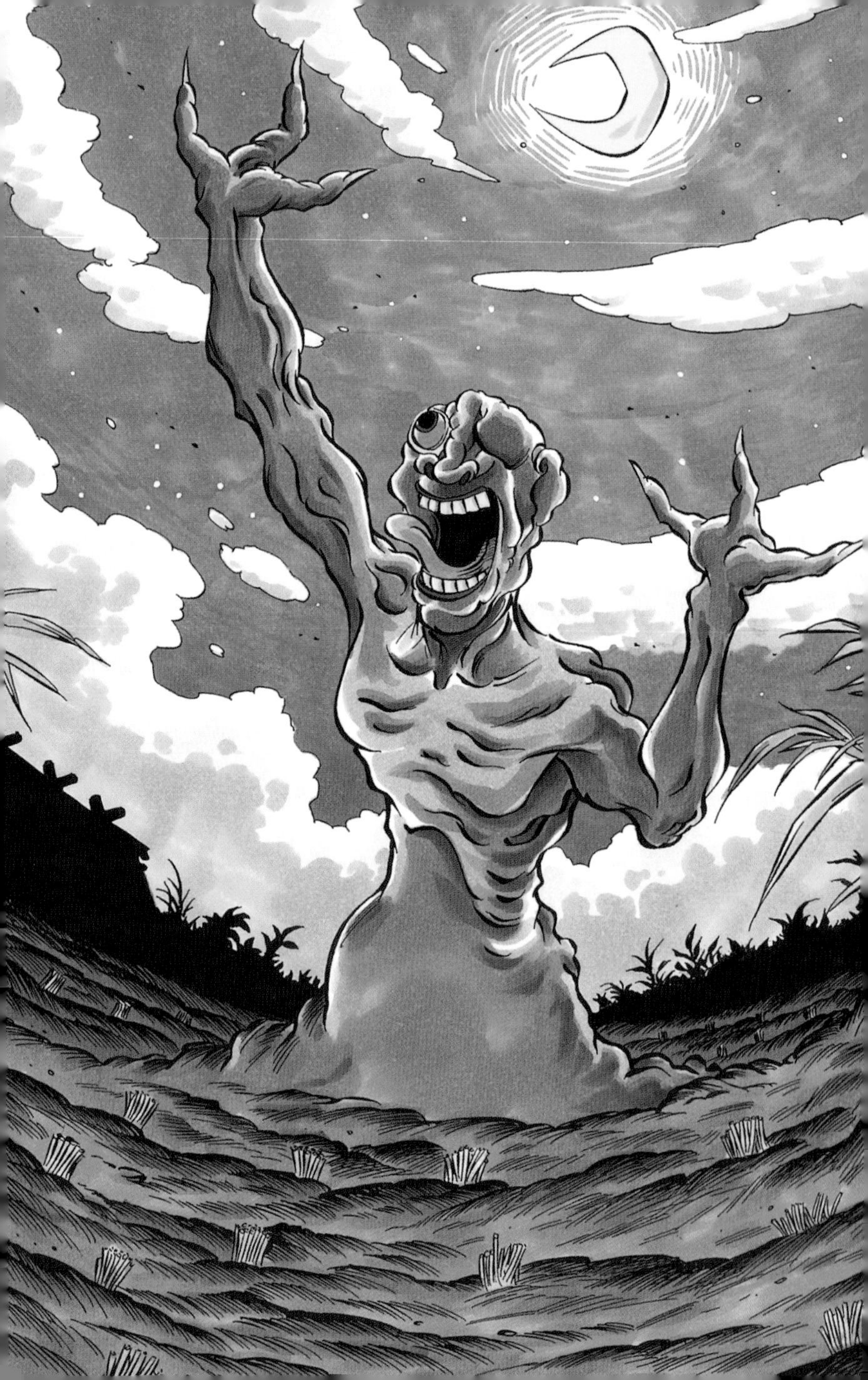

middle of its forehead, it appears spontaneously in rice fields late at night, moaning, crying, and carrying on, generally scaring the hell out of anyone who happens to be in earshot. More often heard than seen, it is a quintessentially rural sort of monster. Although superficially simple, the Dorotabo is actually one of the most metaphoric of the yokai.

According to some tales, it represents the spirit of a hardworking old farmer who toiled to turn a humble plot of land into a productive rice field. In spite of the years spent supporting his family and his hopes of providing an asset for his heirs, upon his death his dissolute son turned around and sold the beloved piece of land to pay for women, wine, and song. Giving the phrase "rolling over in his grave" a new and literal meaning, his father's departed soul returned to the rice field that he had created with his own blood, sweat, and tears, reduced to moaning and wailing to express his eternal dissatisfaction at the hand fate dealt him.

Others describe the Dorotabo as the spirit of a farmer cheated out of his land, returned from the grave to haunt its new owners.

Still other theories hold that it is a pun based on the concept of indulging in one's personal vices (see note below).

SOME SCHOLARS BELIEVE:
Sekien intended the Dorotabo as a silly metaphor for the Yoshiwara "pleasure quarters" (brothels) located to the north of Edo castle in the eighteenth century, as the term "*dorota wo bo de utsu*"—literally, "sticking a pole in the rice paddy"—was used as slang for sexual intercourse at the time.

Spook Season:
Descriptions of this yokai are scarce, making it difficult to pin down when exactly it most commonly manifests. However, analysis of Sekien Toriyama's illustration of the creature (at right) gives us a hint. The field is obviously wet, but there are no signs of rice shoots on its skin or in the paddy around it. Paddies are generally tilled in the early spring, then flooded and allowed to lie fallow for a period before rice seedlings are planted. Specific dates vary depending on the climate of a given region, but if this illustration is any

guide, the Dorotabo is most likely to appear in the period after a paddy is flooded but before seedlings are planted.

The Attack!

The Dorotabo appears at night, chanting (perhaps wailing would be a better term), "Return my field! Return my field!" over and over again until dawn. The Dorotabo is not known to attempt to physically attack human beings, but this is small comfort to those being accosted by its endless, plaintive cries.

Surviving an Encounter:

Knowing that the Dorotabo rarely, if ever, interacts with humans, you might be tempted to head out to the paddy and whomp his head with a shovel, but violence is a lost cause. He's a mudman and thus more than capable of reconstituting himself.

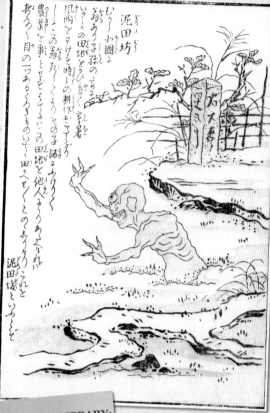

泥田坊

よう小國よ
むかし北國に
翁ある子孫に
このの田地とひさぎて
風雨をきけきくなく気暑
しこと翁別にくらしてのまほ
ふこと翁別にくらしてのまほ
農業と事とせどさるこころの
あろく目の一つあるくろきものいで
田ろへとくとの声するとの
ありれ泥田坊とよぶとき

泥田坊といふなる

Sekien's version of the Dorotabo

The only thing in danger from a Dorotabo attack is a good night's sleep. Invest in a pair of earplugs. Soundproof your bedroom. Or better yet, knock off the dang partying and start tilling those fields, boy!

FROM THE LIBRARY: The Dorotabo made its first appearance in Sekien Toriyama's eighteenth-century book *Konjaku Hyakki Shui* ("Tales of Monsters Now and Then"). Although possibly based on folktales or stories, it is more likely a character of his own creation.

Jinmenju

人面樹

Pronunciation:
(JIN-men-joo)

English Name:
Literally, "Human-Faced Tree"; Tree With Human Fruit

Height:
6 ft. to 35 ft. (2 to 10m)

Locomotion:
Essentially immobile

Distinctive Features:
Fruit-laden branches
Tiny human face on each fruit

Offensive Weapons:
None

Weaknesses:
Laughter

Abundance:
Extremely rare

Habitat:
Isolated mountain valleys

Claim to Fame:
Japan's densely forested mountains are home to a great variety of yokai and other mysterious creatures, including the elusive

Jinmenju, or the Tree With Human Fruit. It takes the form of an exotic but otherwise natural looking tree, its branches laden with what appear to be oversized fruits. Upon closer inspection, it becomes evident that each bears a human face, complete with eyes, ears, mouths, and noses.

Some variations of the story claim that these fruit are capable of speech, either individually or en masse. Usually, however, they are described as totally ignoring attempts to communicate, simply chuckling or giggling as humans pass by. Whether this is perceived as creepy and sinister or simply silly depends entirely upon one's frame of mind.

Jinmenju are said to live in valleys, suggesting that they prefer lower elevations, and resemble trees found in tropical habitats; some accounts describe them as being superficially similar to *Artocarpus incisa*, the breadfruit tree.

Believe it or not, the fruit of the Jinmenju is apparently edible. It is said to have a

ANNOYING NEIGHBORS

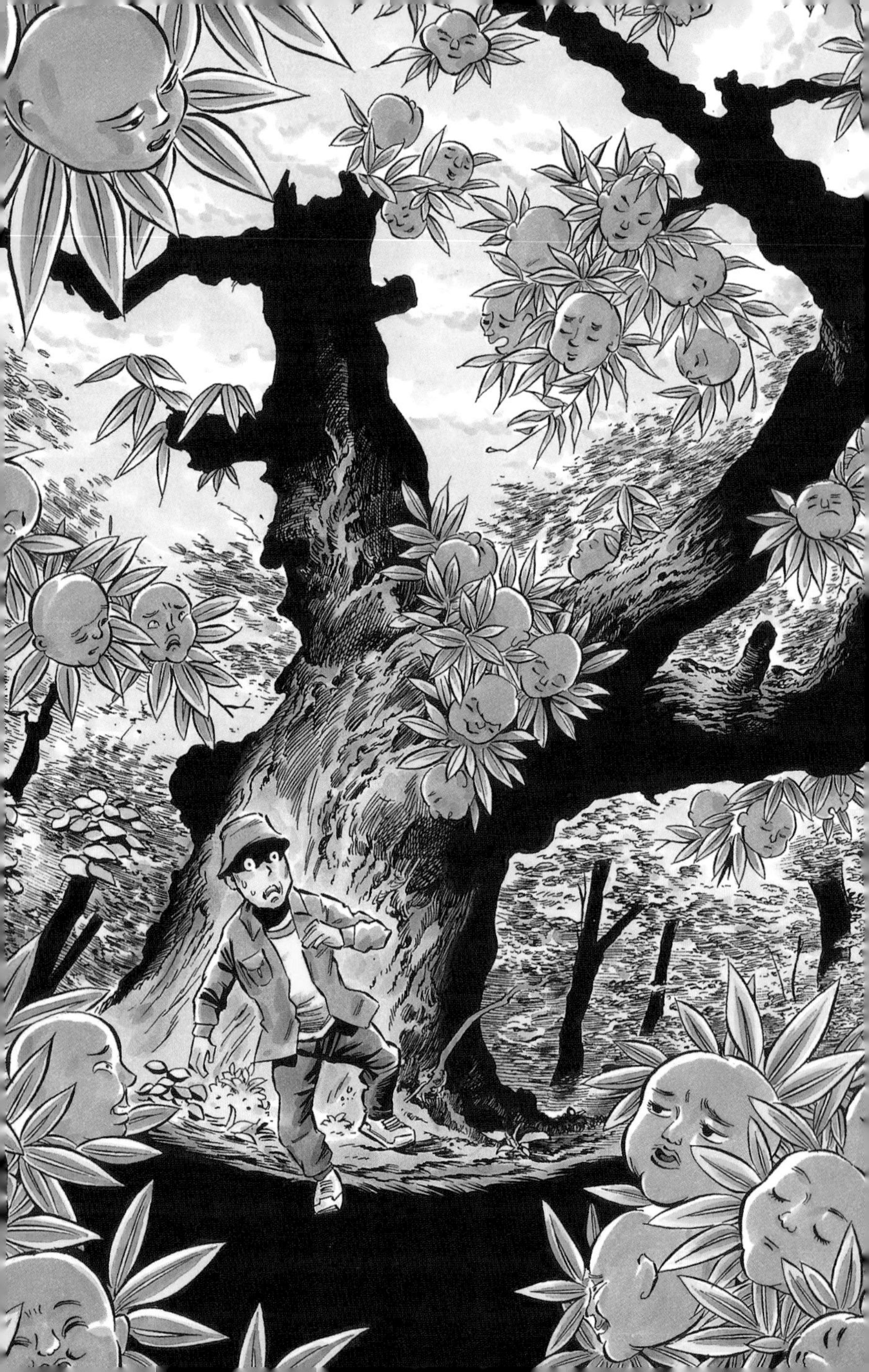

citrus-like sweet and tangy flavor, though we wonder what kind of person would bite into the head of a tiny human in order to obtain this information.

The Attack!

While you probably wouldn't want to have a constantly chortling Jinmenju living next to your window, they are not dangerous in any sense of the word. They are essentially gentle beings whose interactions with humans are limited to voyeurism.

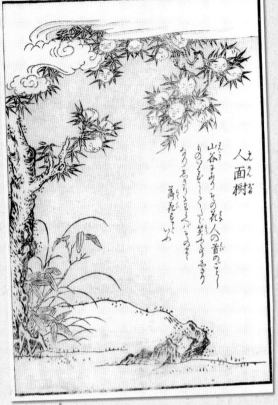

Sekien's illustration of a Jinmenju tree

Surviving an Encounter:

Relax. You are in no immediate danger, and in fact have the upper hand. For if Jinmenju fruit laugh too hard, they fall off their branches. Humans with a mischievous bent might try a little stand-up routine to shake the laughing fruit from their precarious perches.

Scholars Believe:

That the Jinmenju's roots extend abroad, specifically to Chinese folktales (which, in turn, appear to originate with Indian and Persian legends). Indeed, an entire book could easily be compiled about the convoluted path by which tales of the Jinmenju made their way to the Japanese islands.

The Jinmenju was first officially cataloged in a 1712 encyclopedia called *Wakan Sansaizue*, a mixture of myth and practical knowledge compiled over the course of thirty years by an Osaka doctor. He described it as originating "in valleys on a island some 1,000 *ri* [some 2,500 miles] to the southwest," which corresponds to somewhere in the Indian Ocean. It is believed that this could be an indirect reference to the legendary island of Waq-Waq, referenced in a Persian tale from *The Thousand and One Nights* as home of the Waq-Waq tree, which produces human-shaped fruit. Some believe Waq-Waq refers to the Seychelle Islands off Madagascar, others to a forgotten island in Indonesian or Chinese waters. (A few theories tie it to the Korean peninsula or even Japan itself.)

Another potential source of information about the Jinmenju can be found in the sixteenth-century Chinese classic *Journey to the West*. It mentions a tree called the Ninjinka, which is said to "bear thirty fruit that resemble human infants once every three thousand years, which in turn take three thousand years to mature, and then ten thousand to become edible." If indeed related to the Jinmenju, this incredibly long incubation period could explain the lack of any sightings in recent years. Eating the fruit of the Ninjinka is said to extend an individual's life to some 47,000 years, which sheds some light on the otherwise disturbing accounts of the flavor of Jinmenju fruit.

Are the waq-waq tree and the Ninjinka ancestors of the Jinmenju? Are the Jinmenju reported in Japan a distinct indigenous species, or were they imported from China or some mysterious island in the distant past for reasons unknown? We will probably never know for certain, but circumstantial evidence makes for a compelling argument that the Jinmenju is among the most international of the yokai.

YOKAI NO: 027

Namahage

なまはげ

ANNOYING NEIGHBORS

Pronunciation:
(NAH-mah HAH-gay)

English Names:
Literally, "Blister-Peeler"; The Bogeyman

Gender:
Male and female

Height:
Approximately 6 ft. (180cm)

Weight:
Unknown; likely around 180 lbs. (80kg)

Locomotion:
Bipedal

Distinctive Features:
Straw "mino" coat
Bright red skin (males)
Bright blue-green skin (females)
Demonic visage with horns and fangs

Offensive Weapons:
Wide-bladed farm knife or machete

Abundance:
Prevalent

Distribution:
Akita Prefecture

Habitat:
Snowy alpine regions

Claim to Fame:
The Namahage are fierce-looking creatures with a pathological dislike of the lazy and spoiled. Hailing from the snowy reaches of the Oga peninsula, they take their name from the concept of the blisters that appear on the feet of slovenly individuals who sit in front of a warm hearth for too long when they should be working. In fact, Namahage is actually a colloquial contraction of the words *namomi* ("fire-blister" in the regional dialect) and *hagu* ("to peel").

In spite of their ferocious countenances and penchant for tormenting children, the Namahage are seen as harbingers of good fortune, if for no other reason than the threat of a visit was traditionally enough to get a

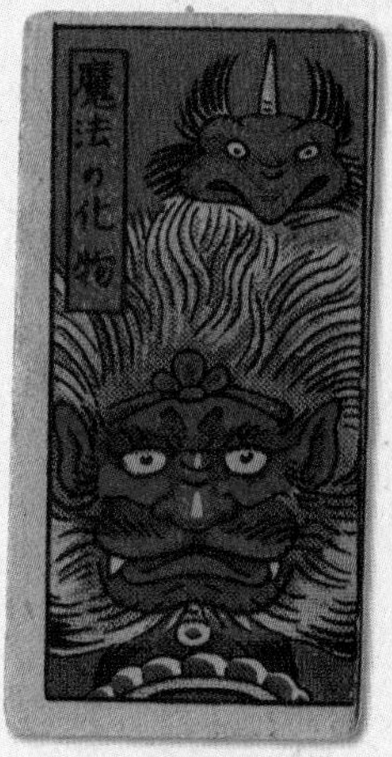

魔法の化物

A 1960s Karuta showing Namahage

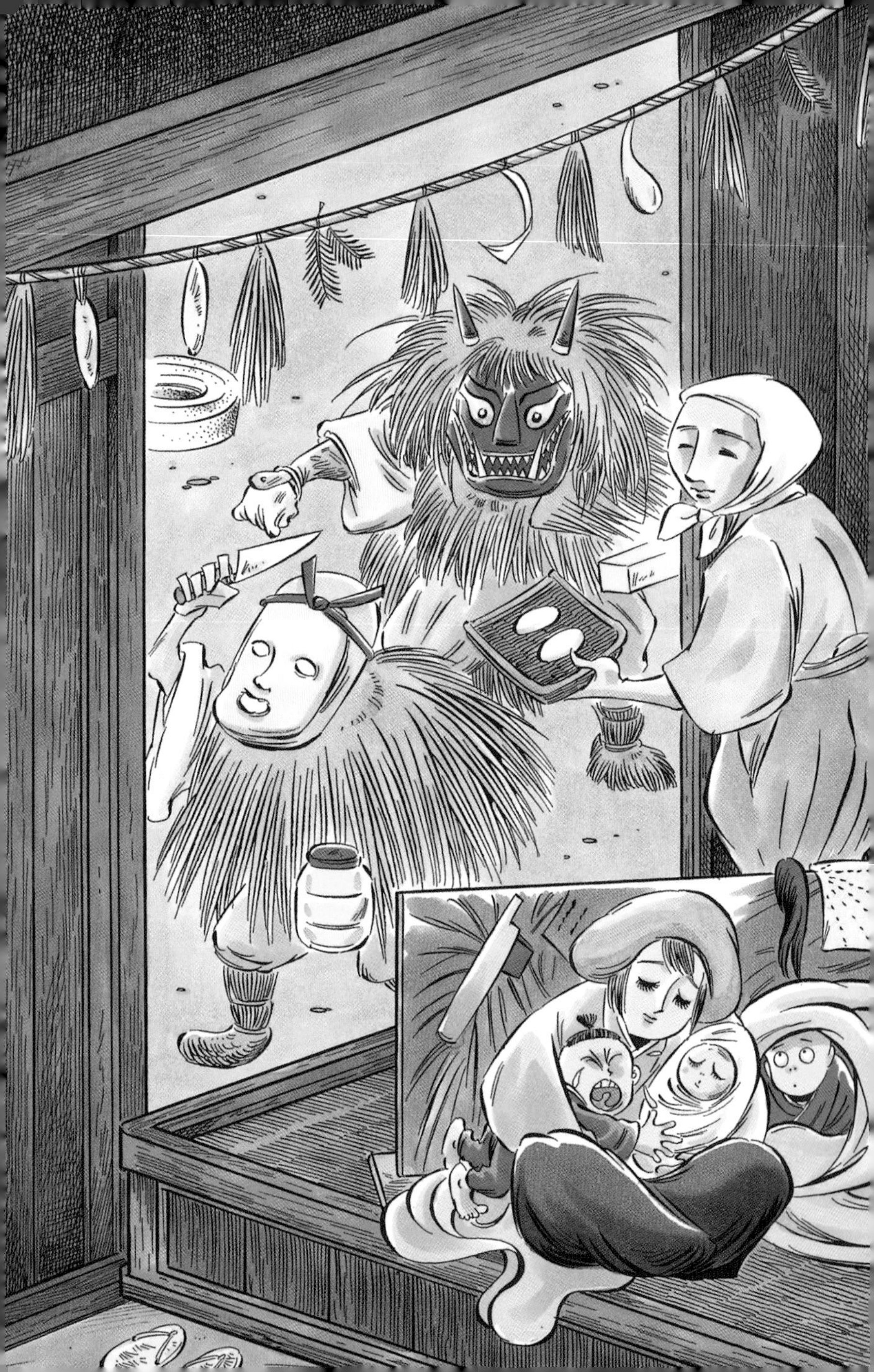

wayward child back to their chores.

Although categorized as yokai, the Namahage can also be seen as a sub-species of Japanese demons called *oni*. Rather than being simple tools of evil (as portrayed in Christian belief), oni are a personification of forces unseen, unknown, and fearsomely powerful. In fact the word "oni" can be a synonym for either "strong" or "evil." The stereotypical portrayal of an oni is of a muscular humanoid with red or blue-green skin and horns on the head, clad in a tiger loincloth. The Namahage are essentially oni recast in the image of farmers, clad in straw snow-coats and carrying agricultural implements such as machetes and buckets.

There are a variety of stories concerning the origins of the Namahage. The most famous local legend claims a Chinese emperor visited Oga in the first century BC in search of a mythical herb said to bestow eternal youth. He was accompanied by five oni that he used for hard labor, rewarding them with one day a year on which they were allowed to run wild. Every year they would use their temporary freedom to descend on nearby villages, stealing food and kidnapping women and children for their own twisted entertainment. After several years of this, understandably fed-up villagers approached the emperor with a wager. If his oni could build a staircase of one thousand stones before sunrise, the villagers promised to hand over a young maiden to them every year. If the oni failed, they would leave the citizens in peace. To make a long story short, at the last minute the villagers mimicked the sound of roosters crowing to convince the demons to abandon their work at the next to last stair, sending them back into the mountains once and for all. Knowing their victory was based on deception, the villagers decided to appease the demons by holding a festival in which they would pretend to welcome the creatures into their homes one day a year.

The Attack!

At the height of winter, the Namahage appear without warning at homes they believe harbor lazy individuals, pounding on doors and demanding to punish any misbehaving whippersnappers. "Are there any crying

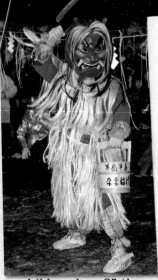

NAMAHAGE NEWS:
In New Year's celebrations in the area, locals dress in costumes to re-enact the rampage of the Namahage, pounding on doors and threatening to punish wayward children. Although these celebrations are not open to tourists, those interested can experience a public version at the Sedo Festival, which is held every February at a shrine in Oga city.

There is also a yearly accreditation test for fans of the creature and its habits. Dubbed the "Namahage Professor Trial" and taking the form of an hour-long multiple-choice test, it allows those who pass to describe themselves as fully qualified Namahage experts.

If you think you have what it takes, go to the (Japanese language) link:

WWW.NAMAHAGE.NE.JP/ OGAKK/NEW/NAMAHAGE/

children here?" they bellow. "Any good-for-nothings? Any children who refuse to obey their parents?"

The very young are excused with a mere scolding, but older suspects face a more painful fate. When the Namahage do happen to encounter someone who's been enjoying the warmth of the fire for too long, they take great pleasure in holding their victims down and peeling the blisters from the soles of their feet.

Surviving an Encounter:

What are you doing reading a book? Get your lazy carcass out from in front of the fire and back to work!

In all seriousness, there is a recommended method for appeasing infuriated Namahage. When they appear at a home, the father of the household must reassure them that his children are all well behaved, and also provide refreshments—in the form of cups of warm sake. Being a fearsome yokai often has its privileges.

If properly treated to this sort of hospitality, Namahage depart without causing any harm, promising to bless the family and home with good fortune in the coming year.

Tanuki

狸

Pronunciation:
(TAH-new-key)

English Names:
"Raccoon Dog"; "Japanese badger"; Tanooki

Scientific Name:
Nyctereutes procyonoides

Height:
1 ft. 8 in. to 2 ft. (50 to 60cm)

Weight:
Approximately 22 lbs. (10kg)

Locomotion:
Bipedal

Physical Characteristics:
Raccoon-like face
Conical straw hats
Enormous testicles

Offensive Weapons:
Shape-shifting

ANNOYING NEIGHBORS

Weaknesses:
Sake (rice wine)

Abundance:
Prevalent

Habitat:
Mountains, forests, cities

Claim to Fame:
One of the three most famous yokai, along with the Kitsune (p. 154) and the Kappa (p. 26), statues of the rotund and well-endowed Tanuki are a common sight throughout Japan. The animal from which the Tanuki takes its name superficially resembles a raccoon but is actually a member of the canine family. Once a common sight in the fields and forests of Japan, its habitat has been greatly reduced by urban sprawl and pollution. Still, the Tanuki remains one of Japan's most enduring and beloved folk characters.

Much like Kitsune, Tanuki are pranksters, fond of shape-shifting and playing tricks. Occasionally they take human form, passing off leaves or other worthless trinkets as money in order to

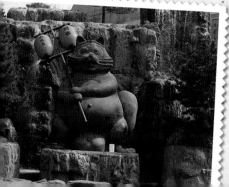

A Tanuki statue at Komatsushima Station Park.

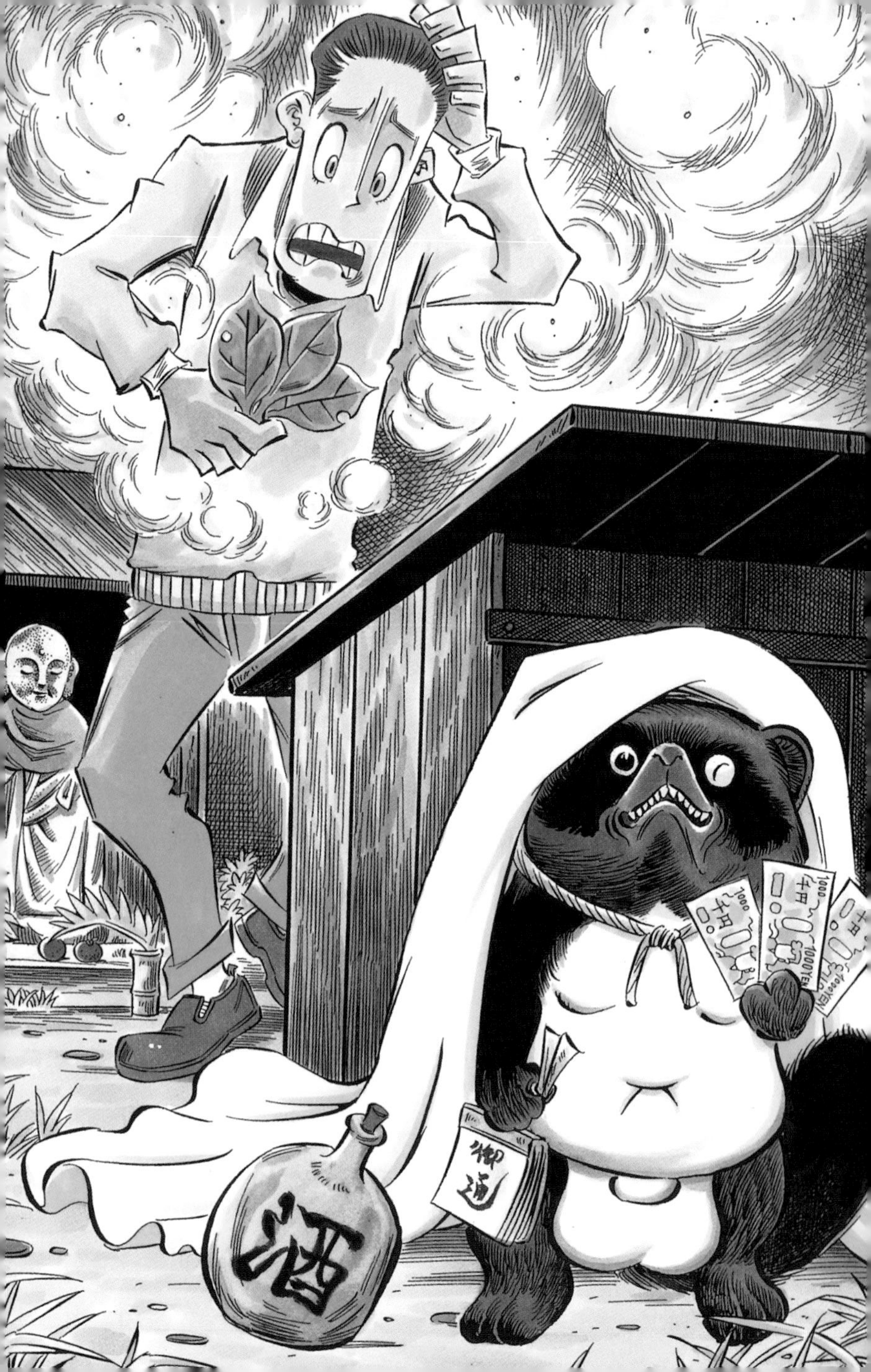

千円
1000YEN
御通
酒

procure food and wine. In other cases, Tanuki transform themselves into inanimate objects to insinuate themselves into the lives of unsuspecting humans. In the famous tale, *Bunbuku-chagama* ("The Lucky Teakettle"), the father of a Tanuki family transforms himself into a cast-iron teakettle, which his wife sells to an unsuspecting antiques dealer in order to save their children from starvation.

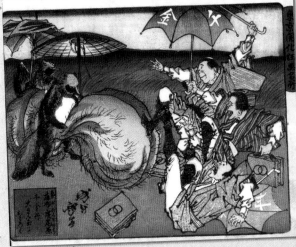

Goin' "nuts" the Tanuki way, in an 1881 print by Yoshitoshi.

No discussion of the Tanuki would be complete without a mention of their extraordinary testicles. Totally flexible, extensible, and mobile, they are a potent tool in the Tanuki's bag of shapeshifting tricks. Tanuki use their testicles as makeshift raincoats and drums, weapons, and even as a disguise to impersonate other creatures and yokai. Some accounts claim they can be extended into a sheet some eight tatami mats in size—more than 130 square feet (12 square meters). That's a whole lot of scrotum. In fact, there is even a famous children's rhyme (set, incongruously enough, to the tune of the Baptist hymn "Shall We Gather at the River?") that goes:

Tan Tan Tanuki
no kintama wa
Kaze mo nai no ni,
Bura Bura

(The Tanuki's testicles
swing-swing even
without any breeze)

TANUKI PROVERBS:

Tanuki Ne-iri: A phrase that translates into "playing possum."

Toranu tanuki no kawa zanyou: Literally, "don't count the tanuki pelts you haven't caught yet," which is of course akin to "don't count your chickens before they're hatched."

The Attack!
Although theoretically capable of causing harm with tooth and claw, a Tanuki almost always eschews violence for trickery and deception. Its shape-shifting powers far exceed those of the Kitsune, but the Tanuki tends towards the mischievous rather than malevolent. It is something like the "wild card" of the yokai world, charming and unpredictable. As such, the actual form of attack is extremely difficult to predict. Bear in mind that the Tanuki is especially fond of rich food and drink, and has even been known to kidnap and impersonate brides or grooms so as to partake of the banquets served at weddings.

TANUKI SIGHTINGS IN HISTORY
In 1795, a Tanuki masquerading as a samurai managed to enter a Nagasaki brothel, making full use of the facilities and enjoying the company of a variety of fine women until he was discovered and ejected from the premises.

Surviving an Encounter:
Your life isn't in any danger, but your bank account and pride may be. Fortunately, the happy-go-lucky nature of a Tanuki means its silly schemes often backfire or collapse before they have a chance to play out. Still, if you find your wallet filled with leaves, or stumble across your newlywed husband or wife hog-tied in the closet just after the wedding reception. . . .

Tasty Tanuki:
Tanuki Soba and Tanuki Udon are two of the most popular noodle dishes in Japan. They contain tiny chunks of fried batter, essentially "junk" left over from cooking more expensive tempura dishes. Some believe they are so named because the thought of paying good money for empty bits of batter is amusingly evocative of falling for a Tanuki prank.

Lucky Testicles:
Ceramic statues of tanuki are common sights outside of Japanese businesses, particularly bars and restaurants. In times of old, craftsmen wrapped gold nuggets (*kintama*, or "gold balls"—also a euphemism for testicles in Japanese) in tanuki pelts for hammering into gold leaf. The association of "tanuki" and "gold" stuck, making representations of these yokai common good-luck charms even today.

YOKAI NO: 0 2 9

Ashiarai Yashiki

足洗邸

ANNOYING NEIGHBORS

Pronunciation:
(AH-shee ah-rye YASH-key)

English Name:
Literally, "Foot-Washing Mansion"

Gender:
Believed to be male

Height:
3 to 4 meters (roughly 9 to 12 feet)

Weight:
Heavy enough to punch through a ceiling with ease

Shoe Size:
80EEE (Estimated)

Locomotion:
Monopedal

Distinctive Features:
An enormous, hairy, disembodied foot and leg
Often muddy; sometimes drenched in blood
Capable of speech

Offensive weapons:
Sheer size

Abundance:
One of a kind

Habitat:
Residential areas

Claim to Fame:
The Ashiarai Yashiki is a yokai to give even the storied Bigfoot a run for his money. It takes the form of an enormous, disembodied, bloody leg and foot that smashes through ceilings without warning in the dead of night, demanding to be washed. Legend has it that it first appeared in a royal mansion in the Edo district of Honjo. Rumors of its existence circulated like wildfire at the time, and the creature remains a staple of yokai tales today.

The legend has been acclaimed in the *Seven Wonders of Honjo*, an eighteenth-century collection of urban legends set in and around Honjo, a district in old Edo that corresponds to Sumida Ward in present-day Tokyo. They are supposedly based on true stories. In addition to the Ashiarai Yashiki, several involve other yokai, mainly Tanuki (p. 126) and Kitsune (p. 154). These include *Okuri Chochin* ("The

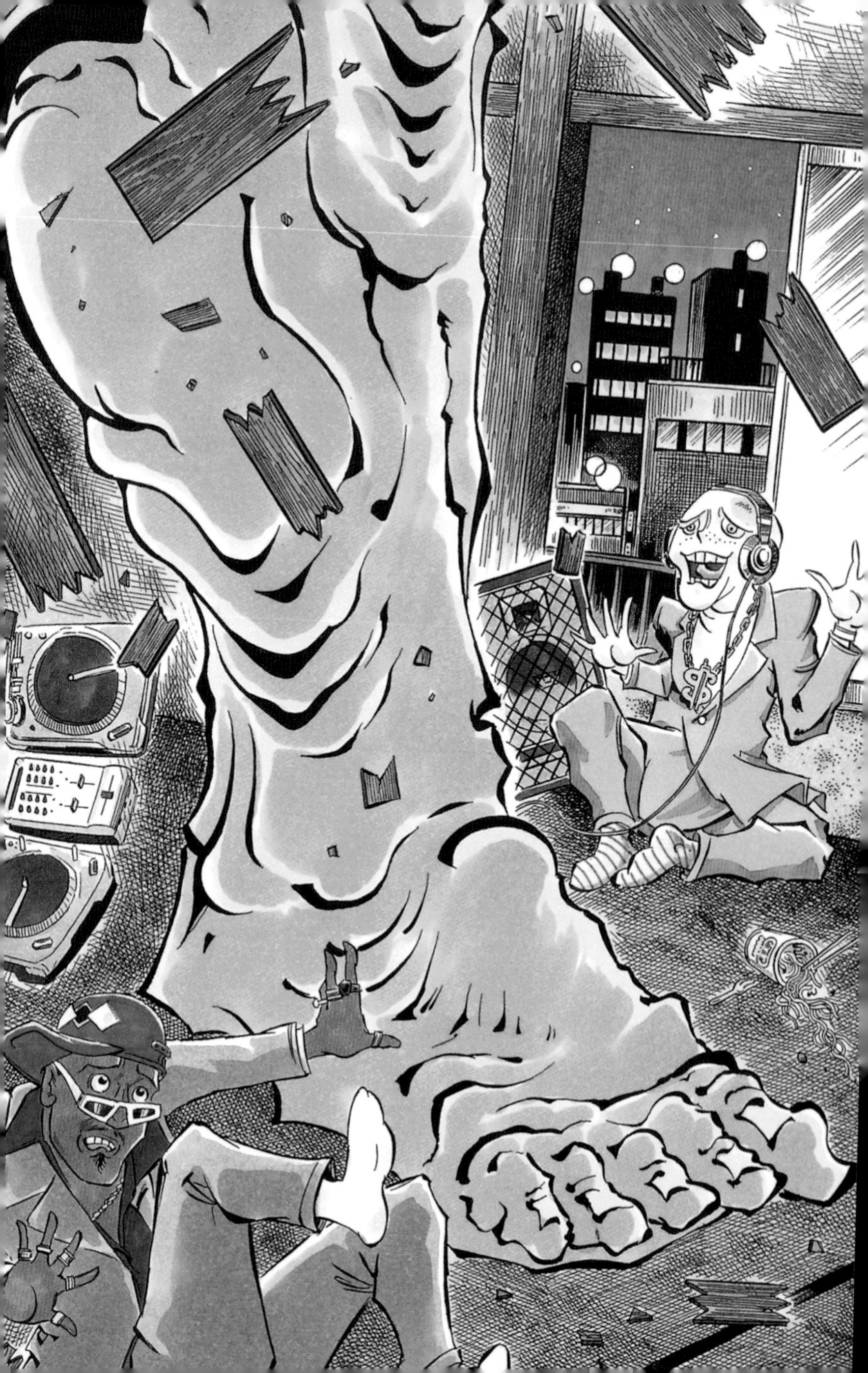

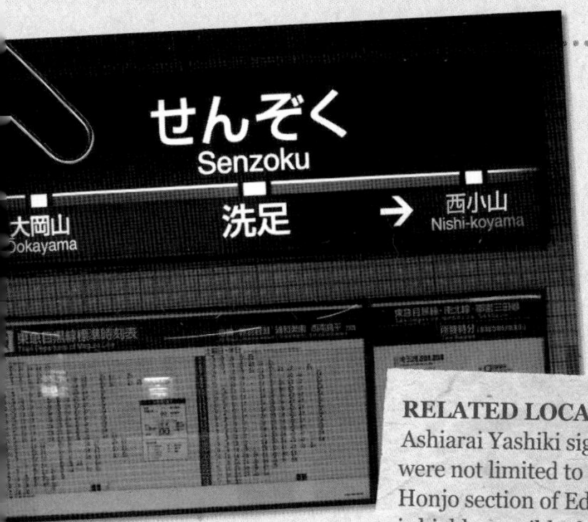
せんぞく
Senzoku
洗足
大岡山
西小山
Nishi-koyama

RELATED LOCATION: Ashiarai Yashiki sightings were not limited to the Honjo section of Edo. It is highly possible that the areas of Tokyo known as "Senzoku" denote places where the creature appeared over the years. The Senzoku area of Meguro is one (and is actually written with the kanji characters for "foot-wash"). And other Senzoku areas in Tokyo, while written with different kanji characters, are a homonym for the Japanese word for washing of feet.

Guiding Lantern"), in which Tanuki and Kitsune lead travelers astray, and *Tanuki Bayashi* ("The Tanuki Concert"), in which individuals become disoriented while trying to track down the source of mysterious music that only they can hear.

The Attack!
An Ashiarai Yashiki appearance tends to follow the same pattern. In the middle of the night, a home—often described as an opulent mansion—fills with strange scratching and thumping sounds. Suddenly a massive foot many times human size appears in the room, accompanied by a booming, disembodied voice that demands the occupant "wash my foot!"

Surviving an Encounter:
Obey and it quietly disappears. Refuse, and it goes on a one-legged rampage, briefly disappearing before smashing through the ceiling again, destroying the contents of the house (and occasionally its owners).

In order to prevent this, we suggest you break out the soap and water, and get ready to put in some elbow grease.

Or you could move. According to one report, a retainer of the Shogunate found himself beset by Ashiarai Yashiki attacks night after night. Tiring of the incessant late-night foot-washing, he arranged to swap homes with

a fellow retainer (under what exact pretense we'll probably never know). The temporary move did the trick, and the Ashiarai Yashiki hasn't been seen since.

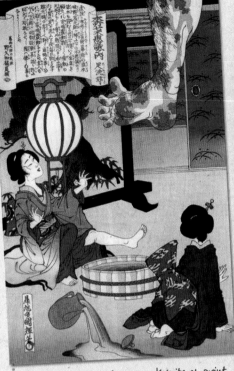

A mid-1800s Utagawa Kuniteru print of an Ashiarai Yashiki encounter.

Another Ashiarai?

According to one theory, the Ashiarai Yashiki isn't a unique form of yokai but rather an illusion created by the notoriously tricky Tanuki (p. 126). In this version of the story, the wealthy owner of a mansion happened to rescue a Tanuki that had been captured and tormented by humans. Years later, the owner was killed by a greedy maid and her lover in a bid to take the family fortunes.

When the man's son found out, he attacked the murderers, but found himself on the losing end of the fight. Out of nowhere, the Tanuki his father had rescued years before appeared in yokai form. Leaping into the fray, it helped swing the battle's momentum, and the son was able to avenge his father's untimely death. After that day, it was said, a giant foot appeared within the mansion's walls whenever its owners unknowingly faced misfortune—an odd harbinger of fate that allowed them to take steps to prevent catastrophe. While this tale is intriguing, its origin and veracity remain unknown, and most experts continue to categorize the Ashiarai Yashiki as a distinct "species" of yokai.

YOKAI TRIVIA:
In times of old, it was common practice for visitors to wash their feet before entering a home. The Ashiarai Yashiki is derived from this custom.

YOKAI NO: 030

Te-no-me

手の目

ANNOYING NEIGHBORS

Pronunciation:
TEH-no-meh

English Name:
Eyes-for-Hands

Gender:
Male

Height:
Average for an adult Japanese male

Weight:
Average for an adult Japanese male

Locomotion:
Bipedal

Distinctive Features:
Eyelids squeezed tightly shut, Eyes on palms of hands, Clad in robes

Abundance:
Perhaps one of a kind, perhaps prevalent

Habitat:
Chasing terrified humans

Season:
N/A

Preferred Habitat:
Rural areas

Distribution:
Pretty much anywhere people go

Claim to Fame:
At first glance, this yokai is apparently a perfectly ordinary sight-impaired human, save for a chilling difference: a fully functional eye on the palm of each hand. The ease of hiding this characteristic is what makes the possibility of an encounter so frightening, for it is all too easy for a Te-no-me to get up close and personal before springing the surprise about its true identity.

There are several theories about the origins of this yokai. One is that he represents the elderly appearance of the Nopperabo ("Faceless Ones," see p. 166). According to this idea, the older a Nopperabo gets, the more rudimentary facial features develop, and eventually a pair of working eyes appear in its palms. If this is the case, it represents the aged form of a (relatively) common yokai,

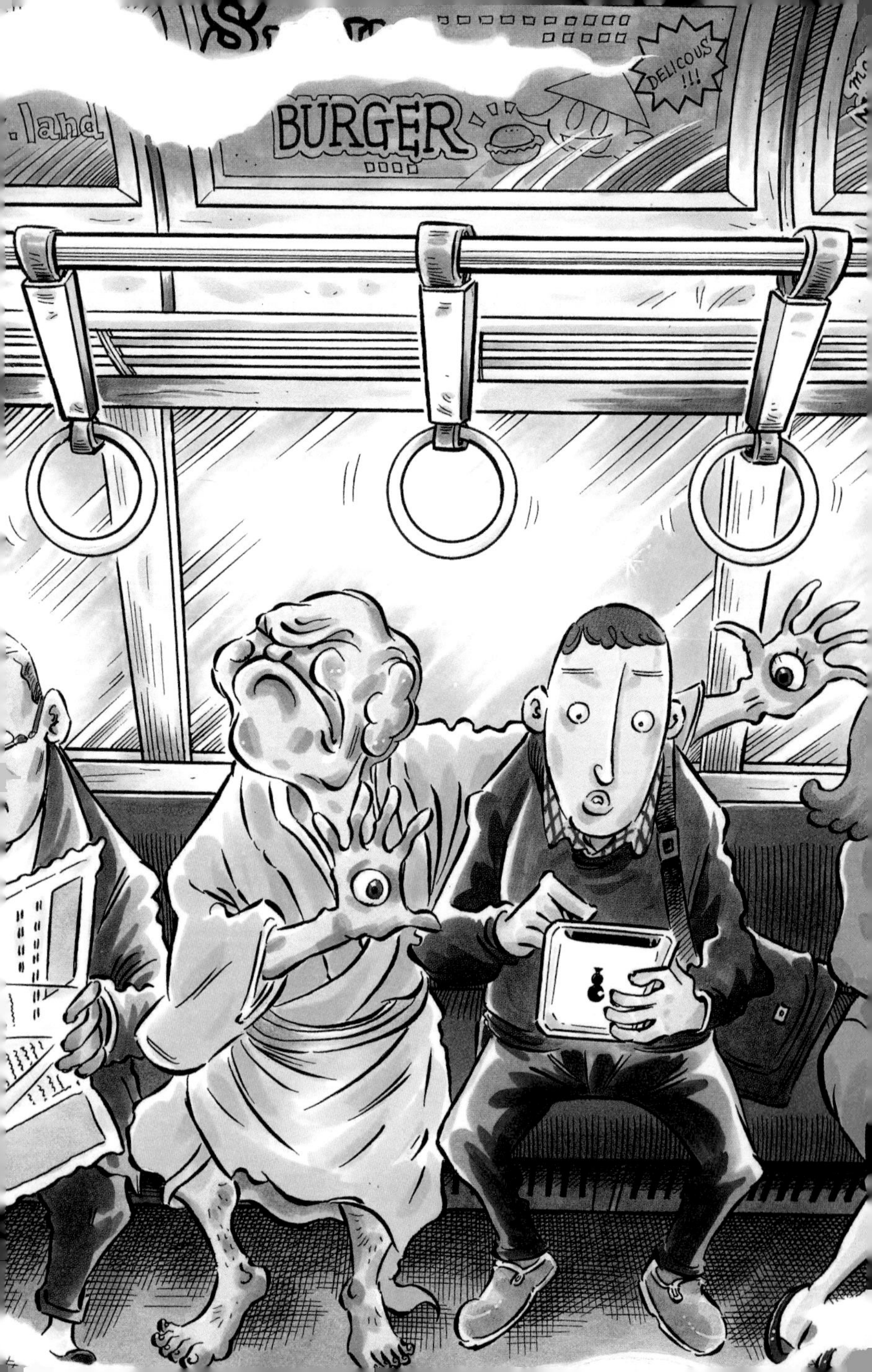
land
BURGER
DELICOUS
!!!

and there are potentially many Te-no-me plying the Japanese countryside.

But another, perhaps more compelling origin story hints that the Te-no-me could be one of a kind. Before we get into the thick of it, remember that job opportunities were quite limited for the physically challenged in times of old. In order that the sight-impaired might make an independent living, guilds arose that trained them in a handful of service occupations, including musician, masseur, and acupuncturist, that would guarantee a relatively steady source of income. Of course, this also necessitated traveling. And the roads of pre-modern Japan were often dangerous places for any traveler, sighted or otherwise.

Visitors to Japan today are often boggled by the sheer density of roadways and train lines connecting its cities. In fact, much of the nation's modern transport infrastructure is built atop a web of ancient footpaths, canals, and trails that connected cities to villages and smaller settlements—much the same way that the human body's arteries give way to smaller blood vessels and capillaries. Many of the smaller roads in particular led through terrifically isolated and often quite arduous terrain. Terrain that provided those with a criminal bent an abundance of opportunities for profit.

Armed robbery was a popular pastime in the deep rural stretches between pockets of civilization. Gangs known variously as tozoku (thieves) and sanzoku (mountain bandits) specialized in shaking down travelers for valuables. Scoundrels of this sort had undoubtedly operated in some form or another from time immemorial, but their activities reached a crescendo in the 1500s, the near century-long period of civil war called the Era of Warring States. Already questionable safety-wise, many roadways descended into total lawlessness as citizenry displaced by endless war grew desperate for any means to survive.

As you might expect, lone travelers represented prime targets, and those perceived to be weak, such as the sightless, juicier quarry still. Somewhere in the mountains up north long ago, a blind tradesman was travelling between jobs. But he was attacked by a gang of bandits. They not only robbed

him of the money he'd made on his last appointment, but cruelly beat, tormented, and finally killed the man.

His body left to rot by the side of the road without even so much as a prayer said over it, the blind man's soul refused to depart for the hereafter as normal souls do. The powerful anger and desire for revenge within his heart fueled his transformation into a yokai that haunted the area, forever questing with a pair of eyes sprouted upon its palms for the sole purpose of finding its tormentors.

The Attack!
The Te-no-me cloaks itself in thickly vegetated areas alongside mountain paths, such as fields teeming with tall grasses, to ambush travelers. When someone happens along, he springs out and reveals his trademark "eyed palms," then gives pursuit when the victim inevitably turns and runs.

Surviving an Encounter:
Interestingly, for all the reports of Te-no-me encounters, there don't seem to be any cases of it actually catching one of its victims! Whether this is because it is

only interested in finding the men who robbed its original incarnation of his life, or because it's actually kind of a softy at heart, we'll never know.

Given Te-no-me's sad past and solitary existence, perhaps it's only looking for a little companionship. A warning to those brave souls who attempt to befriend this yokai: whatever you do, don't try shaking its hand. That would have to seriously hurt.

Where the Sun Don't Shine

Shiri-mé ("Butt-eye") is a similar yokai with a twist: his single working eyeball is located right where a human's anus would be. According to the folklore of Kyoto, from which Shiri-mé hails, it surprises passer-by by disrobing to reveal its eye, then pursuing them on all fours, back-end first. No fatalites have been reported.

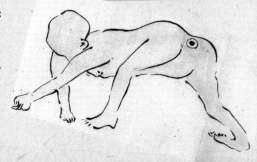

Nurikabe

塗壁

ANNOYING NEIGHBORS

Pronunciation:
(NEW-ree KAH-bay)

English Name:
The Wall, Mr. Wall

Height:
10 to 15 ft. (3 to 5m)

Weight:
Essentially an immovable object

Locomotion:
Variable: Sometimes appears with no legs, as bipedal, or as multi-pedal

Distinctive Features:
Often invisible
Tall enough to discourage climbing
Wide enough to discourage passing

Offensive Weapon:
None

Abundance:
Prevalent

Habitat:
Anywhere humans are found

Origin:
Possibly Kyushu (Tokushima)

Claim to Fame:
The Nurikabe is nothing more or less than the concept of an unseen or unanticipated obstacle that has taken anthropomorphic form. The Nurikabe often insinuate themselves into daily life by mimicking the innocuous wall of a house or other building, but can also be found outdoors, even in remote areas that are totally devoid of man-made structures or buildings. They are usually invisible to the human eye. Descriptions of this type of yokai are manifold; although they are quite well known, it is difficult to pin their attributes down with any specificity.

The Attack!
You're walking in the woods, on a deserted street, or almost anywhere when you find yourself smack up against what seems to be an invisible wall. In fact, it seems to stay there no matter how you try to move. Left . . . right . . . pushing, punching, swinging your bag against it; nothing works. You can't move ahead, or in

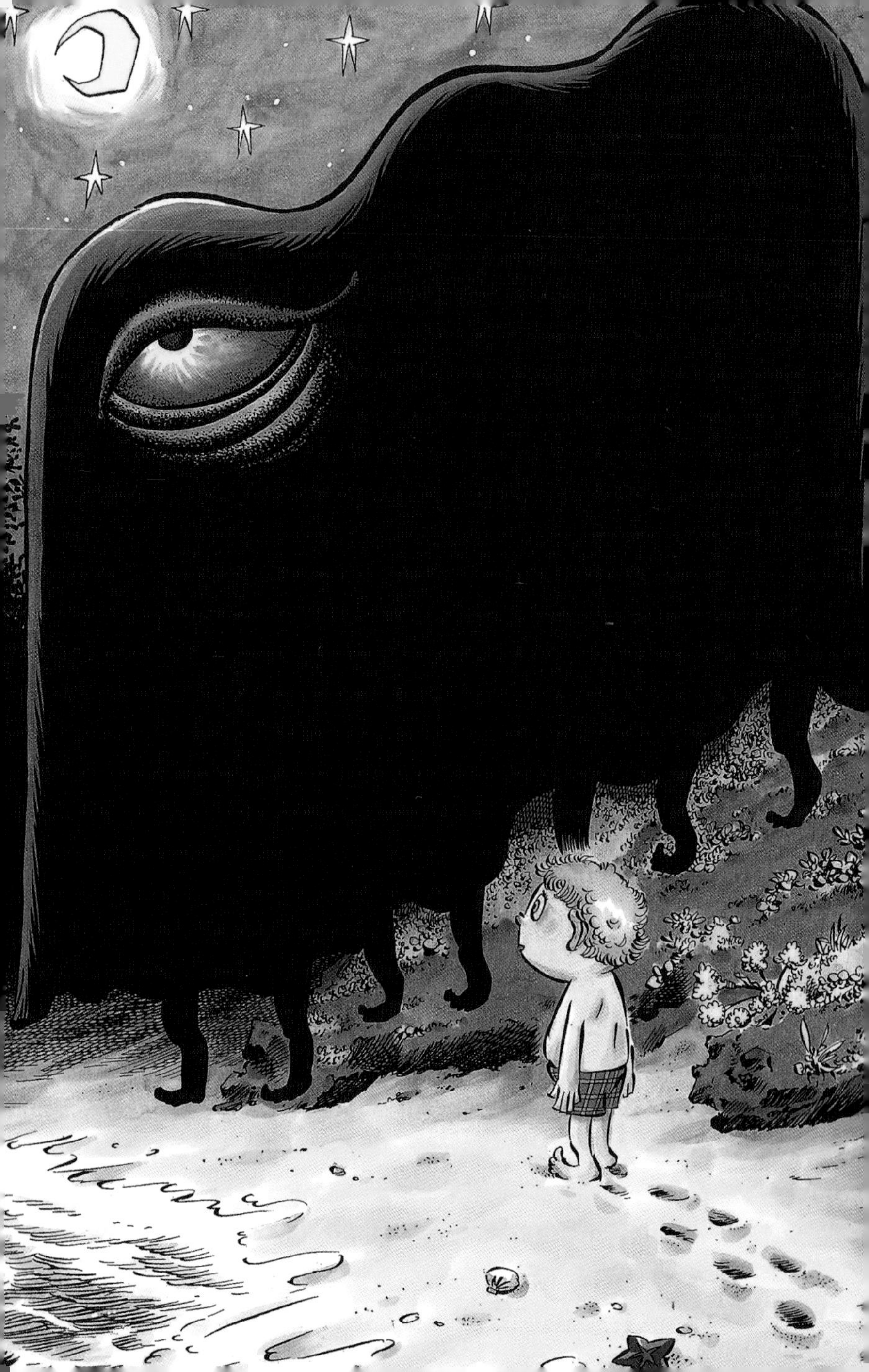

any other direction. You're up against the wall: Nurikabe.

YOKAI TRIVIA: In spite of its wide variety of appearances (or disappearances, given that it is often invisible), "Nurikabe" literally means "plastered wall" in Japanese.

Surviving an Encounter:
Nurikabe attacks are often frustrating and frightening but rarely fatal. This yokai often targets those who are panicked or in a rush. The first and most important thing to do is calm down. Then, wave a stick (or in a pinch, your hand) near Nurikabe's "base," just above the ground. For whatever reason, this action is said to dispel the hold it has on you. Perhaps it simply doesn't like having its "feet" touched. Whatever the case, you should find yourself free to go along your way.

Nurikabe's Pal?
Tokushima prefecture, located on the island of Kyushu, is home to tales of a yokai with a similar disposition to Nurikabe. Dubbed Tsuitate-danuki (literally, "The Screen-badger"), it is often classified as a form of Tanuki (p. 126). However, its modus operandi is almost identical to that of Nurikabe.

The Tsuitate-danuki once inhabited a certain road leading out of the town of Waki, blocking the progress of any who attempted to take the path late at night. Although a few intrepid villagers were fearless enough to press through, the vast majority avoided the road altogether. Finally, the villagers conducted a religious ceremony to contain the creature, sealing it away within a large stone obelisk.

The obelisk stood on the spot for many years, but according to recent reports was stolen by vandals. Could the Tsuitate-danuki be on the loose once again?

A REAL-LIFE ENCOUNTER
Yokai expert and famed comic book artist Shigeru Mizuki recounted a Nurikabe experience in his book *Nihon Yokai Daizen*. The event took place in Papua New Guinea during World War II, when he was separated from his comrades in an attack. As he was fleeing through the jungle, he found himself unable to proceed. "It was as though I was stuck in tar," he wrote. "Left, right, forward . . . it was all the same." For twenty minutes he pushed forward, then collapsed, exhausted. After a brief rest, and "in spite of doing exactly what had gotten me nowhere before, I was able to move again."

The **Sexy** and **Slimy**

Hey, even ghouls can be glamorous. These creatures give "foxy" a new meaning. And talk about beauty and the beast: here they're both.

Rokuro Kubi

Pronunciation:
(ROH-koo-roh koo-bee)

English Name:
Long-necked Woman; Snake-necked Woman; Flying-head Woman and "Rubberneck Woman"

Gender:
Female

Height:
Average for a Japanese woman (when neck is retracted)

Weight:
Average for a Japanese woman

Locomotion:
Bipedal

Distinctive Features:
Youthful, attractive appearance
Traditional dress (kimono)
Extendable neck with purple striations on neck when retracted, or
Head capable of complete separation from body, with small red characters on neck

Maximum Neck Length:
Unknown

Favorite foods:
Lamp oil, human vitality (Snake-necked Rokuro Kubi)
Human flesh (Flying-head Rokuro Kubi)

Abundance:
Prevalent

Habitat:
Anywhere humans live

Claim to Fame:
The yokai known as the Rokuro Kubi takes the form of a beautiful woman by day, but this femme fatale has a trick up its collar by night.

There are two distinct "species" of Rokuro Kubi. The first and arguably most famous has a neck to put an anaconda to shame. Let us call it the "Snake-necked Rokuro Kubi."

Normally all but indistinguishable from human females save for a series of pale stretch-marks on their necks, many of this type of Rokuro Kubi enjoy the masquerade so much that they take employment as entertainers or marry human spouses. Some even come to believe they're people. But

THE SEXY AND SLIMY

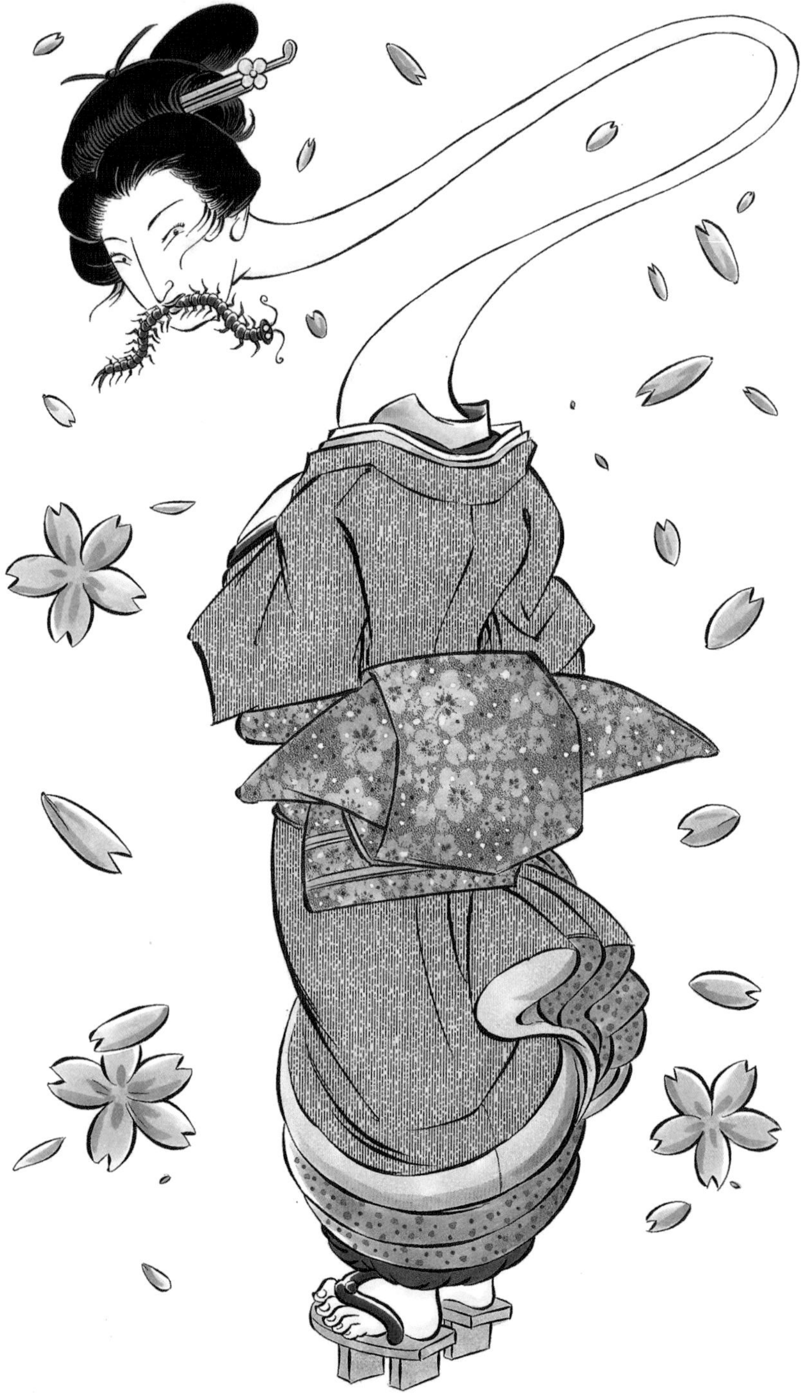

once the sun goes down and it falls asleep, even the tamest Rokuro Kubi can't help but show its true colors. Quietly its head stretches like a snake, further and further and further out of its kimono, worming its way out of the room and into the night, searching for prey. Occasionally the hunt so tires a Rokuro Kubi that it forgets to retract its neck, and falls asleep with its head resting against a roofbeam or other unlikely place.

A Rokuro Kubi's head prowls the forests for grubs, centipedes, and worms, but bugs aren't the only thing on this yokai's menu. It also hungers for *qi*, the vitality that courses through human beings, and men's qi in particular. Rokuro Kubi also has a penchant for licking the fuel out of old-fashioned oil lamps (a trait shared with the Neko-mata, p.38)

The second species of Rokuro Kubi is every bit as beautiful as its snake-necked counterpart, but far more dangerous. Its defining feature is a head that is capable of separating entirely from its neck and taking flight through the night skies. Also known as Nuke Kubi ("Removable-head"), this form of Rokuro Kubi is believed to have originated in China. We will refer to it henceforth as the Flying-head Rokuro Kubi. In fact, this species is also known to occasionally include males, although female specimens are far more common.

SOME SCHOLARS BELIEVE: That the Rokuro Kubi is related to the Japanese idiom "*kubi wo nagakushite matsu.*" Although it colloquially means "eagerly waiting for something," the literal translation is "stretching one's neck out to wait."

Although it is said to consume the same sort of gross stuff as its snake-necked cousin, the flying-head Rokuro Kubi prefers the taste of human flesh.

The Attack!
Snake-necked Rokuro Kubi:
A Rokuro Kubi is a vampire of sorts, seeking the stew of physical and mental desire that brews inside healthy men. It takes it like a thief, coming at night to draw this ethereal force from its unsuspecting prey as they sleep.

However, perhaps the most fearsome aspect of a Rokuro Kubi isn't the prospect of an attack, but rather the idea that you could be one without even knowing it. Who hasn't woken up with a crick

in their neck and a foul taste in their mouth at one time or another?

Flying-head Rokuro Kubi: Attacks inevitably occur after dark, either singly or in "packs" that resemble families. A flying-head Rokuro Kubi launches its head through the night skies, bobbing and weaving as if weightless. Though it can subsist on worms or insects, it prefers human prey. It is known to lure travelers into its home during daylight hours with the offer of free lodging, so that it can attack the unsuspecting victims as they sleep.

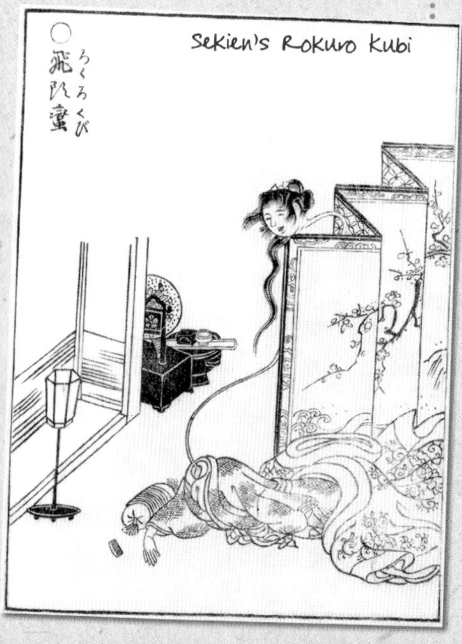
Sekien's Rokuro Kubi
ろくろくび
飛頭蛮

Surviving an Encounter, Snake-necked Rokuro Kubi: Attacks are seldom fatal. As the Rokuro Kubi targets sleeping individuals, victims tend to not even realize they have been attacked, attributing the extreme fatigue that accompanies a feeding to, for example, exhaustion from travel. If you're new in town, avoid invitations from pretty women with odd purple markings on their necks. And if you encounter a woman wearing a scarf out of season, watch out!

Flying-head Rokuro Kubi: This Rokuro Kubi is known to attack and consume human victims. Fortunately, there is a concrete expedient for dealing with them. According to Lafcadio Hearn's 1903 classic *Kwaidan*:

"It is written that if one find the body of a Rokuro Kubi without its head and remove it to another place, the head will never be able to join itself again to the neck. And . . . when the head comes back and finds that its body has been moved, it will strike itself upon the floor three times—bounding like a ball—and will pant as if in great fear, and presently die."

YOKAI NO: 033

Nure Onna

濡女

Pronunciation:
(NOO-ray OHN-nah)

Alternate Japanese Names:
Nure-onago; Nure-yomejo

English Names:
Literally, "Wet Woman";
Snake-woman,
Dragon Lady

Gender:
Female

Length:
At least 100 ft. (30m), possibly several hundred feet

Locomotion:
Slithering; swimming

Distinctive Features:
Snake-like body with a human face
Human-like arms and hands
Long black hair

Preferred Diet:
Human flesh and blood

Offensive Weapons:
Paralyzing stare
Fangs
Powerful constricting muscles

Abundance:
One of a kind

Habitat:
Harbors, coves, and other shallow ocean areas; occasionally rivers

Claim to Fame:
A ferocious, dragon-like creature with the body of an enormous snake and the head of a woman, the Nure Onna haunts shorelines throughout Japan. It preys on isolated fishermen, swimmers, hikers, and the like. So-called because it spends most of its time submerged, its scaly skin has a wet, glistening sheen when it rises from the water. Like the fabled Medusa, Nure Onna is said to be able to paralyze its victims through simple

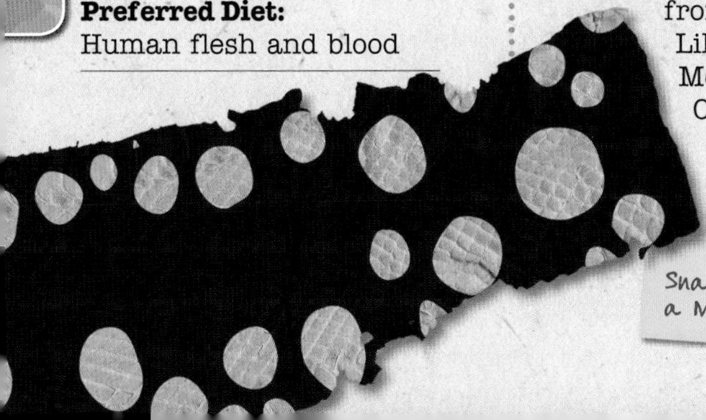

Snakeskin found near a Nure Onna sighting

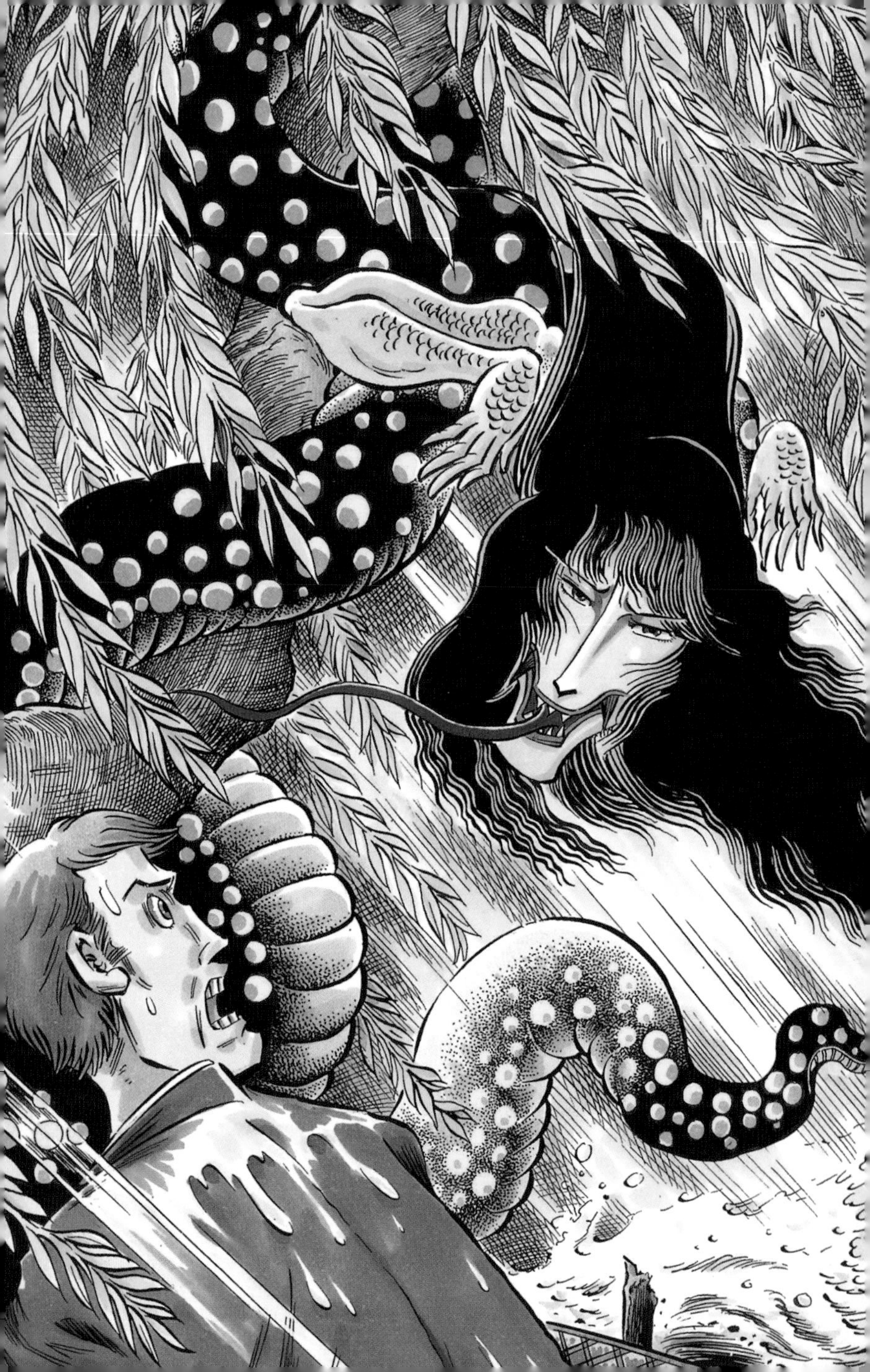

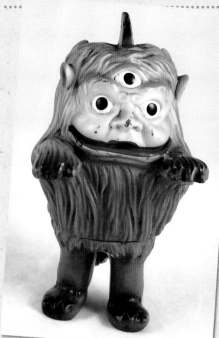

STRONG LIKE BULL

Descriptions of the Ushi-Oni vary widely. Some say it takes the form of a cow's head atop the body of an oni (ogre) or Tsuchi-gumo (see p. 58). A vicious predator, it was so named for its propensity to attack livestock as well as humans.

A vintage soft-vinyl figure of Ushi-Oni, who is described as Nure-Onna's husband in some versions of her tale. This toy was produced by Mtto as merchandise for a 1968 film called "The Great Yokai War."

eye contact (though the effect appears to be psychological or physiological rather than transforming flesh to stone). Some believe that this is merely a metaphor for the fact that none who lock eyes with it live to tell the tale.

Nure Onna is notable for the extreme variance in the way it is described in legends across Japan. On the island of Kyushu, it is described not as a snake but rather a normal-looking young woman clad in white robes and cradling an infant. In this tale, it works with another yokai—the Ushi Oni ("Demon Bull")—to prey on hapless fishermen.

The Attack!
Snake-Like Form:
When an unsuspecting human—often a fisherman—wanders along the shoreline, it strikes and entangles its prey, dragging them into the water before devouring them with a mouthful of fangs. Unlike normal snakes, the Nure Onna has a pair of arms as well, making it all but impossible to wriggle out of its grasp once entangled.

Nure Onna is also known to prey upon those who attempt

to ford streams or rivers, and in spite of its incredible length is capable of hiding in surprisingly shallow stretches of water.

It is also believed to use its human face as a lure, bobbing it on the surface to simulate a swimmer in distress or a floating body, in order to draw victims within striking range.

SOME SCHOLARS BELIEVE:
The Nure Onna is a perfect example of the variability of yokai tales across Japan. It is described as taking a variety of forms, but all of these tales share the ocean as a common factor. (Nure means "wet" in Japanese.)

Young Female Form:
It quietly approaches fishermen while holding a baby, which it leaves under some pretext before turning, walking into the ocean and disappearing beneath the waves as if in a suicide attempt. Before the hapless fisherman can react, he is paralyzed by the infant, which rapidly increases in weight so as to immobilize him. As he struggles on the shoreline, the Ushi Oni (see above) rises from the waters and consumes the helpless victim. In some versions of this tale, the Nure Onna and Ushi Oni are said to be married.

Surviving an Encounter, Snake-like Form:
Save for its preferred saltwater habitat, the Nure Onna is essentially similar to animals such as anacondas and pythons. The problem is its sheer size, for it is capable of extending extraordinary lengths in pursuit of prey. Once you are targeted, it is nearly impossible to avoid the clutches of the Nure Onna. It's best to avoid solitary walks along dark beaches or riverbanks at night. If you do happen to encounter one, avoid making eye contact at all costs—and run.

Young Female Form:
Today, sightings are rare. In this era of cellphones and other methods of rapid long-distance communication, a kimono-clad woman appearing out of nowhere and offering her baby would probably stir up a commotion even in the most isolated of areas. Still, better safe than sorry: if you find yourself in this sort of situation, refuse and contact the authorities. Yokai prey on individuals with no easy escape or method of calling for help.

Kuchisake Onna

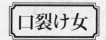

口裂け女

Pronunciation:
(KOO-chee SAH-kay OHN-na)

English Names:
"Slash-mouthed Woman,"
"Slit-mouthed Woman"

Gender:
Female

Height:
Average for a Japanese
woman

Weight:
Average for a Japanese
woman

Locomotion:
Bipedal

Distinctive Features:
Long hair
Surgical mask
Fang-filled mouth extending
from ear to ear

Number of teeth:
130 (estimated)

Preferred Diet:
Bekko ame
(traditional
hard candies)

Like this one →

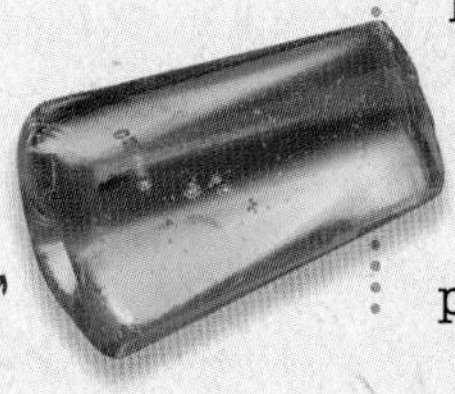

Weaknesses:
The scent of hair pomade

Top Speed:
Capable of running 100
yards in three seconds

Offensive Weapons:
Knife, machete, scythe

Abundance:
One of a kind

Habitat:
Urban and suburban areas
throughout Japan

Claim to Fame:
It is feared by schoolchildren
as a cold-blooded predator
with a mouthful of fangs and
the ability to outrun a speed-
ing motorcycle. In fact,
according to one source,
a whopping ninety-nine per-
cent of Japanese children
claim to be familiar with the
general story. It appears to
be a normal young woman,
but a surgical mask covers a
horrifically oversized
mouth that stretches ear
to ear, filled with far, far
too many teeth. (Wearing
gauze masks is a common
practice for those suffering

THE SEXY AND SLIMY

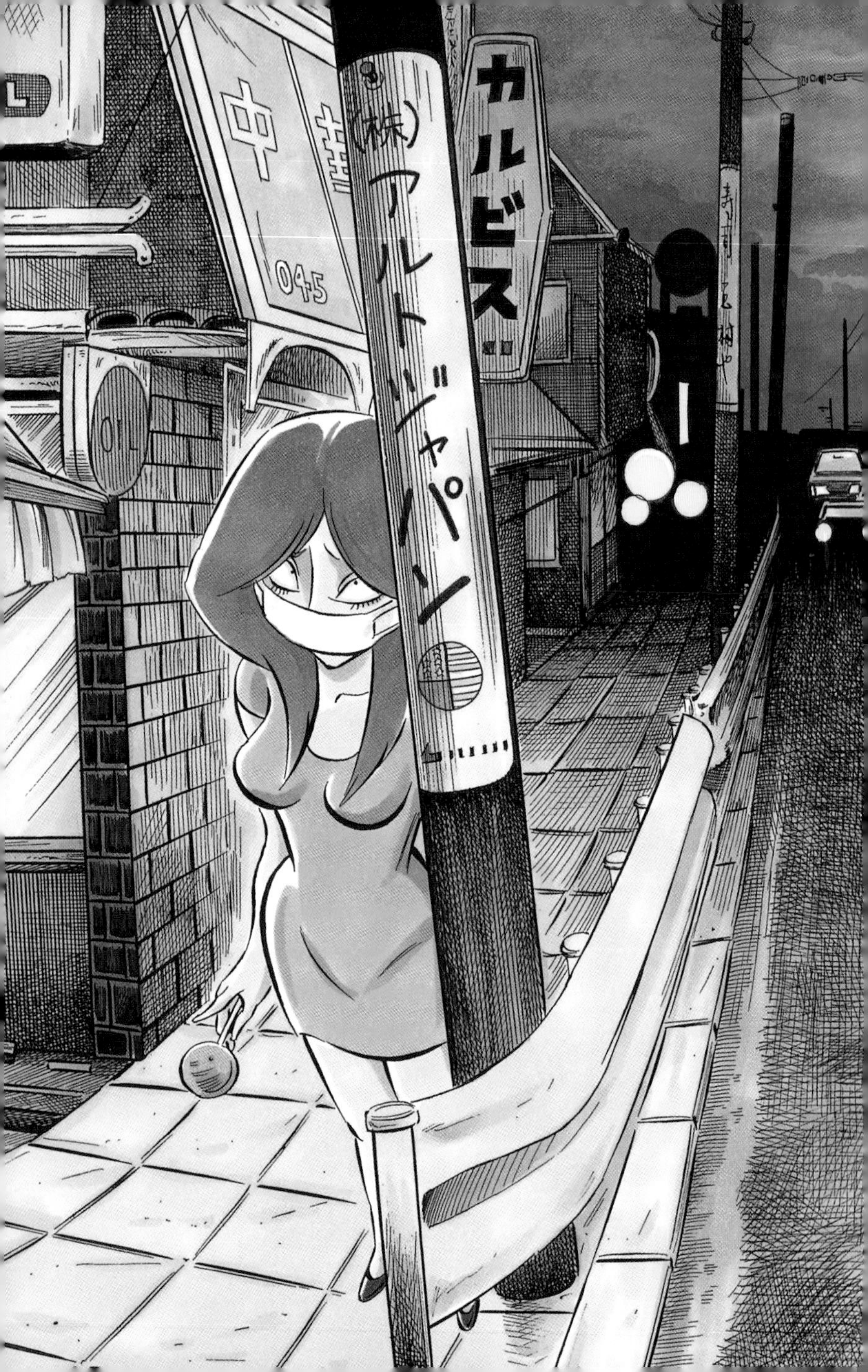
カルビス
中
045

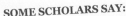

from colds in Japan, a custom that allows the yokai to smoothly blend in with the population at large.) It is nearly always encountered in cities or suburbs, and, unlike many other yokai, often appears during daylight hours—particularly in the late afternoon, when children are on their way home from school.

The Kuchisake Onna is one of the newest members of the yokai pantheon. There are virtually as many rumors as there are those who tell the tale; children in nearly every area of Japan have their own versions embroidered with local coloring. Some accounts claim it is the victim of cosmetic surgery gone horribly wrong. Others blame its mutilation on a botched dental procedure. Still others claim that a homely sister slashed her mouth ear to ear out of jealousy over her beautiful face. Nearly every story claims it is capable of running at superhuman speed. A few rumors, undoubtedly embellished by youthful hysteria, place her as the driver of a screaming red Lamborghini sports car, eternally on the prowl for fresh blood.

SOME SCHOLARS SAY:
That it was born from a sort of mass hysteria, a group hallucination of the specter of parental pressure, driven by the unceasing anxiety children feel to succeed in the hyper-competitive Japanese school system. There is no question, however, that it is a pastiche of traditional and modern imagery. The machete and scythe are typical yokai accoutrements, akin to those carried by the Namahage (p. 122), another creature that preys on children. Hair pomade, Olympic experience, and sports cars are obviously modern touches. This is a perfect example of how yokai imagery undergoes a constant cycle of change and rebirth, even in modern times.

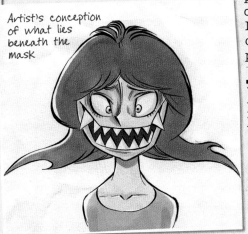

Artist's conception of what lies beneath the mask

The Attack!
Attacks inevitably follow the same pattern. It approaches victims with a single question: "Watashi kirei?" ("Do I look beautiful?") If the

victim answers "yes," the Kuchisake Onna leans in and removes the mask to reveal a grotesque, oversized mouth that stretches from ear to ear. "Even like this?" It takes advantage of its victim's shock to lash out with a knife or scythe, mutilating their face in a manner similar to its own.

If the victim answers "no," it slashes the victim anyway. Damned if you do, damned if you don't.

It is disgusted by the scent of hair pomade. In some accounts, shouting the word "pomade" three times has stunned it long enough to allow victims to beat a hasty retreat. (Rumor has it that the doctor or dentist who mutilated her face had thickly pomaded hair.)

Another popular method of warding it off is to chant the word *ninniku* (garlic) while drawing the kanji character for "dog" on one's hand.

Surviving an Encounter: Running won't help. The Kuchisake Onna is said to be capable of covering one hundred yards in three seconds. (Some versions of the tale describe it as once having been an Olympic athlete.) However, it is also said to be extraordinarily fond of traditional Japanese sweets called bekko ame. Giving, or in a pinch throwing, them will distract it long enough to escape.

The Magic Number: In addition to the rumor that chanting "pomade" three times drives it away, encounters are also said to occur more frequently in places with three in their names or addresses—Mie Prefecture, which is written with the kanji character for the number three, is said to be a favorite haunt—and to those with a three in their birthdates. The origin of this obscure numerological connection remains unclear.

REALITY CHECK:
The Kuchisake Onna remains one of the most well-known urban legends in Japan. The first reports appeared in 1978, reaching a peak several years later. Now it has attained the status of an enduring folk legend, and portrayals appear in a wide variety of comic books, television dramatizations, films, and other forms of entertainment. At the peak of its popularity—or infamy—police departments occasionally received calls from terror-stricken schoolchildren who reported seeing it in their neighborhoods.

Kitsune

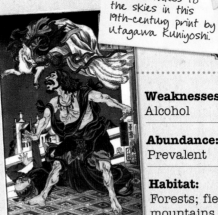

狐

A nine-tailed kitsune takes to the skies in this 19th-century print by Utagawa Kuniyoshi.

Pronunciation:
(KEY-tsoo-nay)

English Name:
The Fox, Demon Fox, the Fox-god, the Fox-spirit

Scientific Name:
Vulpes vulpes japonica

Gender:
Male and Female

Height:
Variable

Weight:
Variable

Locomotion:
Quadrupedal or bipedal

Distinctive Features:
Appearance of normal fox, multiple-tailed fox, or (sometimes) human

Supernatural Abilities:
Shape-shifting and mimicry
Fire-breathing
Spirit possession

Favorite Foods:
Deep-fried tofu

Weaknesses:
Alcohol

Abundance:
Prevalent

Habitat:
Forests; fields; mountains

Claim to Fame:
A proper description of the Kitsune's role in Japanese religion, mythology, and culture could easily fill a book many times over. Literally translated, *kitsune* is the word for the common Japanese red fox. Legends involving this sly animal have been a staple of generations of folklore, based on the traditional belief that foxes possess extraordinary life spans and boast intelligence at least on a par with humans. On top of that, once they reach a certain age and hone their natural talents, they transform into yokai that boast a wide range of mysterious abilities. In their yokai form, Kitsune sprout additional tails as they develop their supernatural skills; a nine-tailed fox is consid-

SLIMY AND

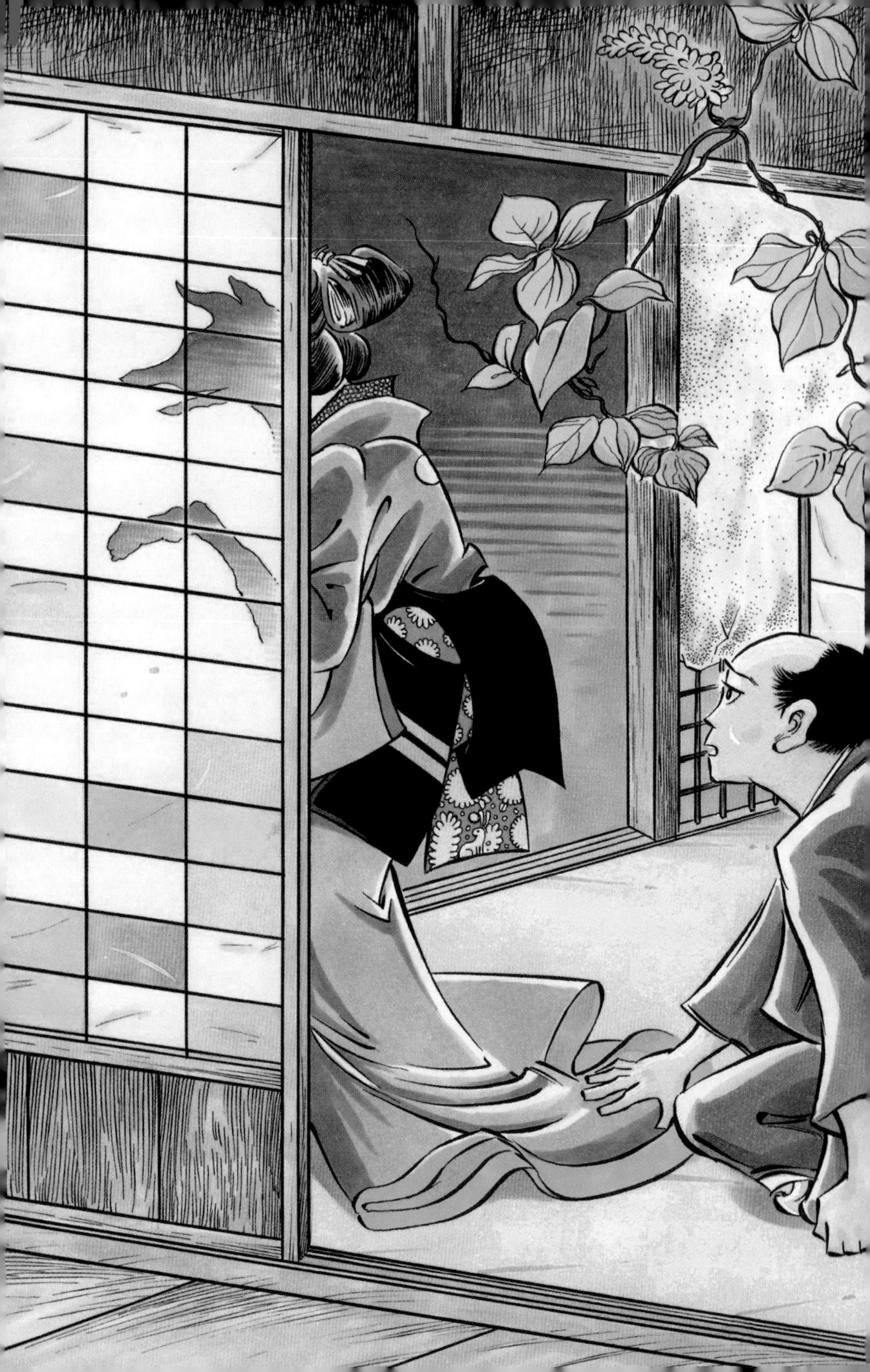

NOTE: See image of nine-tailed fox on page 146

THE SEXY AND SLIMY

ered to be at the pinnacle of its powers.

There are many forms of Kitsune. Some are merely mischievous; others are malicious; and still others are considered divine messengers of the gods. In any event, the general idea is that humans are on dangerously unstable ground when dealing with these capricious and powerful creatures.

The abilities of this yokai are many. Perhaps the most common manifestation is the phenomenon of *kitsune-bi*, or "foxfire," which is similar to the Western concept of the "will-o'-the-wisp." They are notorious mimics and shape-shifters, known for transforming themselves into beautiful women—occasionally for extended periods—in order to seduce their prey. Conventional wisdom holds that a Kitsune needs to cover its head with leaves, reeds, or even skulls to properly mimic the form of a human being.

However, in contrast to the similarly skilled Tanuki (p. 126), Kitsune are considered dangerous and occasionally even lethal adversaries. In a nineteenth-century collection of urban legends referred to as the "Seven Wonders of Honjo," travelers were led astray by what appeared to be humans carrying lanterns but were actually Tanuki or Kitsune in disguise. Tanuki were satisfied to lead their victims far off course; Kitsune, on the other hand, guided unwary travelers over cliffs or into other deadly situations.

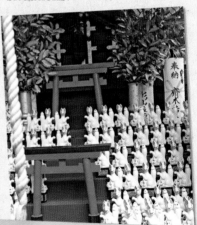

FOXES AND INARI: In Japan's native religion of Shinto, foxes are believed to act as messengers and servants to Inari, the god of fertility and agriculture; representations of foxes are extremely common sights inside Japan's Inari shrine compounds. The sheer pervasiveness of these shrines cannot be overstated. Conservative estimates number some twenty to thirty thousand public Inari shrines, but the figure would be several times higher if "unofficial" mini-shrines found in suburban neighborhoods, on mountainsides, and even on the rooftops of skyscrapers were counted as well.

The Attack!
Typical Kitsune encounters take one of several forms, but they are such skilled shape-shifters that quite often their participation goes undetected until after an incident has occurred.

A Foxy Feast: The Japanese noodle dish Kitsune udon contains strips of fried tofu, said to be a favorite food of Kitsune. This ingredient is also used to make inari-sushi, vinegared rice wrapped in a fried tofu skin.

Kitsune love to play nasty pranks. A classic example involves taking the form of a kindly individual who offers unwary victims what appears to be candy but turns out to be a piece of dung.

Kitsune tales—or is that tails?—often involve a fox shape-shifting into a beautiful woman to seduce a male victim, draining him of life-blood. In some cases, these "foxy ladies" masquerade as humans for years on end.

Kitsune are also said to be capable of possessing human hosts so as to cause insanity or illness. To quote the 1913 treatise *Myths and Legends of Japan*, "The studies of Dr. Baelz, of the Imperial University of Japan, seem to point to the fact that animal possession in human beings is a real and terrible truth after all. He remarks that a fox usually enters a woman either through the breast or between the fingernails, and that the fox lives a separate life of its own, frequently speaking in a voice totally different from the human."

Surviving an Encounter:
Get a dog. Kitsune may be able to pull the wool over the average person's eyes, but canines are more than capable of sniffing them out. Or buy it a drink, since a Kitsune in human form often forgets to hide its tails when preoccupied or drunk. The bottom line, however, is that if you've become mixed up in some bizarre Kitsune scheme, you're pretty much along for the ride.

However, it is important to note that not all Kitsune are considered malicious. Even those who masquerade as humans may not necessarily be doing their partners a disservice. In fact, throughout history more than a few individuals have claimed to have fox-blood running through their veins.

Yuki-Onna

雪女

Pronunciation:
(YOU-key OHn-na)

English Name:
Snow Woman

Alternate Japanese Name:
Yuki-musume, Yuki-joro,
Yuki-onba

Gender:
Female

Height:
Average for a Japanese
woman

Weight:
It's impolite to ask a lady
her weight!

Locomotion:
Bipedal

Distinctive Features:
Youthful-to-adult appearance,
Black hair, Complexion so
pale it borders on translu-
cent, White kimono or other
season-inappropriate clothing
(Sometimes almost naked)

Body Temperature:
Cold as ice

Abundance:
Unknown (see below)

Season:
Dead of winter

Preferred Habitat:
Alpine areas

Claim to Fame:
The Yuki-Onna is one of Japanese folklore's most famous
femme fatales. You know
the old saw about "looks
that kill?" She's got one. She
takes the form of a beautiful
woman who appears before
men trapped in mountain
snowstorms — and is the last
thing they ever see.

Her preternaturally pale
skin, frost-covered tresses,
and dazzling white kimono
seem startlingly out of place
amidst the natural violence
inevitably swirling about
her. Although occasionally
described as the wandering
spirit of a young woman who
died in a blizzard, she is generally regarded as a yokai
rather than a yurei (ghost).
She may even BE snow. In
fact a 19th century physical
scientist named Genrin Yama-
oka theorized that she was
born of the stuff itself, though
his idea was based on the
long-obsolete biological theory
of spontaneous generation.

THE SEXY AND SLIMY

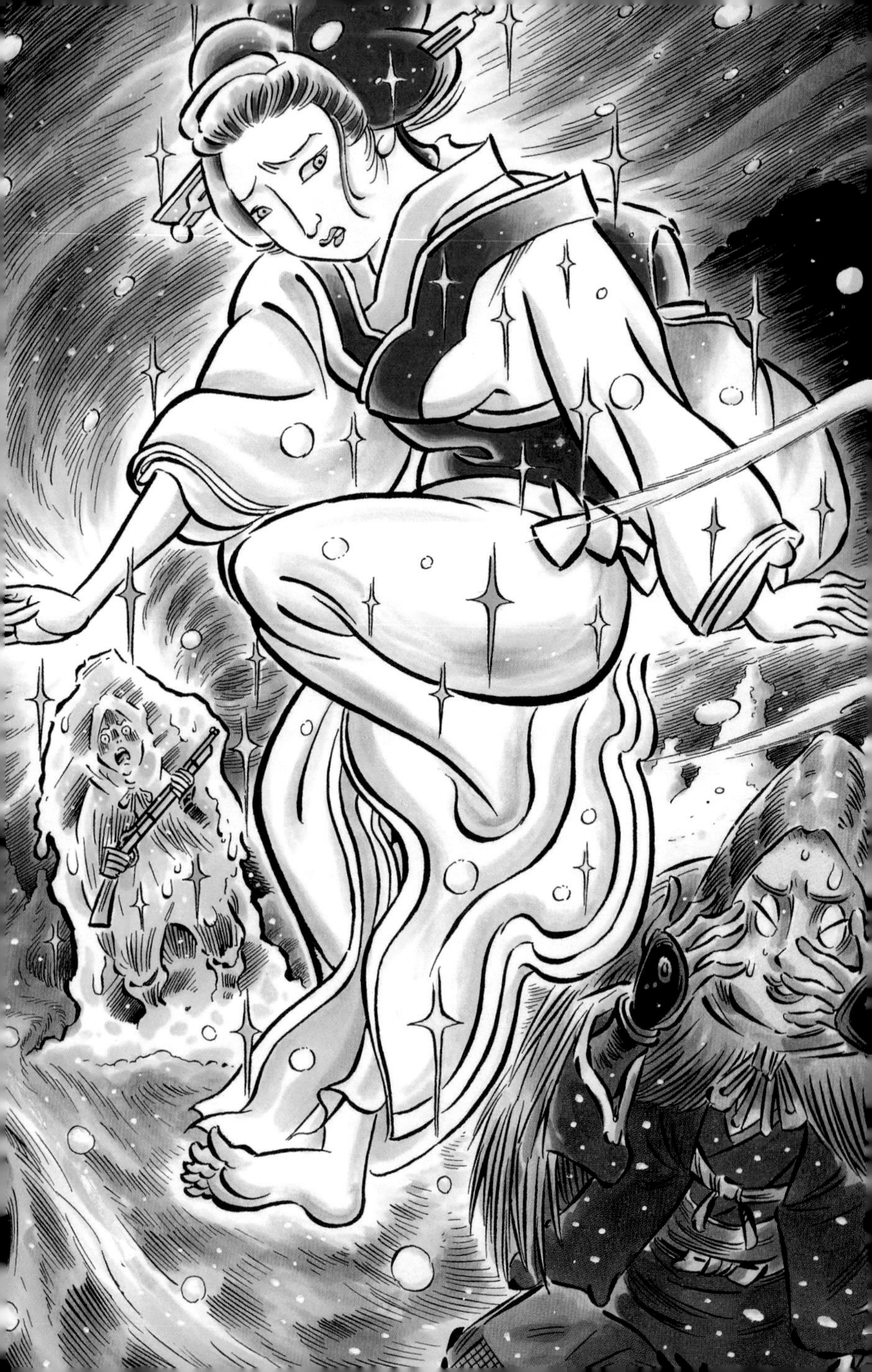

There are as many varia-
tions of the Yuki-Onna legend as there are mountains
in Japan. For example, in
Iwate and Miyagi Prefectures,
Yuki-Onna is said to freeze
unwary travelers solid with a
single penetrating glance. In
Niigata (where she is known
as Yuki-joro, the Snow Courtesan) she is said to specifically target young children,
whose livers she devours raw.
Residents of the mountains
of Ibaraki and Fukushima
claim that if you ignore the
Yuki-Onna's call, she will
push you off a cliff or bury
you beneath a snowdrift.

The sheer number of
reports would seem to hint
that Yuki-Onna represents an
entire species of yokai, but
an equal number of legends
claim she is a lone individual, the only one of her kind.
The truth remains unknown.

The Attack!
In an era of Gore-Tex ther-
mal underwear, portable
stoves, and such, Yuki-Onna
fatalities are rare. But that
doesn't mean you are out of
the woods. Remember that
bit about her being able to
freeze people solid with a
look, Medusa-style? As the
conflicting legends show, we
don't know exactly what

lurks in her bag of tricks.
Typically, however, Yuki-
Onna preys upon those who
have already fallen victim to
the cold and stopped moving
in the snow. She crouches
over her fallen prey and
exhales a breath as white
as smoke into their faces,
removing the last vestiges of
heat – and life – from their
bodies. Perhaps you could
think of her as hypothermia
personified.

Surviving an Encounter:
It's as simple as it is compli-
cated: get hitched!
Allow us to explain. There
is precisely one report of a
man surviving an encounter
with a Yuki-Onna. Lafcaido
Hearn chronicled it in his
1903 book *Kwaidan*.
An elderly woodcutter
named Mosaku and his teen-
age apprentice Minokichi
were overtaken by a snow-
storm in the mountains. They
hunkered down in a hut to
wait out the storm. Late that
evening, Minokichi awoke to
find a woman bending over
his mentor, blowing her fatal
breath upon his face. Realizing she was being watched,
she turned on the young
man. But she took pity and
offered to spare him if he
swore never to reveal what

THE SEXY AND SLIMY

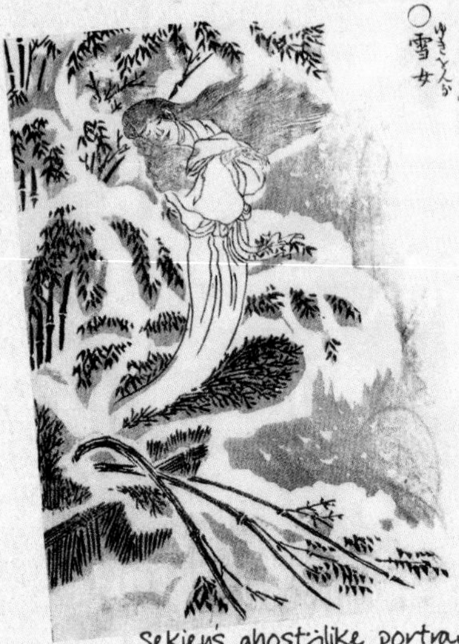
雪女

Sekien's ghost-like portrayal of Yuki-Onna.

he had seen. Should he ever speak of what happened, however, she would take her revenge (a dish, of course, best served cold.)

Minokichi startled awake the next morning. The storm had broken. Had it been a dream? Yet Mosaku was dead, a look of terror frozen into his features. And so the young man resolved never to speak of the incident again.

At roughly the same time the following year, Minokichi happened to run into a beautiful young woman on the footpath leading past the village. Introducing herself as Oyuki (a common name meaning "snow"), she told the young man she was an orphan, on her way to Edo (now Tokyo) in search of employment.

As it turned out, Oyuki never did make it to Edo, because she and Minokichi fell in love at first sight. They married shortly thereafter and before long Oyuki was pregnant with Minokichi's child. Over the next decade, she bore him nine more children, all healthy little boys and girls.

The family lived happily for many years. But one evening, as his wife sewed by candlelight, Minokichi remarked that she reminded him of someone. The story of his encounter in the hut spilled from him, bottled up after so many years.

"It was I!" shrieked Oyuki, flying from her chair into the startled Minokichi's face. "You swore an oath! And were it not for our children, I would kill you where you stand! Take good care of them, for if they ever have reason to complain, I'll track you to the ends of the Earth and make you pay, pay, pay..."

As her tirade reached its crescendo, her body faded into wisps of smoke that quickly spun up through the chimney-hole. Minokichi never saw her again.

Bottom line: if you encounter a Yuki-Onna, you'd better hope you're her type.

YOKAI NO: 0 3 7

Hashi Hime

橋姫

Pronunciation:
HAH-she HEE-may

English Name:
Literally, "Bridge Princess"

Gender:
Female (sometimes male)

Height:
Average for a Japanese woman

Weight:
Average for a Japanese woman

Locomotion:
Bipedal

Distinctive Features:
Human female appearance
Black hair parted into seven loops. Iron "crown" topped with lit candles often topless

Pet Peeves:
Happy couples

THE YOKAI THERAPIST
There is a shrine to the Hashi Hime in the city of Uji, which is often visited by those who wish to cut ties with someone in their lives.

Offensive Weapons:
Furious scowl
Claws and teeth

Abundance:
One of a kind

Habitat:
Bridges

Claim to Fame:
A human turned yokai by the sheer force of jealousy and revenge, the Hashi Hime is essentially an anti-Cupid, a super-stalker, a ferocious force of nature dedicated to the solitary purpose of making others pay for her betrayal. Unlike other yokai such as the Kappa (p. 26) or Tengu (p. 22), it is a lone creature, the only one of its kind.

There are many tales associated with the Hashi Hime. The most famous tells of a married couple who lived long ago near the Uji River in Kyoto. Betrayed by her philandering husband, a faithful wife prayed day and night at a local Shinto shrine for holy retribution.

On the seventh evening, the shrine's priest approached her with news of a strange

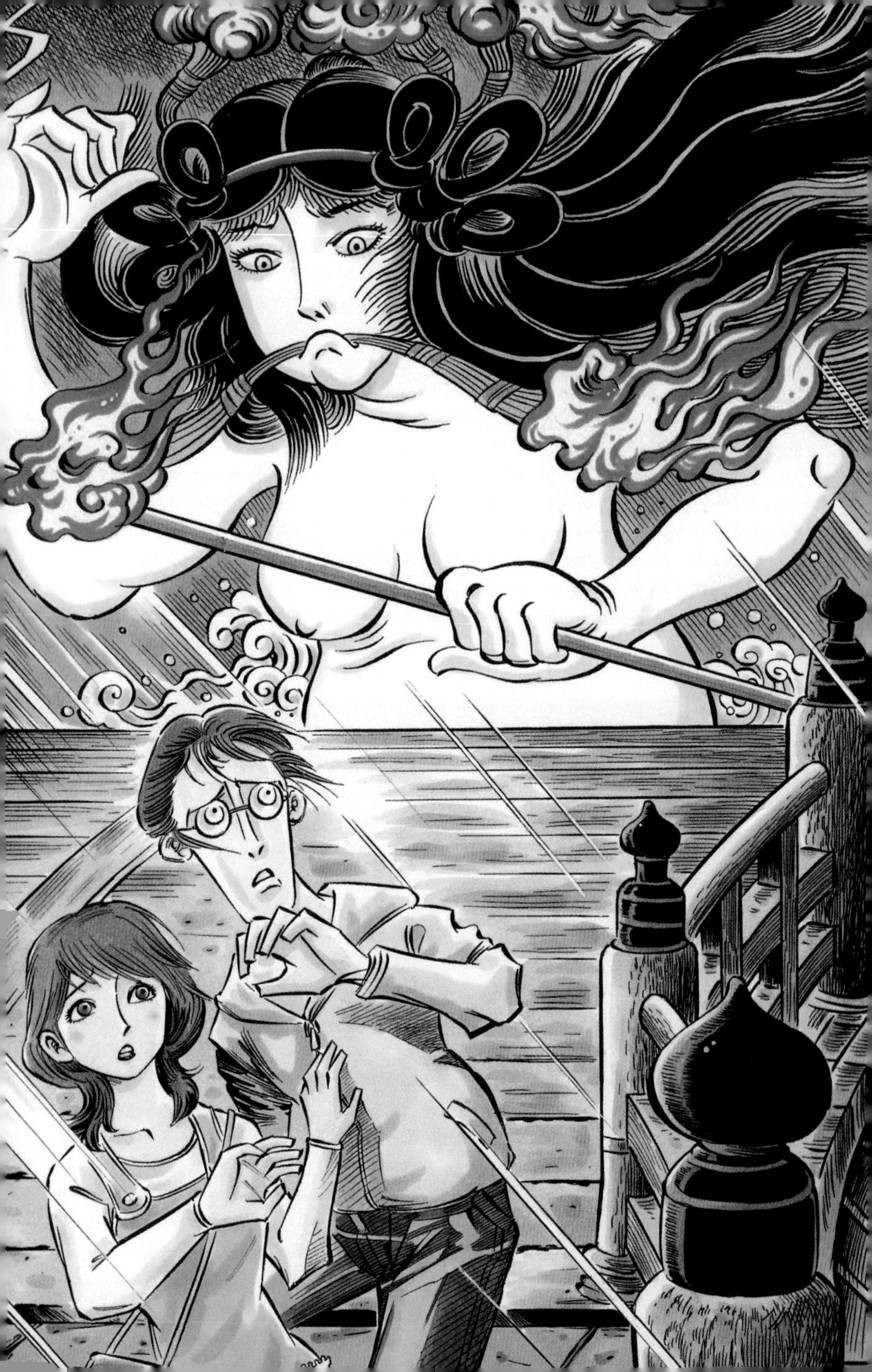

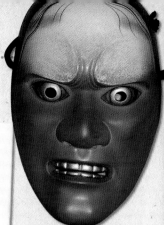

A mask of the Hashi Hime used in the Chofu festival

dream that had awakened him. In it he was instructed of the method by which the woman could take her revenge. She was to dress in red, streak her face and body with poisonous cinnibar, part her hair into seven loops, place an iron brazier inverted and topped with lit candles on her head, carry a rod of pure iron in one hand, and remain at the Uji River for twenty-one days. If she obeyed, she would be transformed into a creature capable of exacting the vengeance she so desired. And the rest, as they say, is history.

IN THE YOKAI LIBRARY:
Hashi Hime is the title of one of the chapters of the *Tale of Genji*, the world's first novel, written circa the year 1000 by a courtesan named Murasaki Shikibu.

The Attack!

The Hashi Hime preys upon travelers who cross bridges; its range spans nearly the entire Japanese archipelago. It is said to appear in female form when targeting men and male form when targeting women. Once you have been enchanted by the facade of beauty, it quickly reveals a hideous true form: that of a furious demon. The sight is said to drive many insane; a handful die outright from shock.

Another type of Hashi Hime encounter involves a request. In one of these cases, a traveler encountered a beautiful woman while crossing a bridge. She begged him to deliver a written message to her counterpart on another bridge elsewhere in Japan. Agreeing to the task, the traveler happened to open the note along the way, realizing with horror that it stated, "Kill this man." The simple expedient of adding the words "do not" to the note allowed him to carry out his duty while escaping an unsavory fate.

Surviving an Encounter:

The Hashi Hime is particularly fond of targeting happy couples. If you encounter one, your only chance to avoid a painful death is to swear to break up with your significant other. Don't have one? Uh. . . .

THE SEXY AND SLIMY

The Wimps

If the previous chapters sent you into a cold sweat, relax. We humans are a far scarier lot than this bunch could ever hope to be.

Nopperabo

のっぺらぼう

Pronunciation:
(NOH-peh-rah BOW)

English Names:
Faceless One, No-face,
Blank-face

Alternate Japanese Names:
Nupperabo, Zunberabo, Nup-
periho

Gender:
Male or female

Height:
Average for an adult human

Weight:
Average for an adult human

Locomotion:
Bipedal

Distinctive Features:
Apparently a normal, everyday individual
Perfectly smooth, featureless
face

Offensive Weapons:
Shock of physical appearance

Origin:
Edo (Tokyo)

Abundance:
Prevalent

Habitat:
Urban, suburban, and rural
areas

Claim to Fame:
The Nopperabo, whose name
evokes the feel of something
smooth and featureless in
Japanese, resemble normally
dressed, apparently healthy
individuals save for one
major difference: a face "like
unto an egg," devoid of any
hint of features.

These mischievous crea-
tures are among the most
well-known yokai in Japan.
In some tales, Nopperabo
simply lack eyes and noses.
Others describe them as
being completely lacking in
features altogether. Although
they appear perfectly human
aside from their faces, they
are believed to be Kitsune
(p. 154) or Tanuki (p. 126)
mimicking human form. Perhaps they represent the first
tentative attempts of young
shape-shifters to assume
human form? Whatever the
case, they seem to take great
delight in scaring people,

THE WIMPS

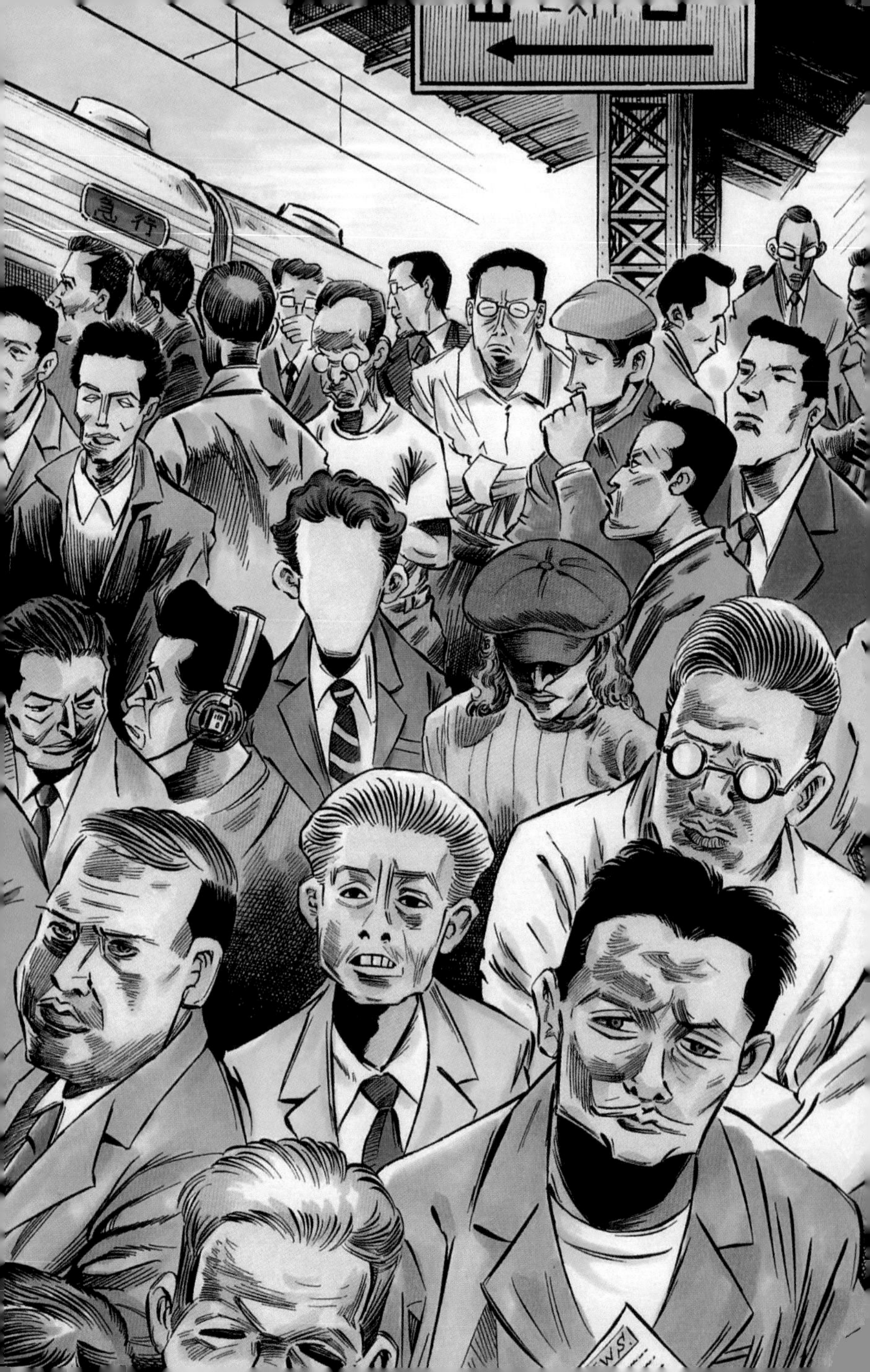
急行

often putting themselves in situations where they know they will be observed by unsuspecting "victims."

Many stories seem to hail from Kyoto. In one, the Nopperabo tugs on the sleeve of a merchant, who runs for his life. Upon catching his breath some time later, he notices a dozen or so coarse hairs sticking to the part of his clothing that had been grabbed. Another tale concerns a certain abandoned house in the Chuo ward of Kyoto, said to be home to a Nopperabo that endlessly pounds a mortar and pestle.

Nopperabo appear to have an affinity for water. They commonly appear near moats, riverbanks, and along canals and the like, leading some to speculate that they are the work of otters or weasels rather than Kitsune or Tanuki. (Incidentally, some believe that otters are behind the yokai called Nobiagari [p. 190] as well. Who knew those fuzzy little guys had it in them?)

The Attack!

An encounter inevitably follows the same general pattern. It occurs late at night,

letting the faceless creature get as close as possible before revealing its shocking lack of features. According to some reports, it is capable of erecting an illusory facade of a normal face for short periods of time, letting it get even closer to potential victims. Its entire bag of tricks, so to speak, is in the sole service of surprising the hell out of the individuals it meets.

Nopperabo often work in teams. One scares the victim, who runs off in search of someone to hear his tale of woe. Inevitably the next person they encounter listens sympathetically before revealing that it, too, is a faceless Nopperabo, sending the victim into even more of a tizzy. A bit sophomoric, perhaps, but good clean fun as far as a yokai is concerned.

LANGUAGE LESSON: Like so many other yokai, the Nopperabo's name is a play on words. It is based on the word *nopperi*, which means "featureless" in Japanese.

Avoiding an Encounter:

Those with heart conditions aside, encounters are seldom, if ever, fatal. The mischievous Nopperabo are content to merely scare the living daylights out of their victims. Once they've done so, they simply wait for the person to

run off screaming.

If you happen to encounter a Nopperabo, try and keep your wits about you and stand firm. You never know: you might be the first person to get a Nopperabo to turn tail itself!

Reality Check:
Ironically, much of the Nopperabo's current popularity is due not to Japanese folktales but rather the translated literature of Lafcadio Hearn (1850-1904), who wrote in English under his given name and in Japanese as "Yakumo Koizumi," the name he took after becoming a Japanese citizen in 1896. Assisted by his wife, Setsuko, who translated and re-enacted the stories for him, Hearn gained fame as one of the first non-Japanese to chronicle many regional folktales and ghost stories. "Mujina," one of the signature short stories in his 1904 book *Kwaidan*, was inspired by tales of the Nopperabo.

Although in reality *mujina* are small Japanese badgers, said in folklore to possess powers similar to the Kitsune, the popularity of Hearn's story has caused the image of the mujina to become intermingled with that of the Nopperabo in Japan.

Intriguingly, there have been reports of Nopperabo-like mujina sightings outside of Japan as well. A Hawaiian urban legend believed to date to 1959 describes a pair of faceless women combing their hair in the restroom of a popular movie theater, the unexpected sight of which sent the observer to the hospital with a nervous breakdown. What could Nopperabo have been doing in Hawaii?

Perhaps even yokai need a vacation from time to time.

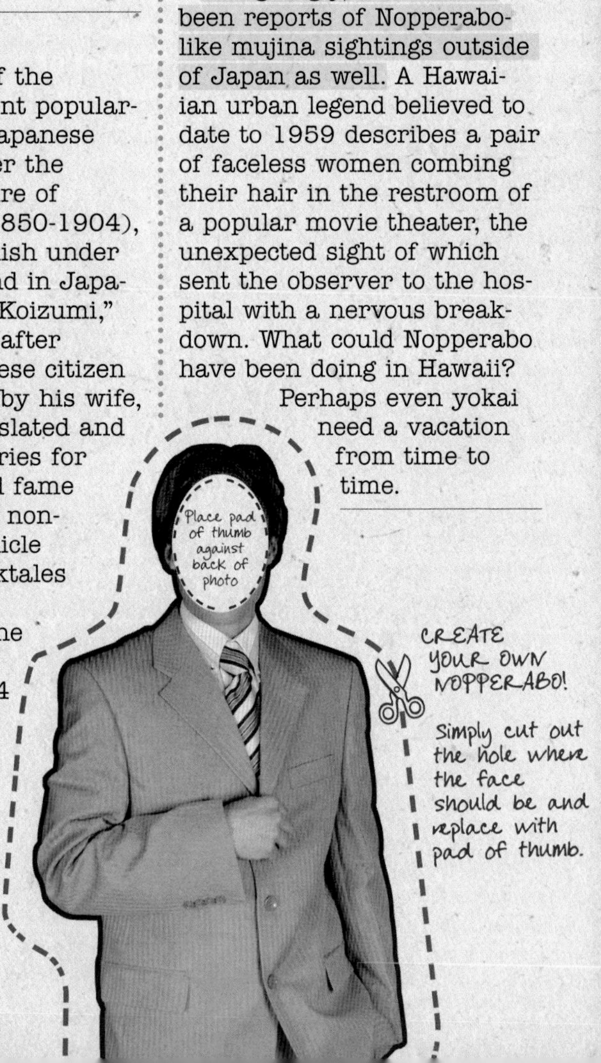

Place pad of thumb against back of photo
CREATE YOUR OWN NOPPERABO!
Simply cut out the hole where the face should be and replace with pad of thumb.

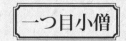
Hitotsume Kozo

一つ目小僧

Pronunciation:
(Hee-TOH-tsoo-may ko-ZOH)

English Names:
The One-eyed Boy; One-eyed Goblin

Gender:
Male

Height:
That of a seven- or eight-year-old boy

Weight:
That of a seven- or eight-year-old boy

Locomotion:
Bipedal

Distinctive Features
Humanoid
Often dressed in traditional garb (kimono, *geta* clogs, straw hat, etc.)
Bald or closely-shaved head. Single oversized eye in middle of forehead

Offensive Weapons:
Shock of physical appearance
Glowing eye

Abundance:
Prevalent

Habitat:
Generally mountainous regions, but also anywhere humans live

Claim to Fame:
Diminutive, cyclopean creatures that are notorious pranksters, either leaping out of the shadows or sneaking into people's homes to scare the living daylights out of them. They are often portrayed as having extraordinarily long tongues, and are traditionally dressed in kimono, robes, or other period garb, often resembling that of a monk in training. Sometimes one is seen carrying a rosary or other articles associated with the Buddhist faith. Arguably one of the superstars of the yokai world, tales of the Hitosume Kozo first began appearing in urban legends

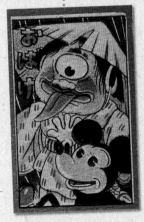

Friend of a certain mouse? A 1960s *Karuta*

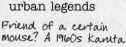

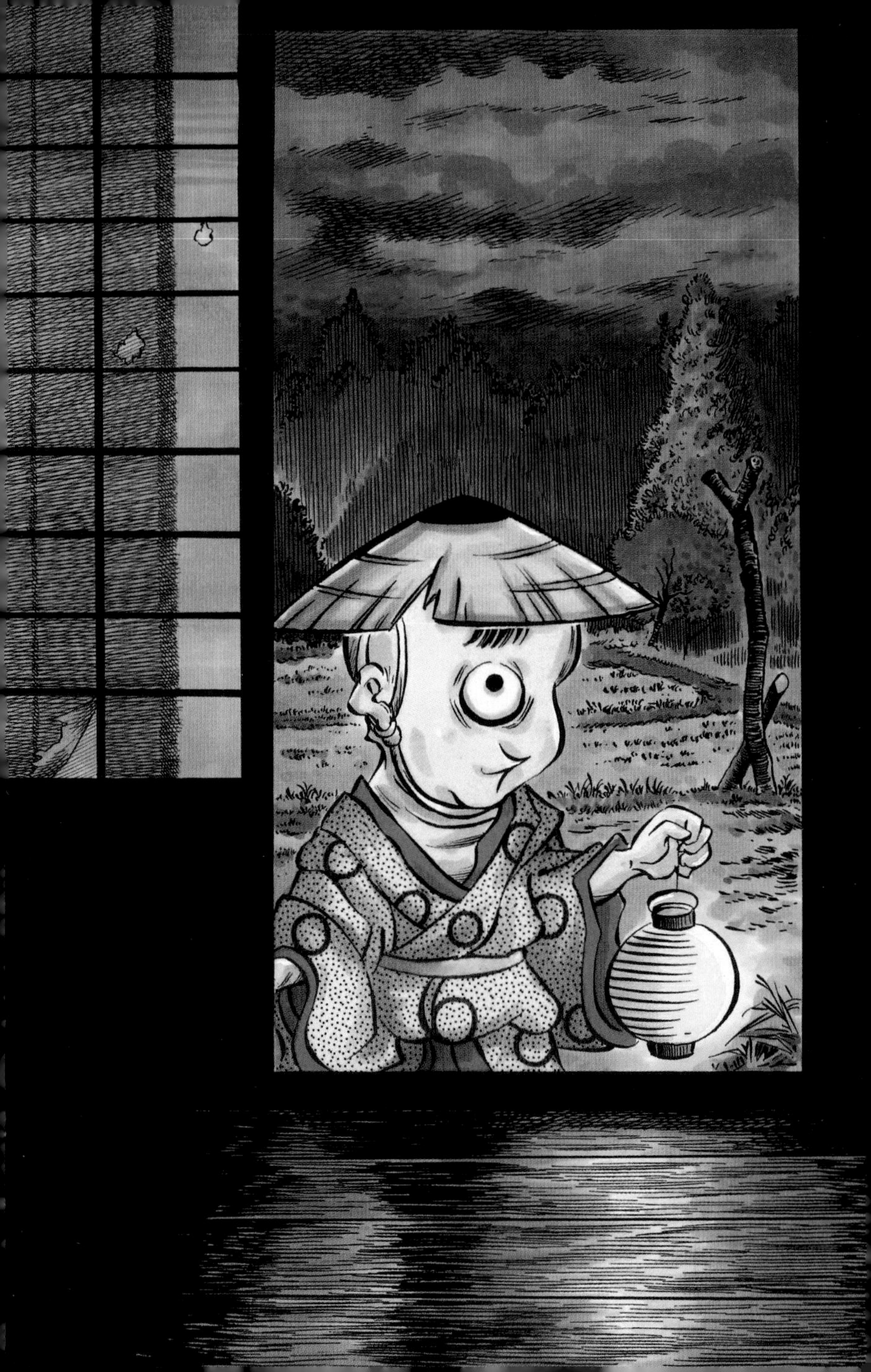

and tales of terror in the Edo era (1603-1868). Playing cards called karuta featuring its visage were popular playthings at the time, making them a precursor to the collectible card games so popular with children today.

Hitotsume Kozo is widely known in Japanese folktales, and many different regions have their own traditions and legends concerning the yokai. In Shizuoka prefecture, for example, folk tradition holds that the Hitotsume Kozo descend from the mountains to visit peoples' homes on December and February 8th. Residents are supposed to place holly leaves (said to be responsible for poking out one of the Hitotsume Kozo's eyes in some tales), baskets, and the white water from the washing of rice outside their homes to keep the yokai at bay, while dining on *sekihan*, a mixture of steamed rice and azuki beans, inside their homes. If a Hitotsume Kozo drops by and sees that a family or resident isn't eating sekihan, it is said, it marks the address down in a notebook, and the location is cursed with poor health and misfortune that year.

Although generally associated with playful mischief, there is at least one case of a Hitotsume Kozo performing a public service. In the monastery on Kyoto's Mount Hiei, it is said that one appeared before a monk who was enjoying himself a wee bit too much in the pleasure quarters of downtown Kyoto, ringing a bell to chide him back onto the righteous path. (Incidentally—unrelated to the Hitotsume Kozo—a pilgrimage to Mount Hiei remains a popular tourist activity today.)

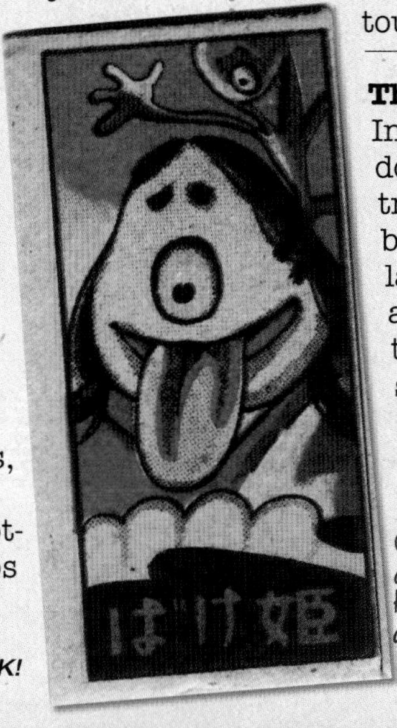
ばけ姫

Could there be females as well? This 1960s Karuta seems to hint as much.

The Attack!

In a traditional outdoor encounter, a traveler is surprised by the sight of a large glowing eye in a tree or alongside the road; when he stops for a closer look, Hitotsume Kozo launches itself

THE WIMPS

OCCULT OVERLAP: Perhaps due to their similar-sounding names and young appearances, the Hitotsume Kozo and the Tofu Kozo (p. 82) are occasionally portrayed as being one and the same (i.e., as a cyclopean boy carrying a block of tofu), but they are in fact two distinct yokai.

from the shadows into the full view of the victim, razzing them with an improbably long tongue all the while.

Although it is rare, Hitotsume Kozo are also occasionally known to cause trouble indoors as well, knocking decorations out of place, stealing candy, and causing other sorts of mischief.

Avoiding an Encounter: Don't panic. Hitotsume Kozo tend to disappear before a victim's adrenaline rush even has a chance to subside. In some regions, baskets or colanders are hung in doorways to repel these little pests, as the numerous "eyes" in the weave of the containers frighten the one-eyed Hitotsume Kozo.

Reality Check: The author Kunio Yanagita (1875-1962), who toured Japan gathering yokai tales for his 1912 book *Tono Monogatari* ("Tales of Tono"), believed that the Hitotsume Kozo derived from folktales of Shinto priests so devoted to their art that they deliberately poked out a single eye, the better to receive mystic wisdom from the gods. In spite of this rather gruesome story, the veracity of which remains unknown, these yokai are generally portrayed as childish tricksters rather than adults.

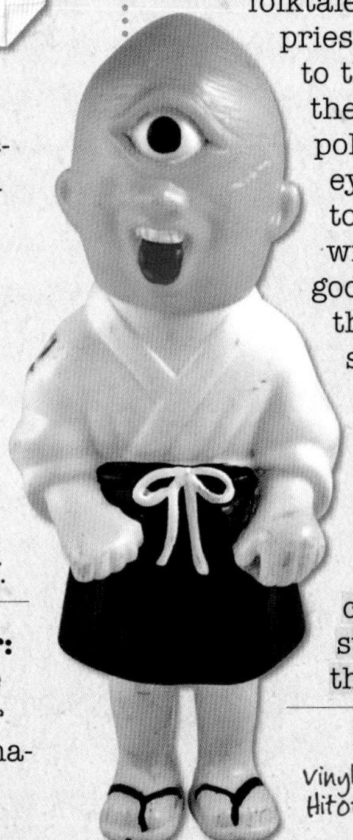

Vinyl toy figure of Hitotsume Kozo

Toire no Hanako

トイレの花子

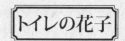

Pronunciation:
(TOY-ray noh HANA-koh)

English Names:
Literally, "Hanako in the Bathroom"; Hanako, Girl in the Bathroom

Gender:
Female

Height:
That of a Japanese elementary schoolgirl

Weight:
That of a Japanese elementary schoolgirl

Locomotion:
Bipedal

Distinctive Features:
Appears to be a young Japanese girl
Bobbed hairstyle
Red skirt

Offensive Weapons:
None

Abundance:
One of a kind

Habitat:
School bathrooms

Claim to Fame:
This yokai is a seemingly normal little girl, dressed in a school uniform, that appears in the bathrooms of elementary schools throughout Japan. Taking female form, it naturally haunts the girls' restroom, although it is occasionally spotted by males in rare situations when boys and girls happen to share the same facilities. The prospect of an encounter is occasionally used as a test of courage for

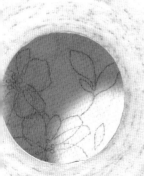

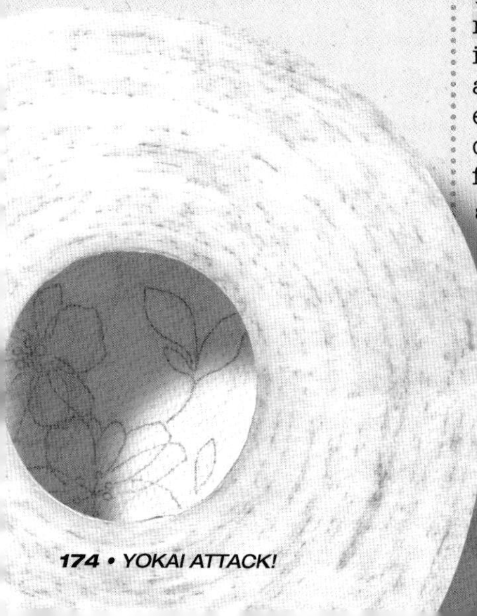

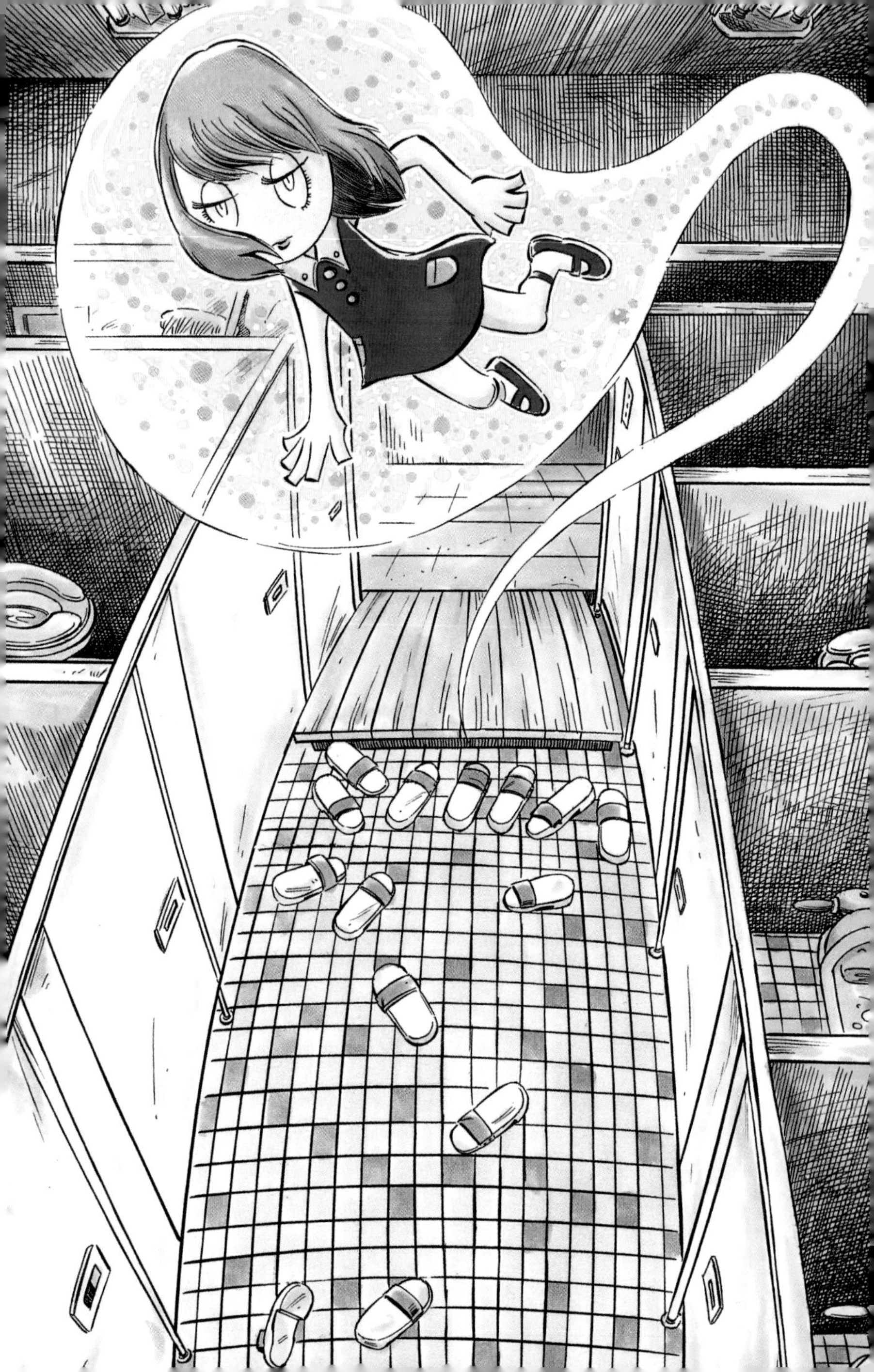

young schoolgirls, who goad each other into venturing into the restrooms it is said to haunt. Little girls have a love-hate relationship with it: while unexpected encounters can be terrifying, it isn't known to cause any actual harm, and some even consider it a school mascot of sorts. It is a classic schoolgirl spook, the kind of monster little kids discuss in hushed tones during slumber parties and on school trips.

Along with the Kuchisake Onna (p. 150), Hanako is one of the "youngest" of the creatures featured in this guidebook. Although occasionally described as a *yurei* (ghost), its modus operandi is sufficiently consistent and yokai-like to warrant inclusion here.

"Hanako" is a common, if slightly old-fashioned, given name for a female. The first recorded appearance of the yokai bearing this name dates back to the 1950s. Urban legends told of a little girl who tried to hide in the school bathroom but was discovered and murdered by her demented mother. Another version describes her as having being killed in a surprise air raid during the war years while playing a game of hide-and-seek with her classmates. Whatever the case, a rash of sightings began circulating among schoolchildren in the 1980s, cementing Hanako's reputation as one of the spooky elite.

Hanako is one of the very few diurnal yokai—most likely to appear during the day, when school is in session, rather than at night when the school is empty.

The Attack!
Hanako only makes an appearance in girls' bathrooms. In a typical

TOILETS OF TERROR
Other entities encountered in bathrooms include the Aka-manto ("Red Cape") whose disembodied voice asks an individual using the toilet if they want a red cape, and if answered in the affirmative, rips the skin off their backs. Akai-Kami-aoi-Kami ("Red Toilet Paper, Blue Toilet Paper") is another disembodied voice that asks victims if they need toilet paper in either of the respective colors. If the person answers "red," they are subjected to a blood-drenched death; if "blue," all of the blood is sucked from their body. And if they answer with any other color, they're simply whisked off to the underworld anyway.

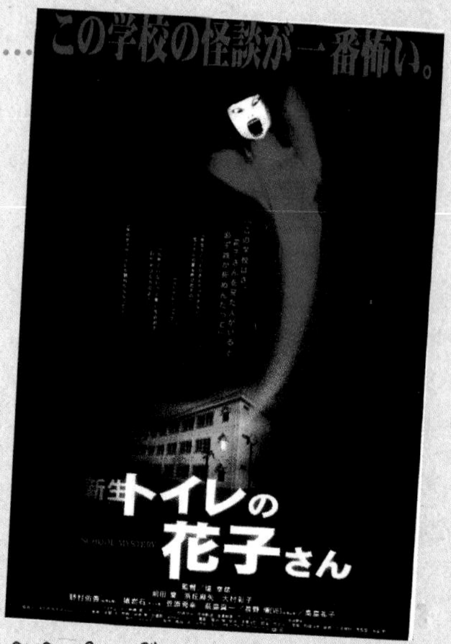
この学校の怪談が一番怖い。
新生トイレの花子さん
DVD of a film based on this yokai (p. 199)

scenario, a schoolgirl calls out Hanako's name when entering an empty bathroom in a school. If Hanako is present, it may respond with an ethereal, disembodied "I'm here." Rare exceptions aside, it generally prefers to remain out of sight. When it does make an appearance, it is often described as sporting a girlish bobbed hairstyle and being clad in a red skirt.

Avoiding an Encounter:
Although the thought of running into it has terrified countless schoolgirls, Hanako is not known to endanger the health or lives of those who encounter it. In fact, it is more of a supernatural mascot than something to be feared. If you happen to encounter it, you might even consider yourself lucky, because there are far worse things to stumble across in Japanese bathrooms (see at left).

Reality Check:
Hanako is a popular subject for Japanese comic books, horror films, and anime, where it is often portrayed in a far more sinister manner than urban legend suggests. In fact "Toire no Hanako-san" is the title of a series of films and television shows featuring this notorious yokai.

Conceptually, Hanako's origins are similar to those of the Akaname (p. 86), another creature that haunts dank bathrooms. Japanese schools are often built according to nearly identical floor plans and feature austere bathroom facilities that can be scary to use, particularly when encountered for the first time by young children. As such they are a natural setting for creepy stories of the sort told by schoolchildren around the world.

Enen-ra

煙々羅

Pronunciation:
(En-en Rah)

Alternate Name:
Enra-enra

English Name:
Smoke-phantom

Gender:
Unknown

Size:
Variable

Weight:
Ethereal

Locomotion:
Floating

Distinctive Features:
An amorphous cloud of smoke

Offensive Weapons:
Smoke

Abundance:
Uncommon

Habitat:
Anywhere near smoke-generating flame (bonfires, etc.)

Claim to Fame:
An uncommon creature whose background is as ethereal as its existence, the Enen-ra is a mysterious sort of yokai that coalesces from the smoke of fires. Never taking actual physical form, it is content to appear in the shape of men, women, animals, and even occasionally other monsters. Apparently composed of nothing more than smoke and air, these creatures are considered completely harmless, if a bit unsettling to actually watch in action.

The Enen-ra is believed to relate to a similar supernatural phenomenon in which the smoke from a fire freezes in place, as if in a photograph, unmoving for a period of time. According to some accounts, only those pure of heart are capable of seeing them.

The Attack!
Generally, it simply coalesces, shows itself, and disappears again. Enen-ra is not known to be aggressive, though it is possible that shifting air

Linguistic Link: "En" means "smoke" in Japanese.

THE WIMPS

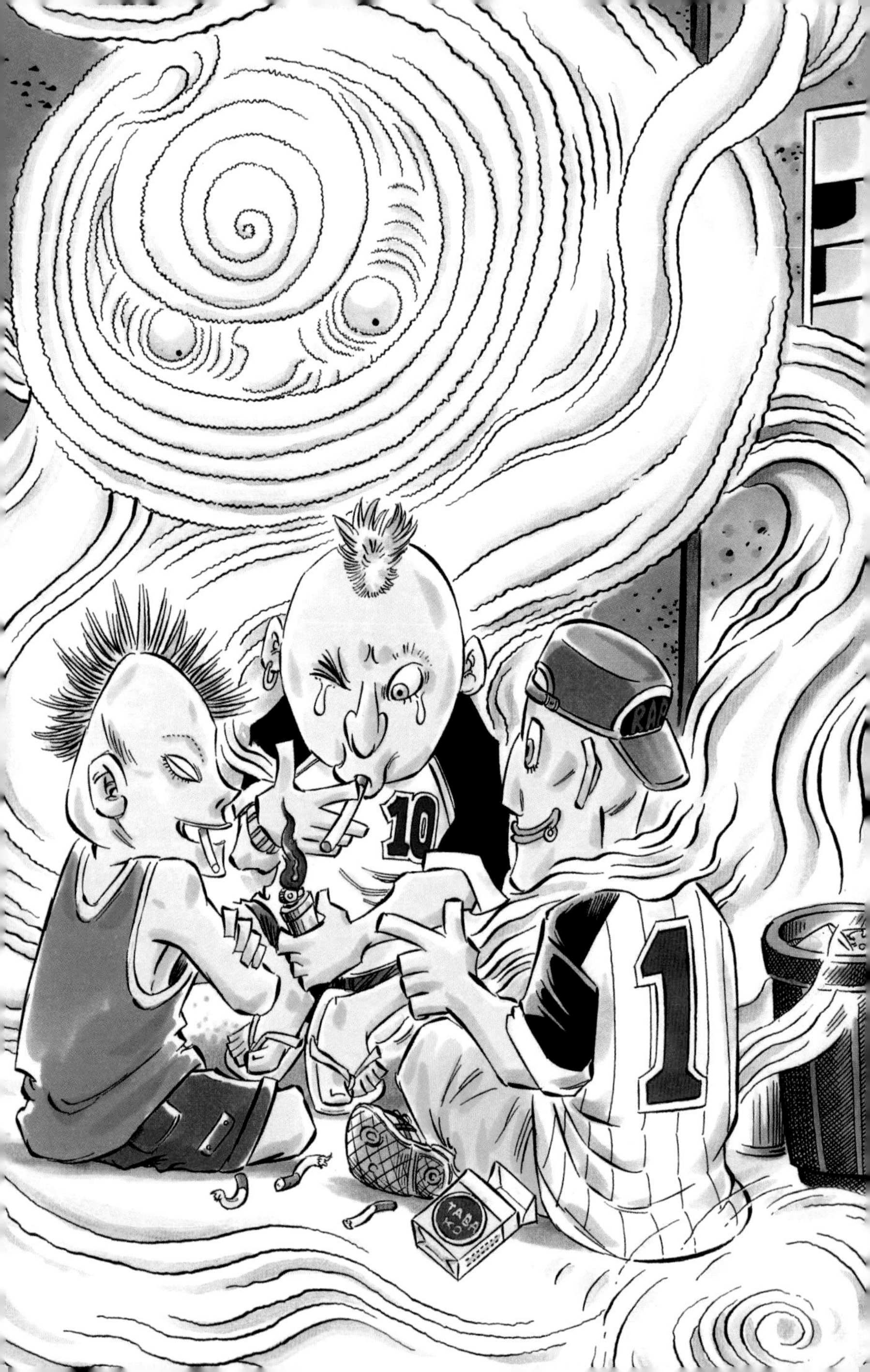
TABA
KO

currents could blow it right into your face. Think of it as being less like an attack and more akin to the dangers of secondhand smoke.

In a recent report of an Enen-ra appearance, the mother of an infant encountered what appeared to be a ghost-like woman leaning over her child as if to comfort it. Surprised by the mother, the apparition disintegrated into a cloud of smoke that quickly swirled, ribbon-like, into the edges of the tatami mats covering the floor. The infant, it is reported, was unharmed.

Avoiding an Encounter: Almost more of a phenomenon than a creature, the Enen-ra need not be feared in and of itself. It is content merely to startle onlookers with its sudden appearance.

However, its presence may be indicative that the location possesses higher than normal supernatural activity, which could theoretically be a good thing or a bad thing, depending on your disposition towards yokai.

If you're asthmatic or otherwise susceptible to breathing problems, consider wearing a gauze mask or painters' mask to avoid

HIROKO SAYS:
When I was a little girl, my friends and I loved playing with a toy called Yokai Kemuri ("yokai smoke"). It was a package filled with sheets of paper impregnated with some sort of chemical substance. When you swiped your fingers across the paper and then repeatedly pressed them together, mysterious tendrils of smoke would stretch between your fingertips. Almost as much fun as the smoke was the gaudy packaging, which was covered with all kinds of weird monsters. Although I don't remember the smoke ever changing into into the form of a person or animal, looking back, the effect was sort of like making my own pet Enen-ra! It turns out that this product is still available in specialty shops, sold under the exact same name and in similar packaging.

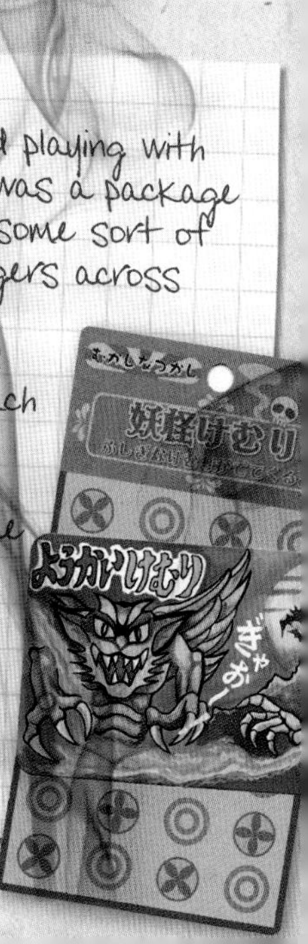
妖怪けむり
ようかいけむり

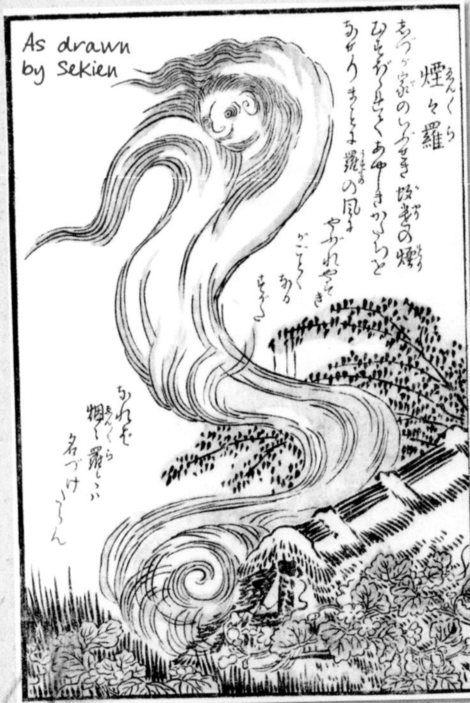
As drawn
by Sekien

inhaling any of the fumes. (Although the Enen-ra itself is perfectly harmless, the Surgeon General reminds you that the smoke from which it is composed could well be hazardous to your health.)

Likely Locations:
Theoretically speaking, Enen-ra can be generated from any kind of smoke, from campfires to funeral pyres to the smoldering end of a cigarette butt.

The creatures are sometimes said to inhabit the eaves of Buddhist temples, apparently fed by the large amounts of smoke generated there. Burning of incense and of amulets made of wood or paper are common practices during Buddhist religious ceremonies. In particular, the practice of *kuyo*, or last rites by immolation, seems a likely scene for the appearance of Enen-ra. In these ceremonies, objects that have spent long periods of time in the company of humans (such as dolls or amulets) or that feature humans (such as photographs) are burned on pyres under the supervision of monks. It is a form of respect and gratitude for the sorts of things that one wouldn't feel right simply tossing out in the trash.

The first depictions of this yokai appeared in Sekien Toriyama's eighteenth-century book *Konjaku Hyakki Shui* ("Tales of Monsters Now and Then"), in which he described one as appearing "from the smoke of fires built to repel mosquitoes," a common act in an age before commercially available insecticides.

Kosode no Te

小袖の手

Boroboro-ton

暮露々々団

Pronunciation:
(Koh-SOH-day no teh)
(BOH-roh BOH-roh tohn)

English Names:
Haunted Kimono Robe
(Kosode no Te)
Haunted Comforter
(Boroboro-ton)

Gender:
Female (Kosode no Te)
Unknown (Boroboro-ton)

Size:
Kosode no Te: 5 ft. to 5 ft. 9
in. (1.5 to 1.75m)
Boroboro-ton: 6 ft. 10 in. x 3
ft. 4 in. (2.1 x 1m)

Weight:
Kosode no Te: roughly 6½
lbs. (3kg)
Boroboro-ton: roughly 11 lbs.
(5kg)

Locomotion:
Kosode no Te: Gliding
Boroboro-ton: Sliding/ shuf-
fling

Distinctive Features:
Apparently normal, if old
and worn, kimono and
futon comforter

Offensive Weapons:
None (Kosode no Te)
Suffocating weight
(Boroboro-ton)

Abundance:
Prevalent

Habitat:
Bedrooms

Claim to Fame:
These yokai are essentially
haunted clothing and bedding,
respectively, taxonomically
making them a sub-species of
the Tsukumo-gami (p. 102).
Often encountered in the
same place—namely the bedroom—they are grouped
together here for convenience.
  The Boroboro-ton's name is
written with archaic kanji
characters that are a homonym for "battered." It is a
threadbare comforter for a
futon bed, often depicted as

WIMPS

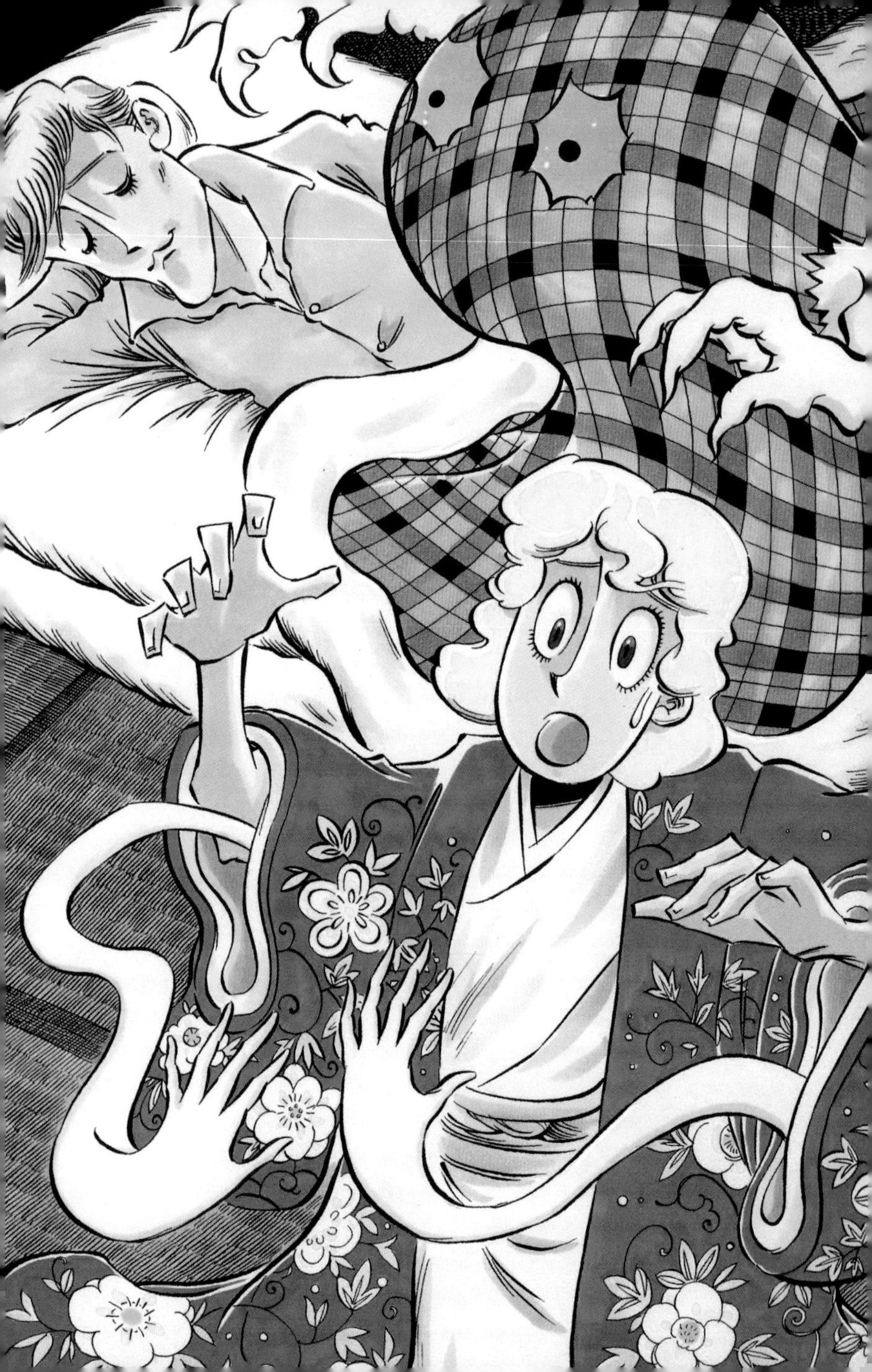

sporting one or more eyes, that shambles around a room in search of prey. Yes, you read that correctly. It's a monster comforter. And not a particularly ferocious one at that.

Literally the "hands in the sleeves," the Kosode no Te is exactly what its name implies: an empty kimono with a pair of ribbon-like phantom limbs extending from its billowing sleeves, fluttering about as it searches for something. Some believe that they are meant to evoke the decorative papers hung at Japanese shrines.

The short-sleeved kimono of the type haunted by Kosode no Te are traditional dress clothes for young girls. In times of old, they were one of the first sorts of things that went to a pawnshop when a family fell on hard times. According to some theories, this yokai represents the spirit of a prostitute whose hands continue seeking the embrace of men long after her death; others feel it represents the spirit of an elderly woman reaching back towards the fondly remembered but distant days of her youth.

The Attack!
Such as it is, occurs when individuals unwittingly use these haunted items: sleeping under one, in the case of the Boroboro-ton, or wearing one, in the case of the Kosode no Te. Encounters take the form of vibrating, rumbling, flying, screeching, moaning, or otherwise behaving in a manner inappropriate to a normal comforter or kimono—preferably in the dead of night, when the victim least expects it.

Avoiding an Encounter:
Although it is theoretically possible to be suffocated by a Boroboro-ton, to date no fatalities—or even mild injuries—have been reported. Still, better safe than sorry.

If you aren't willing to part with your comforter or can't afford a new one, try the following:

1) Wait for daybreak.

2) Collect the offending comforter. If the thought of skin-to-skin contact with a yokai makes you nervous, try a pair of gloves.

3) Air the comforter outdoors in the bright sunlight. (Note to bachelors and students: it's a good idea to do this from

THE WIMPS

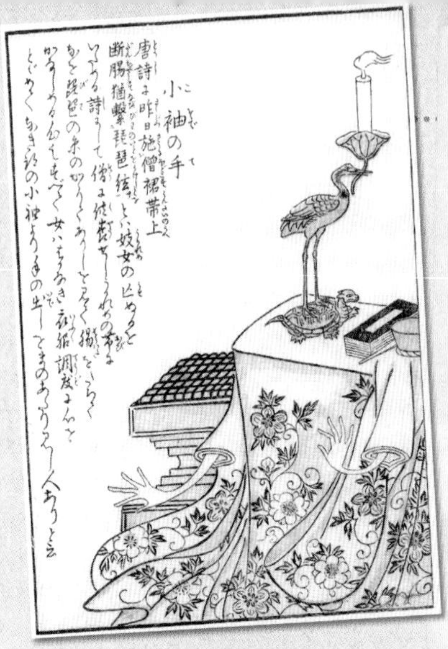
小袖の手

time to time even if your sleepwear isn't haunted by the undead.)

4) When night comes, pray the Boroboro-ton has found someone else's futon to hang out on.

5) If it reappears, follow steps one and two again. But now it's time for a thorough cleaning. Remember: dry-cleaning is recommended for delicate articles such as futon coverlets and kimono, particularly those inhabited by the souls of the dead.

As for the Kosode no Te, take heart: it isn't known to cause anything worse than a good scare, even to those who accidentally wear it.

LITERARY LIASONS

Kosode no Te (left) first appeared in Sekien Toriyama's 1780 book *Konjaku Hyakki Shui* ("Tales of Monsters Now and Then). His description reads:

"There is a T'ang era poem that refers to a man who, grieving at the passing of his favorite courtesan, requests a priest to conduct a funeral rite over the obi from her kimono, whereupon he notices a single biwa string hidden within its folds; this reminds him all the more of what he has lost, serving to further heighten his anguish. Something of a woman's soul remains in the accoutrements and clothing she has worn, and even once she has died it is said that one can glimpse ghostly hands extending from her kimono's sleeves."

The Boroboro-ton (below) appeared in Sekien's *Gazu Hyakki Tsurezure-Bukuro*, "An Illustrated Collection of Many Random Creatures." Precious little is known about its background. Sekien's oblique description mentions a battered futon used by a hermit who has abandoned society, but upon closer reading appears to contain references to several medieval texts. Chances are the Boroboro-ton is based on an obscure literary pun of some kind.

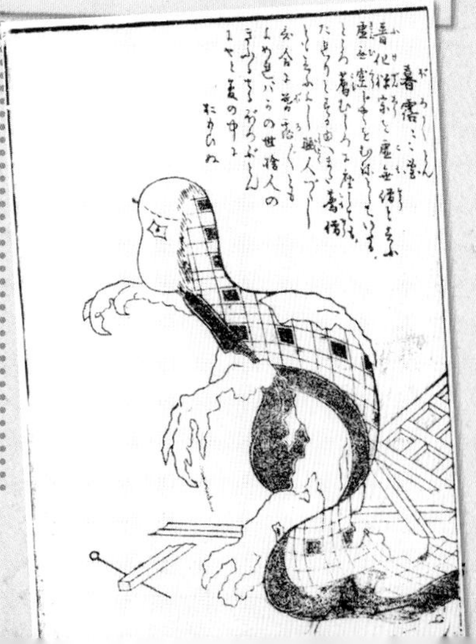

Obariyon

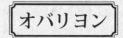

オバリヨン

Pronunciation:
(Oh-BAH-ree-on)

Alternate Japanese Name:
Onbu-obake

English Name:
Piggyback Monster

Gender:
Neutral

Height:
3 to 6 ft. (1 to 2m)

Weight:
Variable

Locomotion:
Bipedal; arboreal

Distinctive Features:
Humanoid
Specific descriptions vary
(see below)

Offensive Weapons:
Variable mass

Abundance:
~~Prevalent~~ one of a kind!

Habitat:
Forests, thickets, and
mountain regions

WIMPS

Claim to Fame:
Obariyon is a strange
humanoid creature said to
inhabit forests and thickets
throughout Japan. Like
nearly all yokai, it is nocturnal, and accosts lone travelers on thickly vegetated and
isolated trails well after
dark. As it is only known to
appear in dim light conditions and always behind the
victim, descriptions of its
appearance vary wildly;
some describe it as being
near featureless, others as
having proportions akin to
that of an oversized infant.
Even its projected actual
physical size is pure conjec-
ture, as its ability to increase
its inherent mass and weight
makes it seem much larger
than it actually is. The portrayal at right is a best guess
as to what this elusive yokai
might actually look like in
the light of day.

The Attack!
The Obariyon waits patiently
for unwitting travelers to
walk beneath its hiding place.
Once in range, the creature
cries "*Obusaritei!*" ("I wanna
piggyback ride!") and drops

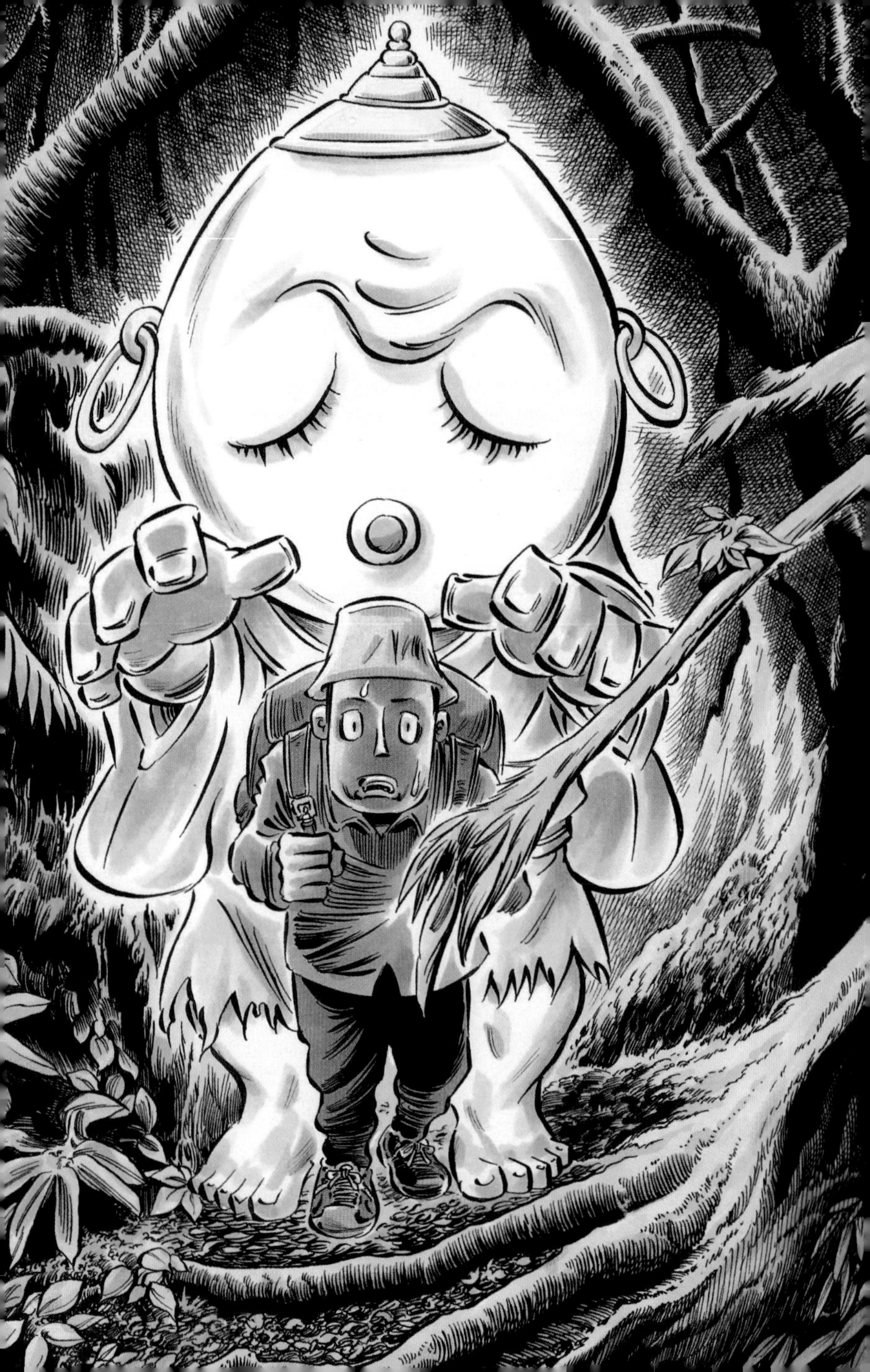

onto the victim's shoulders. Clinging to the hapless individual, the Obariyon slowly but surely increases its weight until the victim is pinned to the ground and immobilized.

Avoiding an Encounter:
Although it is theoretically possible to be injured by the crushing weight of the Obariyon, encounters are almost always more annoying than dangerous. Here are some strategies to help shake it off.

1) If you happen to hear the whoop of the Obariyon, run like hell. This is less to save your skin than it is to avoid the time involved in extricating yourself.

2) If you do happen to find yourself encumbered by the Obariyon, attempt to dislodge it by throwing yourself on your back. Avoid bellyflopping on your stomach, as you will absorb the impact yourself rather than the Obariyon, which will remain attached and make it far harder for you to struggle upright again.

3) Remain calm. Remember that even in worst-case sce-

narios this yokai does not permanently harm its victims; it is content merely to cling to their backs until bored or distracted.

4) The best defense is preventive: avoid entering areas with dense thickets or shadowy overhangs alone, particularly at night.

Reality Check:
Conceptually speaking, this yokai is extremely similar to the Konaki Jiji (p. 62). The big difference is that encounters with the Konaki Jiji are often fatal, whereas Obariyon is simply a pain in the backside. But not all Obariyon encounters end with only a sore back to show for it, as the following legend illustrates.

The Old Man and the Obariyon, A Fairy Tale:
Once upon a time, an old man traveled a footpath deep in the mountains. Suddenly he heard an unsettling voice calling out from the forest alongside the trail: "Gimme a piggyback ride! Gimme a piggyback ride!" Startled and fearing for his life, the old man turned and began running from the source of the strange request. However, no

THE WIMPS

matter how far or fast his legs carried him, the mysterious voice followed at his heels. Before long, it took on a pleading tone: "Please. Give me a piggyback ride. I can't walk. I'm in trouble. I'm begging you."

In spite of his initial terror, the old man was a kindly fellow at heart, and against his better judgment, he took pity on the disembodied voice. Stopping mid-trail, he spoke aloud, and not without some trepidation: "Fine. Climb on my back. I'll carry you." No sooner had the words left his lips than he felt a heavy weight settle upon his back and shoulders.

"My goodness, you're heavy!" he grunted as he struggled under the mysterious load. "But a promise is a promise. Away we go." As quickly as his overburdened feet would carry him, the old man rushed back along the trail to his home.

A likely spot for encountering the Obariyon

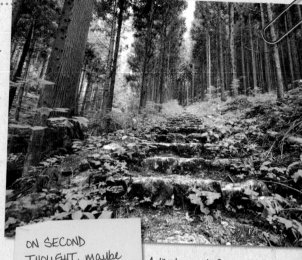

ON SECOND THOUGHT, maybe we should start looking for this guy. Note to self: Start exercise program. Stock up on back-pain relievers.

Many miles he ran along the path, the crushing weight always with him, and it was still present as he crossed the threshold of his humble abode. Trembling, he groped blindly behind him in an attempt to finally release the mysterious load that his tired shoulders had been carrying for so long. Upon setting it on the floor, he was startled to find not a human or a yokai but instead a large earthenware jar filled with nuggets of gold. The old man lived in wealth and luxury for the remainder of his years.

Nobiagari

のびあがり

Pronunciation:
(NOH-bee AH-gah-ree)

English Names:
Shadow-spectre;
Stretching-spectre

Height:
Variable

Weight:
Unknown

Locomotion:
Bipedal

Distinctive Features:
A shadowy humanoid

Offensive Weapons:
Ability to increase in size

Abundance:
One of a kind

Habitat:
Anywhere humans live

Claim to Fame:
Is it a shadow? A wraith-like humanoid? A river or forest creature? Only one thing is known for sure about the enigmatic Nobiagari: it is a yokai that that appears out of nowhere and quickly swells to a massive size. Often stalking its victims from behind and thus just out of clear sight, the details of its origin and physical appearance differ greatly from region to region. Some describe it as an ethereal living shadow; others as a human-like creature, sometimes in the guise of a Buddhist monk; and still others say that it is some sort of animal that has gained the ability to trick humans into believing that it is far larger than it actually is. Whatever the case, the Nobiagari's true form is believed to be that of a strangely proportioned humanoid—perhaps inspired by the strange shapes our shadows cast on the ground late in the day—that leaps into existence and gives chase to startled travelers. They are said to appear more frequently on paths near water, particularly lakes and rivers.

If it truly is a shadow, the Nobiagari is essentially a personification of the sundial effect. According to these legends, the Nobiagari can potentially show up any time

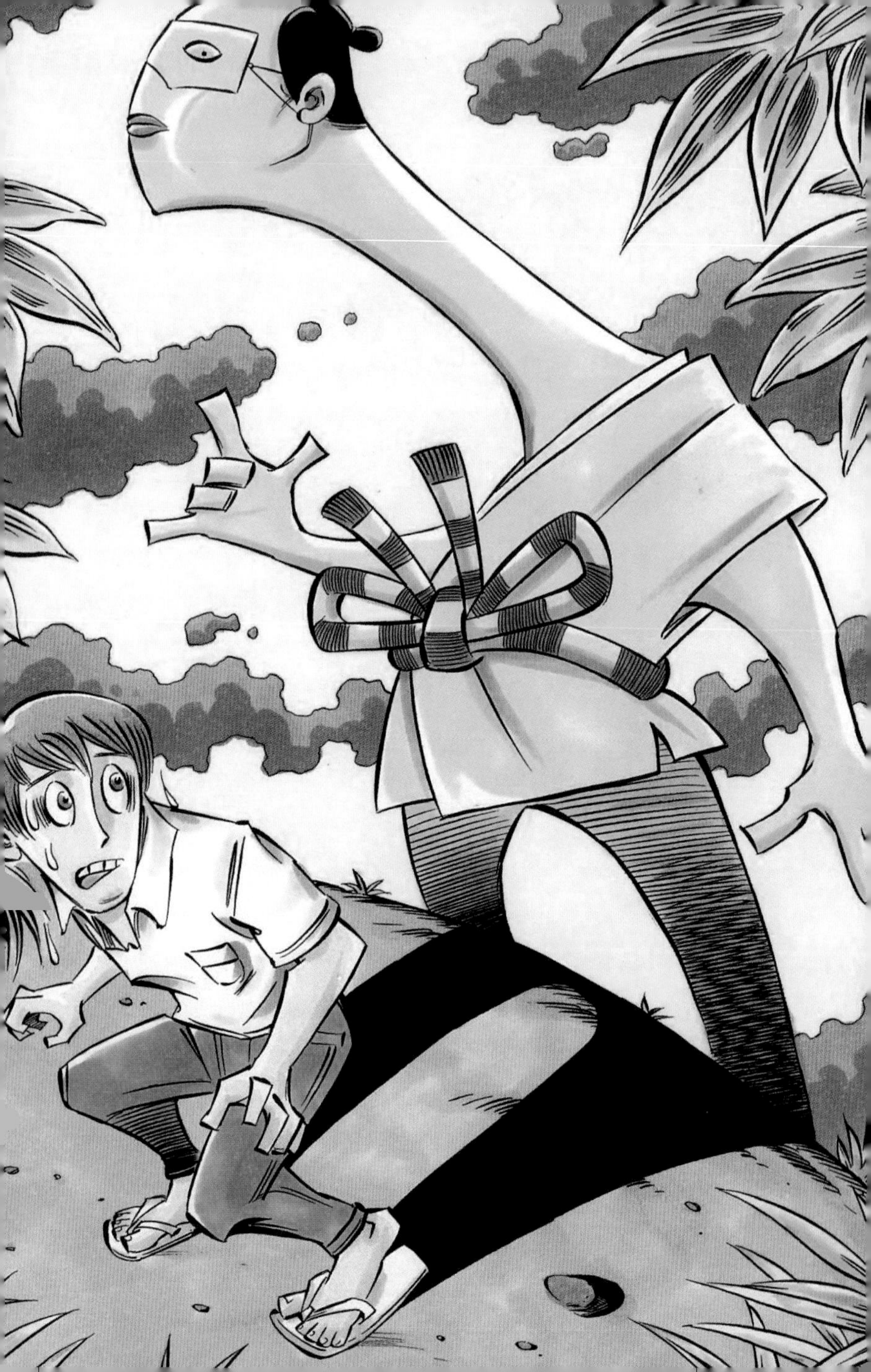

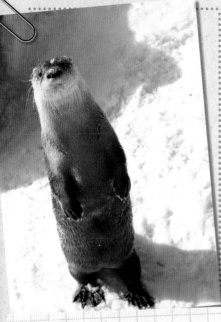

the sun is low in the sky—essentially, just before twilight, the traditional time at which yokai tend to appear. However, logic dictates that encounters are probably more common in the winter months, when the days are short and the sun is low in the sky. (When the sun is at its zenith, directly overhead, there aren't any shadows—and thus no Nobiagari!)

The Attack!

It is not known how the Nobiagari selects its targets; it appears without warning behind lone travelers or other isolated individuals. When the victim nervously looks over their shoulder, straining their peripheral vision in an attempt to get a clearer look at what is behind them, the Nobiagari steadily increases in size. If the victim attempts to flee, the Nobiagari pursues, either by running or elastically extending its neck, torso, or limbs, menacingly leaning in ever closer all the while.

In extraordinarily rare circumstances, the Nobiagari is said to lunge for the victim's exposed neck as they crane their heads back for a higher look.

BEWARE OF OTTER?

Some believe the Nobiagari is merely a mind-bending illusion created by Kitsune (p. 154) or Tanuki (p. 126). However, in Ehime Prefecture, located on the Japanese island of Shikoku, local legend has it that the animal behind the Nobiagari is a river otter. This might explain the large number of sightings near bodies of freshwater. Unfortunately, the last sighting of the Japanese river otter was in 1979, and the species is presumed to be extinct.

Nobiagari is content to threaten rather than injure its victims. Still, encounters aren't pleasant.

Avoiding an Encounter:
Regional legends describe two ways of driving the Nobiagari away. Both involve staying calm and holding your ground.

Tactic One: Turn to face the Nobiagari directly, and slowly lower your gaze to the ground. Its size is determined by the angle at which it is viewed. Looking up makes it larger, while the act of lowering your gaze physically reduces its size. When it has reached a more manageable height, shout "Mioroshita!" ("I look down upon you!"), and it will disappear.

Tactic Two: This assumes that the Nobiagari is indeed a projection created by a much smaller creature. While facing the Nobiagari, kick at a spot in the air roughly a foot from the ground. You may be able to knock the creature off balance, causing the Nobiagari to disappear.

Relatives:
The Nobiagari shares its modus operandi with a variety of similar yokai, most closely that of the Mikoshi (a.k.a Mikoshi-nyudo, the "Look-up Monk"). The Mikoshi takes the form of a Buddhist monk who appears suddenly before travelers on deserted paths or streets, growing to immense proportions as the viewer looks upon him. Like the Nobiagari, the Mikoshi may be the handiwork of a smaller animal; the people of Hinoemata village in Fukushima Prefecture believed the perpetrator to be an *itachi*, or Japanese weasel, though the actual relationship remains unconfirmed. Local legend has it that shouting "Miokoshitari!" ("I can see over you!") at the yokai drives it away.

Other relatives include the Shidaidaka of southwestern Japan; the Taka-nyudo of Shikoku Island; and the Norikoshi-nyudo of Iwate Prefecture in northern Japan. Although the specific habitats, initial appearances, and maximum sizes of these yokai differ from locale to locale, their characteristics and patterns are extremely similar. It remains unknown whether these variations represent different "species," or multiple appearances of the same yokai embellished with local flavor.

Nuppeppo

ぬっぺっぽう

Pronunciation:
(NEW-pep-poh)

Alternate Names:
Nuhehho, Nuppebbo

English Name:
"Blobby"

Gender:
Unknown

Height:
3 to 5 ft. (1 to 1.5m)

Weight:
Unknown, but seriously heavy

Locomotion:
Bipedal

Distinctive Features:
Flabby humanoid appearance

Offensive Weapons:
Pungent body odor

Abundance:
Prevalent

Habitat:
Anywhere humans live

Claim to Fame:
A rotund, humanoid blob of

flesh with the hint of a face in the folds of fat on its "chest," the Nuppeppo is sometimes described as having features such as fingers and toes; other times, only vaguely-defined lumps instead of limbs. In fact, it's often difficult to tell which side faces forward. Widely known throughout Japan, the Nuppeppo is a classic sort of spook.

The Nuppeppo are placid, passive, and unaggressive. Other than their grotesque appearance, the only offensive thing about them is their body odor, which is said to be on a par with that of rotting flesh. Some theories claim they actually *are* rotting flesh. In spite of the stink, there are some rumors that the meat of a Nuppeppo is said to bestow eternal youth upon those who eat it. * see note next page

Nuppeppo aimlessly wander the deserted streets of villages, towns, and cities, often on nights at year-end; or skulk around the grounds and graveyards of abandoned temples that are no longer being used. They often appear alone but are

WIMPS

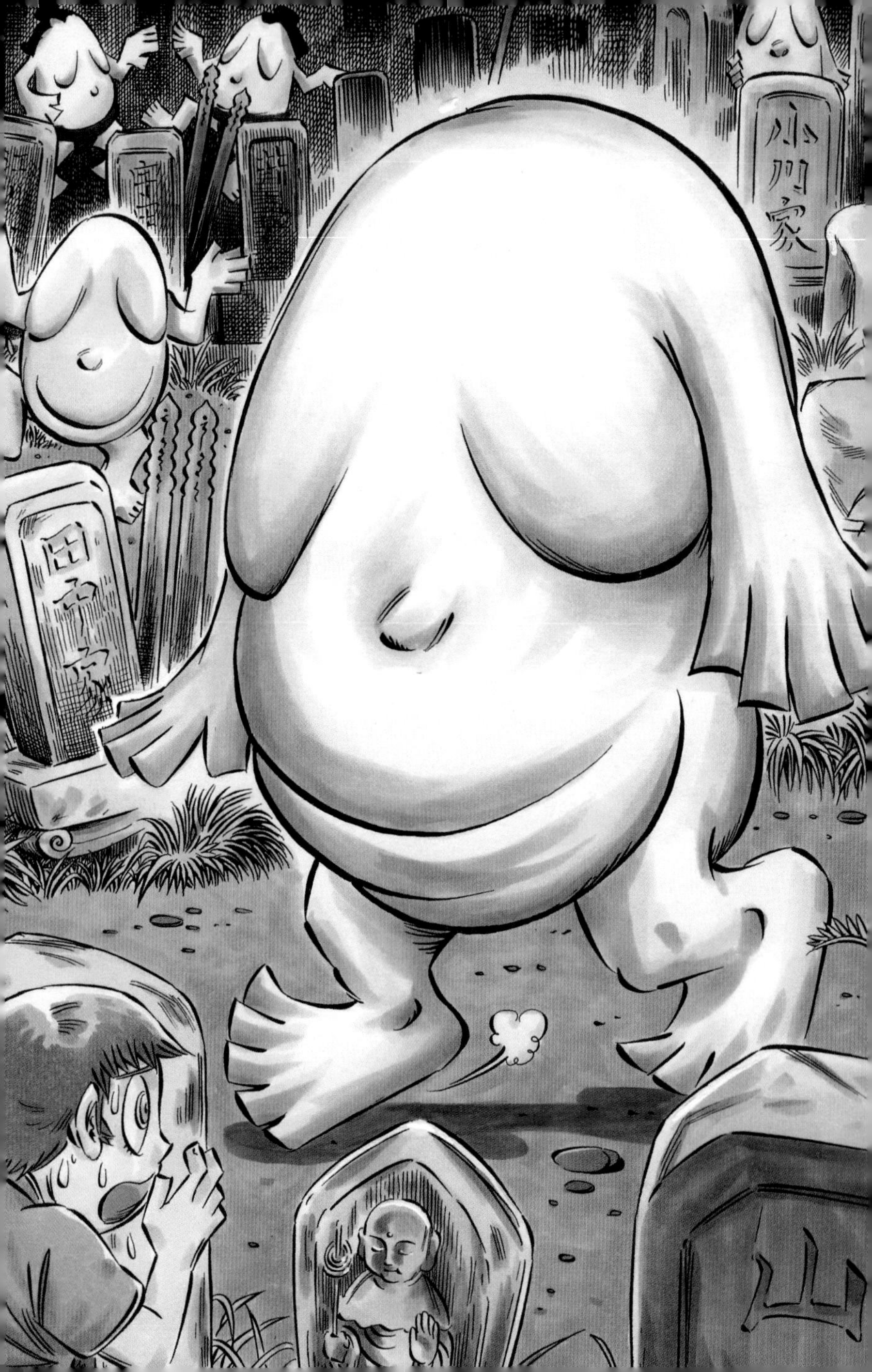
小川家

occasionally sighted in small groups as well.

Some believe that the first Nuppeppo were created long ago from bits of rotting human bodies cobbled together for some unfathomable reason, à la Frankenstein's monster. The record is silent as to whoever—or whatever—was responsible, and there is little to indicate what their motivation may have been.

A word of linguistic caution: Although the Nuppeppo's name appears similar to the Nopperabo (p. 166), they are unrelated save for the fact that both are generally featureless.

The Attack!
You're walking late at night when a ferocious stink fills your nostrils, and you catch sight of blob-like humanoids strolling about. That's about as dangerous as a Nuppeppo attack gets.

Avoiding an Encounter:
It's best to stay away from abandoned temples and old graveyards late at night. But really, you don't have anything to fear, even from direct contact with the Nuppeppo. In fact, this could well be your chance to play with a yokai. Perhaps a little sumo wrestling practice is in order? We'd recommend, however, a clothespin for the nose to anyone wishing to interact with this creature.

And for those with cast-iron stomachs, perhaps a spot of Nuppeppo flesh might cure what's ailing you. Provided, that is, you can bring yourself to slaughter what is, at heart, really quite a gentle and harmless sort of being— and swallow slimy, rotting human skin—and don't mind the possibility of spending eternity as a formless, shambling blob (remember: when they said "eternal life," they didn't specify what form said life would take).

NUPPEPPO SLANG
The derogatory term nupperi is occasionally used for women who apply too much makeup.

The Nuppeppo and the Shogun:
A Japanese scroll written by the eighteenth-century scribe Makibokusen describes what seems to be a Nuppeppo appearing in the castle of shogun Tokugawa Ieyasu (1543-1616). According to Makibokusen, Tokugawa ordered that it be released,

THE WIMPS

unharmed, deep within the mountains far from human settlements. Only later did Tokugawa learn from a scholar that the creature was described in Chinese literature as being a walking "sovereign specific," capable of restoring vitality while bestowing youth on any who consumed its flesh. Easy come, easy go.

Yokai and Eternal Youth:

On a side note, the Nuppeppo is not the only yokai whose flesh is said to bestow eternal life. The meat of a totally unrelated yokai called the Ningyo—literally, "mermaid," though you wouldn't confuse this creature for the buxom beauties Western sailors pined after in legend—is said to have the same effect. In an old folktale called *Yaobikuni* ("The Nun of Eight Hundred Years"), the daughter of a fisherman accidentally consumed the flesh of a mermaid, believing it to be fish. However, immortality proved more of a curse than a blessing. She remained hale and hearty while her family, friends, and acquaintances grew old and died, dooming her to a lonely existence of wandering the Earth for centuries until she finally succeeded in ending her own life. Moral of the story: be careful what you wish for. Eternal life also means eternal suffering.

(*) There is no record as to whether anyone has ever actually successfully harvested Nuppeppo flesh, or what it might actually taste like. If you happen to try it, by all means, let us know. But don't blame us if you turn into a yokai yourself!

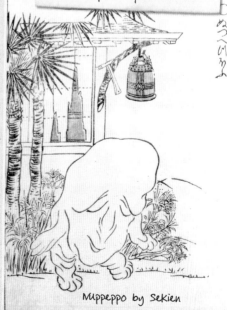

Nuppeppo by Sekien

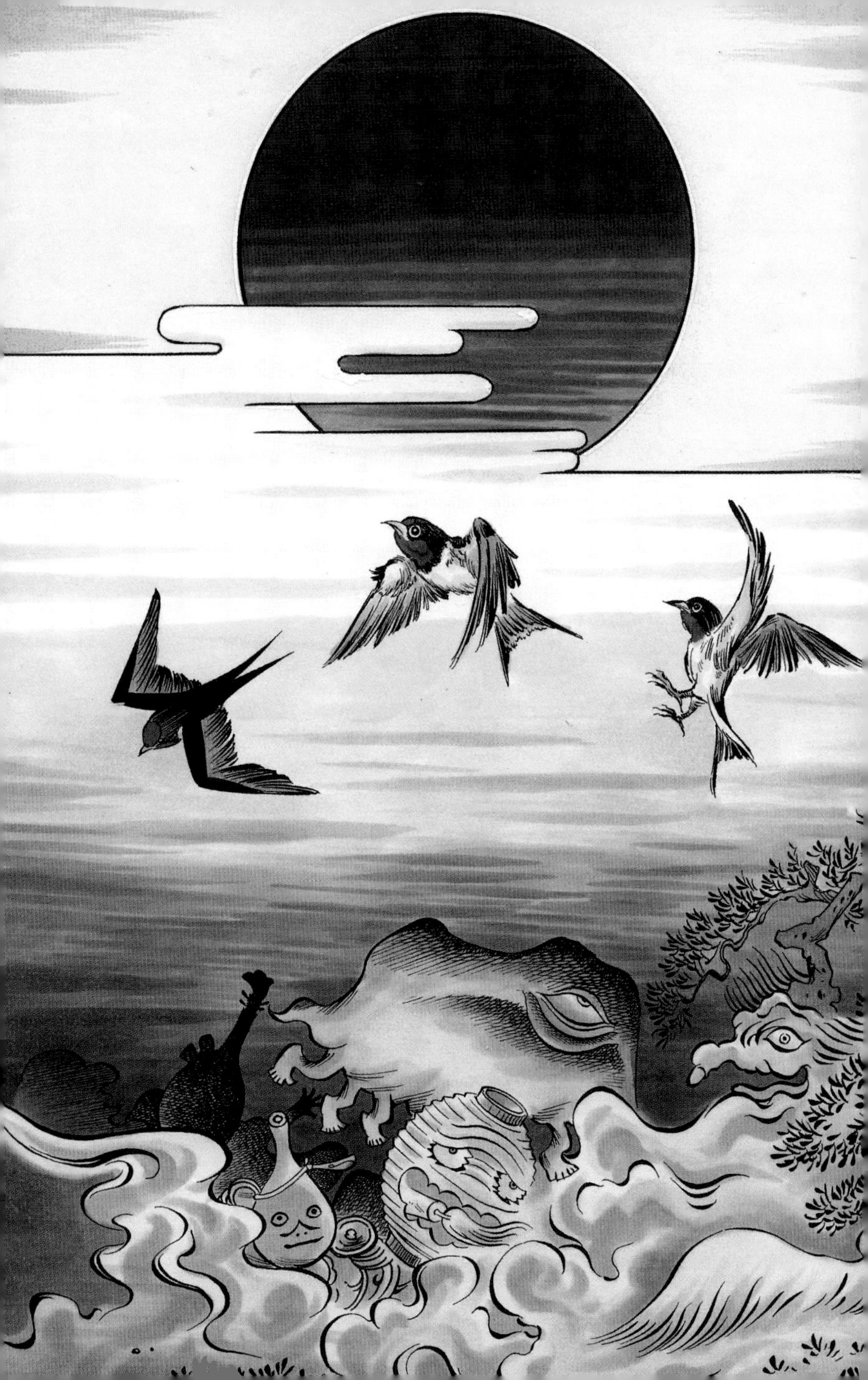

Yokai Resources

CLASSIC FILMS INVOLVING YOKAI

Kaidan (1965)

Director Masaki Kobayashi masterfully adapts several horror stories from Lafcadio Hearn's book *Kwaidan* in this big-screen omnibus. A must-see classic of Japanese horror filmmaking. Available on DVD from the Criterion Collection.

Yokai Monsters: 100 Monsters (1968)

A silly Edo-era period piece featuring several yokai, most notably the snake-necked Rokuro Kubi (p. 142) and a stunningly groovy animated sequence with Kara-kasa (p. 110).
Available on DVD from ADV Films.

Yokai Monsters: Spook Warfare (1968)

His resting place disturbed by treasure hunters, a vampire-like monster from ancient Babylon comes to Japan, sending the local yokai into a tizzy. Campy, borderline-insane fun for the whole family.
Available on DVD from ADV Films.

Pom Poko (1994)

A playful yet thought-provoking film about a clan of Tanuki (see p. 126) whose ancestral home is threatened by suburban sprawl. Beautifully animated by Studio Ghibli. Your chance to see shapeshifting Tanuki in action!
Available on DVD from Walt Disney Home Entertainment.

Shinsei Toire no Hanako-san (1998)

Available on DVD for ¥3990 from Pony Canyon.

Spirited Away (2001)

Although never explicitly referred to as "yokai," many strange mythological creatures populate this exquisitely animated film by director Hayao Miyazaki. Winner of numerous awards, including the Oscar for Best Animated Feature of 2003.
Available on DVD from Walt Disney Home Entertainment.

Kibakichi (2004)

When a wandering samurai encounters a desolate village populated by yokai posing as yakuza gangsters, mind-bending violence ensues. Directed by Tomoo Haraguchi, based on a comic by Takao Shimamoto and Tatsuya Morino.

The same Morino who illustrated this very book!

Available on DVD from Saiko Films and MTI.

The Great Yokai War (2005)

Co-starring Chiaki Kuriyama of *Kill Bill* fame, this represents J-Horror maestro Takashi Miike's first foray into kids' filmmaking. Features legions of yokai.

watch carefully and you might even catch the authors of this book in the crowd!

Available on DVD from Tokyo Shock.

SUGGESTED ONLINE RESOURCES

English-Language

The Obakemono Project
http://www.obakemono.com/

Japanese-Language

怪異・妖怪伝承データベース
(Strange Phenomenon and Yokai Legend Database)
http://www.nichibun.ac.jp/YoukaiDB/

鳥山石燕の世界
The World of Sekien Toriyama
http://www.linet.gr.jp/~kojima/Kyogokudou/Sekien/

妖怪ストリート
Yokai Street
http://www.kyotohyakki.com

BIBLIOGRAPHY

Addiss, Stephen. *Japanese Ghosts and Demons: Art of the Supernatural.* New York: George Braziller Inc., 2001.

Davis, F. Hadland. *Myths and Legends of Japan.* London: George G. Harrap & Co., 1913.

Figal, Gerald. *Civilization and Monsters: Spirits of Modernity in Meiji Japan.* Durham and London: Duke University Press, 1999.

Figal, Gerald. "Yokai Monsters, Giant Catfish, & Symbolic Representation in Popular Culture." Retrieved January 12, 2008 from http://www.east-asian-history.net/textbooks/PM-Japan/ch8.html

Foster, Michael Dylan. "The Metamorphosis of the Kappa: Transformation of Folklore to Folklorism in Japan." *Asian Folklore Studies*, Vol. 57, 1998: 1-24.

Foster, Michael Dylan. "The Question of the Slit-Mouthed Woman: Contemporary Legend, the Beauty Industry, and Women's Weekly Magazines in Japan." *Signs: Journal of Women in Culture and Society*, Vol. 32, 2007.

Fujinuma, Yoshizo, et al. *Yokai Yurei Daihyakka* ("The Big Encyclopedia of Yokai and Ghosts"). Tokyo: Keibunsha, 1982.

Fujisawa, Morihiko. *Zusetsu Nihon Minzokugaku Zenshu* ("An Illustrated Collection of Japanese Folkore"). Tokyo: Akane Shobo, 1959.

Hasegawa, Ryoichi. "The Mysterious Waq-Waq Tree." *Bo Mu Ryo: The Dreamers's Tower* 23 March 2006. Retrieved January 12, 2008 from http://homepage3.nifty.com/boumurou/island/sp02/02Waqwaq.html.

Hearn, Lafcadio. *In Ghostly Japan.* Boston: Little, Brown, and Co., 1899.

Hearn, Lafcadio. *Kwaidan: Stories and Studies of Strange Things.* New York: Dover Publications, 1968.

Komatsu, Kazuhiko. *Nihon Yokai Ibunroku* ("Strange Tales of Japanese Yokai"). Tokyo: Shogakugan, 1992.

Kurotani, Sawa. "Behind the Paper Screen / 'Yokai' Folklore Boom Grips Japan." *Daily Yomiuri Shimbun,* November 13, 2007.

Masamichi Abe, et. al. *Nippon Yokai Chizu* (Japanese Yokai Map). Tokyo: Kadokawa Shoten, 1996.

Mizuki, Shigeru. *Nihon Yokai Daizen* ("A Big Guide to Japanese Yokai"). Tokyo: Kodansha Plus Alpha Bunko, 1994.

Murakami, Kenji and Studio Hard MX. *Hyakki Yako Kaitai Shinsho* ("A New Analysis of Hyakki Yakko"). Tokyo: Koei, 2000.

Murakami, Kenji. *Yokai Walker.* Tokyo: Kadokawa Shoten, 2002. Nakamura, Yukio, et. al. *Books Esoterica 24: Yokai no Hon* ("The Book of Yokai"). Tokyo: Gakken, 2006.

Sato, Kouseki. *Kappa at Play.* Tokyo: Nihon Shuppan Kyodo, 1952.

Tada, Tatsumi. *Edo Yokai Karuta.* Tokyo: Kokusho Kankokai, 1998.

Takenaka, Kiyosho, et al. *Nihon no Yokai Daihyakka* ("The Big Encyclopedia of Japanese Yokai"). Tokyo: Keibunsha, 1985.

Yamada, Norio. *Tohoku Kaidan no Tabi* ("A Journey Through Scary Stories from Tohoku"). Tokyo: Jiyu Kokumin Sha, 1974.

Yanagita, Kunio. *Tono Monogatari* ("Tales from Tono"). 55th revised edition. Tokyo: Kadokawa Sofia Bunko, 1998.

Yumoto, Goichi. *Meiji Yokai Shimbun* ("Meiji Yokai Newspapers"). Tokyo: Hakushobo, 1999.

Yokai Street, "Kodogutachi no Hyakki Yako" ("The Tools' Night-Parade"). Retrieved January 12, 2008, from http://www.kyoto-hyakki.com/web_0317/hyakki-yakou01.html.

Yokai Index

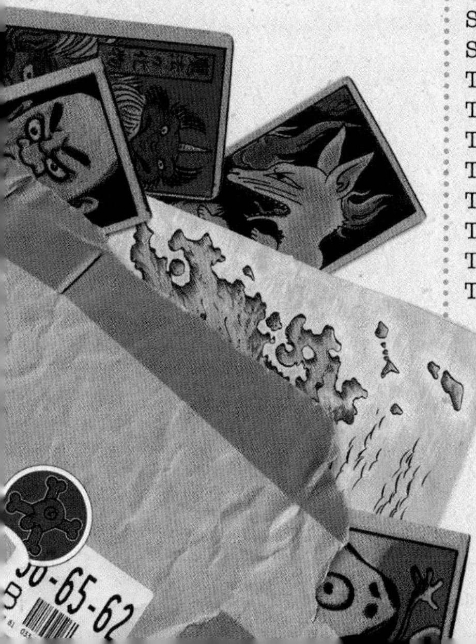

Acknowledgments

Hiroko and Matt would like to thank the following individuals for their help and support in the creation of the revised edition of *Yokai Attack*:

Gregory Starr, for his unwavering support from the very get-go and keeping us in line with his much appreciated editorial comments. Andrew Lee for his infallible sense of layout and design. William Notte and Alphone Tea at Tuttle Publishing, for their editorial and design work, respectively. Yutaka Kondo, for his beautiful calligraphy that graces p. 37. And Rich Amtower, Robert Duban, Tim Hornyak, and Mark Schreiber for a variety of advice and assistance along the way.

In addition, we would like to thank the following individuals for their generosity in lending us imagery for use in the book. Art dealer Jerry Vegder (and his website *www.printsofjapan.com*). The Mike Lyon collection, Kansas City, the Michael Thaler collection, the Izunokuni Tourist Association (*www.izunotabi.com*), Yoshimi Kawada and his site about festivals, (*www005.upp.sonet.ne.jp/omatsuri/*), David Keymont and his toys, and Yoshiharu Kato, a.k.a. "nandemoplamo," and his website (*blogs.yahoo.co.jp/nandemoplamo*). And author Natsuhiko Kyogoku, for penning the ofuda slip for the revised edition of the book.

What book about yokai would be complete without a salute to the supernatural? Hiroko gives a big thanks to that quintessentially modern yokai Kuchisake Onna, who fueled hours of heated childhood discussions, not to mention countless bekko ame purchases. And in true animistic fashion Matt would like to give thanks to his long-suffering laptop, which after pounding out this book is probably well on its way to becoming a Tsukumo gami.

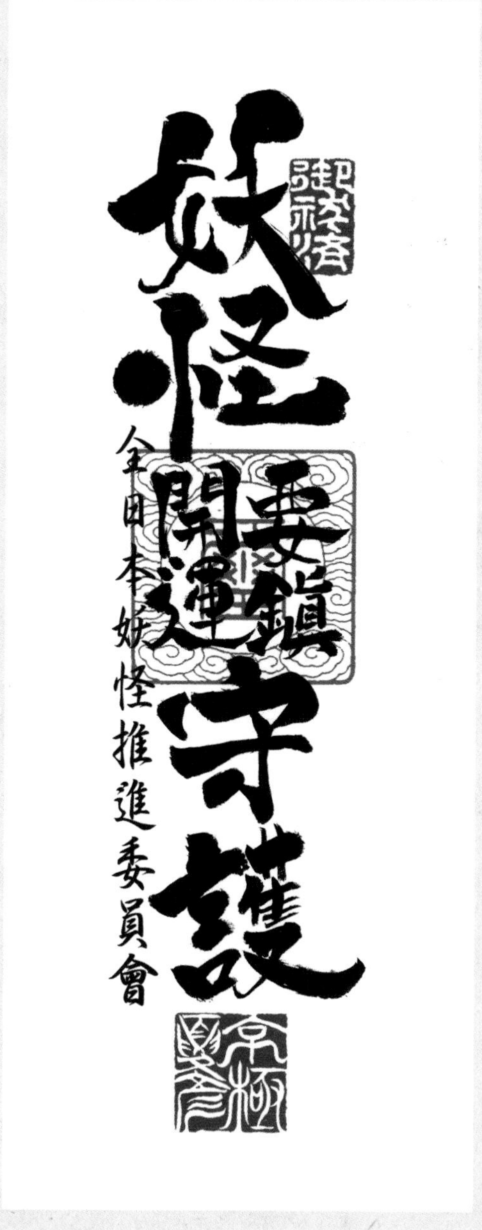
妖怪守護
開運
全日本妖怪推進委員會

An "ofuda" is a traditional paper talisman that can be carried or posted to protect one from supernatural harm. The mystery novelist Natsuhiko Kyogoku was kind enough to pen this one especially for Yokai Attack! It reads: "Yokai Protection: Good Luck from the All-Japan Yokai Promotional Committee." Now you're covered, too!

PHOTO/ILLUSTRATION CREDITS

Tatsuya Morino: Jacket and all main illustrations, plus 73, 152; Adachigahara Furusatomura: 78; Matt Alt and Hiroko Yoda Collection: 38, 62, 66, 122, 170, 172; National Diet Library: 21, 36, 40, 43, 48, 69, 89, 92, 101, 117, 120, 145, 148, 181, 185, 185; Hiroko Yoda: 22, 24, 32-33, 42, 49, 82, 105, 114, 125, 150, 156, 180, 189, 206-207; Mike Lyons Collection: 25, 81, 104, 154; William Shlitz: 84; Michael Thaler Collection: 29: Izunokuni Tourist Association: 45; Visipix: 52, 57, 85, 133; G. Starr: 100, 126; David Keymont Collection: 112, 173; Jerry Vegder Collection: 128; Andrew Lee: 132, 146; Yoshimi Kawada: 164; Pony Canyon: 177; Dave Pape: 192; Yasuhiro Hatabe: 88

WHEN THE LAST RAYS OF
SUNSHINE FADE FROM THE DAY:
THAT'S WHEN JAPAN'S YOKAI
COME OUT TO PLAY.

-AUTHOR UNKNOWN

REVISED EDITION WITH 16 NEW PAGES
AND IN FULL-COLOR FOR THE FIRST TIME!

WITHDRAWN

Yokai Attack!

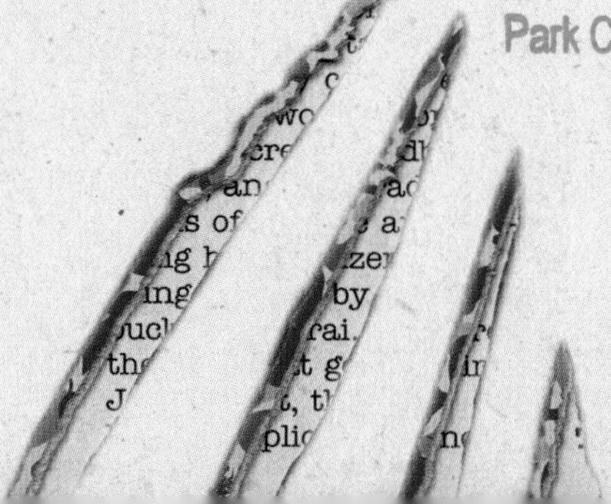